Praise for

THEY COME IN ALL COLORS

"Emotionally acute . . . Eye-opening and rewarding for a wide range of readers."

—*Library Journal* (starred review)

"It's possible to imagine literary recluses J. D. Salinger and Harper Lee coming out of hiding to forge this shaggy, rakish yet haunting account of a smart aleck's coming-of-age in harsh times."

—*Kirkus Reviews*

"Confident and ambitious debut novel."

—*AM New York*

"An urgent and heartrending novel about an America on the brink. With force, Malcolm Hansen writes about race, identity, and the fleeting deceptions of youth."

—Matt Gallagher, author of *Youngblood*

"This is a voice so honest and alive it feels like a stranger whispering a confession in a dark room. Malcolm Hansen's novel is a prodigious debut of a rare literary talent."

—Mat Johnson, author of *Loving Day* and *Pym*

"In *They Come in All Colors*, Malcolm Hansen is not writing about saints or monsters, just vivid human beings. And [he] does so with humor and insight."

—Victor LaValle, award-winning author of
The Changeling and *The Ballad of Black Tom*

THEY COME
IN ALL
COLORS

They Come in All Colors

A Novel

Malcolm Hansen

ATRIA PAPERBACK

New York   London   Toronto   Sydney   New Delhi

ATRIA
PAPERBACK

An Imprint of Simon & Schuster, Inc.
1230 Avenue of the Americas
New York, NY 10020

First Atria Paperback edition April 2019

ATRIA PAPERBACK and colophon are trademarks of Simon & Schuster, Inc.

For information about special discounts for bulk purchases, please contact Simon & Schuster Special Sales at 1-866-506-1949 or business@simonandschuster.com.

The Simon & Schuster Speakers Bureau can bring authors to your live event. For more information or to book an event, contact the Simon & Schuster Speakers Bureau at 1-866-248-3049 or visit our website at www.simonspeakers.com.

Interior design by Michelle Marchese

Manufactured in the United States of America

10 9 8 7 6 5 4 3 2 1

The Library of Congress has cataloged the hardcover edition as follows:

Names: Hansen, Malcolm.
Title: They come in all colors : a novel / Malcolm Hansen.
Description: First Atria Books hardcover edition | New York : Atria Books, [2018]
Identifiers: LCCN 2017052461 (print) | LCCN 2018000086 (ebook) | ISBN 9781501172342 (ebook) | ISBN 9781501172328 (hardback) | ISBN 9781501172335 (trade paper)
Subjects: LCSH: Coming of age—Fiction. | Teenage boy—Fiction. | Racially mixed people—Fiction. | Private schools—New York—Fiction. | Race relations—Southern States—United States—Fiction. | Race relations—Fiction. | Civil rights—Fiction. | Domestic fiction. | BISAC: FICTION / Literary. | FICTION / Coming of Age. | FICTION / Cultural Heritage.
Classification: LCC PS3608.A72226 (ebook) | LCC PS3608.A72226 T49 2018 (print) | DDC 813/.6—dc23
LC record available at https://lccn.loc.gov/2017052461

ISBN 978-1-5011-7232-8
ISBN 978-1-5011-7233-5 (pbk)
ISBN 978-1-5011-7234-2 (ebook)

To Maja, without whom this would not be.
To Ramsey and Wren, without whom this would not matter.

If I've killed one man, I've killed two—
The vampire who said he was you
And drank my blood for a year,
Seven years, if you want to know.
Daddy, you can lie back now.

There's a stake in your fat black heart
And the villagers never liked you.
They are dancing and stamping on you.
They always *knew* it was you.
Daddy, daddy, you bastard, I'm through.

SYLVIA PLATH, "DADDY"

THEY COME
IN ALL
COLORS

1

I ONLY HAVE TO CLOSE my eyes to see that son of a bitch Zukowski, passed out like he was on the dining hall floor. Then came the looks of revulsion on the other kids' faces at the sight of me trying to shake him awake while shouting out for help. After an ambulance came and hauled him off, Mister McGovern grabbed my arm and dragged me down the hall and blurted out, *It wasn't something sexual between you two, was it?*

LISTEN, CLAREMONT PREP may be an all-boys school, but that doesn't make it a gaybo factory. And even if it was, Lord knows I wouldn't be with the likes of Zukowski. For the record, Ariel J. Zukowski wears horn-rimmed glasses. He combs his greasy hair to the side in a desperate attempt to look debonair. But despite his prodigious effort, he's still a dork. Which, believe it or not, has nothing to do with why I wanted to see him dead.

Then there's the issue of his mole-infested face, which is why nobody sits with him. Which, if I may harken back to my very first day at Claremont, five years ago, was how I ended up taking pity on the little twerp in the first place. But what was I supposed to do? Sit at a table filled with those other namby-pambys while he ate in the corner all by himself?

Like a schmuck, I sat down beside him and there I was, brimming with butterflies because it was, after all, the first day of school, and that god-awful quiet between us sitting there together was made worse by the giddy buzz of chatter from the tables around us, where kids were going on endlessly about their summer up the Hamptons or wherever it is they play croquet.

Then, out of nowhere, Zukowski took his sandwich from his lunch tray and pushed it over to me and said that I could have it. He's got some kind of weird allergy and couldn't eat it anyway. I was stunned. You see, sitting there in my wrinkly button-down and wrong-color tie, I'd steeled myself in preparation for nonstop douchebaggery, but that smushed Saran-wrapped triangle gave me hope. Funny thing is, I'd just assumed that Zukowski was sitting there alone like that because he wasn't as, well, shall we say, refined as the others. So you can imagine my surprise when I found out that it was his first day, too. The revelation came as something of a miracle because I thought for sure that I was the only new kid. You see, starting up at a place like Claremont in the fifth grade is a kamikaze mission. The other kids have been going here since kindergarten—not to mention that their fathers and grandfathers all went here since kindergarten, too. So right off the bat we were the oddballs, which was something great to have in common, even if it was the only thing.

Which it wasn't. After school that first day, I discovered that he took the subway, just like me. On the way to the station, I told him that in a way you could say that I grew up around money because my mom was the housekeeper for mattress magnate Zachariah Blumenthal, who lives on the Upper East Side with his fat wife, their twins, and a pet iguana that has his own room. Zukowski didn't care one bit because his dad's just a plumber.

He said that the only reason they gave him a bunch of dough to come to Claremont is because he's some sort of whiz kid. So I asked him, *What's one hundred twenty-one divided by eleven times five add two and take away ten?* He promptly responded with, *Forty-seven.* Thinking that even a busted clock is right twice a day, I fired off another one. *Okay, hotshot, so what's fourteen times fourteen divided by two plus twenty take away three?* He paused for a second, and then said, *One hundred fifteen.*

Sweet mother of God. I bet you're smart enough to bring up the whole school's average!

He curtsied like a real faggot and asked what my excuse was. *I'm NYCHA,* I told him. Of course he didn't know what the hell that was.

When I explained that I had been awarded the honors of a student of outstanding scholarly accomplishment by the New York City Housing Authority, he looked at me like I was joking. The funny part was that I'd left out the corny bit about me having won it in a writing competition among my semiliterate neighbors in the Jacob Riis Houses.

On East Fifty-Ninth Street you have to go underground to board the train. When we got to the top of the stairwell, I told him flat out, *You're a jackass, Zukowski. A real fairy. I've seen kids like you my whole life, strutting around with your glasses on and your head up your ass. And now that I've got you up close, I oughta punch you. But I won't. Because I like you. Don't ask me why, but I do.*

We had what Mom calls *rapport*. Even if he was a blowhard, he wasn't a douche. Besides, Mom had told me that not being too picky was the key to making friends. So we shook hands, and I just stood there watching him prance down the smut-covered stairwell, thinking that all I had to do was to sit behind him in Coach Picareaux's pre-algebra class and I'd do just fine.

Me and Mom eat at the HoJo's up on East Seventy-Second on the days she works late. Seeing as how I only had one token left, I hightailed it uptown on foot and jumped into a booth beside her and squeezed her like she was the very last of the toothpaste. As we were catching up I told Mom that there was another kid there who was just like me, or at least kind of like me, or at least he was more like me than I thought anybody would be!

And for the most part, Zukowski was. For five whole years. Then came the day in the ninth grade when we went more than a few blocks out of our way to check out the St. Michael's Academy girls' field hockey team practice after school. And let me tell you, if Claremont's more of a mansion than an actual school building, St. Michael's is a full-on manor estate with castle and moat. We passed the Guggenheim and saw the girls up ahead, lined up at midfield doing warm-up exercises. We took up our usual position at the wrought-iron bars some twenty yards behind them, which I thought was discreet, but apparently it wasn't because no sooner had they started their windmill routine than one of the girls in the back row caught sight of me from between her legs. She shot straight up and shouted for us to stop gawking. When we didn't just run off like a couple of pansies, she picked up her field hockey stick and started straight for us like she meant business.

Zukowski yelped like a poodle and booked it. The girl stepped up to the fence and just sort of stood there looking at me like I was something her biology teacher had just brought into class on a petri dish. I stood there, fully aware of the entire squad behind her—coach included. They were ready to charge me at the drop of that stick, while I stood there with mouth agape, staring at her like an imbecile. She was friggin' hot.

She rolled her eyes. *You go to Claremont?*

Yeah.

Well, stop ogling us. We don't like it.

Okay.

Before I knew it a screeching whistle sent her galloping back to the field. Zukowski, still in awe that I had talked to a girl, reappeared from behind the sculpted bushes in front of the Russian consulate.

We hopped on the downtown 6 train, hooting and hollering like a couple of lunatics who'd just won the lottery. You see, even if it wasn't exactly a friendly interaction, it was the first time we'd made contact with a St. Michael's girl. Zukowski didn't care one bit who it was she brought when the time came for our inevitable double date. He thought that the best thing we could do would be to take them back to my place and play Spin the Bottle. But even if Mom was hardly ever home, what with her practically raising the Blumenthal twins like she was, there was no way I was bringing them back to my apartment. Zukowski's house was out of the question, too. Never mind that it was two hours away on the Q line; his mom hung their laundry out to dry in the windows, and the whole place stank of goulash.

Instead we decided it was better to take them to a matinee, because we could sit in the back row and get them plastered on peppermint schnapps we'd hustle from one of the drunkards in Times Square, who were rumored to be so desperate for a nip they'd damn near suck on your balls for a spare quarter. Only problem there being that all the theaters were showing *Midnight Cowboy*, which, it turns out, isn't a cowboy movie at all.

So there we were, back at square one, wondering how on earth two kids like us could leverage our status as Claremont boys to nab a couple of St. Michael's girls. We got off at Astor Place and cut through Tompkins Square Park, kicking at the sandy path on our way to my place, because even if neither of us would say it outright, we both knew that our ship was sunk before it'd even got out of port. That's when Zukowski elbowed me in the gut and pointed at this big-bellied woman pushing a stroller coming the opposite way. He said we'd have a better chance getting her.

I smacked him on the head. *Fuckwad. Pregnant women can't fuck. That's how babies get brain damage. Jesus, don't you know anything?*

Zukowski skipped off toward the fountain, yelling *Leggo-my-Eggo-I'm-preggo!* Only I'm not looking back at Mister Dildo Breath scaring away the pigeons but in front of us. I look up toward Avenue C and what do I see but this big-as-hell billboard on the side of the Con Ed Building promoting the one hundredth anniversary of big-league ball. I think to myself, *Jesus. Has it only been a hundred years?* For some reason I just kind of assumed that baseball had been around forever. And that's when the answer to all my problems hit me—the only rub being the extra bread needed for two tickets to a game. You see, even if being a Claremont boy was a big selling point in most quarters, we weren't supposed to be stone broke, and a St. Michael's girl paying her own way was out of the question.

ZUKOWSKI THOUGHT I was crazy. Maybe I was. But he sure was singing a different tune come game day, when we met that chick and her friend on the Fifty-Ninth Street subway platform, where we hopped onto the 7 because the Mets were our team. All of us were chatting on the train ride out to Queens and happy once we hit the elevated because the clouds were starting to break up and we could tell that it wasn't going to rain after all. Me and Suzie Hartwell were already starting to get hot and heavy on the way there, even as more and more people piled on with every stop.

When we finally got to Shea, Suzie and I untangled ourselves to exit. Zukowski and his date, Amanda something, who wore crooked glasses and a ponytail and kind of had the same mole thing going on, spilled out with the rest of the train. We walked past the goony-looking scalpers hawking tickets for an arm and a leg in their singsong way.

The afternoon sun warmed our faces as we sat down, and right smack in front of us was an infield raked as smooth as our Japanese teacher Mister Yamaguchi's sand garden. Everything was so pristine it felt like the inside of a cathedral. Not that I've ever been in one, mind you. It's just what I imagine it to feel like.

By the seventh inning the Mets were getting clobbered. Suzie got up and said she had to use the restroom. Okay, I figured. That was just a polite way of saying that she wanted to make out some more. So I winked at Zukowski and got up and left with her. Only it turned out she really had to use the bathroom. So we threaded our way past the inevitable beer line to the ladies' room, and on our way back she was taking her time, walking real slow and twirling a long strand of brown hair between her fingers. She asked me if anyone had ever told me that I looked a little like Omar Sharif.

Sharif? I didn't know who he played for. She laughed and pulled me behind one of those hulking I beams supporting the grandstands above and we started smooching. A few seconds into it, she took out her chewing gum and told me I was pressing too hard. I promised to do it more softly next time. Only when the next time came, she said for me to stop sticking my tongue so far down her throat. So I told her no problem; I'd fix that, too.

I could tell that I was getting the hang of it after a minute or so because she was combing her fingers through my hair. I made do with planting my hands on the soft angora at her waist because first, it was our first date, and second, we were in public, and third, I was starting to really dig her. Suzie came up for air for the third time in fifteen minutes, which I suppose wasn't too bad, and, after she put her chewing gum back into her mouth, told me that I had an awfully big mouth. I buried my hot face in her cool, soft hair and pretended not to care.

When we got back to our seats, Zukowski handed me back my popcorn with a wink. *What took you so long?*

The line to the restroom practically went out to the parking lot.

You lovebirds missed a whole inning.

I turned to the game at the crack of a bat. Chacón was shouting out for the high, looping fly ball sailing out to shallow left in Spanish. Thomas plowed straight into him, and the ball just sat there in the grass like a hot potato. Ashburn picked it up and threw it in, holding the runner at second. What a circus. The crowd was booing so loud that I couldn't hear a word Zukowski was saying. I tossed a handful of popcorn toward the field, then sat back down and explained to Suzie that Chacón was from Puerto Rico, which is why he wasn't able to call off Thomas in English. She asked if that was where my family was from. *I'm from Georgia*, I answered, half expecting some stupid joke about the South. She gave me a surprised look. *Oh. So—you're American?*

I turned back to Cookie Rojas standing there, digging himself a trench in the batter's box, and prayed for him to knock a line-drive foul ball straight into Suzie's teeth. Zukowski accepted the hot dog being relayed to him by Amanda, then leaned in over me so far he was practically sitting in my lap.

Yeah. His dad's white. His mom's just colored, is all.

The little prick shoved the hot dog in his mouth and sat back to watch the game. Suzie did a double take: first to Zukowski, then to me, then back at Zukowski.

Whaddya mean?

Ouch! Hey! That was my foot, Huey! Whadja do that for? Then, to Suzie: *Whaddya mean, "Whaddya mean"?*

You mean he's not—?

What?

I dunno.

No. He's colored.

Suzie's gum went still in her mouth. I couldn't get myself to look at anything but Rojas and that trench he'd dug for himself. I wished I could climb into it with him. Zukowski kept munching on that damned hot dog of his. Right next to my face. Like it was the best damned ballpark frank he'd ever eaten. When Suzie just sat there speechless, Zukowski leaned in over my lap toward her and said, *You probably just don't know what to look for.*

MISTER McGOVERN SAT back in his chair, kicked up his feet beside Zukowski's lunch tray, and nudged his thin, wire-framed glasses up the bridge of his nose.

"What to look for"?

Mister McGovern looked confused as he puzzled over those words.

I could tell that he felt uncomfortable talking about the fact that most people don't think I look like I'm colored. I slumped in my seat and said never mind. He knew damn well what Zukowski had meant. But how could someone like Mister McGovern possibly understand what it felt like to be outed in the middle of a ball game, sitting as I was, between my friend and my girl having a bonding moment at my expense.

Zukowski's sandwich had one bite taken out of it. Mister McGovern asked how the peanut butter smeared in with the tuna fish had gotten there.

If you don't mind my saying so, sir—he doesn't have a single friend in this place. It could have been anybody.

A pack of Winstons sat in a square glass ashtray on the corner of Mister McGovern's desk. He reached over the lunch tray for them.

Horseshit. You locked him out of the gym naked last week. The week before that, you stuffed his textbooks down the john. Before that it was the dog shit you smeared through the air vent in his locker. Not to mention that you punched him in the mouth at the pep rally. What do you take me for?

THE SECOND TIME I SAW Zukowski, he was standing in the gym with his Keds tied so tight they seemed to strangle his pigeon feet.

Zukowski, right?

Yeah.

How ya doing?

Good. You?

Good. Good.

I took in the dusty light glaring down from the narrow slit windows above the rafters, the cinder walls covered in a thick coat of fresh paint. The wooden stands teetered all the way up to the blue-and-gold banner. I tried to whistle. I mean, wow. Just, wow.

Say, what are you doing here?

Trying out.

You?

A door marked EXIT creaked open, and Coach Picareaux limped in with his duffel bag stuffed with basketballs knocking against one leg. First, we did jumping jacks, which were a breeze. Then came wind sprints—which were considerably less of a breeze. By the end of the fourth one, I was looking at Coach Picareaux like he couldn't be serious. By the middle of the sixth—or maybe it was the fifth—I turned back a few feet shy of the blue lion they've got painted on one of the walls, clutching my gut as I trudged back toward the other side. By the ninth one, I was hacking so hard I was surprised not to see blood when I went down on all fours and spit.

Then came free throws. I hit the rim twice. The rest were air balls.

Coach Picareaux was a heavyset man who wore black polyester slacks up around his gut and a golfing shirt so tight it pinched in all the gray hairs around his flabby bicep. The rest of the guys loved him for his encyclopedic knowledge of baseball, basketball, hockey, football, golf, tennis, lawn bowling, lacrosse, track and field, Formula One, the Tour de France, the America's Cup—you name it. Everything but algebra. Me, I loved him because he once let me win at Shipwreck.

He lined us up on the baseline and called Lichenberger and Vernonblood forward and instructed them to pick sides for a basketball game. A few minutes later, I was wearing a yellow mesh vest over my T-shirt that ballooned like a dress despite my best efforts to prevent it. Zukowski managed to get the ball early on and make an impression with all the fancy stuff he could do. Like dribble without looking at the ball.

The principal problem for me, so far as I could tell, was that I didn't seem to inspire much confidence in my teammates, and, to my great dismay, Zukowski least of all. At first, Lichenberger and Hamilton were the only two on our squad moving the ball up the court, which was bad enough. But then they gave it to Zukowski, of all people. Not only was he shorter than me—by a whole inch—but he wouldn't pass me the ball. It was bad enough the first time. But when it happened a second and a third and a fourth time, I confronted him.

Stop hogging it!

Damn it, Huey! Go under the net!

Let someone else dribble it for once!

We're not taking turns—this is a scrimmage! Now go wait for a pass under the net like you're supposed to!

I said, give it!

The whistle shrieked. I hung back by the goalpost and leaned my ass against it, clutching the tops of my knees, gasping for air, sweating like a pig. My butt hole itched. My ass felt buttery. I felt like I was going to shit myself. I spit a long string so thick the phlegm stretched out like taffy. I tried to wipe it off but only managed to smear it across my face. Then it stuck to my arm. By the time I finally got rid of it, the boys were charging back down the court, full speed, panting like wolves, straight for me.

The ball bounced off Vernonblood's sneaker. I snatched it up before the big goon could recover it and ran with it in the opposite direction like I was going for a touchdown. Everyone in the gym was hollering for me to stop. To get them all to shut up, I halted dead in my tracks and held the ball over my head like I'd seen the others do.

Zukowski was hollering himself red in the face. *Huey! What in hell are you doing?!*

Not so much fun now, is it?

Pass it!

Go to hell!

Goddamnit! Pass it already!

See? How do you like it?

Coach Picareaux was fed up and wanted to know *What in the Lord's name game are you playing?*

Keep Away, Coach!

And boy did it feel good, for all of the fifteen seconds or so that I got to do it. I handed the ball off to Lichenberger, smiled at Zukowski, and hobbled down the court after the others.

I STARTED PACKING up the second the big announcement hit the intercom: Coach Picareaux had finally posted the lineup outside his office door. The fifth period bell rang, and I shot out of my seat and bolted downstairs. Rumor had it that the fourteenth spot was selected by lottery. So even if tryouts hadn't gone so well, I figured I still had a shot. The team roster was up, just like the announcement had said, and Zukowski was standing underneath it. Lichenberger, Vernonblood, and Hamilton were behind him. Bilmore and everyone else shoved past me on their way to the door. They all, every last one of them, crowded around Zukowski, shouting, wanting to know if they had made it or not.

They were all clawing at it like savages. Frankly, I was surprised the stingy bit of masking tape was holding. As Zukowski ran his finger down the mimeograph, with that mountain of assholes slowly caving in on him, I turned around and split. So there I was, walking back down the now quiet hall the same way I'd come, up the flight of stairs where cardboard pumpkin cutouts taped up along the slick wall were decorated with orange and black glitter sprinkled on white glue. I ran my finger along the grout and knocked them down, one by one. I walked out of a pair of swinging double doors and to the right, past a portrait of one of the headmasters from the days of Ye Old Governor William Bradford. I walked up to him and, after careful consideration, lobbed a loogie right between his eyes.

I stopped at the glass trophy case that's set into the wall by the entrance. It reminded me of Dr. No's aquarium except without the water and fish. Among the dusty memorabilia were a collection of daguerreotypes crammed in on the top shelf. And let me tell you, a bunch of fourth and fifth and sixth graders never looked more noble. One of the kids in the front row was holding one of those old-style basketballs, and something about it reminded me of someone I used to know. I dunno. Maybe it was the dark brown leather they used back then.

I passed the janitor on my way out. Clyde was a bowlegged colored man who'd introduced himself to me on the very first day of school. At the time, I just figured Mister McGovern had given him a heads-up about me or something. That sort of thing seemed to be happening all the time since I'd started at Claremont. Me being called aside, I mean.

Huey, here, meet Mister So and So. I told him all about you—what a promising young scholar you are.

And Mister So and So: *Glad to have you—a real fine addition to our school, young man. Can't wait to see you out on the court. Make us proud.*

Clyde was standing at the foot of the steps, holding one of those wide brooms that's really hard to push because of how stiff the bristles are. He was leaning on it, looking over all the sagging garbage bags chock full of leaves that he hadn't yet tied up. As I made my way down the steps, he told me to cheer up. Said he'd worked at Claremont for God knows how long and was awfully glad to see me. Then he held out his hand and slapped me five. Clyde could try and make me feel better all he wanted, but it was no use. I felt like I was the only colored kid on the planet who didn't know how to put a ball through a hoop.

THAT CHRISTMAS MISTER Blumenthal gave Mom tickets to see *The Nutcracker.* Wanting nothing more than to finally meet this new friend of mine that she'd been hearing so much about, Mom kept nagging me to invite Zukowski until I couldn't stand it anymore. So one night after school the three of us were on our way to the show, chitchatting on the bus about this and that—still getting to know each other, I suppose—and Zukowski asked Mom how she liked New York.

I knew that Zukowski was just trying to make small talk, but Mom didn't. She started blabbing nonstop about how she didn't think the city was all it was cracked up to be, how she'd come here expecting a professional life she hadn't been able to find down South and here she'd become, of all things, a housekeeper.

But I suppose I'd do it again. If nothing else, at least now I know what became of all the women who left Akersburg when I was a kid—waves and waves of them. Because I'd always wondered. They had so many dreams. Fantasies, really. And I grew up hearing about them all the time—dreams of finding a sanctuary up here for people like me. Where we could live like everyone else. And I needed to see for myself if that was true.

I suppose I can see where you're coming from, Missus Fairchild. But it's still gotta be better here—I mean, people are living in the Dark Ages down there, aren't they? Killing colored folks left and right. Not just Dr. King, I mean. Ordinary colored folks. Like that one that got lynched just for swimming in that pool. You remember that, right?

Mom looked out the dark window and went quiet. All this time she had been pouring her heart out, I was bursting at the seams, wanting nothing more than for her to shut her big fat mouth. And this was why. Even Zukowski, who was pretty damned inept when it came to reading body language, noticed the uncomfortable silence. I could tell that he was wondering what he'd said wrong. So I slung an arm over his shoulder and told him not to worry about it. It wasn't his fault. Poor fella. How was he supposed to know that he'd just stepped in a pile of dog shit?

There we were—the three of us—sitting on a crowded city bus lurching its way down Broadway on a snowy December evening. Outside, people in long wool coats were caroling down the bright, window-lit street, and us on our way to see, of all things cheery and uplifting, *The Nutcracker*. How was I supposed to tell Zukowski that we only had one pool in all of Akersburg, and come summertime, it was like a second home to me, which was the only reason Dad and I had turned up in our swim trunks the day after the shit had pretty much hit the fan?

EVEN IF THE BILLBOARD OUT front said that the Camelot was the perfect rest stop for snowbirds passing through Akersburg on their way to Florida, it owed its survival to the moms who brought us kids to the pool out back. Mister Abrams opened it to us kids six weeks a year. The rest of the time, it was only for his motel guests. But for those six steamy, hot weeks of summer he practically let us have the full run of the place. I ran in that day expecting to see a bunch of my friends horsing around, only to find the place empty. Dad strolled in behind me asking if anyone was here yet.

I slid the patio door open and stripped down to my trunks while Dad went on like a broken record about how nice it was to have the pool all to ourselves for a change. He eased himself in and held up his hands like he was about to catch a football. The agreement had been for me to jump in on the count of three, but on two a voice boomed out, *You can't be in there!*

It was Mister Abrams. Dad hoisted himself up the stepladder and headed on over to see what was the matter. As the two of them stood there talking, I went to check out the Coke machine sitting underneath the wraparound staircase leading to the catwalk above, only before I'd even reached it, Dad shouted out for me to pack up. *Pool's closed,* he said.

What's more, he was just as tight-lipped out in the parking lot as he had been poolside. So I kept my mouth shut, like I always do when I don't know what the heck's going on; that is, until we pulled back onto Cordele Road.

What was that all about?

Dad started explaining about this time last year when my friend Derrick had lit a brush fire out behind his shed and his mom had called the fire department all the way up from Blakely, when she could just as well have put the damned thing out with her garden hose.

The point is . . . People overreact. Derrick probably just got caught tinkling in it, is all.

Which I knew perfectly well was true. Derrick claimed that it wasn't so bad so long as you did it in the deep end. Being only eight and highly impressionable, I believed him. Besides, it was pretty much what all of us kids did. Which meant that Dad had no idea what the heck he was talking about.

When we got home, Mom was preparing her hot comb over the stove, and the whole house stank of bergamot. I immediately asked her if Derrick had come by.

He wasn't at the pool? She asked the question as if Derrick being there was a given. Dad plopped himself down at the kitchen table and answered with a quick *Nope.*

When the comb was smoking hot, Mom hollered out to Miss Della that she was ready. Mom had been doing Miss Della's hair since before it'd turned gray, which I'm pretty sure made her Mom's longest-standing customer. Anyway, Dad was going on about how we'd found empty deck chairs scattered around the pool and a half-empty beach ball rolling over the terrace like a tumbleweed.

Not a soul in the place. And just as Huey's set to hop in, Stanley comes out and tells us he's closed. Can you believe it?

For business?

No. Just the pool.

The bathroom door opened, and Miss Della appeared in the doorway with her hair in a plastic bag and jumped right into the conversation. *You didn't hear about the two colored boys caught swimming in there last night?*

I stepped back as Miss Della teetered past, the garbage bag wrapped around her neck like a four-sided apron.

Mom pulled a chair up to the sink. *Trespassing?*

That's the question everybody's asking. Why, your buddy Nestor saw them on his way home from work. From what I've heard, he was driving by as they were heading across Cordele Road with a shoe in each hand,

and Stanley's front office lit up like a Christmas tree. When Nestor sped up to get a closer look, they hightailed it on out of there, so scared the one didn't bother coming back for the shoe he dropped. Nestor pulled over. And you know damned well that Nestor being Nestor, he got out of his tow truck and fetched it—then went straight to the police and handed it over, along with the story of what he'd seen.

What kind of shoe was it?

Hell if I know. But apparently the sheriff's wondering if Stanley ain't been letting coloreds in after hours for a small fee.

You're kidding.

Do I look like I'm playing a practical joke?

Akersburg was a nice place to live, but like any place, we had our problems. Mostly with colored people. Anyway, Miss Della was the Orbachs' housekeeper. Whenever I saw her around their house, it was always *Yes, ma'am* and *No, ma'am* and *Right away, ma'am*. But the second she stepped foot in our house, I never heard a woman cuss so much in all my life. She didn't give a damn what Mom or Dad thought—except where it concerned her hair.

Mom eased Miss Della into a chair and sent me out to help Toby clean the points and adjust the timing. Toby had been around as long as I could remember. It didn't matter if it was the cistern or a watch: if a man made it, Toby could fix it. I watched from the open doorway as Mom tipped Miss Della's head back over the kitchen sink and rinsed out the blue grease. All the while, foul-mouthed old Miss Della jabbered on like a windup toy.

Toby had the hood of our truck up and was struggling to get the distributor cap off. He was cussing under his breath because he could only turn the wrench in tiny increments. I walked up behind him and coughed. Toby emerged from the engine compartment with a grateful look on his face. Getting that damn distributor hold-down bolt off was one of the few things I could help him with. My hands were small enough to give me easy access. He helped me up onto the bumper, handed me the wrench, and said for me to *Have at it*.

WHEN IT GOT too dark to go on, Toby sent me inside to wash up. Miss Della was gone, and Mom and Dad were sitting at the kitchen table trying to figure out what colored man in Akersburg had gumption enough to swim in the Camelot's pool. When I said to Dad never mind who, but why, he told me to go back outside and continue helping Toby. When I showed him the grease covering my hands, he handed me a gingersnap and told me there would be another one waiting just as soon as Toby and I finished up.

It was pitch black out. From the front window, Toby was visible under the pool of flickering patio light. He let the hood slap shut and a square of dust kicked out from under it. I let the curtain fall back over the front window. *He's done!*

Then help your mother.

His lazy ass had moved into the den. From the sound of it, he was lying on his back watching *The Price Is Right*. Mom was sweeping crisps of hair from the kitchen floor. She asked me to start in on the dishes. A few minutes later, Toby was standing beside me. He reached over and washed his hands in the sink, then took the Pyrex that I'd been struggling to get clean, scraped off the rice caked on it, and handed it back. Toby then pulled a plate of rice and beans from the oven and limped out to the back porch.

I stood there with that dish in my hand, stunned. Dad stalked in from the TV room cursing Mister Abrams's pool, hot weather, and Mondays. He complimented me on how clean I'd gotten the Pyrex, then asked Mom how much she'd bid on a new-model Westinghouse slow cooker. When she said eleven or twelve dollars probably, he demanded to know when in the Lord's name that old skinflint Stanley was going to get around to cleaning that damned pool of his.

I didn't see what the big deal was, especially considering that everyone trespassed occasionally. Sometimes there was no getting around it. You had to cut through one place to get to some other place. I had. And my buddy Derrick had, too. He bragged about it. Besides, if dirt was the issue, there were plenty of people who could take care of that, Miss Della being the first who came to mind. Missus Orbach was always boasting about how sparkling clean Miss Della got her bathroom.

I dragged a chair up to the cupboard and pulled down a milk glass. *I thought that's what chlorine was for.*

That'd be like using a Band-Aid to fix a broken neck.

Mom dumped a mound of hair in the wastebasket and mused about how Mister Abrams had originally built his ramshackle motel to cater to the countrified Negros who lived on the outskirts of town back in the days of the sprawling pecan plantations. Of course, it didn't have a pool back then.

Never mind all that, honey. The real issue here is that I paid up front for those swim lessons. Stanley asked if I wanted a receipt and I said, 'What's a receipt between old friends?' Son of a bitch if that wasn't a mistake. I want my money back.

You what?

Goddamnit, Pea. Horsing around in a pool isn't the same thing as knowing how to swim! I figured it was a good opportunity to ask Danny if he wouldn't mind giving Huey a few lessons. Hell. The boy was captain of the high school swim team. I thought it was a great idea. Instead of just sitting around on his rump playing lifeguard, he might as well give Huey a few pointers. The money was just to make it worth his trouble.

Mom pulled down a coffee tin from the cupboard and counted what was left. Dad winked at me and asked Mom if there was any more pie left. She pointed to the back porch and complained about him spending money we didn't have.

Although Toby never ate with us, he usually waited in the kitchen while Mom packed up leftovers for him. When he limped past Dad on his way in, rinsed off his plate, put it away, and left by the front door, I figured he was giving me the cold shoulder for pestering him so much to let me file down the points. Even though he was always complaining about how much work it took to keep the carburetor in sound working order—taking it off every other week to adjust it—he never let me do that part. Getting the distributor cap off was one thing, but adjusting the timing was something else. He paused in the doorway and looked my way, then wiped his mouth on the back of his hand and headed out. It wasn't much. Just a look—enough for me to know that he wasn't sore at me.

Mom stood at the stove yapping to Dad about how he just needed rest. She suggested he put his head back down and try his hand at another catnap. Instead, he paced up and down the kitchen, eating straight out of the pie dish while complaining bitterly about how he was too tired to work and too restless to sleep, and how prices are going through the roof, and that thirteen dollars is a ridiculous amount to ask retail for a slow cooker, even if it is a Westinghouse.

Dad was starting to drive me crazy. I helped myself to that second gingersnap and ducked out the back door. About a hundred yards out, a light flickered upstairs at the Orbachs'. I propped myself up by the banister and stood on my tippy-toes to see if Derrick's bedroom light was on; maybe he knew what the heck was going on. It wasn't. I plopped myself down on the stoop and gazed out over the saddest-looking peanut crop you ever did see, all the while wondering what to make of all the fuss.

THAT POOL WAS the only thing I had to look forward to for the entire month of July. It was practically the only time I got out of the house. Six days a week I'd drag my feet from bedroom to bathroom to kitchen and out onto our creaky back porch, where I'd work for most of the day. Then, come Saturday, you couldn't find a happier kid on the planet, goofing off, making waves in that pool as I did. I kicked at the dirt and headed for the silhouette of the Orbachs' house, the light still blinking in the distance.

The Orbachs had a one-eared mutt named Pip. Derrick said they didn't let her inside because she was a work dog. I'd never seen her work a stitch in her life, unless you count the way she ran up to me at the fence posts that separated our fields from theirs. Pip jumped up on me, wagging her tail and sniffing and licking me all over. She pranced alongside me all the way up to Derrick's bedroom window. I told her to keep quiet and knelt down and combed my fingers through the dirt, looking for an acorn or a pebble—anything that would reach the second-floor window without breaking it. But Pip wouldn't let up. Frustrated with me for not playing with her, she barked. Before I was able to muzzle her, the front door opened. Missus Orbach was standing in the doorway glaring at me.

Damn you, Huey!

I bolted. Missus Orbach was on top of me before I'd even made the line of fence posts. She grabbed me by the neck and I squawked so loud birds flushed and field mice scattered. She dragged me across the field, under the clothesline, and around the side of our house. She mounted the bottommost step and banged on the front door.

Dad poked his head out.

I found him creeping around!

On account of the pool being closed, Pop! I swear it! Christ almighty, I gotta come up with something else to do on Saturdays now! Either that or get to the bottom of who did it so Mister Abrams can open it back up!

What'd I tell you about poking your nose in other people's business, Huey?

If not me, then who? The police? The last case they cracked was. Well, Mister Nussbaum still hasn't gotten his pig back.

Dad told me to apologize.

But my lessons! Don't you get it? Danny packs up and goes back to college in four more weeks. No lifeguard, no swim lessons. It's as simple as that. Mister Abrams is always saying that he doesn't trust any of the other teenagers to look after us kids! So unless I get to the bottom of this, and quick, I may as well kiss that pool goodbye! Besides, you already paid for my damned lessons. Said so yourself. You don't wanna lose that money, do you?

Dad apologized to Missus Orbach. He walked her down the stoop and assured her that whatever was going on with me, he'd sort it out. Missus Orbach said that I sounded like a prairie dog scurrying around in her hedgerows and that I was lucky not to have been shot, then disappeared in the darkness.

AKERSBURG IS MORE of an administrative center for all the local farmers than an actual town. So I just assumed that it was like Dad had said: people just get riled up over the least little thing, just to have something to talk about. Gives them a sense of community. So I pretty much wrote off the matter concerning Mister Abrams's pool, hoping that all the hubbub would blow over in a couple of days and that would be that. But after the fifth day, Mom and I were watching TV after supper when we heard a loud *knock knock knock knock knock knock knock knock knock* at the front door.

Mom didn't take late appointments. She turned down the volume and went to see who it was.

Mister Abrams gave an embarrassed grin in the milky light cast from above the front door. Mom opened it further and invited him in. I shot up in my seat, hoping that he'd come to announce that whatever the heck had been going on was all better now and us kids were welcome back. He took off his hat and told her that he'd just come by to have a quick word with Dad. Mom hung his hat up and led him into the kitchen. Dad was out back repairing stack poles with Toby. She went to get him.

I slid down from Dad's easy chair and followed Mister Abrams into the kitchen. When the storm door smacked shut behind Mom, he pulled from his overcoat what looked like a candied apple wrapped in fancy tissue paper. He wiped his fingers on his coat and unwrapped the paper, then held out a baseball. He told me to take it.

I did.

Mister Abrams said that it was a home-run ball. He told me what inning it had been hit and how warm the night.

You know who Roger Maris is, right?

I nodded.

Mister Abrams went on about how Maris had been hopelessly out of position, even though it wouldn't have mattered in the end, unless perhaps Maris had been sitting high up in the bleachers beside Mister Abrams himself. His knuckles went so white I could see the bone as he tightened his fists around an imaginary bat and mimicked the glorious swing of the man who had hit that ball so hard it shot from his bat like a rocket.

A rocket, *Huey, a* rocket! *Willie Mays made that mark, son. Will! Eee! Mays!*

Mister Abrams stood up straight and caught his breath. He wagged his hand at the ball in mine and said that he didn't care what people said about the Babe. Everyone knew in their heart of hearts that Willie Mays was a god among men.

Well. The ball did smell like a pinecone. And the scuff from where the bat had smacked it was beautiful. But I was suspicious. It was the first time I'd heard anyone talk as if it was possible to comment on a game with nothing in mind other than the game itself, and it stunned me. Because the old man slouching in front of me, with breath like camphor rub, had just spoken of a baseball player as a baseball player and nothing else. And just like that, a light clicked on.

The back patio light. Mister Abrams mussed up my hair and told me that he wanted me to have the ball.

Dad walked in with a paper plate in hand and asked Mister Abrams if he'd care for a cup of coffee. Mister Abrams wasn't interested in coffee. He apologized about having been so testy the previous week, then glanced at Mom and said that surely she'd heard how the police were claiming two colored boys had swum in his pool.

Mom made as if it was the first she'd heard of it.

Dad, too. *And all for a lousy dip. Christ, what's the world coming to?*

There's no place for colored folks to cool themselves is what the world's coming to, dear.

Mom was prone to exaggeration. They had the run of pretty much all of Lake Offal. Dad and I had even seen them there once, on our way out to Kolomoki Mounds State Park. We'd stopped to watch them for a minute; Dad wanted me to see that they could swim just fine.

Dad kicked off each of his boots. I went over and stood beside him in the kitchen doorway, wondering why in the heck those people were always getting themselves into trouble. Mom was at the sink with her back to me and her hands in soapy dishwater. Her backside shimmied as she spoke over her shoulder while scrubbing.

Well, did they catch them?

Not yet.

But they know who it was?

Mister Abrams said that the sheriff was still tossing around names but that he had no proof. He wiped his forehead with the inside of his elbow, and the desperate expression on his face softened.

Listen, Buck. I've done every damned thing they've asked: had it drained and scrubbed, even had a newfangled chemical treatment applied that's supposed to keep out mold, figuring, what the hell. Even if it costs me an arm and a leg. If doing it will make people happy then I may as well. But if Prinket thinks that being sheriff means that he needs to keep coming up with more things for me to do, then I got a mind to go into town and tell him that he can pay for it himself. Because there's the day or two it's gonna take for the water to warm back up to think about. Not to mention that all those chemicals are gonna take a few days for me to get just right. Now they're saying that's not enough. I don't know what the hell they want me to do—put up razor wire? An electric fence? Hire out a night watchman? Build a watchtower? Maybe tear it up and start over? What? All I know is that if people don't start coming back soon, my goose is cooked. And I gotta be honest—I thought that you, of all people, would understand.

Dad's face was deadpan. *Well, we don't.*

Mom turned around with a coffee cup in one hand and a soapy scrub brush in the other. Mister Abrams looked searchingly at her. When she didn't say anything, he groped agitatedly through his pockets only to find that his car keys were already in his hand. He winked at me on his way out. As soon as the front door clapped shut behind him, Mom picked up the crinkly wrapping paper from the kitchen table and, folding it, said how it hadn't even been a week yet and Mister Abrams was already acting like a ruined man.

Dad tossed the paper plate into the trash and told her that this should be a lesson to her: greed was a shameful thing. And he wasn't none too happy about Mister Abrams having gone off and put us in a bind.

Not to mention the money he owes me. Shame on him. Of course we can't go back there now. What'd he bring you, anyway?

A baseball.

A baseball? Christ. That old fool don't even realize that being cheap is what got him into this mess. Go on and get yourself ready for bed.

But it's only seven.

Then pick up your room.

Dad just wanted to get rid of me, telling me to pick up my room when he knew perfectly well that I already had. I stopped at the front window on my way. Our driveway was a rutted gravel path covered with dead, rotten leaves from the previous fall and lined with garbage cans and a bunch of junk we never used. I blinked as Mister Abrams backed out his Pontiac. And then blinked some more. I couldn't stop blinking.

IV

As much as I would have liked to tell Zukowski about all that had happened that summer, the truth is, I'd gone to great lengths to avoid talking about anything relating to Akersburg those first few years at Claremont. And I do mean *anything*. Don't get me wrong. It's not that I'm ashamed of where I'm from or anything like that, but I could only take so much of Bilmore and Hamilton busting my balls about the way I talked. So when they kept up their *My Fair Lady* routine all the way through Halloween—*The rain in Spain stays mainly in the plain*—I started to feel that maybe I ought to just throw in the towel and hop on a Greyhound back home to Dad's.

Of course, that wasn't going to happen. But I did forbid Mom from coming within ten blocks of school. I tried to explain to her how the parents of the other kids at Claremont don't talk like we do: how the DuPont kid has this way of talking that makes everything he says sound smart, how Bilmore gets ferried back and forth from school in a black sedan, and how Hamilton lives in a penthouse apartment overlooking Central Park. Not to be mean or anything, but just so she would know that these were high-class people she was sending me to school with. You'd think she'd have understood, based on the amount of time she spent with the Blumenthal twins, but honestly, she didn't.

She didn't even have the sense to change out of that black-and-white maid's outfit the Blumenthals make her wear when I met her on the day of *The Nutcracker*. Shortly after we took our seats, I leaned over and hush-whispered for her to at least have the good sense to keep her coat on until they dimmed the lights. Talk about embarrassing. It was starting to seem like she was doing it on purpose.

A FEW DAYS later, I was sitting in class humming Tchaikovsky's "Russian Dance" when Mister Yamaguchi sent me to Mister McGovern's office even though I instantly apologized and told him I didn't mean to be disrespectful. It was just such a catchy number. You can imagine my surprise when I got there only to find Mom sitting in front of his desk wearing that same full length Windermere coat, nodding—a little too eagerly, if you ask me—as Mister McGovern gave his Sermon on the Mount about all that it means to be a Claremont boy.

Mister McGovern stopped talking at the sight of me standing in the doorway. He pointed to a chair and told me to have a seat, then informed me that certain irregularities had been discovered on my last Japanese exam. Which—I'm not going to lie—troubled me immensely. Aside from Clyde, Mister McGovern was my biggest fan in the place. He held me up as a kind of modern day Horatio Alger.

Now, of course, I'm not saying you did anything wrong. But just as a formality, would you mind telling me how you arrived at this answer here?

Mister McGovern held out my exam.

Mom elbowed me. *Go ahead, cupcake. Tell him.*

Yes, Huey. Just walk me through your thought process.

Thought process? I'd scribbled six different verb conjugations and their associated gerunds in little itty-bitty characters on the back of a grocery receipt on the train ride into school the morning of the exam. When I just sat there staring wide-eyed at the blue booklet in his hand, amazed that Mister McGovern even knew kanji and hiragana—who knew?—he turned to another page.

Tell you what—how about we try another one instead?

I cleared my throat. I had nothing—absolutely nothing.

My God, Huey! Don't tell me you cheated!

I know, I know, I know. Cheating kind of defeats the purpose of going to a place like Claremont. But for crying out loud, everyone does it. Okay, maybe not *everyone*. But Zukowski doesn't need to, and Lichenberger studies so damned much only because he's paranoid he's going to be written out of his grandfather's will if he doesn't. And to make matters worse, Mister McGovern had the nerve to come off like I was the only student in the history of the place to ever cheat.

Mister McGovern sat back and frowned. *You want people to think that's the only way someone like you can get ahead in life? Is that what you want?*

V

LISTEN, I WASN'T ALWAYS ASHAMED of Mom. It was just that she was the darkest white person I knew. I never thought twice about it in the context of Mister Abrams's pool. Heck, what was the difference between her and Missus Burns, who was always slopping on the Coppertone, doing her damnedest to brown up every bit as much as Cleopatra? Which is why I always begged Mom to come along to Mister Abrams's pool. Imagine: here it was, the closest thing we had to a country club, and she, the prettiest housewife in Akersburg, refused to step foot in the place. It didn't matter that the rest of the moms all went—even Missus Orbach, whose one-piece made her look like a beach ball in sunglasses. Mom absolutely, positively, refused. After a while I stopped pleading with her. Then the pool closed, and suddenly it didn't matter anymore.

A few days after Mister Abrams gave me that home-run ball, I was tossing it to myself out front when the door creaked open and Mom stepped out with an armful of laundry.

Poor Stanley.

Dad was sitting on the front stoop, showing me the proper way to sort through a pile of stack poles.

Poor Stanley? Poor us. They got every white man in town complaining about how they're being made to take a bath with those colored boys. They got no choice but to close the pool until they find out who did it.

Close the pool? Don't be ridiculous.

Sorting through a pile of stack poles might seem like a piece of cake, but it isn't. Never mind that the pile went all the way up to our roof and was home to all kinds of vermin—each pole was eight feet tall and strong enough to support five hundred pounds of peanut hay. We literally had thousands of them that we reused every year. When I realized that pitching in was the only way to get Dad to shut up about how important our work was, I squatted down and propped the end of the mangy-looking one I'd kicked down from atop the pile across my lap and tried to decide if it should go into the scrap heap or not. And as I looked it over for what Dad called "seams" or "beams" or "reams" or something—I hadn't really been paying attention—I started to wonder how in the world it hadn't been tossed on the junk heap years ago. The son of a bitch had to have been over a hundred years old for all the gouges, pits, and what looked like whip lashes covering it.

I hesitated. Staring down at the gnarled and knobby end in my hand, I felt kinda bad. I mean, this thing looked like there wasn't anything it hadn't had heaped upon it over the years. Instead of taking it to the junk heap, I dragged it across the yard, over to the truck. I leaned it up against the rear bumper, then hopped up and into the truck bed and lifted it over the tailgate until it was in the truck bed with me. As I stood there looking down at it, sorta proud of myself for having spared it, everything around me was nice and quiet except for the *chick chick chick chiiiiiiiick* of the field sprayer across the road and the squeaky sound of the rusty nails Dad and Toby were pulling from dry sweet gum.

Mom came out with another basket of laundry. *There's a plate of peaches for you on the porch.*

Lord knows I was hot and sticky. The shade felt nice, and the peaches were cold and juicy. Mom was standing in the bright sunlight, wringing out a pair of Dad's boxers like a dishrag. And as I sat there atop the stoop, slurping up slice after slice, she went on about how her grampa had picked peaches in the orchard surrounding the Camelot before there even was a Camelot. How, as a girl, she'd seen him walking down Cordele Road on his way home from work after having stopped off there for an "iced tea," shortly after it had opened, back when it was called the CanTab.

I leaned back against a piece of cordwood. She took a clothespin from her mouth and pinned it up, then explained how her grampa had to scratch the CanTab out of his Green Book shortly after they built Turner Airfield.

I wiped peach juice from my chin. *What's a Green Book?*

It's like the Yellow Pages, only for colored people—listing places where they're welcome. Anyway, the motel's not in there anymore. The furniture— threw it out. The carpet—tore it out. Wood paneling gone—tore that out, too. Anything in that motel that held even a trace odor of Mister Abrams's old customers had to go. Then he outfitted it with a new pool. Been the Camelot ever since.

I sat up. *The Green Book still exist?*

Of course.

Can I see one?

I don't see why not.

Mom reached down into the laundry basket and fished around for another clothespin. The porch floorboards were itchy and creaked under my weight, but that didn't stop me from dozing off. While I was lying there half asleep, Dad came out onto the front stoop, wiping his hands on a red rag. He helped himself to a peach slice and asked if I wanted to go for a drive.

I shot up so fast I bumped my head on the rail. It felt like forever since Dad had asked if I'd wanted to go into town, six days a week of having to go without that pool having turned into seven. I darted into the house for my shoes and notepad before he changed his mind. This was my big chance. Green Book, Yellow Book, Purple Book, or whatever book, there was more to the Camelot than met the eye. That much was for sure. I needed to know more—lots more. Who knew where it might lead?

The sun burned the top of my head before I'd even cleared the three lopsided steps out front. I stood there with my shoes in one hand and a pencil and notepad in the other. Dad disappeared around the side of the house. The sky was a crisp blue, and skylarks swirled about in the trees. The laundry was all up, and the bed sheets wafted in the breeze. Mom was hunched over in her vegetable garden, patting down a tomato vine.

You coming?

Mom tossed her garden shears into a bucket, came over, and took up the plate. The screen door clicked shut, and she was gone. Her voice rang out from inside.

Maybe next time.

AKERSBURG HAS A business route that branches off a two-lane highway that takes traffic straight through the center of town. At its northern edge, Main Street merges onto Cordele Road, and a couple of miles up we passed the Camelot. Judging from the way Mom and Dad had been talking, I expected to find yellow tape strung around it and a bunch of patrol cars out front. But Mister Abrams's Pontiac was sitting all by itself underneath the carport of the otherwise empty parking lot.

How long before we can go for a swim?

Filter's busted.

Busted?

I know. Can you believe it? Probably got clogged or something. God knows from what. Could have been from all those little frogs that are always getting in there, for all we know.

The town council had issued a notice decreeing that the Camelot's pool was closed until further notice. I turned to Dad with my pencil still in my hand. Detective Joe Friday wrote stuff down, that much I knew. But what, I had no idea.

I doodled little frogs instead. *Wouldn't stop me.*

Dad chuckled. *And here that ol' fussbudget went to all that expense of applying a fancy chemical treatment, and after all that headache it turns out it's just his filter.*

Why doesn't he just ask Toby to fix it?

Borrow Toby for half a day—in July? Are you kidding me? Not on your life. That boy's up to his gills with work. But I'm sure he'll buy a new one soon. Probably have it in, oh, I dunno—best case, a couple of weeks.

I looked down at my fingers and counted. *Two whole weeks? But that only leaves eleven days until Danny's gotta go back to Fayetteville!*

The order fulfillment alone is bound to take a week.

Order fulfillment?

You didn't think a pool filter just arrives here magically, did you? No, sir. A stock clerk's gotta package it up first. Likely to arrive with bubble wrap stuffed all around it so it doesn't break in transit. Then he's gonna have to invoice it and ship it. Didn't think of that, did you?

Mister Abrams is gonna turn us kids away all that time?

What choice has he got? Our health is a matter of the public trust. Next thing you know, you have the Black Death getting spread. Could be catastrophic.

The tattered billboard leaning off to the side of the road announced that the Camelot was the only place with a pool for the next seventy-five miles. I screwed myself up in my seat.

Know what I don't understand?

What's that?

You remember how we were the only ones there?

Dad grinned.

Well, how'd everyone else know?

The moms probably called around.

The Norfolk Southern Railway cuts right smack through the center of Akersburg on its way to Blakely. We followed the dirt road running alongside it for a good quarter mile before turning off to park. Dad tossed me a couple of plasterer's buckets from the back, and we started up the dirt road on foot.

There must have been at least five hundred head of cattle in the confinement feed lot, and every single one of them was making such a squawk I couldn't hear myself think. Their handlers were gouging cattle prods into their hindquarters, trying to get them up a ramp and into a paneled boxcar. One ambled over. Or maybe he was shoved, I dunno. I could only see a foot or two into the boxcar. After that, it was a dark well filled with bloodcurdling squeals I thought only pigs were capable of making. Anyway, this one cow was crammed in at one end of the boxcar, sorta pinned in, trying desperately to poke his snout through the slats. I reached up and petted his bristly hair, caked flat with dried mud.

I stroked his rubbery snout and told the poor fella not to worry because with any luck they'd get the dirty business done and out of the way before he knew what had hit him. Then I asked Dad how they did it. But before he could answer, I told him how it'd be neat if maybe someday soon we could setup a sanctuary, kinda like the wildlife preserves they got down in the Everglades for the heron that people love so much, only for cattle. Then I looked into this big, dumb animal's beady eyes and gave it to him straight. I told him that it was nothing he'd done. Life just wasn't fair. The trick was just to be so bony no one wanted to eat you and—who knows?—maybe grow some wings.

I turned to Dad and asked him to level with me.

Like I was saying—there's a beefy fella whose job it is to hold him steady, and another burly fella holding the ax. You always gotta have two. One's just not enough. And they do it from behind so the poor bastard doesn't see it coming. Because the meat doesn't taste nearly as good if he does. And if he can get the blade just right behind the ear here—

I mean, how come no one called us?

Dad kicked at the dirt and grimaced like he was afraid that was something I was going to ask, then looked away.

Huey, there's something about your mother that you oughta know. No matter what she does, she can't help but stir up resentment in this town on account of how good-looking she is. Now, you may not know this, being just a boy, and her son at that—but she's a knockout. Okay? There, I said it. Because it's the God's honest truth. I dunno. You're observant. Maybe you've noticed that it causes her more than her fair share of grief. Which is why she doesn't even like coming into town anymore—it's too much of a hassle. No matter how modest she tries to be about it, people resent her. The other moms see how their husbands look at her, and they don't like it. Doesn't matter that it's unwanted attention, either. No one ever looks at them like that, or offers them the same courtesies, which gets under their skin. And they blame her. So ask yourself: why on earth would they have called her?

Dad shook his head disconsolately. *Huey, I'm not proud of it, but that's the truth, the whole truth, and nothing but the truth, so help me God. Okay? Now you know. And you and me had both better just get used to it.*

BUSKIN BROTHERS WAS the local consolidator and supplier for all the farmers in Early County. They didn't sell a whole lot, but what they did sell, they sold a lot of. Dad stood at the counter shooting the breeze with Mister Buskin's eldest son, Stuart.

Still no leads?

It's like a ghost done it. Personally, I don't even see how that's possible. We've got the boy's shoe sitting in some evidence box, for crying out loud.

Dad took the two buckets from me and set them atop the counter and wandered off to the back of the store. I stooped down to the gumball machine and started fiddling with the knob. Derrick claimed that he knew how to get a handful of gumballs to come out without having to put anything in. After what seemed like a million turns of that knob, I was about to punch a hole through the glass case when I felt a pinprick on the back of my neck.

Stuart leaned over the counter and spit out another sunflower seed shell at me. *Go easy on the machine, squirt.*

Stuart wasn't even a real grown-up.

Aw, go suck on a lemon.

Stuart went back to flipping through a stack of receipts.

Dad was fingering over the sweet gum display case on the far side of some paint cans. *Wanna help me pull the truck around?*

I shook my head no, then turned the knob and jiggled the machine some more. Still nothing. I turned that damn knob round and round, shoving and jerking and tugging at the glass case, wondering what in the Lord's name I was doing wrong, only vaguely aware of the stupid front door opening and closing and our truck's diesel engine knocking as Dad pulled into the loading bay and, above me, some loud-mouthed woman shouting over the siphon pump hee-hawing behind the counter, *Of course you know him! The one Buck always has fix that piece of junk truck of his!*

I looked up, surprised. It was Missus Orbach.

Stuart spiked a receipt. *Toby?*

Yes!

I stood up, brushed the sawdust from my knees, and tapped Missus Orbach on the elbow.

Ma'am? Can Derrick come over to play later?

Missus Orbach was dressed in overalls, and her boots were covered in mud. She was looking down at me kind of funny. Her face was red and sweaty. She didn't look very happy.

VI

TOBIAS WETHERALL MUNCIE WAS A smart-as-hell colored man known for being the best farmhand around. The fact that he worked for us was just pure luck; we'd had him since he was a boy. A week after our Buskin Brothers run, he was standing in our field, plunging a posthole digger into the ground, when we pulled up alongside him. Dad leaned out of the truck's window.

What's wrong with your leg?

Hurt it putting up a swing a few nights ago.

Dad laughed. *You crazy nigger. Don't you know better than to hang a swing after dark?*

Toby had been that way for two weeks. How Dad hadn't noticed it before then is beyond me. It was as if he only ever really saw Toby when he was working in the fields. Anyway, Toby didn't seem to care. He limped out into the field and continued hammering away. For the next several days, that's all we did. After lugging hundreds of stack poles into our fields, Toby worked that posthole digger while Dad and I stood close by with a pair of eight-foot stack poles in hand. When the hole was dug, Dad slid in the long, heavy pole, and I'd get down on my hands and knees and tamp down the dirt around it.

Later that week, I was patting down the last bit of loose dirt for what felt like the millionth time when a car came up the road, past the shade trees. It slowed down and turned onto our access road like it wasn't sure where it was headed. People who stopped off for gas in town usually had difficulty finding their way back onto the highway; I assumed the driver was lost. The car pulled over beside Toby and two men got out—to ask directions, I figured.

Dad was hammering a stack pole into one of Toby's postholes, cussing about it not being deep enough. The two men looked like no tourists I'd ever seen. I hollered out to Dad and pointed. Next thing I knew, he was walking toward them so fast I had to run to keep up.

Dad asked Toby if they were bothering him. One of the men offered him a cigarette and wondered aloud how anyone could hoe ground this dry. They were with the Tenant Farmers' Association and were investigating reports of a Mister Nestor Hines charging things on a farm commissary book and refusing to let his customers add up the figures at the end of the month. The men asked if Dad knew him. Dad nodded, but wanted to know what it had to do with us. He pointed at Toby and told them that they could see with their own eyes that he was happy. Dad and Toby had worked together for twenty years, ever since Toby was my age and Dad was a young man. Dad said that he'd taught Toby everything he knew, and that as far as he was concerned, Toby didn't have a single complaint in all the world. *Isn't that right?*

Toby glanced my way. He was so still I could see the rise and fall of his chest, which startled me. Him being anything less than perfectly happy was a scary thought. The man said that Dad wasn't on the chopping block, Mister Nestor Hines was, and did Dad care to help. Apparently, he'd received word from someone in Albany that Dad was different. All I could think was, different than who? Aside from being the last in town to seed, with the single exception of Mister Harrison, Dad wasn't different than anyone.

Dad was tall and wiry. He had a chronic slouch that was in part due to working all the time, but mostly it was because of his bad knee. He was leaning on his sledgehammer with an exasperated look on his face. If his eyes drooped from too little sleep, they were still cold and hard. The man held out a business card. Pop tucked it in his shirt pocket, and the two men left. Didn't even say goodbye—just kicked their way back toward the flower strip, holding out their arms to balance themselves as they crossed our windrow beds. Their car whined in reverse all the way down the access road. All the while, I stood there watching them, thinking how they never explained how they intended for Dad to help.

Dad ordered me to get my finger out of my nose and called me over to his side. I was caked in dust and sweat and was tired of digging around on my hands and knees in dirt as hard as Sheetrock. I had so much of it caked underneath my fingernails that my hand hurt. I wanted a rest. I braced for him to start chewing me out, but he told me to go wait for him in the truck, which irked me. He never let me listen when he talked business with Toby. The only thing he ever shared with me about it was when he went on like a broken record about how city folks think it's just salted peanuts and roasted peanuts and peanut butter, as if the food we raised was good for nothing but sandwiches and ball games.

I moseyed across the ten or so rows between me and the road, smushing every last peanut I could, thinking how I should've gone over to his side to listen in while I had the chance. The truck's hood was hot. Dad's sideview mirror made me look goofy, and the dusty ring around my eyes made me look like a hobo. All the while, Toby and Dad were standing in the middle of that bone-dry field in rain boots.

I assumed that they were bickering over Toby's insistence on planting after the alders had blossomed. But it had been a while since they'd squabbled about anything like that, ever since Mister Schaefer had drummed up worries that the year's crop wouldn't be worth the trouble of digging out of the ground, but ours had weathered the heat just fine. That was the first time that Mister Schaefer ever conceded how good Toby was.

The beds of withered leaves on either side of them went up to their knees—half as high as they were supposed to be. Even if I couldn't hear what they were talking about, I could tell it was important. Toby's face was rock hard; Dad's, too. Toby snapped open a peanut with his teeth and spit out the shell.

My nubby-toed sneakers were clay colored from the road, and a cucumber beetle was snaking its way around my left heel. I squatted down and picked it up.

Don't worry little fella. I won't hurt you.

I glanced up. The rows of sun-withered leaves stretched out behind Dad and Toby as far as I could see. Our field was almost entirely dug up, and we all needed to pull together to get our vines up on stack poles before they rotted. Toby took his cap off and wiped his brow—didn't even blink.

What in the world was taking them so long? The sun was directly overhead; I was starting to roast. Never mind that there was a shitload of work that needed to get done and no one but us three to do it, and with Dad usually running around helter-skelter this time of year complaining about there not being enough hours in the day to get everything done in time, now here he was rambling on like we had all day when all I wanted was to go home and sit in the relative cool of our den and watch TV.

Figuring that my wiggly little friend might make good fish bait, I was digging around to see if there were other beetles burrowed into the nearby dirt when the damn thing bit me. Can you believe it? Dug his pincers into the tender skin between my thumb and pointing finger. I flicked him to the ground. One twist of my shoe and he crunched like an acorn.

Toby let his posthole digger fall to the dirt and limped off. I wiped the dust from my eyes and stood up. Holy mother of God—that was not something I saw every day. Dad ordered me into the truck. I got in and asked what the heck was eating Toby.

I WAS SCRATCHING at the rash of little pinprick scabs up and down my left arm when Dad strolled through the den, trailing peanut hay. He complained to Mom about how he didn't have time for any of Toby's horseshit and how he'd almost had to knock some sense into him earlier that afternoon. Mom asked what for. When Dad explained about Toby walking off the job, Mom said he was probably just tired.

Dad looked doubtful. When Mom asked if he'd had the decency to help, on account of Toby's busted-up leg and how hard it was to dig postholes after such a long dry spell, Dad stood yawning before a half-empty fridge and said that that's what he paid Toby to do, and that Toby had to have been the laziest damned no-good son of a bitch in all of Akersburg.

No wonder he's broke all the time. The nerve of him, complaining about not having enough money.

Well, did you lend a hand?

What do I look like?

For the next several days, the spectacle of that afternoon was all Dad talked about. Toby sloughing off on the job soon became Toby picking a fight, which soon became Toby menacing him with a sledgehammer. Either way, one thing was clear in Dad's mind: Toby was a hothead who was not to be trusted. There was no telling what he might do next.

I WAS DESPERATE to talk to Derrick, because here it had been over a week since Mister Abrams's pool had been shuttered and I was no wiser than I was then. Mom's old Green Book was useless; none of the places around town were listed in it. When I asked why, Mom said it was because Akersburg had become practically a sundown town after Reconstruction—whatever that meant. All I knew was that I was back at square one. I sneaked out the next morning before the sun had crept over the pine trees lining Cordele Road and waited for Derrick to appear from around the bend. When I saw him, he was munching away on a peach, with Pip strutting gleefully alongside him, licking up the juice drippings from the ground.

I ran over. *Where the hell have you been?*

I could ask you the same thing!

We headed off down the road together and didn't look back until we crossed the thick yellow paint of the center line at the sight of Mister Abrams's Pontiac sitting all by itself in his empty parking lot.

Derrick sank against the slatted chain-link fence surrounding the terrace. *Are you sure it's okay to be doing this?*

Sure I'm sure.

Derrick was the littlest kid in school, shorter than our classmate Darla, who was so short she had thick risers mounted to the soles of her shoes to make her taller. Derrick wore glasses that he was always cleaning on his shirttail because he had the bad habit of pressing his glasses up so close to his face that they got sweaty and dusty until he could hardly see through them. He wasn't exactly the perfect angel, but he looked so studious that no one ever guessed the stuff that came out of his mouth when grown-ups weren't around. Anyway, he was in the middle of wiping off his glasses when I told him to stand up. I climbed atop his shoulders and struggled to balance myself against the pipe-fitted rail at the top of the fence. I peeked over it.

Empty deck chairs were scattered around the fenced-in terrace, and the kidney bean–shaped pool was as still as backwater. The glare from the sunlight dancing over the surface of the water was so bright it hurt my eyes.

What a waste.

Is there water in it?

Yeah. But Danny's not here.

I teetered atop Derrick's shoulders and clutched onto the fence. The yellow cordon draped around a pool so clean it sparkled was mesmerizing. Something creaked, and all of a sudden, the bottom fell out. The next thing I knew, I was holding onto that fence, kicking out my feet, screaming.

Goddamnit! What the hell did you do that for?

I hit the ground with a thud and scampered to my feet. I'd almost landed on Pip. Mister Abrams's wash lady, Aurelia, was standing there with her head cocked and her arms crossed. She'd been coming out poolside with extra towels and fresh drinks from the tiki bar for as long as I could remember.

Can I help you boys?

I clapped my hands clean and brushed off the dirt.

Yes, ma'am. We were wondering if this was the spot where those fellas broke in. Because. Well. You see. I just thought that since the sheriff can't seem to catch them—well, I got a pretty good idea about how to keep them from doing it again.

Aurelia stiffened. *And what might that be?*

I pulled out my notepad and pencil from my back pocket.

Afraid I'm not free to say, ma'am, pending a background check. This is all very hush-hush, as you can imagine. We're dealing with security-clearance issues and the like—all very sensitive stuff.

I waited for her to say something. Instead, she pushed her wobbly linen cart across the gravel lot, propped open the door of one of the ground-floor guest rooms, and disappeared inside with a short stack of towels and sheets in her arms. There was something starchy about Aurelia. I think it had to do with all the clothes she washed.

Derrick walked off.

Where are you going?

You're a crazy boy, Hubert Fairchild. If you think I'm going to hold you up again so you can climb over that fence, you've got another think coming. Bad enough that I got your footprints all over my shirt. Lookit— this was clean when I left my house this morning. You're the reason my mom says I can't keep anything clean. Not me—you. And now, to top it off, I'm in trouble with Aurelia, too. Goddamnit, you just know my mom's gonna find out sooner or later. And then what? I'll tell you what. I'm in hot water, that's what. You hear that, Hubert Fairchild? She's gonna have my ass. And you know why? I'll tell you why. Because I'm not even sup- posed to be here, that's why!

Don't be ridiculous. If anyone knows how to keep a secret, it's Aurelia. Trust me, her job calls for a great deal of discretion. I get an earful every Thursday night when my mama gets home from Bible study and then again on Saturday when she does her hair before church.

I took Derrick by the hand and tugged him back toward the arched front door on the promise of a free cola if we could make it past the lobby undetected. It was one of those medieval-style jobbies with a big brass knocker and required all the strength we had to tug it open. I stood in the cool shade of the air-conditioned lobby with Derrick so close I could feel his breath on the back of my neck. We stood there listening to the hum of the air conditioner and the flapping window blinds. The reception desk was unmanned. The coast was clear.

I crept forward, not sure what my plan was until we were standing right up alongside the pot-bellied coffee urn and the inverted stack of Styrofoam cups sitting atop the reception desk. I thought I heard something, but it was just a young couple, wrapped in white bathrobes, walking past in flip-flops. After a minute of standing as still as a statue, I signaled to Derrick and tiptoed past the reception desk. I signaled again, and we continued to the backside of a sofa, then to the plastic ficus standing beside an issue of *Popular Mechanics* splayed out atop an end table. At last I had the cool handle of the patio door in hand. I gave it a tug, and it screeched.

Huey? Mister Abrams was craning his neck over the reception desk, behind me. He was pouring a cupful of water into the coffee urn while holding the lid in his other hand. *What are you doing here?*

Just a quick dip, Mister Abrams?

Mister Abrams came around from behind the counter and gestured to the front door. I went over and stood beneath the thick stock of the yellow notice stapled to the inside of it. My eyes lingered on the oversized seal stamped over the heading "Cause for Closure." Beneath it a checked box read, "Unsanitary."

Derrick came up beside me, and the two of us just stood there. The reality of everything knocked me over the head like a billy club.

I looked up at Mister Abrams. *How bad can it be?*

Mister Abrams pulled the door open. He said for us to do ourselves a favor and let the grown-ups sort out this mess. I stepped out and squinted in the bright light. The gravel passed slowly underfoot. The parking lot let out to the main road. Pip was taking a leak. It wasn't until we stepped onto hot pavement that we heard the heavy door click shut behind us. The defeat felt worse for the genuine belief that my investigation could have ended otherwise.

VII

IF YOU THINK I SKIPPED out of Mister McGovern's office happy to have gotten a second chance, you're dead wrong. As soon as that bastard lapsed back into something that sounded like a recording, I begged pardon and excused myself on the pretense of having to use the restroom. I headed down the hall and peeked into Mister Needleman's social studies class. Mister Needleman had been wearing the same exact sweater vest every day for two and a half weeks. Zuk and I had been keeping track. His brogues were kicked up atop his walnut desk, and he was sipping coffee from a Harvard Club mug while holding up a magnifying glass to a back issue of the *New Yorker*. His students were all listening to an audio recording of a JFK speech. I tried to get Zuk's attention, but he was too busy taking notes. So I continued down the stairwell lined with portraits of our founders, through the dining hall, and past a bunch of third graders eating with their mouths open and slipped out between two food-service employees smoking a cigarette.

I tossed my blazer into the nearest trash can I could find and vowed never to return. I was pissed. I mean, half the time that Mister McGovern was bawling me out, I had no choice but to keep my mouth shut, knowing full well that Mom would interpret any defense I mounted as back talk, indisposed as she was to draw a meaningful distinction between a sham excuse and a heartfelt one. The other half, I was worrying myself sick about how the heck I was going to get out of the building without anyone seeing me and Mom together. Fact is, rumors of her being a housekeeper had spread like wildfire, and the fact that she insisted on dressing that way everywhere she went wasn't helping.

On the northwest corner of Madison and Ninety-Third Street there was a bank of phone booths that started in front of the corner bodega and stretched nearly halfway down the block. I stopped and slid a dime into a phone and made a discreet call to the local NBC affiliate, informing them of a suspicious package in the second-floor bathroom at Claremont Prep. When the switchboard operator hacked into the receiver and said, *What makes it suspicious, toots?* I said that I could hear the damned thing ticking.

Claremont?

You know, the place where Rutherford B. Hayes went to school? Jesus, and here I thought I was the dumb ass.

When she put me through to the police, I blurted out, *Free Bobby Seale!* and split. I popped into the corner bodega and bought myself a Coke and Devil Dogs, then stood in the doorway and peeled back the wrapper amid the wail of sirens roaring past. There were several bicycles leaning against the side of the bodega's brick facade, right beside me. One of them was unlocked. I did a double take. You wouldn't see a bike like that lying around unlocked in my neighborhood in a million years. It had a green fade paint job, chopper forks, chrome fenders, and a banana seat. It was brand new. I mean, who does that? It was bad enough that these jerks had dough coming out of their ears, but did they have to leave their expensive stuff lying around unlocked right under my nose? I looked both ways and hopped on. I tested the brakes—they were squishy. Good enough. I rode off like a bat out of hell around the block. I crossed Fifth Avenue in a virtual speed wobble and tore ass through Central Park, and on the way it dawned on me that you can't go a block in this city without seeing some bumper sticker slapped across a stop sign.

VIII

I SPENT FOUR MORE DAYS digging those goddamned stack pole holes alongside Toby. I didn't have to, but I felt the need to help because of his busted-up leg. Anyway, I was sick of seeing those holes two and a half feet down and eight inches in diameter. They resemble gopher holes. I was sick of trudging back and forth between the house and the field, sick of the dirt, and sick of the heat. I was practically seeing those holes in my sleep. Sleep sheep were supposed to jump over a fence, but mine fell into stack pole holes. So when I saw Toby out on the tractor, tearing hell-for-leather around our field with the digging blades scooping, sifting, and flipping a mess of roots, stems, and vines, I jumped for joy. I ran and climbed up behind him and took hold of the back of his overalls and yelled out, *Giddyup!*

I've warned you about holding me like I'm a bronco!

Fine, then lemme work the gas!

Toby goosed it so hard I fell off the back and landed on my ass in a puddle of dirt as hard as concrete. Dad was sitting on the bumper of his truck, munching on a sandwich, pretending like he hadn't seen a thing. I limped over and complained. He stuffed the rest of the sandwich in his mouth.

The boy was up nearly half the night getting the wheel bearings filed down just right. Leave him alone.

Leave him alone? One minute he was a lazy, no-good drunk who didn't know how deep a post hole should be and the next he was worth his weight in gold. I wished Dad would make up his mind, because just when I was starting to see how selfish Toby was, Dad would shift course and take his side for no reason at all. *Poof*—just like that, all was forgiven.

Then came the day that I wandered into the kitchen and slid out the newspaper from beneath a glass of lemonade and started reading an op-ed piece by a Mister Ryan P. Nichols, chamber of commerce board member and citizens' council trustee, about how Mister Abrams had permitted a professional "association" to slip into his pool on the sly for a free trim of his hedges.

I sat down and took a swig of lemonade so cold my teeth hurt, smacked my lips to get the sour out, and double-checked the masthead to make sure it was the *Blakely Register* I was reading. Talk about ridiculous. Why on earth would Mister Abrams do something as silly as that? Everyone knows that coloreds work for pretty much damned near nothing.

Then the very next paragraph said something about Mister Abrams running an integrated pool by virtue of permitting coloreds entry after hours for a small fee. I reread it, thinking I'd misread it because the wet ring from the lemonade glass had blurred some of the words. A shadow fell over me, and Mom snatched the newspaper out of my hands. Actually, she tugged at it, trying not to rip it, until she did. I was reluctant to let go. Why would I, when no one would tell me what the heck was going on, and here even the newspaper was saying stuff that made no sense?

They got it backward, Mama. Coloreds fish the leaves out every morning. They don't swim in it.

I couldn't very well tell her that I'd seen it countless times with my own two eyes. That would have been a touch bold, even for me. Anyway, Mom was surprised—even though my elbows were so bony they bored holes in my shirt sleeves, I was pretty damned strong. I wasn't letting go of my biggest clue in weeks. Then she was angry. She grumbled something about not knowing I could read that well, then accused me of pulling the wool over her eyes every time she'd sat down to read with me. Which was only half true. It wasn't that I couldn't read; I didn't want to. The Gospels of Mark, John, Luke, and whatshisface— Matthew—bored me to tears.

She doubled up the newspaper and tucked it under her arm and told me not to believe every single thing I read. When I asked if that applied to the Gospel of Matthew, she slapped me upside my head with the paper and said that God could be wrathful every bit as much as he could be forgiving. I told her that was Zeus she was talking about, not God. What did God have to be wrathful about? He created us single-handedly. Did it in seven days—which some people think is amazing, but I thought curious. What was his rush? If things weren't going right, it was no wonder. He should have just slowed the hell down and taken his time. Rush jobs never end well.

The more I scratched at the surface, the less sense things made. I asked Dad to explain how the pool filter broke, and if it broke by coincidence after the break-in or if it was just old or if someone had done it on purpose or if the burglars had broken it, and why on earth the sheriff was focusing so much attention on the pool instead of the actual burglars. Not to mention that in all this time, no one had mentioned anything having been stolen. Even Mister Nussbaum's mysterious break-in netted the loss of one blue-ribbon heifer named Mollie. And if nothing had been stolen, why not? And now there was all the crazy talk in the paper. Dad always just said *It's complicated* or *I'll tell you later,* but later usually never came, and the few times it did he spread the malarkey so thick even I could see through it. Which was saying something. Truth be told, I still half believed in the tooth fairy. Or at least *wanted* to believe. Because I kinda did and kinda didn't. What I mean to say is, I didn't see how it was possible, but at the same time, I wasn't quite ready to turn down the free nickel.

I dug out my basketball from the shed and slammed it against the backboard, more in frustration than an attempt at shooting baskets. Mom came out and told me to stop. When I asked why, she said because I mostly missed. All the noise the ball made when it banged against the door scared the hens.

Mom went into her vegetable garden and checked after her tomatoes, then disappeared into the henhouse by way of the man door on the side. The two-tiered board-and-batten door creaked open, first the upper half, then the lower. Mom emerged with an egg-filled stewpot and a bunch of hens squawking at her feet.

Now look what you've done.

She shooed them away and closed the door.

If they broke into that pool and didn't steal nothing, wouldn't that be like someone breaking into our house to take a bath? Which, unless

you've got a heart of stone, seems harmless enough. And speaking of col-
ored kids, do they have their own tooth fairy?

There was a moment of quiet. Mom made her way across the yard
and up the steps. I wasn't sure if she'd heard me. I just stood there beneath the chicken-wire hoop mounted above the henhouse door, holding the ball in both hands. The spring-loaded arm of the storm door
hiccuped shut behind her. All I heard was her dismissive voice coming
from down the hallway.

Don't go poking your nose in other people's business.

*Other people's business? It's all anyone talks about anymore! And it's
just as much my business as theirs!*

THINGS DIED DOWN between me and Derrick after our run-in
with Aurelia and Mister Abrams. He said playing detective wasn't fun
anymore and wanted to stop. Who was playing? I think he just didn't
like being Dr. Watson to my Sherlock Holmes. Anyway, just when you
think you know someone, they surprise you. Two days later, something
smacked against my window. I got out of bed and went over expecting to find a bluebottle flailing about on the dusty sill. My hamster,
Snowflake, attracted them. Instead, I found Derrick standing outside
with an acorn in hand and a big grin on his face. He gestured for me
to come out.

I opened the window and poked my head out. *Does your mama
know you're here?*

*That bitch sent me out for cigarettes and matches. I'm probably not
coming back 'til dark.*

That was the Derrick I knew and loved. Listen, he may have been
a little particular when it came to keeping his eyeglasses clean, but he
had the mouth of a sailor. He was a lot of fun to be around. Hell, if I
had to live with that bitch, I'd probably run away for the afternoon, too.
Anyway, Mom had this thing about ticks, which meant that I had to
wear socks, sleeves, and trousers no matter the heat. I slipped on some
clothes and hopped out the window, and the two of us headed off.

On our way through Mister Noonan's orchard, a shiny can half
hidden in a tuft of grass caught my eye. I thought it was an unopened
cola. I dropped the peaches that were tucked within my bulging

shirt and called Derrick over. He wanted to use a rock to get it open, but we couldn't find one pointy enough for a two-mile stretch of Oglethorpe.

We got lucky poking around behind Mister Buford's barn. The bulging can exploded in my face, and Derrick cut his lip on the jagged edge where I'd driven in a rusty screwdriver. The warm beer mixed with blood and dirt tasted like pure adventure. We sat with our backs leaning against the warped pine shingles. The sun was about to disappear behind Mister Noonan's peach trees up the road and gave the blood dripping down Derrick's chin a golden tint. It made him look like some grunt over in Vietnam who'd just taken a round in the gut but who was pressing on for honor and love of country—either that, or something I'd seen in a Coke commercial.

MOM WAS IN the middle of serving up supper when Missus Orbach tossed the front door open and stood there holding Derrick in front of her with a bandage covering half his face.

Your boy did this!

I figured what with all the alcohol we'd sloshed around our mouths it'd stop bleeding by the time he got home, but it'd just gotten worse. Dad got up from the table and asked what had happened. The dumb ass panicked.

He hit me!

With what, a knife? Dad looked genuinely confused.

Missus Orbach barged into our kitchen and explained how that wasn't the worst of it. Apparently someone had seen us chugging cans of beer out behind that old barn that Mister Buford converts into a haunted house every October. Lord knows I couldn't do anything without someone finding out about it. And there Derrick was, cowering behind his mother, pale as a ghost. He didn't even have the decency to look at me.

Mom returned from the bathroom with her first aid kit and offered to "patch Derrick up." Missus Orbach looked like she was about to faint, said she'd just as soon see Derrick harelipped as let her touch him. She declared to Dad that Mom was hardly fit to be a mother and that he needed to rein us both in. Then Missus Orbach stormed out the front door, dragging Derrick and his bloody lip along. Dad shook his head, closed the door, and asked whose idea it had been.

Of course it'd been mine. But what did that matter? Derrick only ever did something if I did it first. Truth is, I was just bored. What else was there to do with the pool closed? Dad sent me to bed without dinner. The rest of that night, I lay beneath a thin sheet with a flashlight and worked on a puzzle I kept hidden under my mattress for times like this. I overheard Mom tell Dad how I should be out swimming instead of drinking rodent-infested cans of near beer and how she had a mind to march me back down to that pool herself just as soon as Mister Abrams opened it back up. Aurelia had warned her that I was up to no good. Then she warned Dad not to expect her to look the other way the next time that crazy woman shouted at her in her own house.

FOR THE NEXT two and a half days, the spectacle of that afternoon was all anyone talked about. Even talk of Mister Abrams's pool died down. The two of us sharing a thirty-two-ounce can of Falstaff became me zigzagging down Cordele Road, unable to hold my head up, which soon became me crawling down the middle of the road, drunk out of my gizzard, which soon became me practically passed out buck naked on the side of the road. Which was the version that Toby had gotten wind of from Miss Della, who'd gotten word of it from Missus Orbach, who probably found out from Mister Buford himself. What do I know?

All I know is that I was helping Toby load up stack poles later that week when he asked me if it was true. I blushed when I said yes, because Dad rarely touched the stuff, and here I was feeling like a boozer at the ripe old age of eight. I braced for Toby to take his turn at being disappointed, but he just asked if it was near beer or rotgut.

What the hell's that?

Well, was it in a can or a bottle?

A can.

How tall was it?

I held out my two pointing fingers about a foot apart from each other. *Yea big.*

Did it have a picture of a mule on it?

A mule? Naw. A lightning bolt.

A lightning bolt? Toby looked impressed. *You sure?*

Sure I'm sure.

Well, was there any writing on it?

You ever seen a beer without writing on it?

Well, what'd it say?

I was a little scared.

Go on. Spit it out.

"High-Octane Hot Springs Distillery. Makes Even the Ugliest Bitch Look Purdy."

And you drank the whole damned thing?

Derrick said it made him walk funny. But I didn't feel a thing.

Toby kept his woolly hair cropped close and had a well-defined jawbone. He was handsome, even when he laughed at me. He stood up straight, rubbed his hand over his head, and struggled to suppress the last of the humor lingering in his mouth.

Oh, boy. And to think your mama said, "Just you tell me how the heck a boy who can't get down a tablespoon of bitters can chug a warm can of beer?" That weren't no beer, son! That was Sam Nelson's rarefied hickory home brew!

By the lights of Toby's reckoning, I had two choices should I ever find myself in that particular predicament again. One was to hunt him down posthaste and deliver it to him for safekeeping. The second was, well, to drink it.

But for heaven's sake, whatever you do, don't guzzle it. You sip that stuff, hear? And stick to the back roads next time. You never do something like that close to home; someone's bound to see you. If you're hell-bent on seeing what it feels like to pass out, do it where no one will find you. 'Cause they'll just wake you up and put you back to work if they do.

WHEN THE TRUCK was all loaded up, Toby and I headed out. I was standing in the back holding on for dear life, with two tons of stack poles skittering around my ankles and feet. Every twenty yards, Toby would pull over beside our field and tap the horn. I'd let a dozen poles spill over the side of the truck, happy just to clear the tires, then slap the side panel. Then he'd go another twenty yards and I'd do the same thing all over again.

We finished setting out our load for the next morning, then headed home. I was starting to get a little worried, because it'd been almost three days and I still hadn't heard a peep from Derrick. On our way past his house, I shouted out for Toby to tap the horn, thinking that maybe Derrick would come to the window. He didn't.

Ever since Toby and Dad squabbled that day out in the middle of our field, Toby just did his work and left. So when we pulled into the drive and he cut the engine, I hopped out of the back and climbed in up front and cornered him. I demanded to know why he didn't hang out with us in the kitchen anymore. Toby just sat there with both hands on the steering wheel and clammed up. When I pressed, he looked over and sighed.

There's a difference between waiting for someone to pack up your food and hanging out.

Which cut me to the quick.

Listen. Your old man's a good guy. He really is. It's just that he's the kind of boss who, if I don't put the brakes on myself, he'd work me until I'm plum out of gas. Okay? So I'm just tired, is all.

I knew what he was talking about. It was true: Dad couldn't resist the temptation to squeeze as much work out of every single day as he could. I reached down and plucked up my dive mask from the footwell and pondered it. I'd forgotten all about it. I must've left it there the day the Camelot's pool closed. Toby leaned over and rubbed his fingers through my hair. He grinned wide.

It's almost as curly as mine.

You've got a dark sense of humor, Toby Muncie. You know that? Dark. And I don't appreciate it one bit.

I WAS STARTING to suspect that Dad's little talk with me about Mom being every Southern housewife's nightmare probably wasn't the only reason she didn't come to Mister Abrams's pool. Early the next morning, Dad shook me awake, I thought to go to the bathroom. My bed-wetting was an ongoing source of conflict. It wasn't like it happened every night, but my folks had let me know that I was too old for accidents like that. Anyway, he whispered in my ear for me to keep quiet. Said he had a surprise for me, then told me to meet him out in the truck. I got dressed and tiptoed out the front door, wondering what the heck was so important that Mom couldn't know about it.

The S&W in town is long and narrow and has booths running along the wall opposite the lunch counter. It was my second time there. I stood in the open doorway for a moment and took in the chrome fixtures. They were all shiny and bright. The checkered tile floor was spotless.

Dad shoved aside two half-filled cups of coffee and an ashtray and uneaten toast someone had left on the counter. He slapped the stool next to him.

Whaddya feel like, partner?

He had this way of talking that made him sound like he could have bought me anything in the place: "Steak and Egg Breakfast." "Triple Stack of Hot Cakes." "Banana Split." "Hot Fudge Sundae." "Vanilla Cream Soda." "Malted Ripple Shake." Which I Knew Wasn't True. But I pretended like it was.

I hopped up beside him and swiveled around. *How about a sundae?*

Two hot fudge sundaes coming up.

I jerked around, surprised. The last time that had ever happened, I wasn't big enough to sit on a stool by myself. I remember him telling the soda fountain boy how we weren't going to be long. I figured it was because of the mess I made while sitting on his lap.

What'd I do to deserve this?

Dad looked at me like we ate ice cream for breakfast every day of the week. He sure could be hard to read when he wanted to. Anyway, it was right about then that a bus pulled up out front. I remember thinking it strange because the bus station was down the street in front of the Rexall; they had a stall inside where passengers could buy coffee and use the bathroom. Not to mention it being so early it was still dark out.

The driver got out and opened the side hatch and started unloading suitcases onto the sidewalk. A colored man got off after him and lit a cigarette and slapped at his rumpled clothes in the quarter light. Pretty soon there was a crowd standing on the sidewalk with him. They looked like Jehovah's Witnesses, all dressed in short-sleeved button-downs and neckties as they were.

It dawned on me that they were probably Seventh-Day Adventists who'd come down for a convention or something—probably for their annual open-tent revival meeting, which they held every fall out on Mister Parker's land. Mister Parker was so devout he burned crosses in his fields like the big ones they had back in the time of Pontius Pilate.

I elbowed Dad. *Looks like they brought the whole congregation.*

Dad wasn't paying me any mind. He was leaning over the counter, asking Tyler if he'd mind giving us an extra squirt of hot fudge. I picked up the salt shaker and started playing with it. Mister Chambers joined Mister Orbach at the front window. I saw him in the mirror behind the counter.

What time does Phil open the ticket desk?

Not until eight.

What time you got now?

Six.

Ted, get Ira on the phone, will you? Tell him to get down here.

He don't usually go into the office until nine, Les.

Just call him!

Next thing I knew, Mister Schaefer slapped the front door open and stormed out and started tossing bags back into the luggage hatch. One of the colored men tried to stop him. That's when Mister Orbach ran out. So did Mister Peterson. And Mister Bradford. And Mister Prewitt. Pretty soon me, Dad, and Tyler were the only ones left in the place.

I stuffed my mouth with ice cream. *What's going on, Pop?*

The words came out in a jumble. No matter how fast I tried to eat my sundae, I couldn't seem to keep it from drowning under all the hot fudge. When I came up for air, Dad was gone, and Tyler was standing with his face pressed up against the front window, looking out. I shoved as much as I could fit in my mouth, hopped down, and ran out with the others. I wriggled through the crowd of men pushing and shoving and barking over each other. It was impossible to hear what anyone was saying, except for Mister Schaefer. He had a shaky old man's voice that could be heard a mile away.

SNCC? What's that?

Student Nonviolent Coordinating Committee!

Mister Schaefer asked Mister Orbach if he knew what the colored man was talking about. Mister Orbach shrugged no. A patrol car pulled up. All of a sudden, I could hear the chirp of a starling flitting gleefully from branch to branch within the thick green canopy of elms lining the street. The sun was just starting to creep up over Missus Henniger's flower shop, but the sky was hardly lit. A colored man with puffy hair and glasses was standing with his back to me, addressing the crowd of coloreds gathered around him with several duffel bags strewn about. He was wearing a necktie and Windbreaker.

Remember, if anything happens, it's hands behind your back, down on your knees, and head down—pray.

Seventh-Day Adventists had never caused this kind of a hullabaloo before. Not to mention that I didn't remember ever seeing so many coloreds among them.

I tugged on Dad's sleeve. *What's he talking about, Pop?*

The sheriff got out of his patrol car and brushed past me on his way toward Mister Chambers, who was barring the open doorway with his arm.

If they want a burger and fries that bad they can just as well go to the Blue Flame, on the other side of the Thronateeska, and be served by a colored just like them, and with a smile to boot.

Or would it kill them to eat in? Spending money they have no business spending on things they can't afford and have no business buying.

No wonder they're broke all the time. Christ.

Tyler brought out a cup of coffee. The sheriff stirred it, then took a sip. As he handed back the spoon, there came the *pop* and *crash* of a bottle shattering against the side of the bus. Glass sprayed over the street and sidewalk. Dad snatched my arm and tugged me through the fleeing crowd. I ran like a bat out of hell and glanced over my shoulder, unsure if he would be able to keep up. I heard his voice.

Looooook ooooooooouuuuuut!

I smacked into what felt like an oven range. What it was doing on the sidewalk, I have no idea. All I know is that everything stopped. I remember lying on my back, floating off toward heaven's pearly gates, ready to make my grand entrance, wondering what in the hell had just happened.

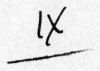

DON'T LOOK AT MY LIPS, look at me. Here, Jerry, you can take these. Smelling salts. Now, how many fingers am I holding up? Not there, here. Good enough. All the way to the back. On top. Just keep squeezing my hand. Atta boy. One hundred over sixty? Jesus. He's going to need some Demerol. Yeah, you can go ahead and get rid of that. No, about sixty seconds. Now, you've got to make sure each of these is snug. On three. Ready?—Umph. I promised Iris I'd take her to the pictures. Because of that swim-in yesterday up in Albany. Where've you been? No, same ones, I think. Just like what they did here, except at the Cozy Oaks. Spoiled everything.

Pop?

Keep your head down, son. And told her may as well put me back on rotation. So I came in to do a quick four. Hours. No, after. When we were at the— Put your head back down.

Mister Peterson?

Atta boy. Hold steady. Over the curb. To the left.

Mister Orbach?

Two steps thisaway. Kitty-corner, steady as she goes. Easy does it. Little bump. Up. Ready. Umph. And in we go.

Mister Chambers?

No, he's gonna be just fine. Not too tight on that strap. You've got to slap that buckle good 'n' hard for it to click in. There.

Where're they taking me, Pop?

I understand that you're concerned, sir, but it's against regulations. And, Jerry, I'll put in a repair order when we get back. No, we didn't see a thing, just picked him up like this. Hey, do me a favor and give us some wiggle room. Yeah. You in? Ain't nothing in the world like a—you've got to slam that door. So, like I was saying. Am I clear on that side? Anyway, me and Iris were at the Cozy Oaks, over on Route 19 toward Leesburg. No, just north of the connector. Three-fifty. For a single. No, all of them have two beds. I just paid for the single.

Pop?

I'm not your pop, son.

Where's my pop?

Right behind us in his truck. He's gonna meet us at the hospital. Now, put your head back down and relax. The medicine should be starting to kick in any second. Anyway, Jerry, like I was saying. We put both beds together and wedged the sheet into the seam. Sure, it's worth saving fifty cents—but that's not the point—the point is we were there last night for our second honeymoon. Huh? Five years. See, and since checkout time wasn't till noon, we figured to stay late for one last dip, only around ten I hear a great big to-do. No, poolside. I thought it was a skunk or something. So I step outside and what do I see but the owner running around the pool, trying to fish out a bunch of niggers. Yeah. Because he was working the front desk the night before. Told me he was worried about getting people to come back. Because it was probably going to be in all the papers. Anyway.

Pop?

Jerry, he's fading back here. You're gonna need to step on it. Of course, you can put the sirens on! No, it's the one on the left. Just above the turn signal. There you go.

Not Jerry. I want my pop.

No, Jerry's not your pop, either. He's up front, driving. I'm staying back here with you. Just hold tight and breathe easy. Stay calm. I gotcha.

Anyway, Jerry, he was running around the pool trying to fish out the niggers, and everyone in the place is out on the catwalk looking down at them in the water, and him in his suit and tie running circles around the pool, hollering like a maniac, and the niggers having a good old time splashing and swimming, and the—Huh? Their hair? Just kind of trickled off. Hell no, there weren't any whites in there with them. Two, as best I could tell. Because I wasn't exactly checking out the colored girls, Jerry. I was about to go down and help the old man, poking his rod with the net for leaves on the end that he was stabbing the water with. Why? Because when I checked in, he told me about how he just spent half his retirement savings outfitting it with a brand-spanking-new diving board and everything.

Po—?

Oh, shit. Christ, Jerry. I'm losing him. Can you reach over and pass me that oxygen mask? No, I've got to hold him steady. Just give it a little tap. There. Got it. This oughta settle him down. Atta boy. Now, breathe nice and deep. Don't talk. Feeling better? Jesus. Anyway. Where was I? Oh yeah. That old retiree. Said it was already in trouble when he took it over and that he'd just finished fixing it up. Jesus. Twenty feet. But just as I come skipping back out of the room with my trousers on one leg, here he comes out of the front office with a jug. Muriatic acid. No, crystals. What they use to unclog toilets with. Of course, it would kill them. Me? To rescue them? No, to help him. I thought it was bleach. But then he holds up the jug and points at it and—and, and, and, and, and reads it to them, and right off the pool goes as still as a backwater, and up goes the jug, and the niggers make like I don't even know what for the opposite ledge, screaming bloody murder as he skips along the ledge with the acid gurgling out, and Iris howling for him to stop so bad I had to drag her kicking and screaming back into the room. Iris was in pieces, so I figured it was time to check us out—No, last night. Where the hell have you been? Around six! Yeah. So when I got home, I called Vera and told her to put me back on rotation. At the training rate. Huh? No, I asked for Akersburg. Figured it'd be mellow down here. Time and a half. Yeah, I got my money back. I suppose he could have called the cops. So I promised to take her out to the pictures instead. I dunno. Whatever's showing. Mouth-to-mouth? On one of them, you mean? Hell n—was that Kitty

Millham's dad's Mustang just passed us on your side? What's she doing out without Myron on a Saturday, driving like that? Was she smiling at me? The flirt. Turn it up, will you? No, we can still hear Vera. Please stay green 'cause she'll get out and come over, smacking her gum at the side of my face, at a red. Always does. You have no idea. Wanted to do things that made me blush. Six months. Me. I wanted something more seriou—who the hell's honking like that? Is his old man still behind us? Making that squawk at us with his horn, you mean? No. Bumper sticker says honk if you're with George. Yeah, all the municipal ambulances do. At first, but now I kinda like it. Why? Because it feels like they're cheering me on—why else?

I MUST HAVE blacked out from the pain because that's the last I remember of Dad, S&W, or Tyler. Sometime later—coulda been an hour or a week, for all I knew—I was freezing my butt off in an air-conditioned room in nothing but a drafty gown, squinting under two fluorescent tubes. Beneath me was something so cold and hard that it could only be stainless steel. Draped over me was something so soft and heavy it made me feel like I was buried up to my neck in sand. Dad was nowhere in sight, but a lady with long, straight brown hair and a vaguely reassuring smile was looking at me through a porthole in the adjacent room or hallway—I couldn't tell which. Her voice was muted by the thick glass separating us. It was so faint I felt like I was reading her lips: *Hold still, sweetheart. You're doing great. This'll be the last one, I promise.*

THE NEXT THING I remember, I was outside, and there was this pungent stench of cigarette smoke coming off Dad as he lifted me into the truck with the help of a colored man. It was dusk out and steamy, and Dad's thick fingers were digging into my armpits while the other guy had me by the ankles. They slid me in like the front seat was a bed, then tipped me up. I was too drowsy to be bothered about being man-handled like that, even by someone I didn't know.

I sagged against the window like a fifty-pound sack of peanuts. I couldn't hold my head up. The orderly backed in through the double doors and returned inside with the wheelchair. Above him, the sign sitting atop the ledge spelled out PHOEBE PUTNEY MEMORIAL HOSPITAL in translucent shell letters. The letters were dimly lit, and several of them were flickering. A couple of them weren't even lit. Of all the things to remember, that's what stood out to me.

My head sagged down to the door panel. I rocked sideways in the gently idling truck. It was all I could do to stay awake as Dad puffed on a cigarette, explaining it all back to me. Some things rang a bell—like my ice cream. I had a foggy recollection of Dr. Hofstetter tapping me gently with his shoe to make sure I was still alive. And the look on Dad's face, his hanky soaked in blood as he wrapped it around my arm. He picked me up and carried me back to S&W and pitched me atop the counter. I was shivering, like I was freezing cold. The white bone sticking out of the flesh against the deep red blood. I was in shock. Dr. Hofstetter scrambling to make another tourniquet as Dad snatched the phone from Tyler with a bloody hand and barked out, *Not for me, Eunice! For my boy! No, I just brought him in. Yeah, he's alive. Now, hurry up! The kid's gone off and busted up his arm something terrible! Now, send someone down here! And be quick about it!*

DAD STUCK TO the windy back roads running alongside the Thronateeska the whole way back. The gentle ripple of the road lulled me in and out of sleep. That winding trough of still water appeared through a stretch of evergreens, disappeared, then reappeared out from behind the blurry low-rise redbrick building that I barely recognized as Ivey's department store, disappeared behind the Trust Company of Georgia bank, or maybe it was the Paramount theater, then reappeared out from behind what I guessed was Freddy Mac Trophy and Plaque. Only there were two of them. Identical and side-by-side, then one on top of the other. Then slightly diagonal to each other. I rubbed my eyes, pressed my hand over my lips, and puked.

Just a mouthful. Dad pulled over, cut the engine, and tapped the horn. I leaned out the open door and spit.

Nestor came over in coveralls unbuttoned down to his crotch. He poked his head into the window and grinned. *Will you look at that.*

Ran into a car.

Ha! Is that what we're calling it these days? I've been telling Myrtle this was gonna happen. We gotta get more stop signs put up, I keep telling her. But she says we don't have more than sixteen intersections in the whole municipality, and besides, it'd be overkill because everyone should know the driver on the right always has the right of way. But what she don't appreciate is that half the dimwits that come tearing ass through here don't know their right from their left, is what I say. Now look what's happened. You sure banged it up pretty good, sport. Remember that plaster jobbie I had back in the fifth grade—went all the way up to my collarbone. What? This one only goes up to your elbow? Consider yourself lucky. Fiberglass? Fancy. Mind if I give it a knock? Huey?

Nestor put his face up close to mine. *Looks like he's drifting in and out.*

Got a concussion.

Don't say.

Ira left his patrol car parked on the sidewalk. Huey slid down it like a stick of butter down a hot tin roof, shuddering and whimpering and twitching like road kill. It was awful. Just fetched him from Putney. Gave him this stuff here for the pain. This to sleep. This so he doesn't throw up. Doesn't seem to be working, though.

I'm telling you, some of the people they give licenses to these days, Buck—I just don't get it. Always in such a rush to get to Boca Raton this time of year. They take a wrong turn off Route 62, looking for a shortcut to get over to US 27, and next thing you know, they're doing eighty in a twenty-five, barreling around combines, wondering where the hell the highway went. How fast was Ira going?

Dad threw me a glance. *It's like the Good Book says, Nestor: everything happens for a reason. What's done is done. What's important is that my boy's gonna be okay. So we'd like to count our blessings and move on. Now, if you don't mind.*

Nestor took the nozzle from the pump and hung it from the truck, then came back around to my window.

You're a better man than me, Buck Fairchild. I don't care what Herb and Carlyle and the rest of the gang says. Walking away from an accident like that carrying a grudge? No, sir. Not you. That's the Buck Fairchild I know. But if you ask me, you need to get out more. We're all starting to wonder how you're doing out there, cooped up like you are. Work, work, work—that's all you do anymore. You gotta learn to live a little, Buck.

My lip was fat, heavy, and numb. It felt like it covered half my face. One of my front teeth was missing. I swirled my tongue around in search of it. Goddamnit if I hadn't wiggled that thing for weeks on end, trying to make it loose enough to come out, and here I couldn't even find it in my mouth. No tooth to put under the pillow. No tooth fairy. No nickel. And to top it off, I was too out of it to even check the mirror to see what I looked like without it.

Whatever it is they're giving him, it don't seem to be working. Just look at him. Are you sure he's okay?

Doctor said that he can comprehend speech just fine. Just a little unresponsive, is all. Might be a few days before he bounces back. Dad removed the top from a prescription bottle with his teeth. *Here. Swallow this.*

Jesus, Buckaroo. Is he gagging or trying to say something? He looks like he's about to keel right over onto the shifter—if he don't choke on that pill first. Can hardly hold his head up. Never mind keep his tongue in his mouth—slobbering all over the place like that.

Dad leaned over my cast and shoved on the door. *Help yourself to some water. Just watch out so you don't trip over them fuses lying around.*

Nestor stepped aside and helped me out. He took two steps with me by the arm before letting go. I teetered uneasily over the oil-soaked sawdust spread out over the garage floor.

To the left of that tool chest! There you go! Keep straight! Watch out for the welding table! And those drills. Is that compressor still hot, Nestor? Get that out of his way, will ya?

The paper cups are in the cabinet, if you wanna take some with.

Bring me some while you're at it, son.

Doctor says moving about is okay?

Jesus—what does a twenty-two-year-old know? Anyway, you had to see it to believe it. I know you think I'm prone to exaggeration, but we were all sitting inside, minding our business, sipping coffee and chatting and playing cards and congratulating Herb on finally having his first load of the season weighed and graded, when they barnstormed the place. And then Ira pulls up. No horns. No lights. No sirens. Nothing. Parks right up on the sidewalk and gets out and shows them three sets of latchkeys for the jail: one for the coloreds, one for the whites, and one for the ladies. Held 'em up and jingled 'em. So all of 'em could see. Then he stated his terms. But they just bulldozed right past him. And all hell broke loose. We hightailed it on out of there—didn't make it to the end of the block before Huey smacked into the damned hood ornament, not looking where he was going.

What the hell was he looking at?

Beats me.

Jesus Christ, Buck. I told you ten years ago that Toby was gonna be trouble, but you didn't listen. Now look at what he's gone off and done. Why, he was in here a week ago with three of them. Walked right through that door with them, stinking up my store with a cologne I never smelled before. Saying whole words I'd never heard before—like they come from money. They held the door open for him, then stood back and watched as he fingered over my peaches for bruises. He held my eggs up to the light, and I got so hot under the collar I told him he could have them for all I cared, just as long as he took the other three with him on out of here. Then one of them is fumbling in his coat, here, there, and everywhere you can hide two dimes on a man, when who pulls up but Byron, with Dwight and Ernie sliding out from the bench seat of his Plymouth, flashing their Kodaks every which way. Toby grinned wide and handed me this here card and said for me not to worry—said he'd be back to see my ledger. My ledger? And I'm looking at this here card thinking, Tenant Farmers Association? Akersburg chapter? Now just who in the Sam Houston does that nigger think he is?

What'd Byron do?

He stayed until they left. To have a word with me.

And?

And he knows I'm no John Brown, but all the same, you can't be too careful these days. Him and his boys had been trailing them all day. Said he thought they were waiting for Farley's hands to get out from work, so as to rile them up.

Byron was following them?

Riding 'em hard—his words, not mine.

And Toby left here with three of them from the bus?

Happier'n a fairy in Boys Town. Christ almighty, you should have put that son of a bitch on a one-way bus outta town years ago. Because that boy isn't going to be happy until he takes the rest of us down with him. You first—and me not far behind.

A CARTON OF milk, two forty-eight-ounce cans of beer, a dozen or so cheese slices, a sixteen-ounce jar of peanut butter, half a loaf of bread, and leftover tuna casserole were piled in the sink, alongside a bunch of half-empty condiment containers whose contents had already started to separate. There was some other stuff spread out over the kitchen table, too, but that was mostly just celery stalks and collard greens, which Mom kept down below in the crisper.

Mom was at the stove, poking at the last of the hot dogs floating in a pot of boiling water. I walked up beside her and just stood there. A second later, the wooden spoon in her hand fell onto my sneaker.

Dad strolled in behind me.

Now, Pea, before you get all worked up—as bad as he might look, he's okay. They just doped him up so much he can hardly talk. Gave him enough Demerol to knock out Mollie. His mouth is in a real fix, too, but it's mostly just swollen. The doctor said it'll go down soon, but don't expect him to be able to talk much in the meantime. I've found it works best to ask him simple questions.

Mom knelt down, looked me over, then hugged me so tight I could hardly breathe. *You told me on the phone that he just hurt his arm!*

The whole drive home, I had promised myself that I wouldn't cry. But when Mom reached down and took me in her arms and carried me into the living room, it was all I could do to stanch the flow of tears. She stretched me out atop the sofa and propped up my head on the armrest. I lifted my head and she tucked a pillow underneath it, then turned on the TV.

WHO'S THE LEADER OF THE CLUB THAT'S MADE FOR YOU AND ME?

Whatever they'd given me for the pain was starting to wear off. Aside from my tear-soaked face, all I could feel was pins and needles up and down my arm. I replayed in my head the moment of smacking into that damned hood: how I put my arm up to brace myself a half second too late. Mom opened my mouth with a tongue depressor and peeked around inside.

Who did this, baby doll?

I blinked.

They didn't do anything to him. He did it to himself.

Mom returned to the kitchen and pulled the door gently closed behind her.

M-I-C-K-E-Y M-O-U-S-E!

His arm's broken, and he's missing a tooth!

That tooth was loose already. Listen—it was some bus full of wackos. They're stirring things up in town.

And?

HEY THERE, HI THERE, HO THERE! YOU'RE AS WELCOME AS CAN BE!

And nothing. Christ almighty! Them showing up at S&W like the damned cavalry to straighten us out—I can't hardly tell if they're here to rescue us from a flood or cause one.

Who?

M-I-C-K-E-Y M-O-U-S-E!

Who do you think? College kids.

What in the world does that have to do with Huey?

He ran into Ira's patrol car.

How fast was he going?

Ira or Huey?

Who do you think?

He was parked!

Parked?

On the sidewalk.

You're telling me that he got this way from running into a parked car?

Mom believed it about as much as Nestor did. Heck, if I hadn't been there, I probably wouldn't have believed it either. Replaying it in my mind, it was like that car had just appeared out of nowhere. But I knew that couldn't be right. Yet I couldn't for the life of me figure out what I had been looking at if not in front of me. What in the world had been more important than watching where I was going? Was it the bus? Or maybe all the people grappling around the bus? It was the missing piece to a puzzle that I couldn't seem to figure out. But I had to. Because who the hell runs into a parked car?

Yeah. Running like a lunatic, trying to get away from it all. We both were. It was bedlam. Everyone panicked.

Where were you?

About twenty paces behind him, trying to get clear of the crowd. Shouting for him to watch out for that damned car. I don't think he heard me. I couldn't keep up. He's too fast.

You and Huey were at S&W—of all places? What, you sneaked out and took him there under cover of the dark, so nobody would see?

Yeah. I mean, no! We were among friends. Caroline and John were both there. Ted was there. So he was safe. Thankfully Carlyle was there, too. I just felt like it was the least that I could do—after all we've been through. And yes, maybe there are fewer people around then. Oh, you know how people are when they get going—egging each other on, saying all kinds of stuff, badmouthing everybody and everything. Talking bad about Toby. I didn't want him to hear it. All that bad language. It's terrible, the stuff they say, just terrible. So I figured we'd go before dawn, while people are just sitting around, still half-asleep, quietly playing cards.

People were hollering at him?

Not at him. But they were hollering—gathered around yelling and taunting and shouting. Throwing bottles and whatnot. Broken glass everywhere. All that terrible language. Terrible, just terrible. And taunting and throwing things and spitting and what all. I don't trust them people, Pea.

Which people?

The people on that bus. Who else? How could they pull a stunt like that when they can see just as clear as day that a little kid was inside?

I asked you once what a Royal Deluxe tastes like. And you said that there was nothing special about a Royal Deluxe and how there was no reason to bother about me being unable to go into town and order one up for myself, because it was just a bunch of hype from uppity colored money with nothing better to do than stir up trouble. And it was right here in this very hallway that you winked at Huey and told me that a Royal Deluxe was no different than any other cheeseburger, even with all that cheese dripping down the sides of that toasted potato bun, and that it was worth neither the trouble nor the expense, and that all that fuss that people were making to eat at some stupid damned greasy spoon was idle troublemaking because everyone knows they could just as well put together a home-cooked burger every bit as good if they wanted one that bad.

Now hold on just a minute.

The back of Dad's head was visible in the doorway. I needed to spit out what tasted like a mouthful of blood. I tried to sit up, but my head was so heavy it fell back onto the pillow. I lifted my arm and banged on the end table. I was trying to get his attention. Then suddenly the room started to spin, and every muscle in my body contracted. I pitched forward, and a spray of vomit shot out of my mouth.

And that poor boy was sitting right here on this very seat fumbling with his shoelaces, looking up at you as you spoke those words, and you winking at him and going on, saying how frankly I shouldn't feel I was missing out on anything because it was just one of life's "little pleasures," you called it, and besides, that special sauce of theirs is probably nothing but a glorified French-dressing-and-mayo mix and you were sure I could figure it out eventually. Now you're standing here telling me our boy has gone off and risked his life for something as silly as a cheeseburger?

Now hold on just a minute. First off, he wasn't there for a burger. I told you, we went for an ice cream. He deserves it. And I figured it was high time, considering how long it's been since the last time we went—and how good he's taken all this craziness. Just ask him! He'll tell you. Tyler even gave him extra hot fudge—so there. And second off, if you want a Royal Deluxe so bad, just tell me. I'd be more than happy to bring one back for you. Goddamnit, that's what doggy bags are for!

The vomit had come in waves. When it finally subsided and I could breathe again, a tangy, viscous fluid hung from my nose, chin, and mouth. I leaned over the edge of the sofa and ran my fingers over the slimy pool spread out over the floor. That damned tooth had to be in there somewhere.

SINCE MY RETURN HOME, THERE had been no mention of any kind of what had happened in front of S&W. No explanation—not so much as a peep. Nothing. Part of me wanted to believe the bus had come to investigate the mysterious circumstances surrounding the closure of Mister Abrams's pool. But that seemed far-fetched in light of the busted filter. Unless, of course, that filter story was nothing but smoke Dad was blowing in my face so that I didn't get my hopes up about the pool reopening before Danny returned to Fayetteville for college. Common sense told me that they had to be at least a little connected—why else would a bunch of college kids have come to Akersburg? Truth is, I wasn't sure about anything anymore. Adding insult to injury, the TLC I got for my broken arm lasted all of two days. It was as if Mom and Dad were in short supply of *How you holding ups*. And I was still waiting for a *Don't worry, we'll try again for an ice-cream breakfast sometime soon*. But that never came, either.

So when Dad and I pulled in one afternoon, after having finished yet another Buskin Brothers run, and he told me to spray down the truck bed like it was business as usual, I went inside and dug out one of his dirty magazines from the hall closet. I'd just about had it. The point is, my arm still hurt, and at the very least I deserved an explanation for all that had happened in front of S&W.

When I returned outside, Toby was standing at the foot of the stoop with his tool belt slung over his shoulder. He was a sight for sore eyes, I thought; if anyone knew what it felt like to be handicapped, it was him.

I figured he'd stopped by to fix the leak in the bathroom. I told him it was about time.

Toby smiled. *Look on the bright side, Huey. At least now it doesn't matter that the pool's closed. You wouldn't be able to go in the water with that thing on.*

A stupid little cast, stop me? Damn it, Toby—shows how much you know. How many times have I told you? I can probably swim across the English Channel with a damned anvil hanging from my neck. Look at this body! I was made to float.

Toby sat down on the stoop, presumably impressed. *Don't you ever feel different from other people?*

Jesus Christ, Toby. I swear—sometimes you amaze me. There's a big difference between being enthusiastic and being stupid. And I'm not stupid. I'm perfectly aware that I have a broken arm.

Toby peeled off his ball cap and said that wasn't what he meant. I leaned over and whispered in his ear about my hardly-noticeable third nipple, but that wasn't it, either. I slapped the magazine down so loud the hens started squawking in the henhouse.

Toby Muncie, you got the devil in you, and I know it. I don't know what about, and I don't care to know, so long as you leave me out of it. Okay? Because ever since you and Pop had it out in the field, you haven't been the same. You've got some sort of ax to grind, and I know it. I can tell just by looking at you. You got that look that says the world owes you something, when the world don't owe you nothing. You think you're the only one with problems? Well, let me tell you, I got problems, too. I got a lot on my mind, without you adding to it. If you can't tell, I'm feeling a little down in the dumps after this here mishap with my arm. Frankly, I still don't entirely understand how it even happened. Okay? Besides, it's still sore and sweaty and hurts like the dickens. On top of that, I've gone three weeks without a dip in that pool, and I ain't exactly happy about that, either. To make matters worse, Pop's acting like everything's hunky-dory. I'm struggling to keep a sense of what Mom calls perspective. What am I saying? You don't understand that junk. Jesus Christ—when you see something from different angles, okay? Hopefully positive ones. That's perspective. Get it? But I just can't seem to get the hang of it. No matter how much I try to pretend otherwise, I just can't. Not in this heat. It's too damned sticky for all that.

Listen, Toby, I'm gonna make it real simple for you. Me and how I feel about that pool is probably like how you feel about—aw, hell, I dunno—watermelons, cheap suits, and white women, probably. Okay? And the last thing I need right now is for you to pile on with your cheap shots, teasing me every chance you get about the texture of my hair or my skin tone, or how I'm getting darker every year and how at this rate I'll be your color by the time I'm twelve. Frankly, I don't appreciate it. It's not my fault I tan easily. So just hush up about that. If I've said it once, I've said it a thousand times: Mama's the dark one in this family. Not me. I'm normal, okay? Get that through your thick skull, once and for all. It's not my fault my skin's more sensitive than most. Mama says there's not a single damned thing I can do about it except to stay out of the sun. Not after that special cream she gave me damned near burned my skin off so bad I could have sworn it was bleach. So I'm warning you—I will tell her. I don't wanna, but I can be pushed to the brink and I know you're just the person to get me to do it. I don't care if she makes me put on that damned cream again, so help me God, if it gets you to shut up. Jesus Christ. You'd think a dark-skinned colored fella with half a heart would understand the misery of tanning easily, but I guess not. Now scoot over, 'cause you're hogging all the shade, and leave me alone.

I sat down beside Toby and flipped the magazine open and marveled at some caramel-colored woman with a bouffant hairdo sprawled out atop satiny bed linens. She looked both happy and sad at the same time. When I glanced up, Toby was still sitting there right beside me, inspecting the brim of his hat. He raked it back over his head, and we just sat there together in silence—me staring at a bunch of nudie pictures and him fondling his hat distractedly.

He took his hat off and wiped his brow, then put it back on. He took it back off. Held it by its visor and rotated it in his hands, then put it back on. I watched him do that three times in a row, before I flipped the magazine closed.

Jesus Christ, Toby. What's with you? You're acting like your old lady's in the house about to pop out another one of your little chitlins. Make up your mind—either put on that raggedy old hat or take it off. All your fidgeting is driving me crazy. How'm I supposed to heal with you sitting there fussing over your cap like that?

Toby reached into his wallet and pulled out a picture. He looked at it for a moment, then handed it to me.

I took the bait. *Who's that?*

Your mama.

I could tell from its condition that it was old—she couldn't have been much older than me in the picture. I scoffed.

Probably stole it, for all I know. Big whoop. I'm gonna tell her you been going through her stuff.

We used to be close.

I leaned over and sniffed Toby, figuring that he must have been drunk. If I hadn't been so sure about him being a bellyaching, muckraking boozer with more pride than good sense, who after twenty years on the job still hardly knew how deep a posthole should be, I would have sworn that he smelled just like calamine. Or was it lye? Oh, hell, I dunno. Something soapy. All I knew for sure is that it made my nostrils pucker.

I examined the photo more closely. There was no mistaking her: bright, intelligent eyes. Radiant smile. Perfect teeth. Pigtails. She was beautiful, that much was for sure. The odd thing was—well, never mind that I hadn't ever heard him talk about Mom before; they didn't exchange more than ten words with each other in a week.

How close?

Toby and I were sitting in a luxuriant patch of mid-afternoon shade. A breeze wafted in from the road and dried my lips. It was a sleepy summer afternoon, one of those very hot ones that's strangely pleasant as long as you can stay out of the sun. Toby sat back and took his time. He spoke in clear sentences and enunciated each word with relish as well as candor—said he and Mom had been very close friends once upon a time. Not boyfriend and girlfriend. Rather, like cousins. The little morsels of his youth that he volunteered up sounded as if from a past life. And just in case I had any doubts about Mom's character as a youngster, roaming wild and free with the likes of Toby as she had, he assured me that my mom had been chaste right up to the time Dad had entered the picture. He said that she was given to look upon boys with indifference and young men with outright suspicion, then detailed her abiding interest in school, nothing working quite so well to debunk suspicion of a tramp as a love of books.

Toby described the lengths Mom had gone to in order to cast off Dad in the early days of his courtship. Dad was fourteen years her senior. She'd mocked him and called him a cradle robber to his face when he refused to stop his advances. But Dad was nothing if not persistent. He worked every angle of advantage available to him. Where his wit failed, he used money. When that didn't work, he used his family's influence. Thus, there came the day when Dad asked young Toby if he could deliver Mom unto him. Toby said that at sixteen, he had little choice but to do as his boss had asked. He'd tried to warn Mom with as light a touch as could be managed, without leaving a doubt in her mind as to what he considered Dad's true nature.

If Toby had technically satisfied Dad's request, he considered himself to have failed Mom. In the end, Dad got what he had wanted. Too bad, then, that when Dad's mother had learned of it and spoke reproachfully about Mom, as she was expected to do, Dad lacked not only the common decency to defend his young sweetheart's reputation among those who had previously thought well of her but the courage to do so among those who had never been inclined to think well of her to begin with.

Toby toed at the dirt and said that he had decided to level with me, as he put it, because I deserved to know about the man whose family assumed the absolute worst about my mother, and the man who had never, at any time, shown the slightest inclination to stand up for her.

I shifted uncomfortably atop the stoop. I was staring into those bright, intelligent eyes, wondering what I saw there. She looked so damned smart—fiercely so. I flipped open the magazine and hid my face. It'd only been a couple of days since I'd sobbed in Mom's arms and Dad had warned me that he hadn't cried nearly as much when he was my age.

Dad poked his head around the screen door and asked Toby to come in. Didn't even notice me. Toby got up and took his picture back. He returned it to his wallet and reached out his hand. I peeked over the top of that magazine but refused to take it.

DAD AND I loaded up the truck without Toby that night. We headed out to our fields without him, too. Dad pulled over beside our field and ordered me out. I slammed the door behind me and dragged my feet, mad as hell that I was the one helping him instead of Toby. I was the one with a broken arm, not him. I thought I should have gotten the night off. I deserved it. I slid out two stack poles from the back, clattered across the road with them splayed in my arms like giant scissors. I dumped them in the flower strip, knowing full well how careful Dad had told me to be—not with my cast but with those poles.

On the way home, he refused to tap the horn on our way past Derrick's, so I leaned over and did it myself. I was starting to worry about that, too. I'd known it might be a while, Missus Orbach having come over to our house twice in as many weeks to give me grief. But it was going on eight days since I'd last seen him, and now he wasn't even coming to the window. I was worried that I might not have a chance to show my cast to him before the darned thing came off.

We pulled into our drive, and I headed straight for the kitchen. Mom wasn't there. Dad came in a minute later, checked the oven for dinner, then disappeared into the bathroom.

Mister Swanson's Plymouth pulled in later that night. I turned down the TV at the sound of footsteps crunching out front. Mom opened the front door quietly and passed down the hall. She made a racket clearing dirty dishes from the kitchen table. I turned the TV back up and hollered out for her to quiet down.

Everything went silent save for the TV. When I looked up, she was standing in the doorway in her coat, holding a dinner plate wrapped in tinfoil. She asked why I hadn't set out Toby's dinner. I said I had and turned back to the movie.

So why didn't Toby touch his food?

I dunno. But tell Pop Toby lets me toss our stack poles out from the back of the truck so long as I reach the flower strip. He made me get out every twenty yards and walk them over. Jesus Christ, if everything doesn't take ten times longer with Dad than it does with Toby.

I wasn't happy about having had to stay out placing stack poles around our field until it was too dark to go on. Dad had blamed the fact that it took us so long on how slow I was. I blamed it on him making me work with a life-threatening injury. We'd gone round and round like that for half the night.

Dad came in from the bathroom with his face covered in shaving cream and announced that Toby was no longer working for us. I whipped around so suddenly something popped inside my cast. Mom stormed off to the kitchen and slammed the oven door shut amid a clatter of pots and pans. I squeezed my eyes shut so tight I saw stars. When the worst of the pain in my elbow had passed, I opened them to the trample of fleeing mustangs and the war whoops of the Indians riding them and the *pop pop pop* of rifle fire from the cowboys shooting at them. I slid down from Dad's easy chair cradling my cast. I turned off the TV, picked up one of Toby's biscuits that had fallen onto the floor, and asked why.

Dad said that Toby had decided it was time to have a go at it on his own, adding that it was a surprise that a man with his experience and talent hadn't done so long before. Then he returned to the bathroom.

XI

I REMEMBER I WAS LYING in bed the next morning, in this god-awful state of not wanting to get up and not being able to fall back asleep, when Dad appeared in the doorway and told me to get up. I told him to get the hell out and leave me alone. I knew that he was going to expect me to fill those size-twelve rain boots that Toby had abandoned out on the back stoop.

Dad strolled in, snapped up the window shade, tugged me out of the cocoon I'd made for myself, and sat me up. When I finally dragged myself out into the living room, Mom was lying on the sofa in her rumpled nightgown watching *The Donna Reed Show*. It wasn't until nine thirty that she trudged off to the kitchen, complaining about a crick in her neck. Dad picked up the pillow and bedsheet from the sofa, fluffed out the crater-sized indentation in the cushion, and grumbled something about it being her own damned fault.

I sat down at the kitchen table and delicately propped my cast up on it. I decided that I needed to level with Dad.

Pop. I know this is the first summer I'm not just getting in the way, and how proud you are of me for it. Because even little boys have to grow up sooner or later. Like you did, when you were my age. But—but—I just wanna say . . . If . . . I mean. You let Toby go because of what happened the other day—in Mister Noonan's orchard, I mean—I just want you to know . . . Well—for the record—that it had nothing to do with him. I swear. I know how every time Derrick lights something afire, next thing you know, one of the Orbachs' hands gets the ax. But Toby wasn't even there. It was all me. You gotta believe me. That can was just lying there in the grass, and one thing led to another, and Derrick started daring and double daring me, and the next thing you know, we'd drank the whole thing. I dunno. I guess I was just trying to act like a grown-up. Aw, I don't know what my hurry is. But I learned my lesson and I promise it'll never happen again. I'll do whatever you need me to to prove my boozing days are behind me. I swear. Just please please please please don't expect me to pick up Toby's load, is all I'm asking. There's no way I'm ever going to measure up. Please. Because after two hours of sorting, stack poles all start to look the same to me. I get confused looking out at all those different piles. I forget which is which. I know I'm supposed to be better than Toby. But I'm not. Never will be, probably. I don't know what's wrong with me, Pop, but I'm not. Okay? I'm just not!

I hid my face behind my cast and quit while I was ahead. It wasn't easy telling Dad the truth about something I knew he wouldn't want to hear. Especially when just two days earlier, I was complaining about him never letting me do anything, and here he was about to hand me the entire kit and caboodle, and I was trying my damnedest to wash my hands of it.

When I peeked up, the look on Dad's face was halting. It took a second before I realized that he was looking over my shoulder. Mom came up beside me with a hot skillet in hand and slid an egg down onto my plate. Dad just sat there with his fork upright and a stunned look on his face. Mom wiped her hands on her apron, pushed my plate forward, and sat down. She pointed at the uncooked eggs sitting in the stew pot on the counter and told him that he could cook for himself.

Dad didn't seem to care. He just snapped open his newspaper and pretended like he always cooked for himself. After what felt like a very long time, he lowered it.

I swear to the good Lord, a lunatic could walk down Main Street, taking potshots at every man, woman, and child in sight, and the first thing you'd want to know was what people had done to make him do such a thing.

Mom had set her plate aside and was catching up on paperwork. She glanced up from her ledger.

What does that have to do with Toby?

Dad reached over, took a sip of my red drink, and turned back to his newspaper. Mom got up, went to the stove and returned with the coffee pot. She set down a cup in front of him and filled it. Dad smiled and took a sip, then spit it out. Mom sat down and didn't look up from her tapping fingers. She scribbled some numbers in her ledger, then *tap tap tap*ped on her calculator some more. They started bickering about how stingy Mom was with the sugar, then about the cost of sugar, and eventually about the cost of anything and everything, including sugar. Money was a topic that engulfed all other topics. Everything led back to money—and, sure enough, like a dog chasing its tail, it led back to Mister Abrams's pool, Toby, and those college kids who'd shown up on that damned bus.

Don't pretend like you can't understand why the police are wondering if the colored boys caught in Mister Abrams's pool aren't just the tip of the iceberg!

That's all just an excuse for a bunch of bigots to take down a man they've always seen as being too kind to colored folks, and you know it! Besides, he was kind enough to let Huey swim in his pool, wasn't he?

I slammed down my fork. *He was nice to everyone. Not just me!* I glared at Mom. *And if you'd have ever bothered to go, you'd know that!*

I kicked out my chair and stormed out the back door. I sat down beside Toby's rain boots and jabbed at the dirt with the frayed end of a broken stack pole. The island of shade elms standing out in the middle of our field was smudged out by thick black smoke. A little to the left, but further out, a pale dust cloud trailed a tractor moving across the horizon a good half mile away. It was the Orbachs'. I would have gladly sought refuge at Derrick's house if I thought there was a chance in hell of not being chased off by his mother.

There was a moment of quiet. I wasn't sure if they'd stopped arguing or if I just couldn't hear them. When I got up and returned inside, they were both gone. The screen door clicked shut behind me, and muffled voices emerged from behind the bathroom door.

He only did it for the money!

So now you're siding with the police?

I went back to my room to see how Snowflake was holding up. I had unlatched her cage, taken her out, and told her not to pay any attention to all the arguing when something crashed. The shattering sound came from the kitchen. I peeked around the doorjamb to see what had happened. Mom was at the sink emptying the dish rack, with her back to me. She'd dropped a dish. Which was a relief—for a second there, I thought they'd stooped to throwing things at each other. Mom pulled the cupboard open with several dinner plates in hand and looked over her shoulder.

You smell like piss.

It's not me. It's Snowflake.

Dad was on his hands and knees, picking up the broken pieces of Mom's favorite mixing bowl, chiding her for being materialistic.

Materialistic? Me not being materialistic is the only reason I've held on to that rotten old hand-me-down.

All their bickering about money was starting to worry me—not about Toby but about us. It used to be like a bus station in our kitchen, what with all those old ladies trooping through at all hours of the day. It had been a while since Miss Della or Aurelia or any other of the other old ladies from Aurelia's Bible study had come to have their hair done.

Dad stood up. *Listen. If I had to stand up in a court of law I'd say that I refuse to believe that Stanley Abrams let a couple of colored boys in his pool after hours just for an extra buck—impossible. I wouldn't do that unless I was dead sure. But standing here, in my house, I know damned well he would. And you do, too. Christ, Pea. It ain't a stretch to think he'd entertain a backroom deal with a few niggers just so long as no one else was any the wiser. It's in the man's blood.*

I was having second thoughts about wanting to ever step foot in that pool again. It didn't seem worth the headache.

Who was I kidding? Of course it was. That pool was like having our own private water park. It was outta this world.

I returned Snowflake to her cage, which I moved over to the windowsill. On the way, I explained to her that it might be a touch warm in the sun but it wasn't to be helped. She stank. I slumped off into the hallway, past their bedroom, one door beyond which was the bathroom. I undressed and, knowing full well that a tub was a lousy substitute for a pool, slipped on my dive mask and got in.

When the water had cooled down some, I submerged my head only to discover that my dive mask had sprung a leak. I snatched it off and rubbed the sting out of my eyes. I must have been under for longer than I thought: Dad was tapping on the door, hollering for me not to make a career of it. I jumped out as soon as I realized that my cast was dissolving. *Yikes.* I thought it was waterproof. I salvaged the soaked remains of my cast and mopped the water from my face. Everything was so peaceful I could hear the lonesome scratch of hens milling around beneath the stoop, out front. They must've gotten out again.

I wrapped myself in my towel and headed for the kitchen. No one was there. So I poked my head into the den, thinking that Mom must have been folding clothes, but she wasn't there, either. The laundry line creaked out back. I figured that she was hanging up clothes. I hopped down from the back stoop and checked. It was Miss Della. She was standing beneath the clothesline strung from the side of the Orbachs' house.

I headed around the side of our house, pissed at having to return all the hens scurrying around to their coop. I stopped at the corner with the drain pipe in my hand. An unfamiliar sound gave me pause. I knew every creak and moan of that house—but this was new.

Dad stored a ladder on its side beneath their bedroom window. I teetered up it and peeked in over the sill. Dad was in bed, grunting like he was in the middle of a calisthenics routine. It took a minute for my eyes to adjust to the shade of their room. When they did, I noticed that Mom's legs were poking out from beneath him. I keeled over backward from the ladder and landed right smack in Mom's petunia bed.

TWO HOURS LATER, Mom was sitting on the edge of her bed, asking me for advice. She wanted to know if she should wear her blue or black pumps with her fancy flower-print dress. It was another hour before she was ready. When she finally stepped out the front door, you'd have thought she was heading down a red carpet. Didn't matter where she was going, even if it was just down the road. And Dad didn't mind one bit. Her getting all done up was one of the few things that he had no problem waiting for.

Dad pulled the truck around, and we all piled in and headed for town. We sat in silence. The puttering of the engine and the buzz of mud tires over pavement was peaceful. I preferred it to their constant squabbling about how cheap Mom had been with the sugar in Dad's coffee, giving it to him black and bitter.

We turned onto Cordele Road and an endless span of peach trees crisscrossed the foothills. Some were jammed in so tight against the narrow road I could practically touch them. One of Mister Noonan's flitted past at eye level, and I lurched out the window and snatched at it. Mom snapped at me to get my head back in before it got lopped off. Dad barked out asking if I'd lost my mind. They sighed in unison. It was the first thing they'd agreed on all day. I pulled my head and arms in and kept quiet.

The peach and apple and pecan orchards that sat between us and town were dotted with wide-open fields separated by thin tracts of acacia trees. We passed the familiar procession of dusty side roads strewn with the rotted wall boards of gutted barns and abandoned feedlots peeking out from the low-lying trees. The muffler backfired, and Dad pumped the gas only to discover that the engine had cut out.

He pulled over and got out. He pitched the hood up with his shirt-tail and a plume of smoke billowed out. That truck was one of the few things that we had that was worth anything. It didn't matter that I had to tug on the inside door handle with both hands in order to open it. Or that the window roller didn't work. Or that springs poked out of the seat cushion. Or even that it stalled out from time to time. I loved it.

I got out and stood beside Dad. I held my palm as close to the engine as I could without touching it. It was hot. Never mind an egg, I could have cooked an entire breakfast on it. Dad shook off the heat of the radiator cap at every quarter-turn, then poured in water from a jug amid all its hissing and sputtering.

Goddamn that Nestor. He gave me his word that those points were new—swore up and down on his mother's grave. Next time, I've got a mind to try out that nigger on the other side of the river. You know the one I'm talking about.

Mom was inside the truck, I think tending to her needlework. *Please don't use that language around Huey.*

You suppose it's the first time he's heard it?

Mom's face appeared out the passenger's-side window. Dad shook the jug empty and let the hood slam shut.

Okay, okay, okay. Fine. But you know the one I'm talking about, right? Missing three fingers. Damned fine mechanic, though. Better with seven fingers than Nestor is with all ten. Next time, I've a mind to have him install them. What's that boy's name? Doesn't he have a girl's name? Lesley, or something? Remind me when we get home to call him.

Dad got back in the truck and gave the ignition another try. The engine sputtered, then died. We were encircled on three sides by a vast expanse of peanut fields that were bordered on the distant horizon by a wall of evergreens. A narrow band of blacktop stretched out in front of us as far as I could see. I spotted three people creeping steadily over the cresting road, so far up ahead that all I could make out was the faint bobbing of their heads in the shimmering distance.

I nudged Dad. *Pop.*

His head was down and he was squeezing the key tight in his hand. He said, *Not now.* The ignition was whirring round like he was trying to will the truck to fix itself. So I turned back to the road and leaned forward. I wasn't sure that I was seeing right. But I recognized his gait.

I nudged Dad again, urgently this time.

I said, not now. She's almost there.

I remember eyeing the scuffed crease at the ball of Dad's brogan as it rolled off the gas pedal. He let go of the key and looked up. Neither of us said anything—there was nothing to say. We just sat there, listening to the ticking sound of an overheated engine, quieted by the sight of Toby heading straight for us.

Dad nudged me. *Ask him for a push.*

Why me?

He likes you.

I hesitated. Dad turned to Mom.

She didn't respond to him so much as to her needlework. *You ask him.*

Dad smacked the steering wheel so hard I blinked. He cranked the ignition a second time, but it just wheezed. And wheezed. And wheezed.

Toby walked past.

Dad rolled down his window and poked his head out. *That the thanks I get?*

Toby kept walking. Dad reached for the door. Mom leaned over and grabbed him. Dad overpowered her and got out anyway.

Fine way to treat the family that gave you the only opportunity in life you've ever known!

All was quiet except for the sounds coming from the fields. They were rhythmic and seemed to punctuate the distant footsteps.

I leaned out the window and slapped the door. *Run, Toby!*

Mom snatched me in and boxed my ears. She demanded to know what in the hell had gotten into me. When I screamed that Toby was right to walk off, she wrestled me down into my seat and leaned out the window.

Buck, get in.

Twenty years! You don't expect me to just sit here and watch him walk by like he's too good to lend a hand, do you?

Dad picked up a rock and threw it.

You dumb ox! You ain't one of them! You'll never be one of them! They ain't your friends—ain't even your kind! So help me God! Whites do not serve niggers. Never have and never will. I don't care how fancy you dress up, you hear me?! Niggers serve whites. Always have and always will. Haven't you read a goddamned history book, you stupid nigger?

Toby turned around and began walking toward us.

I shivered so bad a drop of piss squirted into my underwear.

Pop! Get in!

I locked the door and rolled up my window. Toby walked up beside us with his eyes deadlocked on Dad. Dad stood frozen before him in the middle of the road. Neither man moved. Not their eyes. Or their hands.

The only reason this damned truck has lasted this long is because of me. You know that, right?

You want me to thank you for all your work, is that it?

Too late for that.

The peanut fields surrounding us were wide-open and flat. Several of the field hands stood from their work to watch. One of the two well-dressed colored men accompanying Toby called out from farther up the road. His accent made him hard to understand.

Come, Brother Tobias. A man curses because he doesn't have the words to say what's on his mind. Ignore him, and let us move on.

Toby leaned in and looked at me. Looked me dead in the eye. His eyes were still, but not resting—they were searching over my face for something. God knows for what. He spoke through the glass.

Your papa's whole family thinks that good woman beside you is noth-

ing but a cheap hussy who's been counting on his religion to keep them under the same roof. You deserve to know that, buddy.

I rolled down my window and spat. I fell short by a good two feet. Toby walked off. Something soured inside me as I listened to the fading sound of his shoes gripping pavement. The whole ridiculous idea of truth. The issue that Toby had with Dad wasn't about work or pay or even our broken down truck. It was about the truth of whatever Dad seemed to lord over Mom. I could see that now. And, strangely, none of that mattered to me in that moment. All that mattered was that Dad was just standing there, dumbstruck, powerless to do anything about it. I leaned out the window.

I hope you rot in hell, Tobias Muncie!

The tirade that I unleashed upon Toby would have made Miss Della blush. I didn't stop until Toby and those two men accompanying him were well out of earshot. Dad reached in and put a hand on my shoulder.

It's okay, son. You did good. A little late to the trigger, but you did good. You can calm down now. He's gone. You're safe now. Just settle right on down. He'll have his day. You'll see. He hasn't gotten the last word yet.

I was having difficulty breathing. I couldn't shake the feeling that I'd just lost something that I'd never get back. After all the years that Toby and I had spent working side by side, it wasn't until that moment that I had somehow stumbled on the courage to admit to myself how much he meant to me. It was only as the hateful words left my mouth that I could see how untrue they were. The door groaned and Dad got back in. After what felt like an eternity, he turned to Mom.

All you had to do was ask.

Mom might as well have been made of marble, pinioned under a frown as she was. She gazed out over the cresting road ahead. Toby and the two clipboard-toting bookish types with him disappeared in the distance.

Whose side are you on anyway?

Mom reached down for her needlework. It was lying in the foot well, crumpled and dirty. I lifted my foot from atop it. She picked it up.

He'd probably have done it for you.

Mom wiped off the fabric. *I told you not to get rid of him, didn't I?*

Dad gave the ignition another go. The engine groaned, then cut out—*pfft*. Only the fan belt showed any sign of life, and then even its screeching came to a hissing stop. Mom tucked her needlework into her purse and made as if to get out.

Dad stopped her. *I hope for your sake that he doesn't have anything to do with those clowns on that bus being here.*

The only place that Mom ever went was to Aurelia's Bible study. That was practically the only time she ever got out of the house. I'd even asked to go with her once, but she'd refused—said Aurelia was funny that way. She didn't like kids; all we did was break stuff. Which was ridiculous—I couldn't have told you the last time I broke anything.

Mom closed the door and sat back down. Dad looked her straight in the eyes. *Does he?*

Mom took off her sheer white gloves and, doubling them, bared a finely chiseled jawbone. She fanned herself. *Maybe he does. Maybe he doesn't.*

The heel of Dad's hand bumped the shifter. He got out and ordered me into his seat and showed me how to shift the transmission from outside his open door. I wiped at the tears streaming down my face and slid over into the driver's seat. I took the shifter into my hand and carefully slid the neon-orange slit below the speedometer over two notches to second gear, just like he said. I waited for his next instruction, hiccuping as I struggled to compose myself, all the while smearing the tears from my face.

Mom got out. I could see her in the rearview mirror bickering with Dad. I bumped the shifter again by accident and the truck started rolling backward. Jesus Christ. Even I knew it wasn't supposed to do that. And here I hadn't wanted to give Dad any more of an excuse to be mad.

I'm going backward, Pop!

Dad hollered out for me to step on the brake. I didn't know which pedal that was, so I slid down and stomped on both. The truck bucked and stopped at a sharp angle to the road. A cloud of dust hovered all around. Dad came over and told me to please get out.

Mom was leaning against a stretch of rail fencing in her twisted-up flower-print dress, gazing out over the field. She put a hand on my shoulder and said that I probably couldn't tell, but the sacks slung over the backs of the field hands working in it were very heavy. She'd worked in fields as a kid; she'd once told me with a prideful swagger that she knew how to raise a stack pole and use a posthole digger better than Dad. Her swagger was gone now, though. Mom looked strange to me, dressed up as she was, with those black pumps that I told her to wear all dusty out here in the middle of nowhere. And after all the trouble she'd taken to look nice. She stood like that in the foreground of all those rows of peanuts stretching out as far as I could see.

Her hands were covered in grimy rust from the truck's tailgate. I wiped them off and hugged her. We stood there in each other's arms, looking out over the wide-open field. The hundred or so field hands scattered around in it were so distant they appeared to be still. Mom stroked my hair and told me how dreamy it was. It was in a soft whisper that she conceded her admiration of it. I looked up at her beautiful brown eyes, sparkling through tears.

You know what I'd have given to have hair like this when I was your age?

I shook my head no.

You have no idea. It's so soft and wavy. Doesn't even need straightener.

Mom seemed to be able to find a silver lining in anything. It didn't matter how bad it was, she would find a way to claim that it wasn't. Frankly, it was starting to bug the shit out of me. I wiped my face clean of tears and tried to smile. Running her fingers through my hair seemed to calm her. She smiled through her tears and asked what was on my mind.

Is it true what he said?

Toby?

I nodded.

Never you mind him. He's just upset, is all. People say the most unimaginable, hurtful things when they get upset. I've told you that a million times. And if Toby's not careful he's going to turn into a bitter old man one day. And I don't want that for you.

It was just as I had suspected. Her answer seemed to explain away the childhood picture that Toby had shown me and all that he'd said the day he'd shared it with me.

Mom let go of my hand and picked a flower growing along the rail fence. She held it up to her nose and, twirling it, mused that her big sister had once, when she was about my age, shown her how to sip nectar from a honeysuckle.

Sister?

Mom didn't have a sister.

Mom looked startled. She dropped the flower, took off her heels, and started off up the road. I had no idea what I'd said. She didn't answer when I called out after her. She just walked on down the road's narrow shoulder in stockinged feet and headed off without me.

Mama!

She didn't look back. I started to run after her, then stopped about halfway. Dad was loading up a duffel bag with stuff from the truck bed.

Never mind her. Dad rolled up the windows and locked the door. *You leave your window cracked?*

Uh-huh.

How about your door?

Locked it.

Attaboy.

Dad headed after Mom with the duffel bag slung over his shoulder. I stopped in the middle of a dust cloud settling in the wake of a car that had sped past. Dad stopped and shouted out for me to hurry up. We didn't have all day.

STARS SPECKLED THE sky. The spring-loaded arm of the storm door felt heavy. Dad had a migraine—said it was from having to deal with Nestor on the phone, but I think it was because Mom walked ahead of us the whole way home with her purse and needlework and shoes clutched in her folded arms. I guess she was upset about not getting her stupid damned tin of bergamot. I couldn't imagine that anyone had ever gone to greater lengths trying, and I thought she should be at least a little happy for that.

Dad went over to my dresser, set my alarm clock, and ordered me into bed. I got undressed and slid under the covers and asked what the hell was up with Toby. He told me to watch my mouth. I told him that dumb nigger had left us stranded on a barren stretch of road, ten miles from town, and without a sympathetic soul in sight, and that I never wanted to see him again. Dad put a finger over his lips and told me to quiet the hell down. I didn't want Mom to hear, did I?

It was disturbing, having someone I'd thought of as family turn on me like that. It didn't sit well with me. In fact, it was eating away at me—how that son-of-a-bitch turncoat had looked at me with those searching eyes of his. Lies. Lies. Lies. It was nothing but a pack of lies. The way he made me feel small and helpless with every little thing that came out of his mouth. The meaning of all the years that we spent together being undone in a single afternoon. And after all I'd done for him. It was disorienting.

This isn't over, is it, Pop? It's not the last he'll hear from us, right? We're not through with him yet, are we? Why, I bet he couldn't fix a faucet if he had a full set of socket wrenches, could he? And his leg, you think he was lying about that, too? I do. I don't think he ever said a truthful word in his life. Lies. Lies. Lies. Just goes to show—you can't trust them any farther than you can throw them. Can you, Pop?

Dad told me to calm down—said I was just worked up. When I pointed out that Toby could have fixed the truck with his eyes closed if he'd wanted to, like he'd done that one time with nothing but a safety pin and a book of matches, Dad stroked my hair back and explained that Toby was just being a pigfuc—

He took a deep breath and said that it was no big deal, really. Toby must have been stressed about things being harder than he'd envisioned. Who knows? He could have been in a terrific hurry to get somewhere important, for all we knew. *Can't fault the man for being in a hurry.*

In a hurry?

That took the cake. When I asked if Benedict Arnold was suddenly a hero, too, because that no-good son of a bitch Toby had probably abandoned us for Fat Cat Mister Orbach, he said for me to watch my mouth, and no. So I asked if the turncoat had quit us for Skinny-as-a-Wafer Mister Schaefer, and he said no.

Pushy Mister Peterson?

No.

Follow-the-Herd Mister Bradford?

No.

Don't tell me he's working for Dumb-as-Nails Mister Snales?

Jesus, Huey. No.

Well, who's he working for, then? Don't just stand there and take it sitting down, like some goddamned pushover! You know just as well as me that Mister Orbach hired him away from us. Don't deny it! Because I heard him talking about Toby like he was the goose that laid the golden egg—laughing and joking and saying how our goose was cooked if he ever left us. Saying we were nothing without him. He's gotta be working for somebody, and I wanna know who! I have a right to know. Because they're probably paying him double, for all you know. And Mama told you that was gonna happen—told you over and over again he was gonna get stolen from us if you didn't watch it. But you didn't listen! And now he's gone. Goddamnit, Pop! And after what he said about Mama, and here you didn't even have what it took to sock him one!

I buried my face in my pillow and sobbed.

All you had to do was hit him. You should have at least hit him. To show him who's boss. You can't let him get away with stuff like that. Who does he think he is?

I peeked out from behind my pillow. Dad got up from my bed and stood quietly looking out my bedroom window. Our field was wide-open and moonlit. He drew the curtain and said that Toby wasn't working for anyone. It was just as he'd said a few days back: Tobias Wetherall Muncie was, in every sense of the word, his own man.

I don't like it any more than you do. But that's just the way it is. And the sooner we accept it, the better.

XII

MOM GOT HOME AT TEN o'clock that night. She was supposed to be home much earlier, but the Blumenthals got caught in traffic downtown after some gala event and they needed her to stay late. I was sitting in front of the TV when she walked through the door. She dropped her handbag in the doorway, kicked off her heels, slammed the door shut, and headed straight for the kitchen without acknowledging me. She started snatching soup cans from the cupboards with a slipper in hand, taking out her frustration on the cockroaches scurrying out from behind boxes of macaroni and cheese as if they were the ones who'd let her down.

And maybe I had. But what was I supposed to say to a mother desperate to believe that I wasn't a little cheat, when it turns out I was? I skulked into the kitchen and sat down and buried my face in my hands. I'd had all the chances that she'd ever dreamed of me having and I still couldn't make it work.

I told her that it wasn't all my fault. It had been her idea to come to New York in the first place. I never wanted to come to this crummy city. We belonged back in Akersburg. That was our home, and everything that was going wrong was just more proof that we should never have left.

Mom set a bowl of Campbell's cream of mushroom soup in front of me. She sat down beside me and asked what more she could possibly do that she hadn't already done. Life wasn't exactly a cakewalk for her, either. She looked me in the eye and asked me to think about what kind of hell of a life must she have been trying to escape that working ten hours a day for the Blumenthals was supposed to be a step up.

Do you have any idea what my day looks like? What it's like having to leave my morning shift at the dry cleaners a few minutes early just to dash across town to be on time for that conference with Mister McGovern? After which I ran off to pick up the twins so that Missus Blumenthal didn't miss her pedicure appointment. Do you have any idea how upset she'd have been with me if she missed that on my account?

Mom was tired, disillusioned, and frustrated. She'd come to New York City on the vague promise of a better life, but all she'd done was trade in Dad for the Blumenthals. Mom took an egg salad sandwich from her purse and unwrapped it. It was something that she'd picked up for herself in some vending machine but hadn't had time to eat. She took a joyless bite.

I've had enough twelve-hour days, low pay, late pay, no pay, unpaid back pay, bad checks, mismanaged rental deposits, security deposits, two-faced landlords, slumlords, sham electricians, bogus carpenters, bad advice, bunk promises, unsolicited advances, rude comments, crude comments, backhanded compliments, and backstabbing, not to mention a door slammed in my face. So, yes—it was a mistake. There. I said it. Are you happy now? So it's settled, then. This obviously isn't working out for either of us.

Mom got up from the table and tossed her sandwich into the trash. She told me to clear my own damned plate; she was sick and tired of always doing things for men. *Men, men, men.* Didn't even matter to her anymore if they were white or black.

What in the hell difference does it make to me, anyway? They're both still men, aren't they? Either way, I get lied to, taken for granted, mistreated, exploited, and shit on at every turn. Every damned man I've ever come across in this town has tried to squeeze me for every cent I'm worth. No matter where I turn there is some baby boy, boy, man-child, or elderly man-child asking me to do something for him. Look here. Mom stuck her left hand in my face. *See this? After all those years of dreaming of having one in Akersburg, I had to buy this fake one just to keep them at bay. Men are shameless. I tell them I got a kid, they hear desperate. I tell them I'm separated, they hear easy. What more do I have to do besides wear a ring? Why, just today I was out taking the Blumenthal twins for a walk in the park, and some man came right up to me and asked point-blank if he could buy me a drink. The twins were standing right next to me! Have I got a sign on my head that says, 'Why not?' Do I look like a streetwalker? Trust me, you don't have anything on me in the aggrieved department. So don't get sassy with me. Lord knows I want out, too. But where in the hell are we going to go?*

My soup was cold. The only sound in the house was the thin scrape of my spoon against the bowl and Mom picking clothes up off the floor, cursing men, cold weather, service work, and me. I got up and went into our bedroom. Mom was growing disenchanted with life and was starting to lose faith in everything—especially me. At times like this, it felt like she'd gone from assuming the very best about me to assuming the absolute worst. I took an envelope from atop the dresser and returned to the kitchen table with it. I took out the letter from inside and told myself that everything was going to be okay. Dad was going to show up one day and take me back with him. All I had to do was be patient. I unfolded the year-old letter and read over the passage where he'd proclaimed all the good things he had in store for me. Mom barked out from the bathroom for me to hurry with my dinner—we needed to get to bed; it was late.

I could hear Mom brushing her teeth. I wanted to ask if she'd cooked real food for the twins for dinner but didn't dare. Instead, I flipped open the *Daily News* lying beside my bowl to the personals section and left it there. I half wished she'd get a boyfriend just to have someone else to take her grief out on besides me. I put the letter facedown and picked up my spoon. For all Mom's piety, I couldn't help but wonder if she wasn't a parable for something having gone terribly wrong.

XIII

IT WAS SOMETHING HAVING TO do with the radiator. But it could just as well have been that the alternator was bad, having corroded through, old as it was. In any case, the fan belt had worn clean through in two places. So that was the obvious place to start. Nestor told us that he'd do his best to fix it, but couldn't make any promises.

The next four days were the longest of my life. Having come to believe that Nestor had taken our truck hostage, I marked the fridge calendar for every day that we went without it. Then, on a Thursday unremarkable in every way except for the fact that the truck was finally ready, Dad and I hoofed it into town. We could have taken the tractor, but Dad had convinced himself that he liked to walk—claimed that it felt nostalgic. On the way, he talked about the long treks he used to make into town as a teenager, back when Cordele Road was packed dirt and he spent lazy afternoons sitting atop rail fencing, babysitting field hands hoeing dirt, but mostly watching planes overhead going to and from Turner, with dreams of flying himself someday.

Wait—you wanted to be a pilot?

Who wouldn't?

Why didn't you?

Who says I won't?

I laughed. That was pretty funny. Anyway, his knee locked up by the time we hit the pyramid of pumpkins sitting in a flatbed parked at the top of Mister Buford's drive. Dad slipped on some loose gravel and fell on his behind. I helped him up and brushed him off, and we continued on. I couldn't help but feel sorry for the old guy. Not Dad—Mister

Buford. It wasn't even September yet, and here he was at it again with his pumpkins.

Dad pulled out Mom's shopping list.

Let's see here. A tin of bergamot. Eggs. What else?

Off in the distance, a field hand was walking through an expansive allée, smacking at the lower limbs of a pecan tree with a long pole. I tugged on Dad's hand.

Did you and Mama meet at school?

You know that I'm older than her. She went to a different school anyway.

What was it called?

Dad shrugged and said Eatonton, probably. But he couldn't be sure. Been so long.

Whaddya wanna know for?

I shrugged. *Just curious.*

There was a billboard for the Camelot on either end of town. One of them pictured two geese flying toward a setting sun. It was leaning out from Mister Brumeier's pecan orchard: Y'ALL COME BACK NOW!

I threw a rock at it. Dad smacked the back of my head—asked what in the hell was the matter with me, vandalizing public property like that. Those geese hadn't done anything to me.

WE'D BEEN WALKING since late morning and arrived at Nestor's, sun-battered and sweaty, at the appointed time. Aside from the grocery store, Nestor had a filling station and a full-service garage all in the same one-level sandstone-brick building. He hollered out from his garage for us to come back in an hour. It wasn't ready yet.

Mom had jotted down her shopping list on the back of a Georgia Power envelope. Dad handed it to me. *Remember when you asked what it's like to be thirty-nine?*

That had been a few months back. I'd been grilling him about the process of growing old. You know—what it felt like and when it started exactly and what steps you could take to prevent it. Anyway, there wasn't a single thing on that list for him. Dad joked that it was a thankless job.

Entire families filled the stores and cluttered the sidewalk with bags chock-full of school supplies and new clothes. Farther up the street,

Mister Waters was signing for a delivery. Dad saluted him with two fingers and nodded to Missus Myers as we strolled past, then tapped me on the head with a rolled-up circular, and we turned into the Rexall.

Grampa Frank!

What in the world happened to your arm, boy? Last I knew, you had two!

Dad's mother emerged from the Rexall holding a stapled prescription bag. She walked up beside Dad, glanced down at my cast, then continued to their truck without a word.

Grampa Frank mussed up my hair and told me not to take it personally. I didn't bother telling him that there wasn't any risk of that, me and Dad having hashed that one out every time a holiday came and went and I never saw her. Grampa Frank always made a point to drop by for my birthday, but not her. Dad warned me that his mother wasn't a very nice person pretty much every chance he got—called her a human icicle. *The* human icicle. The upshot was that she never gave herself the chance to be anything to me but a question mark who I only ever knew as Connie.

Dad brought me in close and positioned me between his legs and asked Grampa Frank what was going on down the street. Albeit worse for wear, that bus was parked in the same spot that it had been the morning I'd run into the sheriff's squad car—the Morning of Infamy, otherwise known as the Battle of Broken Arm.

There was lots more activity going on around it now than there was then. Grampa Frank cautioned us not to pay it any mind, then changed the subject, only to have Dad hem and haw his way through an explanation of all that had happened to my arm and how we were getting along without Toby, then work his way around to asking for money.

What for?

Peola says Irma's as big as a watermelon.

You haven't paid Toby yet?

Paid him? Damn it, I haven't paid myself.

Good Lord! Go to the bank!

Dad nodded like he understood and wouldn't press. I studied Connie in the truck, the way she took off that fancy cream-colored pillbox-style hat of hers and delicately scratched at the crease in her hair. I couldn't figure out what she had against Dad. It was no secret that they didn't like each other, Akersburg being as small as it is and we still somehow managed to hardly ever see her. All I knew was that you had to be one hell of a stick-in-the-mud for your own son to call you by your first name.

Dad and Grampa Frank appeared to have a lot of catching up to do. I wandered over to the curb and looked down the street. A small crowd was gathered under S&W's awning, seven blocks down. Directly in front of them was the bus. It appeared to be leaning off-kilter.

Grampa Frank headed off in his truck, and I tugged Dad down the street, toward the crowd of onlookers. He tried to ward me off, but it was no use. The air was absolutely electric. Something big was about to happen. I just knew it.

Dad warned me to stay on the far curb, said he didn't want trouble. I led him through the gawking crowd, just close enough to the bus to get a good look at the gash in the left front tire and three busted-out windows just behind where the driver sits. White people were gathered on our side of the street, coloreds were gathered on the other.

I clasped Dad's hand tight. I had so many questions. I didn't know where to start.

What the heck are they doing?

Protesting.

What's that?

Same thing you do all the time. Especially come bedtime.

What are they protesting?

Everything, son. Chevrolets, baseball, apple pie. You name it. I wouldn't mind it so much if it wasn't so damned un-American.

They weren't doing anything besides hanging out on the sidewalk. But seeing colored people gathered in a coordinated fashion in town like that fascinated me. Even if—truth be told—their khakis, button-downs, and loafers weren't all that different from the kinds we wore, there was still something exotic about them. They weren't just from out of town. They were from the North—that other world. It almost seemed like another universe to me. Actual flesh and blood northern-ers! They were, to me at least, the stuff of a great and often exasperating folklore. Hell, Dad cherished his Margaret Mitchell just as much as the next person.

All the people I knew either were born in Akersburg, dreamed of getting out of Akersburg, or were passing through Akersburg. The far-thest me or anyone I knew ever went was to Blakely, which sounded like another country but was just up the road twenty miles. I'd never heard of anyone coming to Akersburg except maybe for the open-tent revival meeting, the annual Seed and Feed Expo, or Mister Buford's haunted house, which, small though it was, was practically world famous. Rumor had it that someone from Rowena had gotten scared so bad he'd crapped himself. Word spread like wildfire after that, so that by the time the last week of October rolled around, the line of people waiting to get in spanned half a mile down Bancroft Road. It's been that way ever since.

On top of that, those coloreds were doing something they weren't supposed to be doing. Dad had whispered in my ear that they were persona non grata. When I asked what the heck that was, he said unwelcome visitors who were up to no good—which held its own special kind of allure. So yes, I was riveted.

Look!

Christ almighty.

Christ almighty was right. Long live the Republic, and sweet terra incognita. Toby was like some kind of circus-grade Whac-a-Mole. You got rid of him in one place, and he just popped up somewhere else. He stuck out like a sore thumb, standing as he was in overalls and rain boots in the middle of that well-heeled crowd, barking out orders to the other troublemakers, who seemed to be hanging on his every word. A newspaper man shoved his way up close and pressed a microphone into his handsome face. My jaw dropped. I couldn't believe it. How'd he get famous so quick? What was I, chopped liver? Hell, I'd practically been his boss. If anybody deserved to be listened to, it was me.

I picked at my wedgie and ran my tongue over the soft, gummy spot where my eyetooth had been. All I could think to myself as I stood there admiring the ease with which he dealt with all those people vying for his attention was that he was gone and was never coming back. So envious was I of his natural charisma that I plum forgot how mad I was at him for having left us in the first place. I'd even go so far as to say that I admired him—albeit for only a brief moment. And only in direct proportion to my want of courage to walk up to him in the midst of all that commotion and say, *Hey, Toby. It's me.*

What's he doing?

Organizing.

Organizing what?

Dad was suddenly in a hurry to get somewhere. Where, I don't know. Oh yeah—the truck. What we'd come for. I almost forgot. He jerked at my arm like a leash and dragged me down the sidewalk back toward Nestor's, weaving me through the crowd of upset white people still gawking at the circus across the street. Halfway down the block, I rubbernecked just enough to glimpse Toby mount a milk crate. His words boomed out: *BOSS IS NOT YOUR CREATOR! HE IS NOT EVEN YOUR FACILITATOR!* Dad stopped as if in a panic.

THAT SON OF a bitch Nestor had ordered the wrong year's voltage regulator. When Dad asked how that was even possible, Nestor gave his suspenders a tug and explained that his service manual was missing a page. He'd had no choice but to take the part number from a '54 Ford, which was supposed to be pretty much the same as our '53 except for the exhaust system and the lever on the tailgate latch. There might have been a few other differences, but those supposedly related to the drivetrain.

Nestor pulled out the service manual, spread it out over the front fender of our truck, and showed us all the pages that were missing. He then pulled a cup of water from his cooler, handed it to Dad, and explained that on top of that, postal service to Akersburg was suspended until further notice. It usually arrived on the twelve o'clock Trailways, which was being rerouted to Albany via Rowena. The bus company feared for their fleet. After all that had been done to the one up the street, who could blame them? I stood there tugging on Dad's sleeve, wondering what this all meant for Mister Abrams's replacement filter. I tried to ask him, but I couldn't get a word in edgewise.

I left Nestor's that afternoon with the distinct impression that Akersburg was, ipso facto, under siege. In my mind, we were only one canister of tear gas away from martial law, armed checkpoints, curfews, full-body searches, air raids, and who knew what else. Maybe even bread lines. Make no mistake—we were at war, albeit with ourselves.

A BRIDGE HOUSE, having appeared up the road, stood lookout to a covered bridge. For those who have never been to Akersburg—the great majority of you, I am sure—a covered bridge is just a run-of-the-mill wooden bridge with a roof overhead. It's basically a rectangular tunnel structure that spans a body of water—in this case, the Thronateeska River. It had a fancy name, but I can't remember it at the moment. Walter F. George Memorial Bridge—something like that. Anyway, a pair of granaries loomed high over both, bridge house and bridge, from across the river. Dad and I walked across. We didn't talk about all we'd seen in town. There was no reason to. I'd been there, and he'd been there, and we'd both seen it. What was there to talk about? Then, as we exited the covered bridge, Dad muttered something to himself about hoping to dear God, if there was a God, that they'd clear out by sunup.

From the outskirts of town to our house is little more than a forty-minute walk down Cordele Road, across that covered bridge, past several dozen colored people's homes, and on through a corridor of farmland, mostly orchards. The homes that we passed along the way were ramshackle clapboard houses, what Dad called *shotgun houses*, *sharecropper shacks*, or just plain *shacks*. He called them shotgun houses because they were so small I could fire a pea shooter clear through an open front door and reach the backyard. We plied our way past one after the next of these shacks, their sagging front stoops and balding patches of grass. The sky crackled, then opened up.

Mister Goolsbee's shop was so close I could smell the freshly cut rock dust pouring out of his open front door. The rain was coming down hard, and Goolsbee's boy was standing under the eaves, wearing an oversized black brick cutter's apron draped from his neck. He was sticking his hand out to catch the long needles of rain coming down.

I ran ahead and joined him. Goolsbee's boy pulled his hand in and put some distance between us. He kept to one side of the overhang, and I kept to the other—which was fine with me. I put my hands over my ears because of the shrieking noise of an electric saw coming from inside. Dad joined us a minute later. He came over and stood by me, and the three of us just stood there atop the shrunken floor boards, happy to be out of the rain. I had my head angled skyward, anxious for the dark clouds to pass.

It was the happiest I'd seen Dad since the morning Toby had fixed a backed-up sewage pipe that wasn't draining properly. Our house had smelled like a cesspool for weeks until he did. Anyway, I must have said something about hoping that the rain would let up soon because I was hungry and wanted to get home while supper was still warm. Dad looked at me like he didn't know who I was.

Stop? Goddamnit, boy, have I not taught you anything? You better hope for our sake that it rains so much pigs drown.

A truck splashed through the long puddles out front and pulled up beside a stack of cut granite and a wheelbarrow half-filled with bricks. Two men got out of it and ran through the rain toward us. They were drenched by the time they reached the top of the steps. They banged the storm door open and disappeared inside. A minute later, the electric saw stopped buzzing, and another truck pulled up. Dad always said that when it rained, it poured, so I figured they were customers, too.

Someone called out for an *Evan!* I figured it was Mister Goolsbee calling out for his boy to fetch something for one of the customers. When I looked around for the boy, he was gone.

A man appeared in the doorway. He looked both ways and asked, *Where's Evan?*

That was only the second time I'd ever heard that boy's name spoken in my life. He'd never been anything to me but Goolsbee's boy, on account of having been a fixture around that place for as long as I could remember. I had my sneaker off, and my sock was in my hand. I squeezed it, trying to get the water out. Experience told me that Mister Goolsbee only serviced the colored cemetery down the road. That was the only place I'd ever seen his boy hauling stone slabs along with a shovel in that wheelbarrow out front. Why a white man would be buying a headstone from a colored man was beyond me.

I shrugged. When the man disappeared back inside, Dad dragged me down from the porch and ran off with me in tow. It was the second time that day that Dad had dragged me off like that, without the least bit of explanation, and I didn't appreciate it. I was screaming and hollering out, demanding to know what I'd done now.

I hated it when he used his size against me willy-nilly like that. Drove me crazy. It was bad enough being four and a half feet tall and weighing sixty-five pounds without the Jolly Green Giant making me feel more feeble and helpless than I already was. He was running just as fast as he could, dragging me along with him through the mud puddles and into the wood—twice as fast as he had at the Battle of Broken Arm. And me hobbling along after him barefoot through grass and mud puddles just as fast as I could, struggling to keep up, with my shoes and socks in hand. I hollered at him to at least let me get my shoes all the way back on. But he wasn't having it—wasn't even listening to me. I tripped through mud and over stumps and branches and twigs, convinced he'd finally gone off the deep end.

We covered half a football field in the time it'd take Ernie Davis with one point down, two seconds on the clock, and three defensive ends hot on his tail. It wasn't until we were hidden deep inside the wood's thick underbrush that Dad stopped. He was doubled over, clutching his gut, wheezing. His hair was soaked, and water was dripping down his chin, and his shirt was stuck to his chest. I was out of breath, too. My cast felt like it weighed a good twenty pounds. Dad pressed his hand over my mouth. His face was red and munched and he was peering back the way we'd just come.

A loud voice came from Goolsbee's place. Goddamned if I didn't get the heebie-jeebies. I recognized it. The cloud cover was thick, and it was going on dusk. The light was low and there were too many trees in the way for me to see much. Dad pulled back a handful of branches, and a backlit silhouette appeared in the distance. Someone was being dragged out onto the back porch. I murmured under my breath, *Oh Christ*. It was Mister Goolsbee.

Mister Goolsbee was pleading in the open doorway. He went down on his knees, and his hands were tied behind his back. It looked to me like one of the men was holding a pistol to his head. Rain was pummeling the ground and eaves and soaking the backyard, and it took several seconds of Mister Goolsbee going on in a desperate way before it occurred to me that he wasn't pleading for his own life but for someone else's—his boy's. He was begging for the men not to hurt him. He was explaining that he was just a boy, and that he had no idea where he'd run off to, but that if he'd done something wrong or something he wasn't supposed to have done it was only because he didn't know better.

I looked up at Dad for answers. He cupped a rain-soaked hand over my eyes and said, *Hush*. When the pitch of Mister Goolsbee's pleading increased, Dad grabbed my hand, and we continued farther into the wood, splashing through long puddles, and didn't stop until those horrific sounds were gone.

DAD DIDN'T MENTION anything to Mom about what we'd seen at Mister Goolsbee's that afternoon. When I asked, he just said that it was important to pay your bills on time. Of course, everyone was in debt up to his ears, not just Mister Goolsbee. I knew that. Debt was practically all Dad talked about. He had so much of it I just figured he loved the stuff. Anyway, he said it was probably just some unscrupulous loan shark. Who knew what gambling debts the old coot had. When I brought it up again at bedtime, Dad told me to hush and explained that it was best kept between us.

I had an unsettling dream that night, so I sneaked in and climbed into Mom and Dad's bed. I couldn't have been lying there for more than an hour, trying to fall back asleep to the sounds of water dripping from the eaves and an owl hooting outside, when the telephone rang. Dad picked it up and asked who in the hell was calling so late. It was Nestor. Dad whispered his surprise that the truck was ready so soon.

I rolled over. I could hear Nestor's voice coming from the handset. He sounded panicky. He was explaining that he'd had no choice but to get the voltage regulator from Lesley, who apparently kept a mountain of spare parts in his backyard. Said it was important that Dad pick the truck up as soon as possible. Dad sat up in bed with the telephone droning in his hand. His face was an outline in the moonlight. He looked more concerned than he had been after he'd run into Mister Orbach and Mister Schaefer at Buskin Brothers back in May and they'd laughed him out of the store for having planted so doggone late. Mom appeared in the doorway. She'd come in from the living room, where she'd been sleeping. She took the phone from him and hung it up.

Dad told me to go back to my room. When I refused, he told me to at least go back to sleep. When I told him that I couldn't sleep, he told me to count sheep. I put my head down on the pillow and imagined Nestor as a covert operative driving his tow truck through a land mine–riddled countryside, with our voltage regulator shimmying around on the passenger's seat. I told Dad that it wasn't all bad. Even if we lacked Toby, we had gotten plenty of rain and would soon have our truck, too. With any luck, we'd have our peanuts all dug up and up on stack poles in no time. Dad got out of bed and left to put on a pot of coffee. Mom draped her bathrobe over her shoulders and followed after him, complaining about Nestor doing a rush job just to get our truck out of his garage when it had been sitting there for almost a week now.

MY CAST HURT in a strange new way in the morning. I must have slept funny. I got up to check the thermometer out back just to confirm what my body already knew: it was swim weather. Dad was in the kitchen, scarfing down his breakfast. He told me to hurry up, said that he wanted to get in town early, before things got out of hand. I took one bite of toast, and he pulled out my chair. Told me not to worry about finishing my breakfast. He grabbed me by the hand and led me out the door.

We headed into town early enough that I could see my footprints in dewy patches of grass. There was a particular joy I felt in walking down an empty road in the early morning after a heavy rain. After several weeks of dry weather, the surrounding fields were soaked. Life dripped from the trees, clung to cobwebs, and beaded up on tall stalks of grass. Birds dipped and disappeared in stands of sassafras. Pill bugs and centipedes scuttled at the edge of the road. Earthworms emerged from tiny holes and washed up onto the middle of the road. I carried them off in my cupped hands down a narrow road walled off on both sides with trees.

I was shocked to discover that Mister Goolsbee's shop was gone. In its place, a black wood-burning stove stood in the center of a heap of smoldering embers. A wheelbarrow sat with its handle and tire burnt off. Beside it, a row of cinder blocks were vaguely recognizable as part of its foundation. Shingles were spread over the ground, and nails and saw blades poked out from smoldering ashes. Dad pulled me back and said that it looked like it was still hot.

I kicked at a charred patch of grass where thick tufts of little blue-stem and prairie dropseed had been and looked up at Dad. I had no idea what had happened and was too afraid to ask. I waited for him to say something. Dad said that he remembered when Mister Goolsbee had first built his shop. He'd walked past it practically every day as a boy. As small and unremarkable as it had looked structurally, it had stood as a kind of monument. It was not customary, in Akersburg, for a colored man to own and operate a business. It had taken Mister Goolsbee the better part of his life to put that shop together, by which time he was well into his fifties.

Dad didn't say it, but something told me that he wasn't just talking about the expense of time and materials, which were the kinds of things that normally concerned him. Dad explained that Mister Goolsbee was a source of tremendous admiration and inspiration for a great many people. For whites, he was living proof that they offered a way up, if not a way out. For coloreds, he stood out for being the only one in the entire county who'd ever gotten that far in life. Then Dad said that if it was all the same to me, he would prefer not to talk about it anymore, and continued on down the road. After a few steps, he said to no one in particular that a man like Mister Goolsbee had cheated death enough times and that of course it was eventually going to catch up with him. When I ran up to him and asked what he meant, Dad said that clumsy old nigger was just too old to be working as much as he did and had probably just left a loose wire lying around—and that frankly, he was lucky not to have lost his inventory. It was a doggone shame, but the fact remained that I must not fall into the trap of always assuming the worst, no matter how bad anything ever looked. Which was fine with me. I was perfectly happy believing that Mister Goolsbee's shop had been washed away with the rain if Dad wanted me to.

I'd brought along some fliers I'd made, figuring to post them while we were in town. I was down to a paltry two weeks before Danny's scheduled departure and had decided it high time that I took the law into my own hands. I had tried the 221B Baker Street approach, replete with magnifying glass, pipe, and deerstalker hat. Now I was trying the bare-knuckled approach. On our way past the Camelot, I pulled one out and asked Dad if it looked like the genuine article. Dad looked concerned. I assured him that it wasn't so much a matter of me assuming the worst as it was just plain wanting answers. Dad took my hand and asked how I could think about that pool at a time like this. I shrugged. I dunno. It wasn't that hard, really. I just could.

THE THREE SHELL—BACKED chairs lined up on the sidewalk in front of the Rexall were wet. Trailways, having been out of service for over a week, had little use for them. Dad pulled a hankie from his back pocket and wiped off two. He sat down and massaged his knee; he told me to put my ear up close and made it pop just by bending it—called it the sound of middle age. He said there was no preventing it. It had just sort of crept up on him. Like one day he woke up, and that's how his knee sounded when he bent it.

I sat down and swung my legs back and forth. People were starting to gather around the battle-scarred bus across the street. I was convinced that at this rate we'd be on rations of canned meat and powdered milk in a few more days. I'd probably have to learn another way to communicate with Derrick.

Can my bedroom light be used for Morse code?

Any light source can.

What's Morse code for cast, Pop?

Dad had to think, then asked why I wanted to know.

I shrugged. *Just curious.*

The bus was in much worse shape than yesterday. There was graffiti spray painted all over its metallic keel, and more of the windows had been broken. The sun was just now coming over the low-rise buildings across the street. I cupped my hands over my eyes. I couldn't believe some of the stuff written on it.

Is that even legal?

Just be happy your mom's not here to see it.

My cast was a mess, too. My skin was raw around both ends. My fingers were filthy and looked terrible. They were sort of shriveled up and swollen at the same time. Made my face crinkle up when I bent down to smell them—like my feet after I'd gotten home with rain-soaked sneakers the night before.

Where do you suppose they're staying?
Probably under a bridge somewhere.

A coin-operated Laundromat sat next door to S&W. Missus Higgins emerged from it. She stood on the corner, watching the coloreds milling about in front of S&W in their usual aggrieved way, then continued curbside, where a patrol car sat like a fixture. A deputy was leaning against it, quietly reading the paper. She interrupted him, pointed with her cane, and asked if it was legal, what they were doing.

Mister Abrams's filter fixed yet?

The question had just popped out of my mouth, and I regretted it the second it left my lips. I don't know why I even bothered to ask. I knew what was coming. If it wasn't going to be about the coloreds across the street, it was going to be about that damned pool, and if it wasn't going to be about the pool, it was going to be about the fire at Goolsbee's place, and if it wasn't about that, it was going to be about that son of a bitch Toby, who just strolled up across the street, because the fridge had finally conked out on us and had left such a mess that morning Dad had to put on his rain boots just to get at his coffee. He'd spent the rest of the predawn hours with Toby's tools spread all over the kitchen floor, claiming to have fixed it. All the while, Mom was feeling around inside the freezer, complaining that it couldn't cool a cracker.

Meanwhile, I was shocked at the discovery that Toby hadn't come back for his tool belt. Mom had made it for him as an anniversary gift sometime before when I could remember to show how grateful Dad was for his ten years of service. And sure enough, they'd spent the rest of the morning in the kitchen, squabbling about stuff that had nothing to do with refrigeration systems or Freon or whatever frayed wires Dad had been fussing with, and I was so fed up with it all I disappeared into my bedroom and slammed the door shut. All they did anymore was bicker, and it was getting so bad that I didn't care to ask what about.

Dad took out one of his cough drops, popped it into his mouth, and sucked on it. He started in about how much more difficult things had been since Toby had left. Telling me how important it was for me not to buckle under pressure—especially now that Miss Della, Aurelia, and Missus Swanson were no longer coming by to have their hair done, and here it was over a week and the toilet bowl still backed up to the rim every time I flushed it. Not to mention that Mom was starting to come apart at the seams, sleeping out on the sofa every night as she was.

Dad slung an arm over my shoulder and pulled me close. *We've got to pull together, son.*

I can always poo in the outhouse, Pop. I don't mind that. Not one bit. But what about the fridge? Who's gonna fix that? Because we need food! Christ, everybody needs food!

Toby was standing across the street. He took his place atop the milk crate and started going on like a one-man pep squad, lifting the spirits of his devotees with rallying cries and spurring on the slow-moving crowd around him. He seemed to breathe life into what looked to me like a band of devil-worshiping pagans who were single-handedly precipitating the decline of life as I knew it, otherwise known as Western civilization. Dad didn't exactly say it, much less have to spell it out for me, but I suspected they were protesting something having to do with the government. Mom had let it slip while on the phone with Aurelia, asking her where she'd been hiding all this time. But what the government had to do with S&W was anybody's guess.

It was one thing when those college kids had kept me from enjoying an ice cream, but what with Trailways rerouted, businesses up and down Main Street in a slump, and postal service suspended, it seemed like the beginning of the end. As I sat there listening to the foot-dragging rasp of loafers marching back and forth over the sidewalk and the lackluster chant of some uninspired two-four-six-eight number, part of me was surprised to see Toby still able to command everyone's attention as he was. He was a natural. It was like he'd been born to do this sort of stuff. I almost got the impression that it was his calling.

Even though I hadn't seen all that had happened, the episode on the back porch of Mister Goolsbee's shop the night before had put me on edge so bad that I'd only slept a few hours. I still hadn't found out from Dad what it was that we'd run from. I wished he'd just come out and told me, because I had goosebumps lying awake all night with my imagination running wild, never once having imagined that the place would be gone the next time I walked by. I don't care if Mister Goolsbee was up to his neck in debt, how the heck was he supposed to pay anyone back with his only source of income demolished? I knew that money made the world go around, but that was ridiculous.

On top of that, I wet the bed. I didn't blame Mister Goolsbee for that, of course. I would never do that. I put the blame square on Toby. I was mad as hell at him for having undone two years of progress in a single night. An eight-year-old isn't supposed to wet the bed. Mom consoled me by saying, *That's just how your body works, dear. It's not your fault.* Until she realized I'd done it in what she called *her* bed. Then she was mad as hell. I demanded to know what she was so upset about, since she was sleeping out on the sofa. Worse still was the fact that I couldn't even pawn off the stink on Snowflake. Then I told her it was all Toby's fault, for all the stress his self-righteous crusade in town was causing me. It was having real-world consequences for me. I couldn't help it. I was so desperate to be rid of Toby and all those coloreds who now seemed to be under his spell that I cast a hex on him using an old sock monkey that was lying around. I wasn't sure who it belonged to. It was either Mom's or Dad's from when they were a kid.

Even if Dad was coming around to the view that Mister Goolsbee had been the victim of a hazardous work environment, it wasn't lost on me that some people were more prone to having their places torched than others. What was even more amazing, though, was considering the rapid deterioration of the battle-scarred bus. Never mind that it was only the morning after the tragic fire afflicting Mister Goolsbee, Toby had somehow managed to drag still more people into the dispute taking place in front of S&W than he had the previous day. Judging from what I was seeing, I must have crossed my signals with my incantation and gotten my hex backward. Instead of clearing out, the coloreds seemed to be multiplying. The crowd was getting larger right before our eyes, with people constantly arriving, joining in the procession moving around and around in a circle on the sidewalk.

Most of the people yelling back to Toby in a loud and impassioned call-and-response weren't impetuous renegades. They were pious old colored ladies with gray hair, the kind of women who went to Aurelia's Bible study. They wore white leggings and padded walking shoes. They filled the entire street with the sound of their voices. I recognized the stock clerk from the Rexall, along with the woman who used to fold and iron clothes at the Laundromat next door. I wasn't sure if she was working there anymore, though. Maybe not. Who knew? They were all considered the pillars of the colored community. At the sight of Missus Shapely and Missus Greeley over there with him, I leaned forward and spit.

You think he remembers us, Pop?

Of course he does.

Should I go say hi?

Can't you see he's busy?

I had no idea why Toby was with the people across the street. I was trying to figure it out. Aside from the obvious fact that he was colored and so were they. It felt like a betrayal—he'd known us just as long as he'd known any of them. He'd been with us for so, so long. And his father before him. Grandfather, too. After that, it got murky. Dad said people didn't keep written accounts that far back. He made it sound like employment records were a modern invention.

I tried to imagine exactly what I'd say to Toby if I had the nerve to confront him. It wouldn't be nice. Because it felt like he was assuming the absolute worst about me and my whole family. Why would he do such a thing, when we were just doing what people like us were supposed to do? It was what bosses did. And we were bosses. It wasn't our fault. Heck, someone had to be. And quite honestly, I was thankful. Better us than someone else.

Dad claimed that we were the providers of jobs. The way he figured it, Toby and the other field hands jabbing at the air with their picket signs should have been thanking us. What would Toby have done with himself if he didn't have us to provide him with an honest day's work? Besides, it's not like we were getting rich off him. Didn't he know that this was just how the world worked? When they said God made the world in seven days, well, this was the world He made. It was starting to look like we were being scapegoated for the problems of every field hand who ever walked the earth. Dad made his knee pop again. He looked up with a grimace.

I know that man better than anyone, Huey. Known him since he was six. This is nothing but one man's grievance. What you're witnessing is a lifetime of frustration and anger boiling over. My only regret is that I didn't see it coming sooner. And trust me, Toby doesn't care one iota about anyone but Toby. Here he's dragged Missus Greeley and Missus

Shapely into this mess with him, not to mention all those other innocent and unsuspecting old ladies. Only God can help them now.

Gee whiz, Pop. You hear all he's saying? He's making us sound like monsters. Half of it's not even true! Christ almighty, Mom made him dinner practically every night, and I personally wrapped them in tin foil to keep them warm. Son of a bitch, I even hand delivered them to him.

Now, now. You're getting ahead of yourself. Toby's in way over his head. He's got no land. No equipment—not even a damned truck. Not to mention that busted-up leg of his.

He's not using his cane anymore.

So what? All that boy's got are his good looks and natural God-given charm and speaking ability. He'll be lucky if he ever gets one seed in the ground come April. I give him ten days. Ten days, you hear? As soon as these people clear out and things return to normal around here, he's gonna be done with those high-minded ideas of his and come knocking on our door, begging for us to take him back. Mark my word.

Seems to be doing fine now, though.

Dad reached into his pocket and pulled out a cough drop. He lobbed it underhand to me.

Here. They keep me from smoking so much, but they also help with dry mouth. Listen, I got it all worked out. Tobias Wetherall Muncie will come crawling back with his tail between his legs, begging for mercy, just as soon as he realizes that he needs us every bit as much as we need him. That's the plague of the colored race. You understand? They think too much of themselves. Get all high and mighty before they've even troubled to think the thing through. And you wanna know why? Because even he's got sense enough to realize when he's beat. Because being a good field hand is one thing, but running the show is something else. That takes real smarts. Of course, it's all fine and dandy just so long as he lays low and lets me do all the head work, what with the ledger, accounting, applications for various federal and state subsidies, payroll, etcetera etcetera. So don't go getting all worked up over nothing. There's more than one way to skin a cat. You'll see.

I looked up at Dad, surprised—I thought that Mom did all that stuff. Anyway, the cough drop was cherry-flavored, and the wrapper stuck to my fingers. I had to shake my hand furiously in order to get it off.

Is my tongue red?

Dad shook his head no. He folded his arms and turned back to the crowd gathered across the street.

What color is it?

Pink.

That's the normal color, right?

Far as I know.

The neon Coca-Cola sign flashing in the S&W window was making me thirsty. I popped the cough drop back in my mouth. Dad checked his watch and said that the truck was probably ready. He got up and limped over to Mister Brines's shop. I'd hidden all the fliers I'd made in a newspaper. In an environment as untrusting as this, I wasn't taking any chances. Danny only had two more weekends before he had to split for Fayetteville. It was a long shot, but I hadn't given up on the idea of the pool reopening before he skedaddled off back to college. It would require me pounding the pavement in search of a miracle, but it was possible.

I got up, tore off a strip of masking tape, and taped one of my fliers to the seat back of the chair I'd been sitting in. I stepped back and checked to see if it was crooked.

WANTED!

For Trespassing on Private Property of . . .
The Camelot Terrace
AKA "The Pool"
2376 Cordele Road
Akersburg, GA
On the Evening of June 12
Approx 7:30 PM
Suspect last seen walking around with only one shoe.
Possibly injured during flight.
See anything suspicious?
Please call: 876-1492
REWARD: 5 lb bag of boiled peanuts.
THANK YOU!

*Reward pending arrest and conviction.
**Plus reopening of pool by 8/6.
***Reward should be ready with any luck the last week of August.

It was straight enough. I followed after Dad.

How 'bout now, Pop?

Still pink.

Dad hadn't even looked. He stood there with one hand in his pocket and the other twirling his key ring as Mister Brines pulled down a dive mask from a shelf behind the window display inside his shop.

Wanna go in?

I shook my head no.

Aw, c'mon. I thought you said that cheap rubber gasket on your dive mask had started to crack. A boy needs a working dive mask—well, don't he?

I shrugged. *It's okay.*

Dad rested a heavy hand on my shoulder. *Aw, what am I saying? You're probably just down about your mother and me, aren't you? It's no wonder. The trick is to get her off the sofa and back into our bedroom. Then things have a chance of returning to normal. But what on earth will accomplish that, is the question? I'm open to suggestions.*

I dunno. Maybe apologize and ask Toby to come back? Short of that, she probably just needs to get out of the house more.

Dad sighed. *There's no sugarcoating it, is there? Hell, who am I kidding? You probably miss him, too. It's not your fault. Known him your whole life. Probably can't help but feel some affection for the man. After all, he was like a big brother to you.*

No, he wasn't.

Well, all I'm saying is that it's not your fault. So don't feel bad if you do.

I don't.

Only stands to reason. Hell. I probably would, too—if I were you, I mean. He was always nice to you.

Never let me ride on the tractor.

That was because of me.

I looked up, surprised.

Nothing for you to hold on to.

Missus Orbach appeared in front of Ivey's—which was unexpected. We'd been sitting there, squinting in the sun coming over the buildings across the street, for a good half hour, and I hadn't seen her go in. She set her shopping bag down and took a moment to straighten her dress and put on her sunglasses. I leaped into the air at the sight of Derrick emerging from the double doors behind her. No sooner did I have the *D* sound shaped in my mouth than Missus Orbach picked back up her shopping bag and said, *Come along, boys. We don't want to keep Danny waiting. Vincent, you've got your shorts? Don't swing your goggles like that, Cal. You'll break them.*

Derrick walked off without a word. I was stunned. I wanted to show off my cast. It had been two weeks, and he still hadn't seen it. I stood there smiling ear to ear, waving my cast overhead, but he just looked straight through me. It was as if he hadn't recognized me. Half a block down, Missus Orbach and Derrick and Vincent and Calvin all piled into her wagon. I pressed one nostril with my thumb and blew snot from the other, then wandered over to the cool shade of Mister Brines's awning and wondered if I'd seen right.

Theodore Krasinski had curly blond locks, plump pink cheeks, and candy-apple red lips that framed a constant smile. He was a dead ringer for those plump, cherub-like renderings of the Christ child you see all over the place. No matter the nonstop ribbing he suffered for being such an insufferable little suck-up, he stoutly remained the happiest, most pleasantly disposed and good-natured kid in town. Everyone loved him. Anyway, Theo appeared behind Mister Brines's plate-glass door sporting a brand-new dive mask. He hopped down from the front stoop and waved.

Danny made nationals! He's gotta head back to campus tomorrow for time trials. We're all getting one last swim in today! See ya there!

I'd been nursing that cough drop for the last half hour, and then, just like that, it slipped down my throat. Missus Orbach drove past. I stood still as a statue. I struggled to find it in me to wave. I just couldn't. Danny was gone? Already? One look at Dad and I knew it was true. Open or not, there was no way that he was going to let me swim in that pool as long as they hadn't caught the trespassers. I'd only gotten to visit Mister Abrams's pool three times that summer—so few times it hardly seemed to register as a genuine experience. So few times I could almost trick myself into believing that I'd only imagined it. More than the actual visits to the pool, what stuck out was the depth of my yearning for more. I was a boy of words. Many, many, words. And they all, every last one of them, felt dead in my mouth. It was my last chance to visit Mister Abrams's pool for another year.

And to top it off, Theodore was twirling his dive mask by its strap on his way down the sidewalk. As that black snorkel skipped off merrily down the street beside his mom's shifting skirt, tears burst from my eyes, and I hurled my bundle of fliers at Dad. *Why on earth do you care who broke into that damned pool so much? No one else does!*

Tell you what—how about after harvest, whaddya say you and me, we take a little drive up to the old reservoir out by the county line. You'd like that, wouldn't you?

He was talking about Lake Offal. That was where the colored kids learned to swim. Toby'd bragged once about how when he was my age, he just dove in and swam clear across it his first time out. Which gave me goosebumps just thinking about it. Every September, after weeks of heavy rain, its tributaries rose by more than three feet, and at least one person got sucked into its undertow, never to be seen or heard from again.

Phooey. Stop with your damned sulking. It's not as bad as you're making it out to be. Some swim in pools, others swim in rivers and lakes and inlets and such. What the hell difference does it make? I tell ya, you gotta be open-minded these days, son. Because the world's a-changing. Every day it's a-changing. Changing. Changing. Changing. Now, I know what you're thinking. But I'm telling you, what was not acceptable yesterday may be perfectly reasonable today. That's the way of the world. Someone's gotta take the first step. We'll just take an inner tube along and it oughta be fine.

A truck skidded past and veered wildly in the middle of the street. Dad jerked me back from the curb as Mister Bradford's eldest son, Kyle, leaned out of the window and hollered something at me, then raced off down the street. The episode had lasted all of ten seconds, but somehow I'd experienced the wild-eyed look on Kyle's face in slow motion. Along with the smoke spewing from his tires. And hands covering my ears. The pavement was scarred with black streaks, and a fog of exhaust fumes hung in the air. The crowd gathered across the street was still and quiet. Their collective gaze seemed to be on me. Dad lifted his hands from my ears and the distant grunt of a flathead V8 echoed from a mile away. Dad stepped into the street and checked to make sure that

Kyle wasn't coming back, then stepped back onto the sidewalk and started picking up sheets of yellow construction paper.

Kyle's just pissed that he got a 4-F classification. The army won't even let him stamp envelopes. But that's not your fault, okay? Kyle's an asshole. Always has been. I don't care what he says. Your daddy's white, which makes you white. You know that, right?

XIV

THE NEXT MORNING, A BOWL of cereal and a glass of OJ were waiting for me on the kitchen table. I gave Mom a peck on the cheek on my way out the door. She stopped me and said that I wasn't going anywhere until I'd written an apology. I looked up at the clock, then sat down at the table and picked up a pen.

Dear Mister Yamaguchi,
Please accept my sincere apology for cheating ~~in your class~~. I really enjoy Japanese and you as a teacher. It is a fine language, and you are a really ~~fine good~~ great teacher. One of the best I've ever had. I should be so lucky to ever have another teacher as great as you. Anyway, I have had ~~eighteen hours and thirty-four minutes~~ time to think about my mistake and realize now why I should not cheat. How can I get better if I cheat? My mom says ~~that in the long run~~ I'm only cheating myself. I promise you that I will never, ever cheat ~~in your class~~ again. Not in your class or any other.
                                              Yours truly,
                              Hubert Francis Fairchild, the first.

I folded it in half and slid it into my *Japanese–English Character Dictionary*, gave Mom another peck on the cheek, and ran out the door. Mom stepped into the hallway and asked where my blazer was. I jumped into the elevator and yelled back that it was at school.
What's it doing there?
Long story, Mama. Gotta go. Bye!

I hauled ass out the front door past the smell of reefer wafting around the old men sipping *cafes con leche* out on the front steps. Discarded potato-chip bags stirred in the breeze coming off the East River. The sun reflected off the backboards in the ball court, the chain-link fence on my left, and the chrome bumpers, hubcaps, and door handles on my right. I cleared some broken glass and cut through the long cars parked on either side of a fireplug.

The train felt like a tin can sliding over sand. I squeezed into a seat between some woman in scrubs with a lanyard around her neck and a man in a bow tie with a cane poking up from between his legs. The woman in scrubs had a bag from the dime store Mom had worked at after that job cleaning office buildings. It was a family-owned five-and-dime with a bunch of crazy-looking windup monkeys that play the cymbals in the front window. It was up on East Twenty-Third Street, and even if the old man who owned the joint gave her discounts on all sorts of worthless trinkets and kitsch, he rarely ever paid her on time. After that, it was one of those dime-a-dozen diners up in Columbus Circle, where she was always dropping food and spilling stuff and her boss habitually called her at home with some off-the-charts last-minute shift change that he expected her to be able to accommodate. Then there was the bowling alley out in Brooklyn, which took a whole hour just for her to get to. God, she'd had a lot of jobs our first year here. After that, she took a job in housekeeping at the Days Inn downtown, where the hours were set in stone and they paid her for every single minute that she'd punched in and out for and the commute time wasn't so bad. After a year of cleaning bathtubs and toilets, her boss came into a guest room while she was tucking in bedsheets and said that he could see that she was too smart to be making beds and that he was going to see what he could do for her. After several months, the promised promotion just kept getting pushed out. Meanwhile, other chamber maids came and went, and Mom's boss stuck her with having to hire, train, and schedule their replacements. Then he started making her check their work, validate their time cards, and cover for them when they called in sick. Even if Mom was starting to feel that she was getting a raw deal, she hung in there. She was looking forward to the day she got transferred to the front desk, where she could show off her bookkeeping and people skills. Not to mention her smile. But as the months passed, Mister Reinhardt just kept piling on more work, telling her how much he liked her and didn't want to lose her and for her just to be patient because he was waiting for something special to turn up where someone as good as her could really shine. She was not to worry. He was working on it. Then came the day that Mom walked through the lobby and saw a new girl standing behind the front desk who looked like she'd just graduated from high school, had no front-of-the-house experience whatsoever, and was, well, white.

That night, Mom brought home a dozen of those little bars of soap and mini bottles of shampoo and conditioner. The next morning, she followed up on some job openings she'd come across in a brochure somewhere. She figured what the heck, she had nothing to lose. One night a few weeks later, the phone rang. Mom's voice went up an octave when she answered it. I was in the living room, watching Don Rickles on TV. She wound the cord around her finger and disappeared behind the doorjamb, into the kitchen. I could tell by the look on her face that it wasn't anyone from school, so I turned back to Johnny Carson. What a hoot. I was chuckling like an idiot at some gag they were doing. A few minutes later, the phone clicked into its cradle, and Mom called me into the kitchen. I told her to hold on a minute; Johnny Carson and Don Rickles were hilarious together. She came in with the Yellow Pages and opened it to a full-page advertisement, which she spread out over the coffee table. She turned off the TV and asked if I'd heard of Blumenthal, the Mattress Maven. Of course I had. His signs were everywhere—on buses, in telephone booths, on park benches, on subway platforms, in weeklies. I couldn't go a block without seeing one of his ads. I'd turn around and there it would be, staring at me, telling me how lousy my bed was and that I needed a new one. It claimed in big, bold letters that that was why I felt so grumpy all the time. I wanted to tell him that it wasn't the bed at all, but it was pointless to shout back at some larger-than-life-sized ad shellacked to the side of a brick building.

Mom was fingering over the ad, admiring it, saying how she'd accepted a position working for him. She wouldn't be working for one of his store locations or warehouses or anything like that, but the actual family. I had no idea that she was even considering working as someone's personal nanny and housekeeper and sometimes cook. Turns out, she'd pursued it on a lark. Anyway, the Blumenthals had twin baby boys. As they put it, they could use an extra pair of hands around the house. Who couldn't? It didn't matter to Mom that she had no idea what she was in for. She was just happy to finally be able to tell Mister Reinhardt that he could take his job and shove it.

As sweet and adorable as those twins had turned out to be, it didn't compensate for the fact that the money wasn't that hot. Which is why Mom had to hold on to her job at the dry cleaners. No matter how much I'd beg just to be able to check out the iguana living inside the Blumenthals' home, she'd just pull her hair into a bun so tight it stretched out the little wrinkles from her forehead and shake her head and say that there were no ifs, ands, or buts about it. It was strictly verboten. I couldn't even pick her up there after work. I was starting to wonder if maybe she wasn't somehow embarrassed of me. I couldn't figure out if her concern was about the twins seeing her around me or me seeing her around the twins. All I knew was that I had to meet her at the HoJo's after work. At least Mister Reinhardt would let me come by after school and do my homework in a vacant room.

Mom had been with the Blumenthals for a year before I started at Claremont. Even if she and I rarely ever saw each other after that, what with her away at work and me studying all the time, it wasn't like it was all gloom and doom. If she'd entrusted my education to Claremont, she'd left everything else to Mister McGovern. He'd become something of a father figure. I was a knobby-kneed pipsqueak who couldn't fight his way out of a paper bag, but Mister McGovern talked to me like I was a grown man. Of course, a kid's going to love a guy like that. What's there not to like?

The worst part was that as much as Mom and I missed each other when we were apart, we drove each other crazy when we were together. She complained that I had no idea what her day looked like, and I rebutted that she had no idea what mine looked like. I was always off doing my thing and she was off doing hers, barely home long enough to throw something together for me to eat, check my homework, and tell me to go to bed. She was stretched so thin she wasn't even able to send me off to school on the mornings she had to leave the house before dawn. It was starting to feel like I hadn't just lost Dad with our move to New York. I was losing her, too. Which felt wrong. She was all I had left.

I got off at Ninety-Sixth Street and dashed up the stairs to street level. I ran down the block and dug around in the garbage can on the corner, pulling up to-go boxes, Styrofoam cups, candy wrappers, tissues, yesterday's *Daily News*, the *Village Voice*, and empty soda bottles until at last I found my blazer buried toward the bottom. I pulled a banana peel from the sleeve and shook it out. I held it up and tried to figure out what I could claim all the splotches were from, then brushed it off and put it on.

Clyde slapped me five on my way through the service entrance. Past the nurse's office, up the stairs, around the corner, down the hall. I caught my breath in the doorway and strolled into class. I bowed politely and apologized for being late, then dug out my apology letter and handed it to Mister Yamaguchi with both hands. I asked permission to move up to the front row, where he could see my every move.

Mae no hoo ni suwatte yoroshi desu ka?
Hai.

XV

THE ORBACHS, KRASINSKIS, AND SCHAEFERS shared Miss Della. She might have worked for others, but those were the three I knew about. Later that week, I was on my way out to clean the henhouse when she came running up the road, waving her hands like it was about to rain and our laundry was still up. She called out for me to get Mom. I tossed a handful of dirt and feathers into a garbage can and told her that she was inside. Mom poked her head around the front door. Miss Della labored up the stoop. Next thing I knew, Mom disappeared inside Miss Della's arms.

Are you sure you heard right?

I'm sure, baby doll. I'm sure.

I went about my business of scrubbing the slimy black-and-white chicken shit from the walls, frustrated with how long it was taking with just one arm. The henhouse was dimly lit, and there was crap everywhere: on the side of the water jug, in their food, even on their eggs. Loose feathers shifted at the slightest movement so that I practically had to corner each one.

When I stepped out for air, the two of them were still standing in the sliver of shade beneath the rusty metal awning, rocking back and forth. Miss Della was holding Mom still, and tears were streaming down Mom's face. I had never seen her cry like that. Miss Della let go and rushed past me and hollered out from the road, saying how she wished she could stay, but she couldn't afford to be late. And to turn on the news—that was the main thing. She kept repeating herself on her way up the road, urging Mom to check the news. Telling her that it was on TV and everything.

Mom called me inside. As curious as I was, I also kinda didn't really want to know what was going on. I hollered out that I was busy and demanded to know how I was ever gonna finish up, what with her calling me in every other minute. Mom stormed down the steps and snatched the scrubber and hose out of my hand, tossed them aside, and marched me inside.

She disappeared into the next room. She and Dad huddled in front of the TV and clicked through the channels. They settled on one and just stood there. No sooner had I shoved past them than Mom turned the TV off and left the room. Dad followed after her. I went up to it and was standing with the power knob in my fingertips when Mom reentered the den. I was covered in loose feathers, cobwebs, and chicken shit. She sat me down in Dad's easy chair and knelt down in front of me. She told me that there had been a tragic accident in the peach grove adjacent to the Camelot.

Toby fell from a ladder.

Is he okay?

No. Mom didn't say this so much as squeak it.

Well, how'd it happen?

He was fixing Mister Buford's weather vane, and he slipped.

Is he dead?

Mom wiped at her eyes and nodded. *Yes.*

I fiddled with the button dimpling the section of seat cushion between my thighs, then looked up. I felt like an idiot for not knowing how to react. Mom's chest collapsed.

Listen, baby. People are going to talk. And they're going to say all kinds of stuff. But I want you to remember that it was an accident, okay? Just a silly old accident that could have happened to anybody.

The button was fastened to the seat cushion by a single loop of stretched-out thread. I tugged on it and fell back in the chair, having decided that she was lying. Mom stroked the top of my head and got up.

I'm going to make some collard greens and corn bread. Do you want some?

I shook my head at the TV. A wordless moment passed before I realized that she was still standing there, staring down at me.

Well, we're going to take some over to Irma. Okay?

Who's that?

Missus Muncie.

Toby had mentioned her once or twice, but only in passing. Our TV was the shape of a peach crate, with three big knobs that clicked like a ratchet when I turned them. I looked back at it and nodded. I continued staring at it amid the sound of pots and pans clanging around in the kitchen, then got up to see what Mom was doing. She was wiping spilled batter from the counter. Dad was pacing behind her, going on about how her principal defect was that she always just settled for any old pot within reach, and when was it going to occur to her that if she just dug around in the back of the cupboard a little more she'd find something better suited to her purpose. I turned back to the TV, but didn't dare touch it.

MOM HAD DUG out a notebook for me earlier that morning. She wanted me to write my feelings down in it. Actually, she was trying to get me to express pretty much any feeling. I dunno. I guess maybe I just felt a little numb by then and had clammed up. Anyway, I was sitting in the den writing in it when Dad poked his head in the door. He lifted it out of my hand and said that my Ts looked like Fs and my Ss looked like twos, then asked if I wanted to go for a little drive. Said getting out some might do me good.

When I asked where to, Dad explained that Mister Orbach was short-staffed and could use some help. Our phone had been ringing off the hook all morning. Mom was standing in the doorway behind him with the steaming iron in her hand, demanding to know how he could think of work at a time like this. Dad said he was as sorry as anyone, but that life still went on for the rest of us. Mom said she knew. Which was why he should drop us off at Irma's and not stay himself. It wouldn't take her but a half hour to finish with her hair and get the food ready, if that.

I put my notebook down and followed Mom to her room. I leaned against the doorjamb and watched her change into a dress, wondering what I'd have done if I'd stumbled upon a dead body instead of that can of Mister Nelson's moonshine. I pictured the investigators taking me to the precinct downtown and sitting me down in a smoke-filled room and offering me a cigarette while grilling me about where I had been just before having found the body and where I had been headed and all sorts of other questions. Then I imagined Toby's eyes open as he lay there and knew that I'd have pissed myself and fled.

ATLANTA GAS LIGHT Company was replacing old gas pipes around town, and the mile-long trench running alongside Oglethorpe looked like an open wound of red dirt. Mister Barnsdale was bicycling down the road with his fishing pole dangling from one hand. Dad tapped the horn, and I waved.

It was nice to be just me and Dad together in the truck. Mom was a bundle of nerves and had been driving both of us crazy. For once in her life, she'd been all ready to go, dressed up and everything, but Dad refused her—said it wasn't safe. Everybody in town was hunkering down with the curtains pulled and the doors locked, waiting for the storm to pass. He told her to do the same.

The sun was out and the sky was crystal clear. I didn't know what storm Dad was talking about. I didn't understand why he'd been so nervous about dropping off Mom at the Muncies'—until we hit Cordele Road. Coloreds were pouring down the roadside in numbers I'd never seen. Field hands were a common sight on this stretch of Cordele, especially on weekends, when they headed into town. But never like this. Especially not on a weekday.

Dad put on the brakes. The flood of field hands, stock clerks, and service women taking up half the road weren't paying attention to where they were walking. Dad slowed down some more, careful not to bump Mister Goolsbee, hobbling along with his boy at his side. We passed Aurelia. And Mister Swanson, too. He didn't even bother to look at me, which was unusual—he was one of the nicest men I knew. I leaned out the window and waved at him, but it was impossible to get his attention.

The further we got down Cordele Road, the more there were. I wanted to say something to Dad but wasn't sure what. They were filing in from every side road, access road, footpath, and walking bridge in sight. Some were crossing over from the surrounding fields, past stacks of peanuts drying under the morning sun. Some were alone or in pairs. Others were in small groups. Women filed out of rundown shacks with babies in their arms and small children at their sides. They

turned in from Jackson Street. Others appeared from within Mister
Brumeier's pecan orchard. Another group was turning at Front, being
the final turnoff before the covered bridge. All of them looked grim
as they boiled over the sides of the road, with peanut stacks spread out
over the fields on either side of them.

I struggled to take it all in. Dad zigzagged around them slowly, offering them as wide a berth as he could. We shared a quiet moment as
we made our way through the throng of people. We continued past a
procession of dusty side roads interspersed with Pentecostal churches
and still more peanut fields. Dad nodded, but didn't explain what they
were doing or why they were there or where they were going. He didn't
have to. It was all right there in front of me, just as plain as day. I knew
without having to ask. That road only went to one place. It was in the
trample of their feet—this was for Toby.

We forked off at a side road, and Dad picked up speed. The very
last of the coloreds disappeared in the rearview mirror. I couldn't shake
the picture in my head of Toby sprawled out on his back next to Mister
Buford's barn, dead. I pulled my head in from the window and wiped
the dust from my eyes.

Did he die right away?

Who?

Toby.

I have no idea.

I wonder if he suffered.

Dad shook his head. *I doubt it.*

Well, who found him?

Probably Lance, I imagine. It's his orchard, right?

Last night or this morning?

Jesus, Huey. What difference does it make?

*Remember the time he was climbing up the ladder with an armful of
shingles we'd picked up for him in town? Remember that? And when he
got to the very top of it, how he leaned against the side of our house and
set the stack of shingles atop the roof with only one foot still touching the
topmost rung of the ladder? And how you went out and warned him to
be careful—said it was still slippery and you couldn't afford to have him
break his neck? And how he laughed and told you to go back to your TV
show, because he'd worked atop that ladder since before he could walk?*

And how you came back inside and assured Mom that he knew his way around a ladder better than any monkey?

What in the hell are you trying to say?

How could someone as good at climbing a ladder as Toby fall from one?

It was probably dark out.

That's what I thought. But—

But nothing. Even monkeys slip and fall.

We clattered up to a fingerpost leaning in a tuft of crabgrass on the side of the road. It was an unfamiliar stretch of road to me. I asked Dad what the GA in Hwy GA 331 stood for. He stared at me like I was dumb as bricks. Off in the distance a dust cloud–enshrouded combine was moving slowly over the horizon. Dad sighed and said that Toby was a good man, but that even good men lose their footing and make mistakes, then pulled forward.

Half a mile up, Mister Daley's field ended and the Orbachs' field began. Dad eased right at the first turnoff and continued along a stretch that ran parallel with another of their fields. A little further up, a squat house came into view. It was set back from the road and appeared lonely for the absence of any other houses around it. Its rickety front porch seemed to be propping it up. A yellow curtain slid back. A very old colored woman peered out from behind a busted-out window.

Mister Orbach had fields all over. He had all kinds of equipment, fancy irrigation systems, and lots of people working for him. The only thing we had had over Mister Orbach was Toby. Anyway, the little ripples in the road rocked me as I gazed out at the rows of peanut vines fanning out as far as I could see. I wanted to ask Dad why he was so eager to help someone who never did anything for us. I turned from the window and stared at him.

What's the matter now?

Derrick called me a half-breed once.

Derrick said that?

Called me a scraggly-haired muffin-top half-breed.

Your hair ain't curly.

That's what I said.

Nothing a haircut can't fix.

Toby said I could straighten it if I didn't like it. Said it just burns a little. Said a spoonful of mom's bergamot would do the trick.

A haircut's better. We'll get you a haircut.

Said that's all Mom does all day, is burn colored people's hair straight. Said that's all her life has amounted to—trying to get colored people's hair as straight as yours. But Mama says mine doesn't even need berga- mot. She thinks it's perfect just the way it is.

You want it as short as mine? Nice and flat on top. Here, feel mine. Flat and stiff as a horse brush is how I like it. You like that? We can do the same for you.

Day and night. Burn, burn, burn. Toby said that's all she does.

You've got a lot more to be proud of than you think.

I turned back to the fields. They looked burnt, too.

Other than my hair, you mean?

Like your great grampa, that's what. That should mean something to you. It does to everyone else.

That's your grampa.

You want to know about your mother's, is that it? Well, you know that her grampa used to work for us.

You mean, for you.

What?

He didn't work for Mama. He worked for you.

And you know that her mother did, too.

What was she like?

For crying out loud—I was your age, son. You can't honestly expect me to remember. Seemed nice enough, though.

What about her dad?

She never got to meet him. Because—well, damn it, he pissed off with someone else. Say, what is this?

Dad looked over, frustrated. We clattered up to a line of cars and trucks and wagons and tractors parked alongside Mister Orbach's field. Mister Bigelow, Mister Daley, and several others stood out in the field in coveralls, smoking cigarettes and chatting.

Dad slapped the shifter.

Listen, Huey. Your mother's proud as hell of her grampa. She really is. But she still thanks the Lord that you're a Fairchild. You know that, right? So whenever I talk about "Grampa" or "Great Grampa" or anyone like that, it's my folks I'm talking about. Okay?

A thresher sat in the middle of the field. It was like a giant wooden jalopy humping along full-bore, rattling and shimmying and wobbling like it was about to go off the rails. Dad got out and headed over to it. He shook hands and cracked jokes. He had to shout over the thresher's loud rattling.

Mister Orbach had been out since first light. He wanted to know if we'd seen any of his hands on the way.

I wriggled up front.

I saw 'em. Hundreds of 'em.

A thick cloud of diesel exhaust hung in the air. The thresher was engulfed in a haze of gauzy light. Mister Bigelow emerged from the side of it, dragging a sack of peanuts behind him. He pulled it up to my side and, having placed it into my care, slapped straw and dirt from his coveralls. He shook his head and asked what I was doing with a soldering mask on.

It wasn't a soldering mask. But I kept quiet and didn't say anything—it was easier that way. Bits of peanut hay hung suspended in the air, and the ground was covered with the stuff. I stood there struggling to keep that hundred-pound gunnysack from falling over, all the while scratching the crud out from under my cast. I raked my fingernails over the skin just above my cast so hard red streaks covered the entire top half of my arm.

Dad came over and helped me get some of the grime out from under it, cursing Mom for not having put me in long sleeves. Mister Bigelow stood there shoveling dried peanut vines into the mouth of the thresher with a pitchfork, harping on to anyone who'd listen about how Toby was to blame for everything from the sticky heat to lousy contract prices.

Lord knows how you put up with that boy for so long.

Dad pulled me aside, looked me up and down gravely, and asked me how I was doing. I looked over his shoulder at the men working the thresher, then said that I was doing fine. Dad nodded, pleased. He asked if I knew the way home. The broken-down farm equipment scattered along the rutted road and collected in the drainage ditches seemed to point the way.

Dad dug into his pocket and pulled out some money. He stuffed a dollar bill into my hand. I stared down at it, then peeked up, wondering what it all meant. I didn't ask because I was overcome with the spooky suspicion that I already knew. It was more money than he'd ever given me at one time. I unfolded it and held it in both hands. George Washington's mouth was pressed closed tight, like he was hiding those grim-looking teeth of his from me. I suppose everybody's got something they're ashamed of. I put the bill up to my nose. It smelled like kerosene. Dad reminded me that whatever I'd heard any of the others say, they were still our closest neighbors and friends, then patted my ass and told me to run along.

Straight as an arrow. Do not pass Go. Do not collect two hundred dollars. Is that clear?

Dad didn't want me hearing the sort of language Mister Orbach and the others were using. Mom had asked him a gazillion times not to use it around me. Called it poison. It was more than a pet peeve with her—it was the one wish of hers that she demanded he respect. I'd stood by his side watching as she made him promise, wondering what the big deal was. He wasn't the only one. There was just something about it that seemed a little like trying to mop up the Mississippi.

It's because of what Mister Orbach said, isn't it? All that "nigger" talk—nigger this and nigger that; nigger, nigger, nigger—isn't it?

Dad knelt down and held me in his eyes. *Yes.*

I ain't gonna rat you out, Pop! I promise! I ain't a snitch. Don't you believe me? You gotta believe me. I swear I won't tell! Please! Don't make me go! I don't wanna go! I wanna stay with you!

The fucker just looked at me, then returned to the others. He didn't have anything else to say. The thresher was shaking and creaking like a popcorn popper. Mister Bigelow was standing beside the chute, filling the sack in both his hands, holding it under a whir of peanuts spraying out. He powered it down and joined Dad, who was sitting beside Mister Orbach on the rusty rear bumper of our sun-faded mustard-yellow truck.

I stormed off toward the thresher and kicked over a peanut-filled sack, then another and another, until eight were lying on their side with heaps of peanuts spilled out everywhere. I expected Dad to come over and whup my ass. But he didn't. No one even noticed. Dad was sitting there with Mister Bigelow, Mister Orbach, and several others gathered around him, going on about all we'd seen on the drive there. He asked Mister Orbach when was the last time that anyone had done a census count of all the niggers living out in the shady back wood outside town? Because all of a sudden it seemed like there were more niggers than white people in Akersburg. There had been more than he could shake a stick at on our way there. They'd seemed to come out of the goddamned woodwork. And frankly, he didn't know we had that many.

I kicked over the last standing sack of peanuts and headed off. Dad had intended for me to take the bus. He didn't say it—the dollar did. I preferred to save the money and walk. When I got to the main road, several colored boys were walking up ahead in the direction of town, carrying armfuls of placards and pickets. I hollered out for them to wait up, figuring that if we were going in the same direction, I'd walk with them. They didn't seem to hear me. So I held back and let them continue on by themselves.

A car sped past, so close I'd had to step down into the sheer slope of the road's narrow shoulder to avoid getting hit. Twenty yards down, its brake lights flared, and it pulled over. I didn't recognize it, but I ran up to the window anyway. It was an old Dodge. It had a black-and-white handshake painted on the door—which gave me pause. That was not something I saw every day. The driver talked like the president.

What?

Town, boy. The way to town.

I pointed. He asked if I needed a lift. The front passenger's seat was empty, but three coloreds were crouched down in the backseat, so low I almost didn't see them. I stepped back. *No, thank you.*

The car pulled back onto the road. Why those coloreds were hiding in the backseat was beyond me. Besides, town was so close I could walk there blindfolded.

There were Pentecostal churches up and down this stretch of Cordele Road. Along the far edge of a field sat a row of bungalows connected like barracks. They sat sort of lopsided and were boarded up and empty. Two old colored men were sitting on the front stoop of one, beside the posts from which livestock and slaves had once washed. Everything out this way was beaten down, half dead. Two toddlers were running around naked, chasing each other in play. The droopy-eyed old men watched as I passed by.

A street sign down the road was pocked with bullet holes. I stopped and marveled at how the sun glinted off the peeled-back metal where the bullets had torn through. Some colored boys walked up. They said that I looked to be a few feet shy of the deep end and laughed.

I snatched off my dive mask. I didn't realize that I still had it on. Dad had warned me against bringing it—said it made me look like a goofball. I told him I couldn't see a thing without it because the thresher spewed so much crap everywhere I had to cover my eyes just to get within ten feet of the thing. All that grime and soot floating in the air made me tear up. That's what clinched it. Dad had practically put it on me himself—couldn't stand the sight of tears. Still, I felt like an idiot.

The boys continued down the road without me. I wondered, as if for the first time, if being a loner was such a bad thing. I gave the faceplate a spit shine and put it back on. I decided that it wasn't.

A narrow band of road stretched out in front of me for as far as I could see. Telephone poles lined the roadside, and drooping wire hung from pole to pole. I headed down the road and thought about how the one picture I had of me and Mom had been taken by Toby when he was a teenager. Mom would always tell me about how she had set me atop the roof of our truck in nothing but diapers and told me to hold still. I'd banged my heels on the windshield, crying my eyes out, because it was hot. Mom told Toby to snap it anyway. It didn't matter that the truck didn't have an engine or that I was pouty. She was proud of us both.

I followed Donner Road all the way up to Frontage Road, past my school. Crows were feeding in the adjacent field. Mister Daley rumbled past on one of Mister Orbach's tractors, with two trailers in tow piled high with peanut pods sifting down in thin drifts. Mister Daley didn't see me, so I chased after him and shouted, hoping to catch a lift. He disappeared around the bend going so fast his left side lifted. I tossed a clump of the dirt he'd trailed at the crows and wondered what the heck he was in such a hurry for.

The muddy brown water of the Thronateeska threaded in and out of view behind each slowly passing alfalfa crop. After I'd walked half an hour along Oglethorpe, a cathedral of pine trees converged high overhead. Inside, gauzy bands of light shone through the branches and between the papery trunks of the birch trees lining the side of the road. I hesitated at the sight of a fingerpost leaning out.

EATO TON COL RED SCHO L

It had been fashioned from an oar. Much of the paint had faded, but most of the letters were legible. It fell over on my way past. Fifty yards in, I pulled down a slumping fence and cut through tall stalks of grass. Exposed cinder blocks and tattered beige shingles peeked out from the thinning foliage up ahead. I headed around a derelict clapboard building, not at all convinced that it was the school that the sign had indicated.

I brushed back cobwebs and peeked into a dark window. The interior was completely gutted. I clapped the dirt and flakes of paint from my hands. The building opened onto a glade around back. Two colored boys were stooped over in the middle of a grassy field, with their backs to me. They caught me off guard—I thought I was alone. They looked no different than any of the other hundred or so colored boys who lived in Akersburg—or was it a thousand? I couldn't really say. All I knew was that I didn't have much to do with any of them. Neither did Dad. But Mom was different.

Around them a sea of lush grass and clover bent gently under the breeze. They were combing through the grass, looking for something. I walked up to them and just stood there. They raked their fingers through the grass, and every now and again, one of them plucked a little purple flower hidden under the clover or between thin blades of grass and laid it gently into the ball cap sitting between them.

Whatcha doing?

Neither answered.

Hey, you're Goolsbee's boy—Evan, right?

The boy shook his head no and continued raking his fingers through the grass.

Yes, you are. I saw you walking with him just this morning. Dontcha remember me? I was at Goolsbee's shop when those men came.

He ignored me. I stood up, exasperated. I knew it was him.

Fine. But there's a flower shop in town, you know—Missus Henniger's. She's got much nicer ones than these. I knocked my sneaker against the ball cap. Evan picked out another flower from the grass and gently laid it inside. When he didn't look up, I pulled out my dollar bill and held it out to him.

You can buy a lot of tulips and roses with one of these. What's wrong? Dontcha want something bigger and brighter than these? I got plenty more where this came from. I don't even want it. Honestly, I prefer the crisp, new ones. Go on. Take it. Listen, goddamnit. I'm only trying to save you the trouble of having to dig around on your hands and knees in the dirt for some little piece-of-shit flowers. Hell, I know old Goolsbee ain't paying you nothing anymore. So you may as well take it, because it'll probably be a while before you see another. You'd better take it before I change my mind. Lord knows I'm only doing it out of the goodness of my heart—

Evan stood up and took a swing at me.

Christ! Whaddya think you're doin'? Can't you see I'm only trying to help? Besides, I got a cast on, you idiot! You come one step closer and I'm knocking you to smithereens! I'm warning you! One blow from this and you're out like a light!

Evan yanked me to the ground. I was swinging my cast wildly, trying to knock him in the head with it, but he somehow managed to wrestle himself on top of me. His friend was pulling on him from behind.

Get off him, Evan! Goddamnit, he knows your face! Now he's gonna tell his daddy, and everyone in town is gonna come after us, just like they did your daddy! You hear me? You let go of him right now!

You know how many times I seen him and that goofy white boy with the glasses walking past old man Goolsbee's on their way back from swimming? You know how many years I've wanted to catch this here little fucker alone? And now I got him! And I ain't letting go, so help me God, until I've broken his arm in two!

Evan slammed my cast against the ground.

You're a crazy fool, Evan! A crazy fool! He ain't moving anymore. Check his pulse! I think you killed him! Christ, Evan! He's dead! Cantcha see the boy's dead? I ain't gonna be here when they come for you, Evan!

I must have passed out from the pain and then come to. I was vaguely aware of Evan's friend's voice. He hollered something, then turned tail and ran. I could hear the padding sound of his sneakers over the grass. Evan let go of my arm and squeezed my neck just above my Adam's apple. My eyes popped open. I was choking.

Say mercy!

It's hard to talk when you can't breathe.

Mmmmmrie!

I had only been able to say the first letter; the rest had come out as a wheezing sound. He rolled off me, then got up and stood there looking down at me, heaving. He leaned over and picked up the ball cap, then stepped on my dive mask as he walked off.

I LIMPED ALONG the train tracks running alongside east Oglethorpe, feeling around for my teeth. My cast had split at the elbow, and the plaster was unraveling around my thumb. The skin around it was pink, and my arm was completely numb. I tried to imagine myself crawling through a tangle of crabgrass with a broken neck on the slim chance that if I made it to the roadside someone might see me lying there. That must have been what it was like for Toby. It wasn't until I was standing in the middle of the railroad bridge that it hit me who all those purple flowers were for. Mister Barnsdale was farther down toward the Baker County side, sitting in the sun with his feet propped up on the iron railing, jiggling his fishing pole. I leaned over one of the crossbeams and gazed down at the slow-moving river below. I sat down, pooped.

I shook the dirt out of my hair and slipped my dive mask back on. I didn't give a damn that it was completely busted and now lacked a faceplate. It helped me think. Besides, it was fixable. Everything was fixable. That was the first tenet of my life—right alongside its companion tenets, "Where there's a will, there's a way" and "Try harder." My thoughts were as muddy as the Thronateeska, thinking about Evan: how all these years we hadn't spoken two words between us and still he hated me to bits. How I'd always seen him standing in Goolsbee's doorway wearing that crummy old Dodgers cap low over his eyes, with that heavy black stone cutter's apron draped from his neck and all that putrid dust from the cut stones settling on him like a layer of silt. God only knows how he put up with it.

And then the fear that his friend had of me telling on them. Tell on *them*? Christ, I was still trying to figure out how I was gonna explain my messed-up arm to Dad. I wondered if maybe Evan had broke it again because my fingers were fat and blue. I tried to wiggle them, but they just sort of hung there, limp and lifeless. They hurt too much for me to even scrape out the dirt crammed under my fingernails. I knew that if I said the slightest thing about that to Dad, he'd probably just think that I was trying to get out of doing work and say, *Of course it hurts. It's broke. It's supposed to hurt.* Not to mention that no one that I knew had ever got his ass whupped by a colored boy. It just didn't happen.

Then there was that bit Evan tossed out about me and Derrick strolling past on our way back from Mister Abrams's pool with our towels slung over our necks and our hair still wet, taunting him. Which, of course, was true. Except that it was always Derrick who laughed and yelled out that there was plenty of water for him to cool himself by under the river bridge. I was the one flipping him the bird—at which point Evan's eyes would darken, and he'd disappear inside the doorway amid the shriek of Mister Goolsbee's power saw.

A fire engine bellowed down Cordele Road behind me. It must have come all the way from Blakely because we didn't have our own. Wherever it was going, it was in an awful hurry to get there. I checked the sky for any sign of smoke, wondering what had burnt down now. There was none. Mister Barnsdale had a bottle propped between his legs, and he was reeling something in. He looked at me blankly, as if he didn't know what to make of the wailing siren trailing off in the direction of town, either. He propped up his fishing rod and left that poor little fish dangling there on the end of the line as he stood up, unzipped his fly, and pissed in a long arc. He hiccuped and said, *Captain Nemo, am I right?*

Mister Barnsdale had a big grin on his face. He shook his head, shrugged off the noise echoing out from the fire engine, and sat back down. Not me. I ran after it—or at least I attempted to. My legs were so stiff I slipped between the railroad ties and damn near fell into the river. Mister Barnsdale seemed to enjoy that immensely. He laughed, held his bottle out to me, and declared that it was a little early for Halloween.

I limped past and told him that if Mama ever saw him pissing in that spot it'd be the last time he pissed in anything. I headed up the slippery embankment and hobbled down the adjacent road just as fast as my legs could carry me. A hundred yards down my arm started to throb so bad my eyes teared up. A bus whooshed past. I stopped. Another one just like it was barreling down the road behind it. I jumped up and down and waved, trying to flag it down, but it blew past me, too.

So there I was, standing on the side of the road, covered in dried sweat and bits of sticky grass, with both of my pockets stuffed with shards of glass from my busted-up dive mask that I'd rescued from the dirt. My cast was covered in dirt and jangled around my arm like a bangle that I could rotate halfway around in both directions. A column of wild flowers like the ones Evan and his friend had been picking were poking out from the rock bed between railroad ties running alongside the road. I picked one and looked it over. Damned thing wasn't even that pretty.

I limped down the middle of Cordele Road, past chunks of dried tractor mud lying on the pavement, praying for another car to come so I could hitch a ride. I passed the charred ruins of Mister Goolsbee's— still no car. The Camelot looked abandoned. Still no car. I was so hungry I plucked a dandelion and chewed on its stem to tide me over till home, only to discover that the milky gunk inside made the inside of my cheeks raw, and no matter how much I spit, I couldn't get the acrid taste out of my mouth. I rounded the bend where Cordele turns into Main Street and stopped. Missus Foley was a mild-mannered white woman who wore glasses and kept her hair in a tidy bob. She was a calm, pleasant woman who was always very nice to me whenever I saw her at the pool. She was running up the road at full speed, heading in my direction, with her baby carriage bobbling in front of her.

A hundred yards behind her, a patrol car sat parked with its lights flashing. It had pulled over the two buses that had passed me back at the railroad bridge. The deputy was nowhere in sight, but Mister Buford seemed to have things under control. He was manhandling a colored man who'd stepped off one of the buses. A group of white men were gathered around in a semicircle, cheering him on. The colored man was banging on the door, trying to get back on the bus, but he couldn't. The driver had shut it and wouldn't open it back up for him. He jerked the bus into gear and pulled away. The colored man grabbed a hold of the sideview mirror. One of Mister Buford's cronies took him by the legs and tried to yank him down. The bus lunged forward and carried the colored man off with it; the man holding on to his legs let go. The bus stopped twenty yards down, and the door popped open. The colored man leaped in with the help of several others inside. Mister Buford and his cronies were hurling rocks and yelled out for it never to return.

I had advanced a hundred yards and was now standing very near to the northernmost edge of downtown Akersburg, the town where I was raised—the one that I knew more than any other and loved with all my heart. I must stress this point, because I feel that it deserves emphasizing. It was the last block of storefronts on Main Street before town tapered off into the quaint countryside filled with rolling hills and orchards from which I'd emerged. A crowd of townspeople were lined up along the two blocks that mark the picturesque entrance to town, not far from a sign that read:

WELCOME TO AKERSBURG
POP. 3,708

They were shouting and yelling for the second bus to turn around and go home, too. Only there was nowhere for it to go. It was stuck in the mud on the side of the road, rocking back and forth, trying to free itself from a ditch. I took an impulsive step back and bumped into Mister Pendleton. He was Darla's dad. I think he was a lawyer or judge or something, but it could just have been that he wore bifocals and smoked a pipe. Anyway, Darla was nowhere in sight, and her dad, who had bought boiled peanuts from me once or twice, rested a hand on my shoulder and wrinkled his face at the sight of the bus. He said something that I couldn't make out over all the shouting going on and the cry of the bus's grinding gears. I only heard Missus Thomas, standing beside me holding a half-filled grocery bag, say *Really?*

Next thing I knew, ten other grown-ups were standing around me. We were all waiting to see what that bus was going to do next, because people were throwing stuff at it—anything they could find, really. Mister Pendleton was explaining to Missus Thomas that it had gotten stuck trying to make a U-turn on the narrow, two-lane road. Of course it was. Anyone could see that. It was blocking half of the road, just sitting there like a beached whale. He pointed and said that it had pulled too far forward, and the front tire had gotten stuck in the drainage ditch running alongside Cordele. The road was much too narrow for it to swing all the way around in a U-turn without backing up halfway through the maneuver. He was explaining everything to Missus Thompson like she was a complete idiot.

The bus's gears crunched, and the engine was hissing and moaning and making all sorts of strained noises, but the driver didn't appear to be getting anywhere. People were starting to trickle in from Main Street. They were lining up alongside the bus, and some were coaxing others into rocking it sideways, even as its engine roared and its wheels spun free. Others didn't need convincing. They jubilantly joined in. I had the strange sensation that they weren't going to be happy until they'd tipped that bus like it was a cow. I could tell that things weren't going to end well for the people on the bus, and I didn't want to be around to see it.

Having started toward Main Street, I was heading upstream, against the kind of influx of people I'd seen during Buskin Brothers's annual limited-time-only end-of-year everything-must-go we-will-not-be-undersold close-out sale. When I got there, I was shocked to discover even more of an uproar than the one I had just fled. Cars were lined up in both directions. Some were pulling in from side streets. Others were parked at odd angles. Some sat with their doors flung open, abandoned. People were swarming among them on their way down the street. I knew I had to get out of there but wasn't sure where to go. That's when I saw the patrol car. It was parked in front of the Laundromat. I ran up to it, but the sheriff wasn't inside and the radio handset was sitting on the bench seat, squawking, with a voice on the other end hollering out, *Mayday! Mayday! Alpha One, do you copy?*

The car behind me was getting its windows bashed in. Someone jumped on the patrol car's roof, directly above me. A crowbar suddenly appeared right before my eyes. It had smashed through the windshield like a pickax. I backed out and hopped atop the rear bumper of a neighboring car. It was one of those long turquoise sedans with a spacious trunk. I grabbed a hold of it by the tail fin. Main Street is as flat as a pancake and cars were lined up, bumper to bumper, as far as I could see. A man was climbing the streetlamp on the sidewalk beside me, and several others were standing on the rooftops across the street. Two men were shouting out to them from atop the Paramount theater's marquee. I couldn't hear what they were saying and I had no idea what they were doing, until I realized that they were all looking in the same direction. One of them was even pointing, like a barrelman who, having spotted land from high up in a galleon's crow's nest, leans out into the breeze, pointing at it. The red light of the patrol car swept over a crowd of people concentrated beneath the Coca-Cola sign hanging from a beam-and-cable line. I caught sight of something in the front window of S&W for a split second but quickly lost it amid all the waving placards. There were too many in the way to be sure what it was. I was sure that I hadn't seen right. But it looked like—well, I figured it was probably just Tyler.

I scurried onto the sedan's trunk. Dad would murder me for pulling a stunt like that, but I didn't care. Well above the crowd now, I cupped my hand over my eyes and craned my neck to see around the raised signs and placards swaying back and forth, blocking my view. Having gotten a glimpse of what was going on, I hopped down and bolted straight for it. I shoved my way under a thick band of yellow tape and into the tightly packed crowd. I was one of hundreds of people packed into that small section of Main Street, struggling for a view of all that was going on. An uproar of catcalls erupted. I strained for another glimpse and jumped to see if I could possibly make out anything more, but buzz cuts and ball caps and ponytails blocked my view. It was no use. The only thing I could make out were the placards clapping, smacking, and knocking up against each other, and the beam-and-cable line of the sign overhead. Glass crunched underfoot as I inched closer to it. I pressed on and squeezed through jostling arms and elbows. The massive and chaotic collection of shifting people up in arms grew more dense with every step, until at last it was impenetrable. The Coca-Cola sign was directly overhead. So I got down on all fours and went for it. I hadn't crawled five feet, zigzagging my way through a dense thicket of denim jeans, saddle shoes, bobby socks, and high-tops when my arm gave out. A purse crashed down atop my head.

What'd I tell you about creeping around, boy?!

I stood up.

Missus Orbach? Thank God!

She had on a polka-dot dress with pins up and down one side; she must've been in the middle of a fitting. She jerked me toward her and pinned me up against the storefront window. I assumed she was trying to shelter me from all the craziness. Mister Rinkel, the tailor, was standing beside us with a tape measure flapping wildly around his neck as he banged on the plate-glass window and yelled, *Boooo! Go home!*

He was shouting at the people inside, and his constant hollering was distracting me from whatever it was that Missus Orbach was trying to tell me. The neon Coca-Cola sign in the window was turned off and it was dark inside. Directly behind it, one, two, three—*four* coloreds were sitting at the lunch counter with their arms folded, anchored fast in front of the soda fountain, in neckties and windbreakers. Possibly a fifth, but four that I saw clearly at the counter. Except for the girl. She had on a cardigan and looked like she'd just come back from church. She looked like she'd fallen in with the wrong crowd. I didn't recognize her, but the rest were with the group who'd been hanging out in front all these weeks. I tried to see if there were any others, but I couldn't tell. The lights were off, as was the overhead paddle fan. It was jam-packed inside and every single stool in the place had been tipped over, except for the four stools the coloreds occupied. A crowd of whites was pressed against them, and there was so much pushing and hollering that the front window was rattling.

Mister Chambers was on the other side of the counter, in front of the coloreds, stiff-arming its beveled chrome ledge with one arm and shaking his head. Missus Orbach shouted out to him through the glass for him to kick the niggers out. They had no business there; it was time to be done with them already. Mister Rinkel volleyed that they had no respect for the law.

I was thunderstruck. This seemed to be exactly what Dad was talking about when he had said that the world going to hell in a handbasket. I pressed my face to the glass. I knew that S&W burgers were good, but I'd had no idea they were that good. I yanked at Missus Orbach's sleeve.

You gotta be kidding me! All that for a lousy burger?

Listen, you scraggly-haired love child, I've got news for you! Your days here are numbered! I've had just about enough of you! You hear me? Numbered! You were born in sin, son. Sin! And I want you nappy-haired mongrels out! All of you! Out!

A shrill peal of laughter erupted. It was deafening. In the next instant, all I could make out was *which makes you a love child. A little scraggly-haired, muffin-top, snooping, up-to-no-good love child. And I never want to see you around my house again. Do you hear me? You'll be shot, no different than the groundhogs and prairie dogs that come sniffing around unwelcome! You hear? You are not wanted here!*

Missus Orbach's face was a yelling pink mass of outrage. She turned abruptly back to the window and pressed her face against the glass. She was worked up something terrible. It was like Mom said—people can't think clearly when they get that mad. They say things they don't mean. Mom called her mean-spirited, but I felt a little sorry for her. She couldn't fool me. I knew she was just scared. That's what happens when people think that everyone else is as nasty as they are. They get scared.

Missus Krasinski was inside, working herself up into a fit of her own. She struck at that young colored woman's ear with an open hand, so hard the girl was cradling the side of her face. *My God.* I stood on my tiptoes. That was a first. I'd never seen a woman hit another woman before. I pitched forward. Missus Orbach had shoved me. Her purse was practically in my face. So shrill was her voice that it cut through the din of the crowd. But try as Missus Orbach might to get my attention, my eyes did not move from that window.

Two, four, six, eight! We don't wanna integrate!

I was mesmerized. I could see them all now, directly beyond the unlit neon Coca-Cola sign in the window. I was pinned up against the glass. I tried to get that purse out of my face, desperately trying to hold onto the little bit of space I had. Missus Orbach reached over my head and continued banging on the window, shouting in my ear. *Go back to Africa!*

And as I stood there, mouth open, face not but three inches from the plate-glass window, the darkness inside transposed my reflection over the sign leaning on the sill inside. And as I pulled back from the window and stood there contemplating my reflection amid the chaos swirling around me, I knew that everything that Dad had ever said to me was a lie. Just like I knew that those colored people inside didn't want to eat with us any more than we wanted to eat with them. Just like I knew that the law was the law and that two wrongs did not make a right. Missus Orbach was right there, telling me to my face. I was a phony.

I wanted to be different from those four colored people. I was sure that I *felt* different from them. And I sure didn't look like them. The thing is, no matter what Missus Orbach shouted at me, I wanted to be different from everybody there but her. But that stupid fat old bitch just didn't realize how similar she and I really were. So I had to prove it. I pressed my face back up against the glass and started banging on the window with my cast so hard sharp pangs shot all the way up to my teeth. I shouted at the top of my lungs. I banged and banged and banged and yelled and banged myself hysterical, until little glistening bubbles of spit spewed from the corners of my mouth.

I got a second look from Missus Orbach. She took me by the shoulder and shoved me in front of herself, up front and center, so all could behold my indignation at the obscene villainy taking place before us.

Segregation now! Segregation tomorrow! Segregation forever!

Where you belong, you goddamned orangutan! No apes allowed!

Missus Orbach pushed me forward. *Lookit here! Do you see this? Even this little scraggly-haired mongrel wants you out! Go on, Huey! Let them know what you really think! Say it loud and say it proud! Say what you were saying just a minute ago! Nice and loud, so all can hear!*

Missus Orbach slammed me against the window. *Louder, Huey! That's not loud enough! I want them to hear you all the way up in New York!*

Missus Orbach wasn't going to be happy until I went straight through the glass. My arm was hanging limp at my side now. Every time I smacked it against the window, an electric shock shot through my entire body. Inside, Missus Krasinski was upending a sugar jar over the colored girl's hair. She was shaking it out furiously, like it couldn't come out fast enough. The colored girl's hair was pulled back in a tight bun. She bowed her head and shielded her eyes, and all that sugar just cascaded down onto the counter and floor. I banged on the glass and yelled and banged and yelled and banged so hard that even my good arm started to hurt. The colored men seated on either side of that colored girl weren't doing anything to help her. They were just sitting there, looking straight at the pastry case, stoic. *Cowards!*

She was getting the brunt of it, like the wounded antelope of the herd, the one the crowd had singled out. Which was alarming. I could see the reflection of the two colored men seated beside her in the wall mirror mounted behind the counter. Missus Krasinski clenched her teeth and snapped up the mayonnaise dispenser, gripped it in both hands, and unraveled a long, spiraling yarn over each of their heads. *Jigaboos!*

I banged on the window hard and shouted at the top of my lungs, but no matter how loud or how much I shouted or what I said, the four colored men and that girl remained seated, eyes forward, arms folded, just sitting there, silent, still, and passive. I couldn't hold back Missus Orbach. She was shoving me against the window. It was about to break. I hollered to Missus Orbach that I needed some breathing room.

Inside, Missus Krasinski angled herself between two of the coloreds and tugged at the backs of their shirt collars amid a flurry of hands lashing out. People were swinging and punching at everything in sight. They tugged, ripped, clawed, and tore at their clothes. One of the colored men was wrenched from his stool. He struggled to hold on. Someone blindsided another one. He winced, checked for blood, and wiped the sweat from his forehead. His eyes were filled with panic. He pulled his jacket over his head, but it did little to shield him from the onslaught of punches showering down on him. Someone wrenched him from his stool, and he teetered over onto the floor. I lost sight of him as a gang of teenagers swarmed over him and seemed to swallowed him up like in a feeding frenzy.

I cheered. The celebration among those of us gathered around the window and in the doorway and on the sidewalk echoed down the street. It was electric. I wiped the fog from the window in disbelief. I stopped banging and just took in all the craziness. There appeared to be a fifth colored man seated at the counter. I cupped my hand over my eyes. My lips parted in disbelief. *Toby?*

He was sitting on the farthest stool from the window. He must have been obscured by the man who had been seated to his left, the one who was now in a tussle on the floor. Toby was covered with every variety of condiment in the place. He had one hand clamped onto the counter, holding on as if for dear life, and did not budge except to shield his face and hold on to his seat as all hell broke loose around him. He was as dirty as refuse, as abused as sin, and appeared as stiff and unbending as God's will. I was mesmerized.

Sweet mother of God. Toby's alive!

I jerked at Missus Orbach's purse. That got her attention.

You're not gonna believe this! Toby isn't dead! They got him inside! Don't ask me how, but they do! I tell you, that's him! He's inside! I see him! Look! He's right there! C'mon! I gotta get him outta there!

I didn't know how he'd done it, or why he'd done it. All I knew was that he'd somehow done it. There was not a doubt in my mind. For there could not be two men on this planet who shared his indomitable spirit. Missus Orbach looked at me like I was talking in tongues. On the other side of the window, the man lowered his hand from his face. It was not Toby. I backed away from Missus Orbach, turned on my heels, and ran.

XVI

DAD WAS IN THE SHED, repairing stack poles. He let out a *What the—* when he saw me.

I cut him off. *It's okay. I just slipped.*

I explained that I fell on my arm going down a gravel embankment, on my way to the river. How I'd seen a bunch of kids playing on inner tubes. It looked like fun, so I'd decided to join them. Dad knelt down and looked over my face and inspected the green stains and red splotches covering my cast. He shook his head with concern.

By where Artie fishes?

Farther down.

Where the geese nest?

Down more. Where we saw Mister Slappery's terrier doing it with Mister Marnin's collie—up against the tree, where no one but us could see. Remember?

Oh. Well, I know what it's like for you boys. You're growing by the day—don't know where your body starts and ends half the time. Whaddya say we get some ice for this?

Dad wiped the dirt and tears from my face, suggested that I not tell Mom, then led me inside. Miss Della was on her way out. She walked out the front door, down the steps, and out the driveway without saying a word. Mom stood in the doorway quietly watching her first hair appointment in weeks disappear through the elms lining our drive.

We didn't have any ice in the house, so I dug out a hand towel and wet it with cold water. I could hear Mom out on the stoop telling Dad that she didn't care how little things had cooled down in town, Tobias

Wetherall Muncie had never done anything but good, and that no matter what Dad's opinion of colored people, it was important to show our respect to folks who had been good to us.

Dad didn't think "it" necessary. Mom acknowledged that "it" would be awkward, but insisted. I had no idea what they were talking about but I was inclined to side with Dad—Mom tended to overdo things. There was a moment of quiet. I headed for my room and slipped into bed with that wet hand towel draped over my face. I was a mess. I pulled the covers up to my chin and just as I was starting to drift off, I was startled awake by a door slamming shut and someone snapping, *Fine. I'll drive there myself.*

I lay in bed the next morning with the vague memory of Dad having come in during the night and given me some aspirin. And of Mom asking if I was sure I didn't want any dinner, and me answering, *But you don't know how to drive.*

I'll learn. So help me God, I'll teach myself.

But where would you even go?

THE NEXT COUPLE of days were a blur. All I remember is being startled awake one morning by the sound of Mom barging into my room. She riffled through my dresser and set out a pile of clothes, then disappeared into the kitchen with my white button-down flapping behind her like a flag. My arm was still aching, but at least the swelling had gone down enough to inspire the belief that the worst was past. Dad put two rubber bands around my cast to keep it from slipping off and called it good as new.

I changed into a clean undershirt and reached for the tie that Mom had set atop my dresser, fumbled it into a slipknot, then slung it around my neck. The look of horror on Mom's face when she walked past my room was worse than the time she'd discovered I'd used the last few drops of her eight-year-old bottle of Chanel perfume that Dad had given her for high-school graduation.

She jerked it from around my neck and told me I wasn't ready for a real tie yet. I left the house that morning in a short-sleeved button-down and clip-on tie, carrying an aluminum baking tin as heavy as a cat. Mom teetered down the steps in pressed hair, heels, and a dark dress that covered her ankles and buttoned at the neck. Dad was at the top of the steps in his coveralls and boots, checking his wristwatch. It wasn't until we all piled in the truck that I realized I didn't even know where Toby had lived.

Our driveway let out to a road of packed dirt. The open field across it was ours, too. Dad turned right. Half a mile up, our field ended and the Orbachs' began. Dad eased right at the first turnoff, then continued along a stretch that ran parallel with a rutabaga field, and a little farther up, their big house came into view. Then came the Schaefers' fields. Their peanuts had been out of the ground a month already and two dozen convicts were laying pulled peanut vines out in neatly lined rows. Armed guards were standing on the field's perimeter, watching as they worked. Dad slowed on the appearance of our turnoff, which we were approaching from the back side. He was taking the most round-about way possible—claimed that it was the easiest way to sidestep the trouble in town. We pulled back onto Cordele Road, and as we passed the Camelot, Dad noted that Mister Abrams's fortunes had sure taken a turn for the worse in recent weeks. Mom wasn't concerned with Mister Abrams.

It won't be long now until they bury that poor boy.

Della told you that? That kooky old maid. Her family tree may as well have roots in everyone's front yard, for all she knows about who has done what to whom.

Mom gazed off to the side of the road. She didn't seem to care about anything Dad had to say as we passed the charred remains of Goolsbee's shop.

Mark my word. People won't forget.

Dad clenched the steering wheel and we crossed the river. I leaned over Mom and rolled up her window. The stink of low tide passed by the time we emerged from the *chuh chuh chuh chuh* of the covered bridge. A procession of peach trees flitted past, and it took all of five family orchards before I realized that she had been talking about Toby. A checkerboard-style arrangement of trees passed by. Eventually they thinned out and were replaced with a span of flat pastures crisscrossed with haystacks. Dad looked over and winked.

You know you're from Akersburg if you like the smell of manure. Do you like the smell of manure?

Mom turned away. Me, too. Dad sighed and said that it was just as well to get the condolence call taken care of. *Suppose it's better this way.*

Couldn't live with myself otherwise.

Dad looked over but said nothing. Asphalt turned into packed dirt, and somewhere along a tight, winding back road scattered with old leaves, we pulled in behind a tractor leaning in a drainage ditch. Mom stepped into the reedy grass, careful not to trample the wildflowers. I got out at her prompting and stood on the side of the road.

> *Hoe, Emma, hoe.*
> *You turn around, dig a hole in the ground.*
> *Hoe, Emma, hoe.*
> *Emma, you from the country.*
> *Hoe, Emma, hoe.*
> *You turn around, dig a hole in the ground.*
> *Hoe, Emma, hoe.*

A curtain slid back in the squat house in front of me. A colored woman I didn't recognize peeked out from behind a tile of cardboard fitted shabbily over a busted-out window. Dad rocked himself out of two-day old mud, then turned around. Our truck never seemed the time-traveling spaceship that it was at that moment, its trail of exhaust thinning in the distance.

He's not coming with?

No.

Why not?

Mom undid her shawl and bent down in front of me. She adjusted my tie and told me to close my mouth. *You're gonna be just fine. People are people. Remember that. Now you just watch your mama and do what I do, hear?*

Is Toby's family in there?

Of course they're in there. Where else would they be?

I pointed to the open field. Twenty or so colored men were out threshing. Mom adjusted my sling, licked her fingers, and pressed my hair straight. She led me across the dirt road and up the front stoop. She handed me the baking tin and knocked on the door. A colored woman pulled it open. Mom directed me inside and thanked the woman she called Myrna.

Mom tossed her handbag into a chair and headed for the kitchen. She pulled the refrigerator open and set the baking tin inside like she owned the place. I knocked into one of the flower vases crowding the doorway on my way in. I stooped down and groped over the floorboards to pick it up. The woman named Myrna stooped down beside me to help. The back door creaked open, and I heard Mom scream *Evan!*

Evan?

A colored boy—*the* colored boy—stood in the open doorway in rolled-up overalls, no shirt, and bare feet. It was the same Evan who nearly tore my arm off. Mom knelt down in front of him, and all I could think was, *Evan? What the heck is he doing here?* When Mom introduced him to me as Toby's son, the bottom seemed to fall out from under me.

What are you talking about? "Toby's boy"? That's Goolsbee's boy.

Mom gave me a look. I knew that look, and I didn't like it one bit. It made me feel stupid.

He never mentioned having a son! That's Goolsbee's boy!

It was Goolsbee's boy. Goolsbee's boy was Goolsbee's son. He only had one, and that was him. Goolsbee's was the only place I ever saw him, so it only made sense. Mom's look told me to stop while I was ahead. I felt like my worst nightmare was coming true. Damn it all, Toby barely even mentioned having a wife, never mind a son. I glanced at the fridge. I wondered if Irma was the one who was busy trying to make room for all the food we'd brought. No. Wait. That was Myrna. I looked down at the little purple flower in my hand, then up at the back doorway. Mom and Evan were looking at one another in a dusty shaft of light coming in through the back doorway.

Huey, there's someone I'd like for you to meet.

I took a step back.

Never mind him. If you ever want to come over to our house and spend time with me, you're welcome to. Or even just to borrow some toys. You just let me know, okay?

Another woman entered the room. She was a small-framed woman, shorter than Mom. Her belly was so big I thought she was about to fall over.

Little Huey? What happened to your arm?

I was hit by a car.

And what's this?

I was distractedly looking for the TV. There was none. I felt out of place in a house without a TV.

Oh, this? This is just old newspaper. I unwrapped it. *Here.*

What is it?

Well, nothing really. But. Well. It's something Toby told me to fix once. Ma'am. And that I—or—Well. I glanced at Evan coldly. I couldn't even think his name without a feeling of deep fury welling up inside me. *Well, I recently broke it again. Even if it can't be fixed, Toby—I mean, Mister Muncie—was the rightful owner. You see, it belonged to him, ma'am. In a manner of speaking. Because he told me to fix it. It may not look like it, but I did. And now I'd like for you to have it. You see right here? I tried to glue this. But as you can see, it still isn't quite right. But I tried. And Toby said that's what counts. Which is how I know that he'd have appreciated this—because I tried. Boy, did I try. I know it doesn't look like much. But—well—I tried, ma'am. I really did.*

I held up to Missus Muncie an abomination of my once prized dive mask, which the young colored boy standing in the opposite doorway, charming my mother, had so ruthlessly destroyed not but a few days before. Shards of glass were poking out. Elmer's was smeared across it so thick the face plate wasn't even transparent anymore. Never mind seeing through it, you couldn't wear it without poking out an eye. I suddenly felt silly for having brought it.

I handed it to her. *It would have had tremendous symbolic value to Mister Muncie. I just know it. He'd have looked upon it no different than if it were one of those fancy new ones. He always said that, ma'am. If something broke, don't matter what, you fix it.*

It pained me to have to give it to her in that awful condition. I apologized a second time for the fact that glass didn't glue so well. And that I hadn't been able to find every little piece. Missus Muncie received it tenderly in both hands and led me to the sofa beneath the front window and set it alongside an assortment of family photographs and keepsakes.

She stroked her big round belly and pointed at one. *Do you know who that is?*

I paused, suddenly uneasy. *What am I doing there?*

Evander Erraticus Muncie, you bring Huey here some iced tea. You'd like some iced tea, wouldn't you? Along with a graham cracker from the cupboard. And you might as well bring Peola here some coffee while you're at it. Don't bother heating it, though. She's used to it cold.

Irma pushed aside the flowers cluttering the coffee table. Everything seemed a great effort for her. She sat down and patted the seat cushion beside her.

Darker hair and eyes—and softer features, for sure. But child, you look just like your daddy. But enough of that. Now, what's this I hear about you being at Good Intent?

Yes, ma'am.

Lucky you.

I still had the picture in my hand. I glanced up from it. Now she knew where I went to school? Something stank—and not the fatty smell of ham hocks boiling off on the stove. Mom sat down between us and interrupted me midsentence. She started saying how unfair life is, and how sorry she was, and how near and dear Toby was to all our hearts, and how lucky we were to have had a chance to get to know him, and how sorely missed he'd be, and how he'd been a sorely needed beacon in difficult times like these.

Buck didn't have to tell me what an upstanding worker he was, Irma. I saw it myself—how he didn't mind, not one bit, being out there on those long days. Under that hot sun. In its heat, covered in sweat. To provide for you and Evan. Whatever happened, you can be proud of that.

Missus Muncie's face went flat. *Where is he now?*

Never could stand tears. You know that.

Mom was making up the same old garden-variety nonsense people say after someone they didn't much care for while alive is dead and gone. When my drink didn't come, I got up and went to the back door. I pressed my face against its pushed-out screen and wondered whether it was to Mom's credit that she didn't care what color people were. Evan was standing in the middle of a clearing, heaving an ax. He grunted as he brought it down—*crack*. I stepped out. He looked up at the sound of the door.

Shoulda seen it a week ago. TV people. News people. Radio people. Magazine people.

Movie people?

He paused. *Yeah. Movie people, too. Couldn't fit 'em all in. Cars and trucks lined up and down both sides of the road. It was like Main Street on a Sunday, so many of them coming and going. Made my head spin. See this?* He stroked his fingers along the visor of his stiff, new ball cap. *Robinson saw me with my old one on the TV. Said it was a shame a fan like me should have to wear something so shabby. Sent me this here new one. Even signed it and everything.*

Jackie Robinson sent that?

Evan whacked it into shape and slid it back on. He left the ax in the chopping block and signaled for me to follow him. So I did. He guided me past a lean-to under which wood was stacked, past a chicken coop and underneath the shade of a tarpaulin hanging above a clutter of hubcaps, car rims, and bicycle tires.

I followed Evan over to a swing hanging from the high branch of a red maple across the way and past a stump of salt lick. He shoved the swing out of the way and pulled some shrubs to the side. Inside was a clearing. The ground was covered with curlicues of wood shavings, and chisels, handsaws, wood planes, and squares of sandpaper were scattered about. Evan picked up one of the bow staves stacked up against a chair and held it out to me. Said he'd made it himself.

I rubbed my fingers over it. I'd never felt anything so smooth. I couldn't believe it. I could read cloud cover and wind direction for rain, fold a parachute, tie a noose, clean Dad's Colt with nothing but a Q-tip and a toothbrush, identify the Tupolev Tu-4 bomber, evade capture by communists, and administer a lie-detector test to one, too, but I could not—I repeat—could not fashion my own bow from a tree stump.

Your pop taught you this?

Evan slid an arrow from a quiver leaning against the same chair. He put it to the bow, pulled it back, and let it fly. *Thwangggg*—the arrow smacked into a tree about thirty yards away. A squirrel was hanging from it about forty feet up, twitching. I looked at Evan with dismay and asked what the hell his problem was. He slid another arrow from the quiver, put it to his bow, and aimed it directly at me.

You're like Topsy, if Topsy was a little faggot fucker who acted white just because he looked like a cracker. Your mama's a no-shame gold-digging house nigger like that yellow bitch Cassy. And your daddy's like Massa Shelby, if Massa Shelby had no fucking idea how to raise so much as a patch of grass. What? You don't think I read? Well, fuck you. If it was up to me, you wouldn't even be here!

Evan went quiet. The back door creaked open. He pointed the bow to the ground and whispered, *I'm here to stay. You hear? Those cowards ever come after me like they did my daddy, it's gonna be one of these right between their eyes. If they ever come around here at night, carrying on with their torches lit and honking their horns, throwing exploding bottles and tearing ass around the front of my house, I'm letting the arrows fly. Now shuffle along like a good little Sambo and report back to them that I ain't going nowhere!*

Evan disappeared into the shrubs. Mom called out. I wasn't sure what had just happened. Evan was acting like it was me who'd pushed his daddy off that ladder. I made my way back in a fog, stumbling over tufts of grass and gnarled and knobby tree roots girding broad tree trunks. I tripped over a bicycle frame and followed a string of hoof prints in the mud until I picked up a footpath no wider than a leaf. It led straight to the back stoop.

Mom was on the porch, promising a flat-faced Evan that she would return just as soon as she could. Evan disappeared inside. Mom chewed me out for having wandered off. I kicked at a chicken clucking past on our way around the side of the house. Mom asked if I didn't feel a little silly about having been nervous. Said she was happy to see us boys get along so well. It was the first time I'd seen her with anything resembling a smile in quite some time. So I didn't say anything. She took my hand, and we made our way up the dirt road.

My whole arm felt like it was set to explode. I tugged on the plaster to relieve some of the throbbing. The frayed part up at the bend in my elbow split even more. It helped a little, but my arm still felt pinched in places. I slid my fingers underneath it and started jerking.

Is something the matter?

I hesitated. *What would we do if that ever happened to Pop?*

Mom stopped. *If he fell from a ladder?*

I nodded yes. Mom cautioned me not to trouble myself with thoughts like that and continued walking. After a few steps, she said that she didn't know, but we'd figure something out. *People always do.*

Are you sure Toby liked us?

Sure I'm sure.

Because we were good to him?

Of course.

We don't owe him any money, do we?

Just his back pay. But we're pulling that together.

So Dad was a good boss?

Mom stopped.

And what exactly does it mean if someone says you live off the spoils of your family name? And what's a gold digger? Is that good or bad? Because it sounds like it oughta be good, but then people say it in a way where it doesn't. And just who the hell are Topsy, Cassy, and Massa Shelby, anyway? And is Evan part Chickasaw? 'Cause I got the impression he might be. They were the best with arrows, right? Like, that William Tell fella was modeled on a Chickasaw Indian, right? And what's all this business about the legions of slaves that used to live out this way that I keep hearing about? Did that really happen? And now that I'm thinking about it, why don't you and Pop wear your wedding rings, anyway? It's a little embarrassing, if you ask me. Everyone else does.

What on earth were you two boys talking about back there?

I paused. *And I thought crackers were just food.*

What in the world did Evan say to you back there? Mom stopped. *Wait. Hold it right there. I think I know what's going on. This was bound to happen someday; I suppose today's as good as any. Here. Listen. I know what people think—and what they say. Okay? I do. I really do. And how they talk. Okay? I know all that. You think I don't know that? Well, I do. Listen. Your father's not perfect, okay? But who is? What matters is that he is decent. Okay? I can tell you that much. So don't let anyone tell you different. Ring or no ring, I wouldn't be with him if he wasn't. Now, some people in town talk, is all. They say mean things. Like, that we don't deserve to be together—your father and I. Or they say the complete opposite, that we deserve each other, but they mean that in a mean-spirited way. Okay? Does that make sense? No? Kinda? Well, let me put it to you this way. See, some people say that your father allowed himself to fall for me because he was too simple-minded to know better.*

Okay? There. Make sense now? That was in the beginning. Then they said that he was staying with me only on account of—well—an accident, let's just put it that way. Okay? Say, like I played a trick on him. That sort of thing. What kind of trick? Well, never mind that. But they were wrong about that, too. Nobody played a trick on nobody. There were no tricks involved, Huey. None. You'll just have to take my word for it. There was nothing but love. One hundred percent pure, unadulterated love. But that's hard for some people to accept. They just figure that something else unsavory had to be mixed up in it because according to them he was too good for me. They've been stuck on that belief and refuse to believe otherwise to this day. But they are wrong. So they have no choice but to say that it won't last. And that's more or less where we are today. But they are wrong about that, too. Because here I am. And there he is. And we're still together. And no matter all the mean, nasty, and hurtful things people have said and done to try to tear us apart, here we are. Just as strong and in love as the day we met.

There. Feel better? Sometimes people just have their own ideas about who should be with whom, Huey. That's all. And they have a hard time letting go of those ideas. You could even say they're married to them, in a way. So what do people say now? Well, I wouldn't exactly know because I'm not around those people anymore. And frankly I don't care. Because it's all just idle talk from a bunch of folks who believe that I must be some piece-of-trash gutter girl who could never do better. Okay? I know all that. And now I guess you're starting to know it, too. But right now you're going to wash all that stuff out of your head and pretend like you never heard it, okay? Because it's poison. And when poison gets into your brain, it can be hard to get it out. No, you don't have to mention it to your daddy. In fact, I would prefer it if you didn't. It would just upset him. Because it's nothing but mean and nasty and spiteful stuff that we're trying to put behind us, but that the people who don't want to see us together keep putting in the way.

Listen, Huey. You're gonna hear people say things about us—your father and me. But you shouldn't believe it all. The bottom line is that your father is going to see to it that you have the bright future that you deserve. To me, all that matters in this world is that you're provided for in that way. To have the honest-to-goodness chance to make whatever you want of your life. All that empty talk about pride coming from poor single women in broken families, without a hope in the world for themselves, much less their babies? Let them snicker all they want. Let them believe that I don't have something they do. Because at the end of the day, their pride may only be good for their sleep, and sleep is overrated. I live for the waking hours. Phooey. You want pride? I'll show you my pride. He's standing right here. There's not a thing in this world that I wouldn't do for you, boy. You know that, right? I don't have to do anything in the name of pride that I can do for you.

I turned back to the road.

What now, sweetheart?

Your rings?

Rings? We don't have rings.

Don't have rings? What kind of answer's that? Why not?

Rings cost money, you know. And what's a ring got to do with love, anyway?

And I suppose that's why everyone one else has four or five kids, whereas you just have me? You know damned well I've wanted a little brother for as long as I've been stuck cleaning out the henhouse by myself, washing dishes by myself, shucking corn, peeling potatoes, scrubbing pots, cleaning the windows, sweeping out back, chopping wood, stacking wood, pruning shrubs, baling hay, sorting stack poles, cutting down trees, and pulling weed thistle.

Mom smiled. You're a slow learner, but you're coming along.

It's not funny! Money, money, money. Shoulda known. Everything is about money. Always money! I stopped. Even Missus Muncie had on a ring! The man who used to work for us! And who's dead now! His wife! And don't think I don't know about what you and Dad do in your room! All that, and no baby to show for it! And here you always go on about scripture, and Bible this and Bible that. Well, what ever happened to the Lord, he proclaimeth on the fifth day that man shall go forth on this day and multiply, so that his kin, too, may inhabit the earth, with all its earthly splendor? Because that woman's belly was poking straight out to here. So don't try and fool me with that business about the stork bringing babies when it's as clear as day that something's about to pop out of her any minute!

Mom walked off without a word. I ran up to her, grabbed her hand, and pressed it tight. She forced a smile, but I could tell that it was too little, too late. The road was a narrow, rutted path of red dirt. It was littered with derelict hand plows and old wagon wheels, and lined with brush, garbage cans, and other rusty metal junk. The colored men across the way were still spreading peanut vines over the wagons lined up along the side of the field. Evan's ax echoed out—*crack . . . crack . . . crack.*

> *Emma, help me pull these weeds.*
> *Hoe, Emma, hoe.*
> *You turn around, dig a hole in the ground.*
> *Hoe, Emma, hoe.*
> *Emma, work harder than two grown men.*
> *Hoe, Emma, hoe.*
> *You turn around, dig a hole in the ground.*
> *Hoe, Emma, hoe.*

Our truck was sitting at the very end of the road, about a hundred yards away. Dad was behind the wheel, reading the paper. He folded it up and shoved the door open. I hopped in, cradling my arm like a baby. Mom squeezed in beside me. When I asked why he'd parked so far away, Dad said that he didn't want to get stuck in the mud again, and pulled out.

XVII

IRMA'S GOT TWO DAYS TO find the courage. Evan was inside shining Toby's shoes when a man from the county coroner's office stopped by—said that she ought to just have the body cremated. Imagine! Evan's thumping away on one of his father's boots, all the while Myrna's in the next room, sewing buttons onto his suit for the service, and that Mister Wyatt T. Blake, blocking the damn sunlight coming in through the front doorway, is explaining to Irma how an open casket is a terrible idea. Said that Irma ought to just have him taken straight to the crematorium; they can't allow her to go laying that body out in the state it's in. Called it irresponsible. And you know what Irma did? She took that tin of shoe polish from Evan and gave him a hatchet instead. Told him to go out back and split wood. That boy's been splitting wood ever since.

I'd been lying in bed nursing my arm, half-dead to the world, when Mom barked out at me from the kitchen.

Rise and shine, young man! Time to get up! Chop-chop! All play and no work makes Jack a poor boy! It's a big day, and there's lots to do!

She strolled in two minutes later and sat down beside me. She kissed me on the head and told me to get up. A look of concern overtook her face. She placed her palm on my forehead.

You feel warm, cupcake.

She looked at my arm.

Is it getting worse?

I felt feverish. I knew that I was supposed to have been getting better for the last few weeks, but I didn't feel like it. My fingers had ballooned. She touched them, and a sharp pang shot up my arm. I jerked my cast away.

Stop it!

Honey, I don't think this is healing right—Buck!

Mom examined them more closely. She was dismayed by the discoloration of my fingernails. They were almost black. Dad strolled in holding a razor. He stared down at my cast, then bent down for a closer inspection. He winked.

His fingers look like Vienna sausages. But other than that, he looks fine. Probably just slept on it wrong. I'm sure he'll be fine just as soon as he gets up and about.

Mom had never seen anything like it. She wondered if I should have it looked at. Dad suggested a wait-and-see approach.

Mom looked at him like he was crazy. *Wait and see what? His arm fall off?*

Mom demanded that something be done and marched off. Dad asked if it hurt. When I said yes, he hollered out for her to get some aspirin, then dragged me out after her. I stood in the middle of the kitchen, scratching my upper arm. Mom soaked the red spots in castor oil, but it still itched like the devil. She wiped a wet washcloth over my face, gave me two aspirin, and told me to get back in bed.

So I did. Something smacked against the window. I put down my comic book and went over to it. Derrick was standing outside. He gestured for me.

I opened the window and poked my head out. *Why didn't you say hi the other day?*

When?

Don't "when" me.

Jesus, Huey, you know how she is.

Don't ever do that again.

Okay. Well, don't just stand there looking at me like a dummy. Lemme have it.

I paused. *Danny gone?*

Yeah. Miss Lambert had to drive him because the buses still aren't running. Aw, c'mon. Everybody's saying all kinds of stuff about what happened. I came to hear it from you.

I hung my cast out the window. *About this?*

Yeah.

I got hit by the sheriff. He was flying down Main Street, sirens blasting, and bam! I flew over the car. Must have been going at least eighty miles an hour, in hot pursuit.

That's not what I heard.

Says who?

Everyone.

Well, they didn't see the toxicology report, and I did. It was in big, bold letters: EIGHTY MILES PER HOUR.

Derrick looked impressed.

BLOOD PRESSURE: ZERO. HEART RATE: ZERO OVER ZERO. PULSE: ZERO, ZERO, *and* ZERO, LATERAL, VENTRICLE, *and* DORSAL. *So there. Bone was poking out. Lost tons of blood. Even lost a tooth. Here—see? Stung so bad I blacked out. People thought I was dead. But then I came back to life. Kinda like Jesus, only quicker. But no, I didn't meet any angels, so don't bother asking. Saw the light at the end of the tunnel, though. Decided it wasn't my time yet. So I turned around and jogged back. I should probably sue. I dunno. I am a lot better now, though. So maybe not. Except for the purplish color here and the rash here. Spread from my thumb all the way up to my elbow. Here—see? The doctor says I'm lucky to be alive. Says they're gonna put me in medical books. So I'll probably get some residuals for that.*

Looks like a zombie hand. What in the hell did you do to it?

Oh. You mean the rubber bands? They're just to help keep it in place.

No, that. Did you take it off and put it back on?

Nah. Just tore some.

Does it hurt?

Throbs sometimes. Mostly just when I bang it in the doorway. You know how your fingers usually move when you want them to? Well, these two don't.

Lemme see.

I showed him, after which I explained the frustrations of being a one-armed cripple. Like having to do everything with an arm that I wasn't used to using, and how everything from pouring milk to opening the cookie tin was twice as hard and took twice as long. And how even something as simple as tying my shoelaces made me furious with frustration.

Is it waterproof?

What the hell do I look like? You think I'd let them put something on me that wasn't waterproof?

You're so lucky. Jesus, what I wouldn't do to be in your shoes. You get all the excitement. I can't wait until I break my first bone. Which reminds me—I also came to tell you to be on the lookout. My mama's put the double-barreled shotgun by the window. She's claiming she'll shoot at the first sign of anyone creeping around. Said she's gonna shoot first and ask questions later. So if you come by to talk, hide behind that old root-choked tree out front. Say, what are you up to later? Maybe we can meet up.

Nah. Toby's service is today.

You're going?

Of course I'm going.

Derrick looked at me funny.

What? You wouldn't go to Sheldon's service?

Sheldon hasn't reported to work in over two weeks. Which makes him a traitor. So no, I wouldn't.

Okay, Miss Della, then?

Jesus Christ, Huey. Miss Della does what she's supposed to. My mama says she hasn't missed a day of work in fifteen years. Sweetest old lady I ever knew—even came to work the day God took her baby back. Never mind the time she worked straight through Easter Sunday so that my poor little sister Claire was able to get her new outfit in time for her baptism. Not to mention that she's the only colored in town who's still standing by us. And thank goodness for that, because my mama doesn't even know how to boil an egg. Talking about how long they're supposed to boil for and if you're supposed to put salt in with them like you do potatoes. Now she's got Miss Della running around doing the work of Harriet, Ora, Ross, Gladys, Shapely, Donovan, Lester—all of them. If that's not loyalty, by Jove, I don't know what is.

Miss Della, a sweet old lady?

The question you need to be asking yourself is, would you have gone to Benedict Arnold's service?

I had to think. I know what you're driving at. And the same thing occurred to me. But he didn't. Trust me. I just know it. It's all just a big misunderstanding. Sure, he fixed Mister Abrams's filter that one time.

But he just put a finger in the water to check the temperature. That's all. I doubt he ever even put his arm in up to his elbow, never mind swim in it. Didn't even like the stuff. Niggers don't like water, you know that.

We got forty more niggers working for us than you do, Huey, so go figure. Miss Della doing the wash. Harriet cooks up supper. Ross keeps up the yard. And whatshisface—the new guy—goddamnit, I can't even remember all their names. We got so many coming and going, sometimes I'd swear I know them better than they know themselves.

Doesn't matter. Your daddy even said so—I heard him. Called Toby "the goose that laid the golden egg." Remember when the sewage line backed up, and someone fixed it? Well, that was Toby. And how that one morning we woke up and all those red-winged blackbirds were lying out in the road, bloated and stiff, and no one knew why, until someone figured it out? Well, that was Toby, too. And who fixed the water main when no one else could? Toby. It was all Toby.

Derrick was very generous with his knowledge of practical matters. Among other things, he taught me stuff he knew about colored people. And I was grateful. Mom and Dad rarely touched the subject—which was just as well, because whenever they tried, they just complicated it. But with Derrick, everything was always cut-and-dried. Which was what frustrated me most about Mom's having taken me to Toby's house. Don't get me wrong. I wanted to pay my respects. I just wished I could have done it in a way such that I'd never had to actually go visit the goddamned place. It would have made life so much simpler. Because as unsettling as Evan's threat on my life had been, I couldn't help but admire someone who could not only make a bow but shoot it like he had. Didn't matter if it was cruel. It was amazing. It instantly put him up there with the legendary warrior chiefs and the great Eastern mystics. At the end of the day, I didn't know whether I should be angry at Toby for the headache he was causing me or feel sorry for him because he was dead.

Derrick held his nose and made fun of me for having to suffer through a three-hour-long, nigger-filled service. Mom called out for Dad. Derrick and I froze, listening. Derrick stepped closer to the window and broke it all down for me, explaining how Toby had been in league with those college kids all summer. My bedroom door was closed, but we could still hear Mom and Dad rummaging around in the kitchen. It sounded like Mom was setting out breakfast plates. I leaned farther out the window and whispered.

And?

Derrick went quiet at the sound of Mom's voice.

. . . said Toby always thought you a lackluster overseer who could do no better than live off the spoils of his family name—the man who lacked the wherewithal to prod a field hand into the strenuous labor required of him either by example or force. Who could respect a man hardly capable of fulfilling the duties of the job that had been handed to him on a silver platter? Called you a small man who had taken the easy road in love as well as life and frankly thought I deserved better.

She said that?

And plenty more.

Toby didn't say that, and you know it. He'd never say a thing like that. That boy loved me. Listen, people say mean things when they get upset. Besides, Irma's probably just jealous. Okay? You know that. We've been over that a million times. Comes with the territory—being a diamond in the rough in a small backwoods community such as this. She probably just resents you for it. Probably wants what you have—sees all you've got and wonders why she can't have the same. Honestly, she probably expected that Toby ought to have been able to provide for her like I provide for you. Who knows? She may even hate you for it. And you and I both know it. Mean-spirited women like Irma make it their life's work to undermine people like you and me. Frankly, I'm used to it.

I looked down at Derrick. I tried to say something funny but came up empty. Derrick put a finger to his lips. Dad was in the kitchen, admitting to Mom that Toby had once asked if he could sharecrop a couple of acres of our land, but that he had said that he couldn't afford to do that. Derrick laughed. I hung out the window and took a swing at him. He shut up and there was a moment of quiet.

When I leaned back into the house, he blurted out, *You can always come work for us!*

I whipped my home-run ball at him, but my left-handed throw was clumsy. Derrick disappeared through the bedsheets drying on the line. My door creaked open.

Huey?

Dad poked his head in from the hallway, clean shaven and stinking of aftershave. He asked what the hell I was doing out of bed and what all the racket was about, then told me that if I busted my cast, my arm could set as crooked as a coat hanger for all he cared. I wasn't getting a new one. I stormed past him and plopped myself down at the kitchen table. Mom was washing her hair over the sink.

Was that Derrick stirring up trouble again?

None of your goddamned business.

Neither Mom nor Dad flinched, which was unexpected. Mom lifted her head out from under the faucet and wrapped a towel around it and told me to go wash up. I didn't budge. She was in the middle of greasing her scalp. When she finished, she set the open tin of berga-mot down in front of me and asked what I was staring at. She knew I didn't like how it smelled but did it anyway. Which irked me. I held my nose and said that it stank, then put the lid back on and held it up. The woman on the label looked like she could have been Mom's sister. Mom turned away from me and set the steel prongs on the stove and dialed up the knob.

I slammed the tin down on the table. *That goddamned nigger of ours broke into Mister Abrams's pool, didn't he? He did it, didn't he? Go on. You can tell me. Just admit it. For God's sake, can't anyone tell the truth around here?*

Mom's hot comb fell to the floor. She picked it up and smoothed over the nick it made in the linoleum, then stood up and snatched the tin of bergamot out of my hand, slammed it on the table, and marched me into the bathroom. *That is not a word we use in this house!*

Out came the soap. I closed my mouth.

She pried my lips apart. *Do you hear me?*

I held my breath, but it still stung. I kicked and screamed bloody murder so bad she nearly shoved it down my throat. I tried to get her to stop, but she just kept swishing it round until I was foaming at the mouth, all the while hollering out at the top of her lungs.

It's every bit as blasphemous as shit, cunt, fuck, bitch, kike, mother-fucker, Chink, penis, *and* vagina. *Nod if you understand that!*

My watery eyes were suddenly wide open and astounded. She had my undivided attention. I nodded. With my whole body, arms, fingertips—everything. Over and over again. Several times, and vigorously. Besides being terrified, I was shocked. She knew more cuss words than me.

Dad came in and wrestled the soap from her. He led her out and sat her down in front of Bill Cullen on the TV, then returned to the kitchen and put on a pot of hot tea. I was pitched over the bathroom sink, coughing and gagging and spitting out white chunks of soap cake stuck between my teeth and in the crevices of my premolars. I kept rinsing my mouth, but that damned bitter soap taste just wouldn't go away.

That boy's wearing a real tie! Look! Bill Cullen's got on a real tie. Everyone important has a real tie on. Why doesn't my boy wear a real tie? Answer me that? I want my boy to have a real tie, too! He's practically a grown man! How's he gonna get a good job without a necktie? For goodness's sake, when are you going to get around to teaching your boy to tie a necktie? How's he supposed to make it in this world if he can't even tie a necktie? When all you do is get on him about sorting stack poles? Teach him something useful, like how to tie a necktie!

I riffled through the cabinet for something to help me get rid of that disgusting taste. I found the bottle of pills that Dad took for his knee—not what I was looking for, but maybe they would help my arm. When I finally got the cap off with my teeth, they spilled out all over the floor. I popped two and scooped the rest back up into the bottle.

Of course, funerals were no fun. And Toby had been close to us. But what the heck was up with Mom was anyone's guess. I turned on the water in the bathtub and staggered to the open doorway. Dad was standing at the stove, watching water boil. He looked a little lost. I told him I needed help tying a bag around my cast. Dad followed me into the bathroom and slipped a garbage bag over my arm and wrapped some duct tape around it. He consoled me with the admission that Mom was a little tense, then started talking about life not being fair and needing to grow up in a hurry sometimes because life was filled with the unexpected.

Unexpected indeed. When I finished with my bath, Dad picked up the necktie from the chair back, called me in, and slung it around my neck. A warm, fuzzy feeling spread throughout my entire body as he tied it into a fancy knot. The pain in my arm melted away, and the room was spinning just a little, but I felt great. When he finished, I went into the bathroom and jumped up and down in front of the mirror. I was laughing because of how important the stupid necktie made me look.

Dad brought my suit coat in from my bedroom closet. He dusted it off. Mom laid it out over the kitchen table, sat down with needle and thread, and let the right arm out. And as she sat there, quietly letting out hem after hem, all I could think to myself was that Toby's service required the same getup as Easter, which put it right up there with the Resurrection in my mind.

Dad stood in the kitchen, ironing a dark tie, in nothing but a white T-shirt, boxers, and black socks. He was good with an iron—said he'd learned it in the ROTC. Never told me anything about what else he'd learned, though. Mom sat hunched over the kitchen table with a nest of pins and rollers in her hair, blaming the fact that we were running late on all the time it was taking her to fashion my suit coat to fit over my cast.

My fingertips tingled, and my hand was purple. When I showed Mom, she answered by telling me that we had no ice in the house and to talk to Dad about fixing the freezer, and then took hurriedly to the back door. She returned with my wind-blown button-down, snatched the iron from Dad, and began ironing it, all the while quizzing me about all that was going on in town.

I held my hand up over my head because that seemed to relieve some of the pressure.

All I know is that someone broke into Mister Abrams's pool. And the police are still trying to figure out who did it. And that everyone in town is betting their bottom dollar it was Toby—coloreds included.

How can you be so sure?

Derrick.

Mom wasn't surprised. She seemed to know Derrick better than she let on. Anyway, my fingers felt a little better. At least I could wiggle them a little. Mostly my middle finger, which I was starting to think was the most important. That warm, fuzzy feeling was making me bold.

I'm guessing because he was the only colored ever close enough to it to ever actually have a shot at getting his whole body inside, not counting Aurelia. Or Edna. Or Mister Hardee, for that matter. But they're too old, probably. Besides, Edna never left the laundry room, and Mister Hardee was always out front, clipping the hedges. But what really gets my goat is that Pop's the only damned person in town who's still upset about it and won't let me go back. We ran into Derrick and the guys last week, and they were on their way there. Why, I bet they'd probably been swimming in there the whole time, splashing around and having the time of their lives.

Mom was standing at the ironing board, talking with her back to me. *Huey, that pool's done for. I assure you, it's a ghost town back there right now. Stanley may as well fill it in with dirt and plant petunias. Because they're never gonna find who did it, and no one except maybe a few kids is ever stepping foot in that pool again until they do. That's just how people are around here. It's Blakely or bust for all of Akerburg's swimmers from here on out, I can promise you that. So you may as well just put it out of your mind and forget it.*

I kicked the table leg so hard I nearly busted my toe. Mom set the iron down and held the suit coat out. I was still trying to wiggle my cast into a shirtsleeve as stiff as an envelope.

If you ask me, it was a harebrained idea for Mister Abrams to have ever built that pool in the first place. That pool was never anything but a place for fat, lazy old white men to twiddle their thumbs and sip drinks as they chatted about the weather in between spraying their crops. If you ask me, your father's silly insistence on giving you swim lessons there when he knew good and well we didn't have the money for it is partly to blame for this mess. I don't give a hoot about four generations of Fairchilds having been varsity swimmers, either. It's as much to blame as all the rest of it. Never did get his money back, either. My word. Opportunity of a lifetime, my A-S-S. And the stupidity of paying up front! I never will understand that. Will you just look at the fix it's gotten all of us in? Maybe if people like him hadn't, Toby would still be alive.

I'd been bracing for Mom to say those words ever since we came home from the pool that day ten dollars poorer and with nothing to show for it but a bruised ego and a canceled swim lesson. A big part of me was relieved that she'd finally come out and said it. I hopped over to her, dragging my suit coat behind me.

I'm sorry, Mama. I really am. I don't care about that pool or swimming. Don't care if I never learn to swim. I'm done thinking about that pool. Done. Done. And done.

XVIII

WHEN MOM ASKED WHY I hadn't ever invited Zuk over, I told her that I wanted to wait for our circumstances to improve. When my second year at Claremont came and went and we were still living in the Jacob Riis Houses, she said that maybe it was time for me to swallow my pride and invite him over anyway.

The problem was that I was in the midst of creating a persona at Claremont that bore no resemblance to the reality of my life in the projects. Claremont was changing me: having been introduced to the possibilities that came with erudition, I began speaking, acting, and even dressing differently. In the short span of two years, I was hobnobbing with the distinguished alumni, colleagues, and friends in attendance at our quarterly meet and greets. There was the artist M. C. Escher and Minoru Yamasaki, who designed the new World Trade Center towers being built downtown. Even the secretary-general of the United Nations was there once. My favorite had been Professor Barnard, who had recently performed the world's first successful heart transplant. He stopped by on a visit from South Africa, and stood beside the buffet table munching on cheese and crackers, telling me about how he'd hummed Mozart's *Symphony No. 40* to steady his hands during the procedure. He wiped his lips on the back of his hand, took a swig of wine, and said every surgeon did it. Not to that particular song, of course, but they all had their own personal please-God-help-me-not-fuck-up-this-one song. He chuckled. That was exactly what he called it. The acronym swooped over my head when he read it back to me, perhaps because I was thunderstruck. The whole idea of the world's leading heart surgeon having someone's heart pulsing in his hand as he hummed like a kid gluing his model plane together—*fuck*. That little piece of trivia felt like a gift. It brought the most historic medical procedure the world had ever known so close to me that I could practically smell it myself. For a second, that beating heart was right there in my hands and I knew deep down that maybe I could do something cool like that one day, too.

Of course, I brought every bit of insight I culled from those gatherings home with me. My newfound presumption of equal standing in my relationship with Mom was alternately troubling to her and the source of immense pride. What Dad had withheld from me, Claremont seemed to be holding out to me with an open hand. I seemed to be in store for something truly special, and the last thing I wanted to do was to let my guard down. So no, I wasn't in a hurry to surrender my meticulously crafted persona only to become universally known, *reductio ad ignominia*, as the kid who schlepped in on the 6 train from the projects every day.

By my third year, I realized that something had to give. I told Mom that I was open to the idea of having Zuk over in principle. I suggested a neutral venue, perhaps something unassuming, like a pizzeria over near Tompkins Square Park. That was sort of in my neighborhood. At least we could walk there. It wasn't a well-to-do area by any stretch of the imagination, but it was becoming artsy, which lent it an aura of acceptability. But none of that would do for Mom. She desired nothing short of hara-kiri, or, as she called it, *authenticity*.

She wouldn't stop trying to convince me that it was worth doing, and her constant badgering endured past midterms and continued through the Easter recess, at which point she lured me to some storefront church uptown on the promise of finding God. Who apparently lives up in Harlem. And as a preacher splattered his faith over the unoccupied chairs in the front row, she sat beside me with the big, bulbous afro that she only ever wore uptown, pestering me under her breath until she'd worn my defenses down to a nub. I was sitting on a foldout chair in the back, breathing in the frankincense wafting in from the street vendors outside, listening to the steady beat of African drums in the distance, and watching the men in full-length tunics and bow ties passing down 125th Street greeting each other with *as-*

salaam alaikum when Mom whispered in my ear, *What's the worst that can happen?*

Poor Mom. After two and a half years, she still didn't comprehend what it meant to be a seventh grader at Claremont Prep. Mayor Lindsay's son wasn't thought sufficiently pedigreed to warrant admission that fall, which was a source of tremendous pride to the rest of us. We despised the mayor's antiwar rhetoric. Several notable alumni were on the board at Lockheed, and military conflict was good business. We'd talk about it in the restroom while drying our hands and fixing our hair in the mirror. Not the military-industrial complex, but Mayor Linday's ragtag son. And even as I joked with the others about that poor SOB who'd had to settle for the Dutching School, I knew perfectly well that when I exited the banter would turn to me. The kid who some viewed as the dark-skinned charity case delivered at the behest of the United Nations from the South, which was like a Third World country to all of them. To others I was the poor, underprivileged, minority boy who was living with his mom down in the East Village. As vexing as all that was, somehow it didn't keep me from harboring the view that there was nothing left to learn about me that couldn't in some way be viewed as compromising. Not only was Dad not the CEO of General Electric, Exxon, Shell, Mobil, Dow Chemical, or DuPont, he wasn't even acting like a dad. So yes, I kept my cards close to the vest.

I might have scoffed, but in the end, I magnanimously forgave Mom her ignorance concerning the nature of privilege and the importance of a well-maintained image. How could she possibly understand? I was quite happy to continue my charade indefinitely if need be, and here she was hell-bent on exposing me. After a great deal of reluctance, I waved the white flag and surrendered.

The collection basket was slowly making its way back to us. Mom dug out two dollars from her coat pocket and dropped them in. She handed me the basket. I peeked inside, took a couple of bucks out for myself, and relayed it across the aisle.

I WAS HAVING second thoughts. On the day that Zuk was supposed to come over for dinner, it occurred to me that there was so much that could go wrong—and would. So I did what any twelve-year-old desperate to protect a highly vulnerable reputation would do: I drew up a term sheet and handed Mom a pen and pointed to the kitchen table. In front of her was a list of topics that I thought damning and therefore deemed inappropriate for polite dinner conversation. I unilaterally forbade her to discuss any of them in the company of one Ariel J. Zukowski. The sheet read,

> I, Peola Jezebel Hicks, do swear to abstain from any conversation of a partisan nature and pertaining to, or that may include mention of, the following topics (referred to herein as "the Black List"), listed here in no particular order, under penalty of death, or so much money that I will never, ever be able to repay it.

All "isms," including, but not limited to,

Communism

Capitalism

Zionism

Judaism

The Black Panther Party

The Nation of Islam

Palestinian statehood

The Vietnam War

J. Edgar Hoover

The Johnson administration

COINTELPRO

Executive Order 10925, aka affirmative action

Quota systems, interpreted broadly

Race ~~as a factor in intelligence~~

Any US president ever

The Mets' first-round draft pick

Race

The transit workers' strike

The best bagel in the East Village

Race

Tobias Wetherall Muncie, etc., etc., etc.

Signer: Witness:

Peola Jezebel Hicks   Hubert Francis Fairchild, the first

What can I say? It's a minefield out there. Admittedly, the list was a little longer than I had expected. But at the end of the day, these were the things that got argued over in class, were debated at lunch, and spilled out onto the sidewalk after school. In other words, I knew exactly where Zuk stood on current events.

It'd be a shit show if I allowed Mom to say whatever popped into her head. It'd been a couple of years now that she'd embraced feminism wholeheartedly and had, as a consequence, been given to reckless proclamations on a whole raft of issues. Ever since, her progressiveness had been growing at an unsustainable rate. But lately it had accelerated to such a degree that even I hardly recognized her anymore. She was becoming radicalized in a whole new way. It was like she'd transmuted overnight from lowly sheep to big bad wolf. I don't care how good her cooking was, Zuk wouldn't be able to keep it down. Because even if she'd only recently adopted many of her views on the Johnson administration and the politics of imperialism, she spoke in a way that left no room for debate. It was getting so bad that I expected her to come home any day now wearing a black beret, dark sunglasses, and wielding an assault rifle.

Zuk and I, on the other hand, had a different outlook. Debating was more a sport to us than life or death. Maybe that was because we shared an innate optimism about world affairs. We believed in the imperturbability of human progress—that is, that things just kind of worked themselves out on their own. We viewed ourselves as being living examples of the success of the working class. As screwed up as things were, we still believed that the country was fundamentally on the right course. A ruling class was a necessary evil. Imperialism was human nature. No matter how good one's intentions, you couldn't please everyone. Our job wasn't to try to change the nature of things but to make sure we ended up on the winning side. While Zuk and I made plans for the houses we would own one day, picturing their circular driveways, sprawling yards, tennis courts, and pools, Mom talked like she wanted to tear all that down. She spoke dreamily about a revolution that would obliterate the very establishment we saw it within our reach to join. I couldn't fault Mom for being bitter about the opportunities she'd never had, but I wished that she could just be happy that all of that could be mine. We just had to let go of the past and embrace the golden future that being at a place like Claremont would ensure.

Oh. And race—well, that just never seemed to come up. Which meant that Zuk and I agreed on most everything except which Mets batter would be better to have at the plate in a pinch.

Even if I'd become something of an organ grinder's monkey, I cherished my status. Whether by hook or by crook, I can't honestly say which, I had somehow joined the ranks of the buttoned-up crowd. Aside from not being able to gloat to Dad, things weren't all bad. I was learning what mattered in life, and understood how I fit in. It was nice being among the people for whom life was going according to plan. Frankly, it didn't matter so much to me that they weren't members of my immediate family. I was learning to take what I could get.

So when I explained to Mom why I felt that the Black List was necessary, she had the nerve to act like she was doing me a favor just by agreeing to put on a pretty dress instead of the denim trousers she'd intended to wear with a turtle neck and hoop earrings. I vetoed everything but the earrings. It was bad enough that Zuk was going to see our twenty-third-floor shoe box with its bleak view of the sooty buildings across the courtyard and the morass down at ground level. Of course, I was concerned. From my point of view, anything could happen.

I told Mom that it wasn't exactly her, per se. It was just as much our building and the surrounding public housing complex, our neighbors, our block, and the entire garbage-strewn, rat-infested slum of the East Village. In fact, it was everything. Her budding militancy annoyed me, but that was just part of it. In truth, it was *us*. It was who we were. It was the very idea of public housing and the frictional drag on civilization that people like us represented in fabled institutions of learning across the globe.

Mom sat down. She took her time looking over the Black List. She made a motion to sign, then hesitated. She saw Toby's name at the very bottom. She tapped it with the pen and looked up, puzzled.

Toby?

Oh, Mother. For heaven's sake. Please, not now.

I looked at her flatly and said that as heroic as Toby may have been, he just wasn't flattering to my self-image. Hurt welled up in her eyes. So I explained matter-of-factly that it was nothing personal. He simply didn't portray me in the light in which I desired to be seen. It was a difficult concept for me to have to convey just then. I could see the defenses rising in Mom's darkening countenance. She wasn't nearly as receptive to it as my friends at school had been.

Listen. It's just not how I want to project myself into the world, okay? The associations he calls to mind are all wrong. I know that you may not get it. But these are choices we make in life. And I want the things that I surround myself with to suggest skyscrapers, not garden hoes. Does that make sense?

Mom recoiled. *Jesus Christ, Huey. What's that school done to you?*

I composed myself. *Okay. Fine. You want to have it out? Suit yourself.*

When I asked if Hamilton or Lichenberger or any of the other fellas I went to school with were descendants of slaves, she said probably not. When I asked Mom who in his right mind would choose to be the descendant of a slave if given a choice, she gave me a contemptuous look.

You don't have a choice.

Don't be silly. Of course I do. We all have choices. Everything *is a choice.*

She called me, of all things, a disgrace to my race. I asked what she was referring to, precisely. Only the week before, she was peddling the idea of the whole concept of race as a sham concocted by a few eighteenth-century white men with powdered hair to more conveniently consolidate power, and now here I was, not having even had time to shit out the food I'd been eating at the time, come to find out that I was betraying it. I asked if it was possible to betray something that didn't exist. Because I was starting to feel like she'd drawn me into one of M. C. Escher's sketches, where the thing being drawn was itself a physical impossibility, yet there I was, looking right at myself standing inside it.

I sat up in my seat, unfazed. I explained that the very notion of an immutable identity was a foreign concept to me. Everything was negotiable, and infinitely so. To be sure, I might have felt differently if the identity presently being forced on me conferred even a hint of admiration from my peers. But in point of fact, it was the subject of considerable derision. So I'd cast it off, and after having done so, I'd joined in on the fun. It came so easily to me precisely because I'd pulled that page right out of Mom's old playbook. It was a time that she hardly cared to recall but that I remembered vividly. Ironically, she'd once recast herself as the person she needed to be to help me at a vulnerable moment in our lives, and now here I was doing pretty much the exact same thing. Now, come to find out, she'd had a crisis of conscience, albeit too late to do me any good. To her I was a lost cause, but I preferred to see myself as a self-styled creature of my own invention who had come to the determination that my relation to Mister Tobias Wetherall Muncie, or anyone else on the maternal side of my family, for that matter, wasn't anything that I could gain material advantage from in this lifetime or quite likely any other. And as such I was dispensing with it, forthwith and for all time, etcetera, etcetera, etcetera. Case closed.

I offered Mom a tissue. The point is, everything she was trying to impose on me felt like a pair of shackles buckled tightly around my ankles. I, on the other hand, desired a self-image with broad wings and long, glorious plumage. I wanted to tell her not to give in—to resist. I was still working out the details, of course, but in the meantime, she shouldn't let herself be constrained by an anachronistic classification system that was a holdover from the days of phrenology and which took a monochromatic view of our humanity. No, I was a citizen of the world, free to make myself into whatever I chose, and it was my considered opinion that a few conveniently overlooked branches of my family tree didn't warrant any unnecessary sentimentality. There were so, so many inconveniences in life. One had merely to learn which to prune and which were worth troubling over.

All I'd ever wanted to do was to fit in somewhere. And I finally felt I was making inroads at Claremont. Aside from a few difficulties with binomial expressions early on, there was nothing those other kids had over me, and I knew it. It had taken me a year to see through the self-confidence of my peers, but once I did, it had been like getting a peek behind the velvet curtain to see the Wizard for the small, feeble, and vulnerable man that he was.

It was strange to me that for the last two and a half years, all Mom could talk about was how she had hoped that I would find friends at Claremont in a way that I never had in Akersburg—how much it had saddened her that it wasn't working out that way—and here I was finally making headway, and all her *power to the people, burn baby burn* bullshit was making it damned near impossible for me to do just that. My poise was becoming labored.

I shoved the paper forward, suddenly irritated.

Either sign the frickin' thing or I walk!

The phone rang. Mom got up and answered it. Zuk's dad was calling from a gas station. He'd gotten off at the wrong exit on the crosstown expressway and landed way up by the natural history museum. He was just a few minutes away.

My chair dropped out from under me. Mom disappeared into the bathroom. I took down the brown baby Jesus hanging over the wall clock in our kitchen, just to be safe. That thing bugged the shit out of me—the way it looked down at me at all hours of the day with those judgmental brown eyes. I shoved it all the way to the very back of the utility drawer, imagining an indelicate slipup from Zuk, him saying, *Jesus was no nigger. Isaac, maybe, but not Jesus.* Personally, I didn't care if Jesus was brown or not. I had no skin in the game. He could have been a pimp for all I cared.

I ferreted out an open bottle of Chianti from the cabinet and hid it under the sink. If she took even a sip, I'd be doomed. On second thought, I poured it all out and buried the bottle in the trash. Couldn't be too safe. Then I collected our entire collection of mousetraps and roach motels from corners and behind the trash can and from inside cabinets and stashed all twenty-three of them under the sink.

Mom had a collection of books a mile high. She particularly liked memoirs and biographies. I took a stack from the kitchen and another from the sofa end table and a third from the bathroom floor beside the john and tossed them all onto my bed, then closed the door behind me and did a quick once-over to make sure I hadn't missed anything. I took a deep breath. In through the nose, out through the mouth. Just like Mom had taught me. *Oh shit.* I snatched the last two issues of the *Final Call* from atop the fridge and tossed them onto my bed. I debated momentarily whether Zuk would have occasion to enter our bedroom. I decided that he had better not and closed the door.

I took up position on the windowsill between the radiator and the TV. It was dark out. I had a bird's-eye view of the basketball courts below. They were lit by the floodlights girding the courtyard. Kids were out playing a pickup game. Mom hollered out from the bathroom for me to be on the lookout for a green Chevelle.

On second thought, it'd probably be better if I just went downstairs and waited for Zuk there. I hollered out to Mom that I was heading down. I stood inside the heavy steel double doors in our brightly lit lobby, looking out. When the car drove up, I pulled my forehead from the wired glass of the sidelight and went out. Zuk opened his door. He had his back to me and was saying something to his dad in Polish. I greeted him with a pat on the back and leaned into the open door and shook his dad's hand. He was wearing blue coveralls streaked with grease, and his hands were not so much large as rigid, like a claw. I told Mister Zukowski that my mother sent her regards and assured him that it wasn't worth his trouble to come up. He'd have to find parking and everything, but I was happy to escort Zuk up alone.

Mister Zukowski looked hesitant. He glanced over my shoulder at the crowd of colored kids gathered around the basketball court behind me. He seemed to be inspecting the older kids who were hanging out along the chain-link fence, sipping beer and passing a joint around.

All zis talk about gateway drugs. I'm starting to sink that's what basketball is. First they're in the courts. Then they're hanging out along the fence by the courts. Then they're out in the streets next to the courts. And from there they get picked up by the fuzz, never to be seeing from again.

Actually, it was pretty calm for a weekend night. But I didn't say anything. Still, I found myself wishing that there was some way for me to cover it all up. A car squeezed past Mister Zukowski and honked. Mister Zukowski put his car into gear. I assured him that everything was going to be okay. He said *pa* one last time to Zuk and pulled back into traffic. He stood at the stop sign at the end of the street. The FDR and the East River were dead ahead. Zuk and I watched him wait for an opening, then entered my building. On the way up, I told Zuk that it was good to see him. He said that it was good to see me, too.

It was weird seeing him in my home. Something about it made him seem like a different person, like somehow I was getting to know him all over again. Zuk had both hands in his pockets and was quietly looking over the cork board hanging beside the elevator. The arrangement of the index cards thumbtacked to it was haphazard, a hodgepodge of things for sale, babysitters needed, and the telephone numbers of building managers, custodians, super, and staff, emergency medical services, and social services. Toward the bottom were pest-extermination dates, water-outage warnings, and large-item collection days.

The elevator chimed and the door slid open. Jimmy was sitting inside in his wheelchair. I had forgotten to warn Zuk. Jimmy was a Vietnam vet who hung out in the elevator all day playing doorman. Mom told me that Jimmy was convinced that he was getting paid for it but that he really wasn't. Anyway, Jimmy pretty much said anything he damned well pleased, which was a nightmare for someone like me. Otherwise, there was nothing out of the ordinary about him. He was just another angry paraplegic who had an opinion about everything under the sun and who'd come to figure it all out twenty years too late for it to be of any use to himself. And even if I didn't like him because his wheelchair took up half the available space in the only working elevator in the building, and because bitter arguments often erupted when more than four of us tried to squeeze in—God forbid any of us had laundry or groceries—it was too damned bad. Jimmy was just a fact of life. He came with the building.

Zuk was waiting for Jimmy to get out, and Jimmy was looking at Zuk like he was a dumb shit. Jimmy asked what the hell he was waiting for. I took Zuk by the elbow and told him that it was okay, he could get on. I led Zuk into the shiny steel box and pressed 23. Zuk looked confused, probably trying to figure out why Jimmy hadn't gotten off on the ground floor. The elevator door closed, and we lurched before starting upward on our slow, lumbering ascent.

Jimmy was wearing a black leather vest with little parachute pins all over it. He had on dark sunglasses and driving gloves. His wheelchair was old and beaten up, and the three of us were jammed in so close he was breathing his warm lunch breath on me. His dark sunglasses were angled my way, and I could feel his eyes raking over me behind them. I closed my eyes and waited. I knew what was coming.

Who's this?

A friend.

I'd answered him with my eyes closed. Somehow I could feel him mulling it over, swishing it around in his mouth, like wine. I'd handed him a bottle of Pinot and he was considering what best to pair it with.

From school?

Uh-huh.

Jimmy was going to have something to say. Jimmy had something to say about everything. I opened my eyes and kept them open. There was no point fighting it.

You one dem fancy niggas that go to some real bullshit school, aint-cha? What they teach you about the war? Go on, lay it on me, brutha. All that bullshit learning your school teaches you about the war. I guar-antee you it's bullshit. Every last word, bullshit. So you tellin' me you spend aaaall that money to learnnn bullshit? You fancy niggas sure are some dumb muthafuckahs.

Jimmy turned to Zuk. His face crinkled up, and all he said was, *You got to be fucking kidding me.*

We should have taken the stairs. The doors opened and the elevator seemed to spit Zuk out. I stepped out and turned around.

At least I got all my limbs.

Fuck you! You punk-ass muthafuc—

The elevator door closed. The hall was long and dimly lit. We started down it.

Zuk turned to me. *Well, he seems nice enough.*

I laughed. *He's a four-star loudmouth.*

At the end of the long hall, a thick Plexiglas window made looking outside feel like I was looking through one of those brightly lit but hazy fish tanks they keep in the back of Chinese restaurants. That's where our apartment was. I stopped at our door and knocked our secret knock. Mom opened the door. She was wearing her hair natural. Which sur-prised me, because she only ever wore it that way on her weekly pilgrim-age to the bookstores and hair salons uptown. Not that it looked bad or anything. Mom looks terrific no matter how she wears her hair.

I hesitated in the doorway, then entered. Mom's hair was less shock-ing to Zuk on account of him only having seen her once before. Be that as it may, Mom was a hit. She entertained in bell-bottoms, platforms, turtleneck, big hair, and hoop earrings. She looked like Angela Davis, only without that space between her two front teeth. She played the role of cultured, charming, and gregarious host to perfection. She lit candles and incense. She even served up fondue. Zuk loved it. As we sat there dipping bread in melted cheese that we really didn't have the money for, he said he'd never felt more at home away from home, which made Mom glow. She flashed me a smile and winked. Everything went swimmingly, right up until after dinner, when Zukowski handed over his dirty plate.

That was delicious, Missus Fairchild. You are so talented. And you clean houses, too, if I understand correctly. Wow. How fascinating. Cooking and cleaning, and then raising those twins on top of that. You really are something else, Missus Fairchild. Must be simply fascinating work—the view you get into other people's lives. Really. I mean, if you think about it, you probably get more insights than professionally trained clinicians. People probably don't self-censor half as much with you as they do with their shrinks. You should really figure out some way to turn that into a money-making enterprise—maybe take more of a consulting angle. You could offer home-based therapy as an add-on. You know, at an extra charge.

Mom turned around from the sink. *Oh, it's nothing, really. I give the twins tips here and there, of course. And Missus Blumenthal advice about her husband—when she asks me. I just do it to be nice. And because I like them. I wouldn't think of charging for that.*

And your accent—it's so homey. It has a real 'we, the people' feel to it, if you know what I mean. I really like it. And to think that Huey used to talk like that. You'd never know it now, would you? If you don't mind my asking, where are you guys from again? I think you told me before, but I forget. I'm just curious because Huey here's always getting ribbed for being from the South. He won't talk about it, but I'm dying to know all about it. You wanna know what the kids at school call him? I'll tell you—oh, c'mon, Huey. Lighten up. It's not a big deal. Because it's funny, that's why. Get this, Missus F. They call him Mister Nobody from Nowhere. Can you believe it? On account of the fact that he never talks about himself. He's like a black box. You are so, Huey. You gotta admit, it's sort of true. Zuk turned to Mom. *Won't speak of himself in anything but generalities, Missus F. We gotta help him open up. Oh, c'mon, Huey. You gotta be able to poke a little fun at yourself in life or you're gonna go crazy. How many times has Mister McGovern said that? You gotta be able to laugh at yourself more. If nothing else, it takes the piss out of it. Anyway, I'm getting off track. I wanted to know about your accent. Not sourpuss over here. Where exactly does it come from?*

Mom held a hand to her heart and her face lit up. *Moi? Oh, I thought you'd never ask. You wait right there, darling. I've got just the thing I'd like to show you. You just stay put.*

Mom set out a dessert plate, dried her hands, and disappeared into the bedroom. Zuk gazed around blandly at our humble little digs and whistled to himself. I looked up at the dustless outline where the brown baby Jesus had been and prayed I'd get through the evening without having to show him the bedroom that Mom and I shared. Mom reappeared with a newspaper clipping. She pushed the cheese, crackers, and grapes aside and laid it delicately over the kitchen table.

Do you know who this is?

The problem with Mom was that she couldn't respect a basic agreement. Never mind that she wasn't wearing the pretty dress she'd promised, she talked peace and love but then came out swinging with her gloves off. She took the viewpoint that Toby should be, if not of universal importance, then at least a household name, right up there with Roosevelt, Stalin, and Churchill, probably. I guess I still didn't see what the big deal was. I mean, the people I went to school with seemed to be doing just fine without having the slightest clue as to who those "instrumental" people were. Toby never got debated, never got argued over, much less celebrated. He was hardly even a footnote. As far as Claremont was concerned, he never existed.

In the center of a big block of text in the article was a photo of Toby, squinting in the sun with a stack pole in hand, handsome faced, with a wide, toothy grin. He looked genuinely happy. Scrawled in the margin were the words *Blakely Register, July 22, 1962.* It was one of the few things that Mom had bothered to pack up and bring with us.

No, Missus F. 'Fraid not.

Well, he was in the papers and everything—even made the national news. Anyway, he was from Akersburg. A real firebrand. We're from the same town. Akersburg. It's in southwest Georgia. 'Bout three hours' drive south of Atlanta, a half hour north of Florida. Deep South.

Mom was staring at the clipping. I could tell that it was taking her back.

So many colored people lynched down there, Missus F. You'll have to excuse me for not being able to put a name to the face.

And why would he? Nothing in that photo of Toby conjured a sense of the impact he'd had on our lives. I suppose that to Zukowski, Toby looked no different than any other colored field hand poking at the dirt as he humbly tended to someone else's beans. So I didn't fault him for that. It just saddened me. Even if it was expected, it saddened me. There was something about his politeness in our conversation about Toby that made his comments feel like they were wrapped in polyurethane.

I got up and pushed in my chair. *C'mon, Zuk. It's almost nine. Whaddya say we wait for your old man downstairs?*

Zukowski pulled the clipping nearer. *Is he a relation?*

No.

Why, Huey!

Blood relation. He meant blood relation. That's what you meant, right?

Mom came over, shoved me out of the way, and pointed at that obituary like it was a cross and she was exorcising me of some cockeyed notion I'd been harboring for once and all. Further down, around the fourth paragraph or so, my name was listed among Toby's surviving family members. She snatched up the nearest pencil and underlined it, repeatedly, until the line was dark and bold.

Of course he is. It's Huey's uncle. He was my half-sister's husband. We're related by marriage. Then to me: *Shame on you. And I will not tolerate you talking about your uncle Toby that way.* Then back to Zukowski: *And if you ask me, it's a crime there isn't a monument to him. Why, he should be buried in Arlington, not some patch of dirt behind the outhouse of a church like some ordinary beggar.*

I had known something like that was going to happen. Just knew it. It was the dark cloud that followed me everywhere. Zukowski cocked his head, looked at me askance for a moment, as if noticing something for the first time, then turned back to that clipping.

What's this?

Just a pile of stack poles.

Stack poles?

Yeah. We used them to hold up our peanut stacks. That's our field there, and those are the peanut stacks. Can we go now?

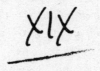

XIX

G̲O̲O̲D̲ M̲O̲R̲N̲I̲N̲G̲,̲ B̲R̲O̲T̲H̲E̲R̲S̲ A̲N̲D̲ S̲I̲S̲T̲E̲R̲S̲. Good morning, Rector Stern. Deacon Willemot. And in particular, I'd like to thank Minister John Stevens for letting us borrow this wonderful church, as well as all the ushers and deacons who have been so generous with their time. As many of you know, there has been great interest in this service. It was not easy to make the necessary arrangements. We've done our best to accommodate as many of you as we can, and so here we are.

The line outside extended all the way around the corner. An old colored man recognized Mom when we got into it, gave her a big hug, and whisked us inside the church. Everyone was sitting down, fanning themselves. Mom was taking her sweet time in the entrance, whispering on and on into that old man's ear.

My apologies in advance to all of you who have been unable to secure a seat. I trust the younger among us will volunteer their seat to that elderly gentleman I see standing there. I see some space over near the back, and here, if anyone would like to claim it. Oh, and here. I see a few latecomers. Please make room.

The old man led Mom down the aisle. Dad pulled me along after them.

By way of a few introductory remarks, I would like to acknowledge Irma Muncie. There are many who did not want this service to proceed. Yet she prevailed in imparting its importance to us all. Needless to say, we would not be assembled here today without her unflagging insistence. I would also like to thank you all for being in attendance. These are tough times, and our accommodations are cramped. Nonetheless, it is an impor-

tant day, and your presence is appreciated. As I said, we are not accustomed to hosting such a large crowd. But interest was overwhelming and, inspired by Irma's steadfastness, we resolved to do what we could. Please accept my apologies in advance, especially to those of you in the back. I've been told that there are still a great many others gathered outside. Know that we're doing the best we can to make room for everyone. Now. Please, folks. Now. The outpouring of sympathy has been tremendous. Irma, my wife, Agnes, and I have been scrambling to deal with the onslaught of reporters. I would like to thank all of you, naturally. These are merely a few of the thoughts that I have had time to jot down for the occasion.

The pastor tapped a sheaf of papers.

The circumstances that bring us together today are quite difficult, as all of you gathered here know. Late Saturday night, a respected member of our community was murdered in cold blood.

Mama, he said—

Shhh!

Now. Now. I would like to emphasize, at this point, that this is not a matter of conjecture, as some have suggested. The police report, which I have examined with my own eyes, states that. Tobias Wetherall Muncie was one of us. Like many of us, he lived in this town his entire life. Akersburg was all Toby knew of the world. And those of us assembled here—the farm hands, janitors, mechanics, and gas-station attendants, and the one stonemason among us—who had the good fortune of knowing Toby know that he did not deserve such an end. But Tobias Muncie was a colored man born into a world where we humans prey upon each other. And so we consequently find ourselves gathered here today asking, are we not all equals in the eyes of God?

Now, brothers and sisters, I recount this brief history of one of our native sons to you with great pain in my heart. But I do so in order that you may better understand the Akersburg that we must deliver from the hands of our shared oppressor. Because Tobias Muncie was a good man. A hardworking man. A family man who stood out only for having asserted his rights. And as we gather here to pay tribute to the uncommon bravery of one who would not submit to their predations, still, we find ourselves asking, are any of us safe in an environment such as this?

Hallelujah!

It was hot and stuffy, and the trickles of sweat crawling down my temple itched. I couldn't wipe them off fast enough. I leaned over and whispered to Mom, asking if she had something for me to fan myself with.

And as we march up Main Street bearing his casket on our shoulders, let us remember that the slander made against the character of the man lying in this box of tinder is a symptom of the many problems ailing our community. As we lay white carnations gently down upon a slab of etched granite, let us remember that the crumbling world of segregation has everything to do with the violence wrought against Tobias Wetherall Muncie. As we stop to shed a tear of remembrance, as our white brothers and sisters heckle us as we join hands in a sliver of cemetery off Ogle-thorpe, let us remember that in a small farming community such as ours, those who are fortunate enough to be blessed with a small holding fear nothing more than the Negro tenant farmer coming into his own form of productivity.

Yessa!

Let us remember, brothers and sisters, that the violence wrought against Tobias Wetherall Muncie is a necessary extension of this fear— that what begins with the right to swim in a white man's pool, or the right of a Negro to work his own bit of land with the same equipment as his white neighbor, ends with a farming contract that was previously white-only. Let us remember, then, when we depart the site of our dear friend's eternal resting place, that those jeering us from within the shade of aging alders have no patience for any brand of justice that threatens their tenuous social standing. But most of all, brothers and sisters, when we're tossed into the back of a paddy wagon, let us remember that fairness may mean nothing to a man holding on to his last grain of food, but it means the world to he who has not even that.

My suit coat felt like a straitjacket. I was struggling to undo the topmost button of my shirt. Mom slapped my hand still.

Let us also remember, then, that brave foot soldier who once said, "I paid my damned twenty cents and I can sit where I want." Let us remember his indomitable grin and unquenchable spirit. Oh yes. It has been a long summer here in Akersburg. There has been too little rain. The hoeing has been difficult, and crop yields stubborn, and tempers running high. Many of the field hands have been at work not out in the fields but in the streets—so have the service women, stock clerks, and attendants. Many of you. Bus service has been suspended, restaurants closed, businesses shuttered and burned. The public library is in a state of indefinite hiatus. Everything is in flux. And still we have had great difficulty winning concessions from the town council, the local merchants' board, the chamber of commerce, the county commissioner, the board of supervisors, and Mayor Simon McDowd himself. But we must not give up our fight. As we look them in the eye, make no mistake—it is a staring contest. And we must not blink. We must continue to fill Mayor McDowd's jails, knowing full well that when they are full, he will call his cousin Asa Grenall in Calhoun County and his brother-in-law Roger Claymore in Baker County and his fishing buddy over in Dougherty and have us taken to one of their jails instead.

And I will have you know, kind brothers and sisters, that so long as not a drop of blood had been shed, I resisted the temptation of inviting outside involvement. Many of you questioned that judgment but accepted the wisdom of not provoking our illustrious sheriff—so long as not a drop of blood had been shed. But, brothers and sisters, what was simmering has now boiled over. And what was bloodless is no longer so. And so I have come to the determination that if justice is frail in our community, then let our brotherhood with the outside world be strong. And so today, we stand together with those who have come from distant places to stand at our side. Yes, brothers and sisters, it has been a very long summer here in Akersburg, indeed.

The pastor stopped. I stood up because I thought he was done. Mom jerked me back into my seat.

Now, let us take a deep breath. And let us take this opportunity to remember that people are tense, that nerves are frayed, and so we must remain calm. Let us carry the Lord in our hearts with every step of our journey. Because Prinket, in all his cunning, will exercise great restraint. But he will do so not out of a sense of decency but out of a desire to undermine us. The eyes of the world are upon him, and his singular boast will be that he has dealt with us "nonviolently." But make no mistake, brothers and sisters, the ends he seeks are the same as those who are trying to put us down in Montgomery. And Selma. And tonight, as we stand, eighty-eight of us in one room with twenty steel bunks and no mattresses, you can judge for yourselves how much more humane. And those of you who aren't in jail with us, please yell out through the thick steel-mesh window and over the cinder-block walls topped with barbed wire that you hear us. Lift our sagging spirits by calling out to us by name. And as we stand inside, shoulder to shoulder, stewing in our own sweat, listening to your voices, let those of us not from these glorious native woods of southwest Georgia remember that the sheriff knows that many of you have hometowns and families and will seek to return to them one day. Yes, I speak to you. And to those of you over there against the wall, bright-eyed and fiery-spirited and filled with hope, who have come to us from places like Missouri and Des Moines and Sacramento, distant places—to all of you whom we are fortunate to have with us: know full well that he will sit back and patiently wait for the day when you grow tired and dispirited, and leave us the way that you found us.

Lord, let us now go peacefully into the light. And whether we take our place in the sheriff's outhouse or that of some other, do not let us forget that there will be busloads behind us filled with mothers and fathers, sisters and brothers, grandmothers and grandfathers, aunts and uncles, nieces and nephews just like all of you, lining up to fill another man's jail. If not today, then tomorrow, and so on, until we achieve the liberties that we seek. Brothers and sisters, are we not tired of the endless accusations made against us? Tired of the contempt felt for us? Tired of living in fear of men hiding under sheets as they burn sticks in a man's front yard? We have had enough. And like our friend, that brave foot soldier, Tobias Wetherall Muncie, who would dare to defy the bit part consigned to him on this, life's grand stage, we too must defy the script others have assigned to us. Akersburg is not a slave ship, brothers and sisters. Akersburg is no plantation. And Boss is not your Creator. For the Lord alone is God of all men.

Let us march off not with spite in our hearts but with love. Now, please, let us bow our heads and pray for peace and reconciliation. That Tobias Wetherall Muncie, a humble man whose memory looms large on this, the twenty-fifth day of July in the year of our Lord nineteen hundred and sixty-two, may somehow bring our beloved community together as one. That we may find the courage to claim our rightful place in this, a community of equals. Amen.

I WAS THE first out of the church that afternoon. I jerked off my coat and mopped the sweat from my face and stood at the top of the steps and looked out over a gathering of what seemed to be every single white resident of Akersburg. Two horse-mounted policemen were stationed on the periphery. Mom snapped at someone behind us to please stop pushing. There was nowhere for us to go. The sheriff's deputies were struggling to keep the mob behind a barricade. I couldn't understand why Toby's death had made them so angry.

Dad headed down the stairs and crossed the street without us. I looked up at Mom. It felt like Armageddon had finally arrived, and he'd forgotten to take us with. The sheriff was leaning against an Oldsmobile parked on the far curb with a helmet on and his arms folded. Mom handed me off to Irma and pressed her way down the steps and across the street, after Dad.

I tried to run after her, but Irma snatched me back. She held me fast against her big, round belly. Mom disappeared behind a patrol car, then reappeared beside the sheriff. Dad was shouting at the sheriff, asking when he was going to clear a path for the people in the church. The sheriff said, *Soon.* Dad was saying, *Now, damn it. There's a pregnant widow back there.* There was no way for her to leave safely. The service was over, and it was important that we all get home before dark. Mom tugged at Dad's arm, yelling for him to stop making trouble. Next thing I knew, she was on the ground. Irma clapped a hand over my eyes. By the time I managed to pry it off, two deputies were hauling Dad off, and Mom was sprawled out in the middle of the street with a bunch of people gathered around. They were taunting her. I hollered out, *Stop!*

The pastor appeared at my side. He begged pardon and made his way down the steps with two deacons. The crowd at the foot of the steps parted. He made his way across the police line and calmly gathered up the stretched-out folds of Mom's dress and picked her up and brushed her off.

Get over here, Pea!

It was Dad. I looked around but I couldn't see him. The pastor returned with Mom in his arms. Her hair had come undone and was twisted out of shape. He propped her up at his side and led her through the crowd, up the stairs.

I'm right here, Mama!

I jumped into her arms and squeezed her tight. She was okay. The people across the street were stabbing the air with their battle flags.

Over here, Pea!

It was Dad's voice again. He was hidden and obscured by the hundreds of people lined up out front, leaning over the sawhorse barricades, pumping their brass knuckles and waving bats. I knew he was close, but I couldn't see him. I slapped the dirt from Mom's front and sat her down on the steps. She was gazing vacantly out at the faces shouting angrily at us. I couldn't bear to even look up. Because I knew them. I covered my ears so that I didn't have to listen to their endless ranting about what awful people we were and how we were to blame for ruining their country.

I looked over my shoulder at the small white clapboard church. The double doors were wide open and a large number of colored people dressed for the service were hunched up together in the doorway, looking out. I didn't even know the pastor, never mind the rest of his congregation. I knew more of them across the street than I did those cowering in the church behind me. It dawned on me that I was sitting on the wrong side of the street. I was supposed to be on the other side, where Dad was. I pulled Mom to her feet and tugged at her arm, figuring that we just needed to cross the street and everything would be okay.

Pea!

I searched the crowd, but between all the shouting faces competing for my attention and Mom resisting my help, there was no way I could find him. There was a convulsion within the crowd of people standing directly in front of me. The crowd swelled briefly, and everyone jumped back.

Dad was suddenly standing right in front of me. I stood up in disbelief. Mister Buford pushed him out of the crowd toward me. *Go on back to your nigger!*

I forced my way down the steps and through the crowd, all the while shouting out to Dad that I was coming. Mister Buford had jumped on top of Dad and started punching him. I squeezed past a tangle of policemen standing beside a tipped-over barricade. I could tell that Dad had heard me because he held his hand out. I reached out for it but was jerked back just as I touched it.

It was Missus Orbach. She barked out that she was sick and tired of seeing me everywhere and jerked me around by my necktie and dragged me off with her. I stomped on her foot and scrambled away before she knew what had hit her. But it was too late. Dad was sprawled out over the wide asphalt street, shielding his face. Mister Buford was still on top of him, slugging away. Missus Krasinski was standing there, beating him with her purse and hollering out so loud little bits of spit were flying from her mouth. *Get him, Lance! Get him good!*

I jumped onto Mister Buford's back and yelled for him to stop. I hadn't gotten two licks in when Missus Krasinski teed off on Dad's face with her heeled shoe. Dad went limp. I let go of Mister Buford and reached out for Dad's hand. I clutched it, but his cold and clammy fingers slipped away. I knelt down beside the gash in his face, put a hand over the blood spilling out, and shook him.

Pop? Wake up!

Dad groaned. I looked up at Missus Krasinski.

LOOK WHAT YOU'VE DONE!

She was heaving, her purse strap doubled up in one hand, and her face was expressionless. I turned to the other men and women standing beside her.

Missus Henniger? Mister Chambers? Mister Hildebrandt? Mister Orbach? Missus Baxter? DON'T JUST STAND THERE! DO SOMETHING!

When they didn't move, I stood up, smeared the tears from my face, and started dragging Dad through a pool of his own blood. Mom appeared at my side. Together we got him across the street. Aurelia, Evan, and Irma were waiting for us. They stepped aside and let us in.

THE EARLY-MORNING SUN FLICKERING AROUND the edges of the broken front window seemed to cast Toby in a different light. I was sitting against a wall inside the church, staring at his casket. It wasn't until the gray hours before dawn that the uproar outside had ebbed and a smoky sunlight washed out that of the torch flames that had raged outside all night. I couldn't see much, but I could hear everything. I had sat huddled beside Dad in a back corner of the church, far from the front windows. Dad was on his back, holding his nose straight. Mom was dabbing his forehead with a damp towel. Mister Swanson popped up at one point and suggested that it might be light enough to leave. Dad hesitated, but I begged him please. My arm felt like it was about to fall off.

Yet another heckle and jeer rang out. A brick crashed through the window. Glass sprayed over the floor. There was renewed commotion about how best to avoid the few lingerers remaining outside. I gazed around at the others crowded inside the church. Most were intent on waiting for help to arrive from Albany. They didn't want to be caught out on back roads alone before full light. Which left me and my aching arm. We bid the others farewell and left by the back door.

When we got to our truck, we found the windows busted and the tires slit, so we got a lift from Mister Swanson. The sun hadn't crept over the horizon yet, but the sky was lit. The fresh smell of dew seeped in through Mister Swanson's cracked front window. And as we made our way down the windy back roads that I knew so well, I thought about how strange it felt, after all these years, to be riding shotgun in Mister

Swanson's Plymouth. It wasn't new, but the window roller worked, and there were no springs poking out of the seat cushion. Mom and Dad were jammed into the backseat along with Irma and Evan. They were each looking out their respective windows with blank expressions on their faces. No one seemed to have anything to say.

Mister Swanson dropped us off at the top of our drive and sped off. A gush of fatigue hit me like a tidal wave. I headed straight for my room and dove into bed. Didn't even take off my suit.

I don't know how long it was before Mom or Dad came into my room, but I remember a lot of wet washcloths and Mom pleading with Dad to call Mister Hofstetter. She couldn't bring herself to call him "Dr." on account of some comment he'd made to her when she was a young girl. Things came back to me in dribs and drabs, like the feverish dreams that replayed the image of Toby in that open casket. I had visions in my sleep of having been held hostage in that church, with a crowd gathered outside trying to rescue me. Flares zipped across the night sky. Rappel lines hung from swirling helicopters. Hand grenades and tear-gas canisters were tossed through the window.

My bed was soaked. I was burning up. I think my temperature spiked to 200 degrees with the realization that the crowd wasn't there to rescue me but to hang me alive. There was a bounty on my head, and every single white person in Early County, with the single exception of Dad, wanted to string me up out front. It was set up in my dream just like those public hangings you see in cowboy movies, where the actual hanging is nowhere near as bad as all the hate-filled invective that precedes it.

I also had a foggy recollection of the racket Dr. Hofstetter made tripping up our front steps and the loud thumping sound his shoes made across our creaky pine floor before my bedroom door swung open and he sat down beside me with that stale cigar in his mouth and fumbled through his medicine bag.

Hold still, son. This is gonna hurt.

That's my good arm!

I yelped, then fell back in bed. Dr. Hofstetter gave me a congratulatory pat on the shoulder and said that the needle was supposed to go in my good arm. He took one look at Dad and told him to take me straight to Putney.

Dad was in a pickle because the truck was still sitting in town, vandalized. He had no choice but to take the tractor. All these years of me wanting to ride on the back of that thing, and here my overprotective dad was tossing me on the back of it, limp as a sack of peanuts and with a fever of sky high. I was in and out of consciousness the whole way. But what I remember of it was good. It was so thrilling, I almost didn't mind nearly falling off at every bend.

Dad carried me through the front door, where a nurse took one look at my arm and asked how long it'd been like that. I'd broken out in a cold sweat, and my breaths were short. Next thing I knew, they put me on one of the unused gurneys lining the wall and rolled me off to some ICU room and pumped me full of penicillin to fight some sort of blood poisoning. How I got that, I have no idea. The doctor pulled out a jigsaw and said he was going to have to remove my cast to see what was going on. I thought he was about to take my arm off and screamed in panic. Two nurses held me down, and the doctor said something about the rubber bands that I couldn't hear before he cracked my cast open with his bare hands. Several of my stitches had opened up and seemed to have festered. A thick white mucousy goo was seeping out and smelled so bad that the nurses made faces.

The doctor said that the infection had spread from the wound to my blood and that Dad had gotten me there in the nick of time. He asked me if I'd experienced joint stiffness and then nodded when I said yes, like he wasn't one bit surprised. Said I was lucky not to have any neurological complications, whatever that meant. Dad asked if I'd have to get my stomach pumped. The doctor said no, he'd just put me on a heavy regimen of antibiotics—at which point my mouth went dry. The doctor took Dad by the arm and led him into the adjoining room. Said that he wanted to have a look at the gash on his face.

It wasn't until my third day there that they got the infection under control and someone realized that the bone wasn't healing right. This doctor was apparently some sort of bone specialist. The young Dr. Beck (or Smeck or Heck—something like that) speculated that I'd experienced some sort of highly unusual form of blunt trauma early on to the proximal region of my arm. He turned to me and asked if perhaps I'd fallen off a bicycle—said it was okay for me to admit to having ridden a bicycle with a broken arm. I wouldn't be the first to have done so. He glanced at Dad and said that I wouldn't get in trouble, right? I shook my head, no. I didn't have a bicycle.

He cleared his throat and held the radiograph up to the light, then explained how it showed that there was a highly irregular rotation of the flexor digitorum sublimis so that the bone's normal orientation was skewed. Called it a displacement fracture, or re-rupture—said it was the result of my arm having been twisted radially with the cast on. He demonstrated on Dad the vector, angle, and force necessary to cause such an abnormality. I didn't understand any of it, of course. All I knew was that my arm hardly felt connected to my shoulder.

When Dad responded with a blank stare, Dr. Beck said that my ulna was healing out of whack and wasn't properly aligned with the radius. The upshot was that disfigurement was inevitable unless something drastic was done.

Whoa, whoa, whoa. Slow down, Doc. You just took a hard left on me. Did you just say "disfigurement"?

Dr. Beck took off his glasses. He looked Dad straight in the eye and said that the only thing he could do to make my arm heal straight would be to break it again. In response to which Dad walked a small circle while pinching the topmost part of his nasal bone.

I know I'm just a peanut farmer, Doc, but wouldn't that be the third time? And on the same arm?

Dr. Beck took a good hard look at Dad. *I'm not here to sugarcoat things for you, Mister Fairchild.*

Dr. Beck explained that our only hope was that maybe it would heal straighter the third time around. To do that, he'd have to effectively start from scratch. I suddenly felt light-headed, like I probably shouldn't be hearing this. I closed my eyes and imagined my arm in a vise, with some doctor in a lab coat taking a baseball bat to it. I heard Dad whisper, *Isn't there some sort of limit to how many times you can do that, Doc?*

Dr. Beck called Dad aside. They moved farther down the wide, shiny tiled hall, out of earshot. After a lengthy conference in the midst of nurses busily entering and exiting the rooms on either side of them, they were both towering in front of me, agreeing that a third break wouldn't be necessary. Which, in a sense, was good news. Or was it? All that medicine must have been making me stupid. I didn't even know the difference between good news and bad news anymore. I mean, sure I didn't want to have it broke again, but neither did I want to be—well. You know. The *d* word.

What about, you know—the deformity?

Dr. Beck said that it would be merely an aesthetic concern. The functional impact to my elbow, wrist, and fingers would be negligible. Dad seemed to think it'd be okay. So I did, too. The doctor had me stay one more night, to be on the safe side. The next day, they ran some more tests, after which they plastered me back up and sent me on my way.

DAD DIDN'T SAY a word on the drive home. We sat at the railroad crossing, watching a wall of ochre-colored boxcars and rust-colored boxcars and navy-colored boxcars rumble past, one after the next. It felt weird being stuck in that truck with him, in silence, after three whole days of having a chatty hospital staff wanting to know every last thing about me. Part of me wished my fingers would swell up again if it'd get him to say something.

So you fixed the truck?

Hm.

New tires?

Hm.

All of 'em, or just the ones that got slashed?

Dad looked over, distracted. *Huh? Oh. Not the windows, though. They're still busted. I just keep them rolled down. Until we get some more money coming in.*

At least the truck was still good for getting a few words out of him. The caboose whooshed past, and the *clang clang clanging* railroad crossing gate lifted. We crept over the double bump of the railroad tracks. Dad looked over and said how happy Mom would be to have me home. After that, he scratched at the thick scab set across the bridge of his nose and went quiet again.

Dad tapped the horn as we pulled into our drive. Mom appeared in the doorway before the engine stopped knocking. I jumped into her arms. She held me tight and said she was sorry she hadn't been able to come to the hospital. It was only because she didn't want trouble. It'd been three days but it felt like two months.

Dad and Mom looked at each other and hugged. Then they kissed, and we all embraced. It was the first time I'd seen them do that in a long time. We all just missed each other. We headed inside, and Dad pleaded for Mom to please go easy on me. He understood the temptation but thought that kind of gushing love was only good when applied sparingly. Thought I might still be adjusting and didn't want to see me in shock or something.

Mom told Dad to hush and tucked me into bed and brought me a tray with chocolate milk and oatmeal cookies and a tiny little vase with some of her petunias from out back. She placed it on my nightstand and told me to get some rest. She kissed me on the cheek and stroked my hair and told me again how great it was to have me back. Said it was the longest three days of her life. I dozed off before she finished drawing the curtain.

I slept like a rock that night. I remember waking up groggy from all the medicine and being half asleep and slapping around on my end table in the dark for some water and overhearing Mom and Pop talking tenderly and sharing in laughter in the kitchen. Whatever problems we'd had seemed to be all fixed. Somehow the events at Toby's service, along with my subsequent hospital stint and maybe even Dad's fistfight with Mister Buford, had brought us all together. I was happy to have my family back.

I felt like a new person the next day. I sat up in bed with my comic books and let Mom and Dad wait on me hand and foot. All I had to do was to cough, and one of them would poke their head in the room and ask if I needed anything. Seemed that every few hours, one of them would stick their head in the doorway and remind me to take my medicine.

The new cast the doctor had put on me was somehow getting the respect the first one never got. No more scrubbing dishes—I didn't even have to carry my dirty plate to the sink. No one bothered me about the mess in my room. Mom even offered to help me brush my teeth that first night. I finally had the time I needed to finish the puzzle I'd started at the beginning of summer. Dad didn't leave the house, which was unusual. He usually went out at least once a day to do something important in town. But he just said that he was working on something out in the shed and that he wanted to stay close to me.

Then, after dinner, Dad told me that I could stay up and watch a ball game with him if I wanted. "If I wanted?" He never let me stay up late. I sat down on the sofa and kissed my new cast. It seemed to have the power to work miracles. Mom was in the kitchen, doing Miss Della's hair. They'd been in there for a good hour or so together. Miss Della was going on about all the people she'd known who had left and were now living these interesting lives up North. Dad turned up the volume of the game. He wasn't interested in hearing Mom gabbing on to Miss Della about how she had no delusions about his family. I popped into the kitchen to scrounge myself up a cookie. I froze at the mention of Connie. Mom never talked about Connie.

Mom had a comb in her teeth and was combing out Miss Della's hair in her fingers, saying how she did what she always did in the face of slander—especially when it came from one whose primary grievance was a pitted heart. Miss Della said, *Oh child.* Mom said she simply swallowed her pride and took what little comfort she could from the fact that the man sitting in the other room hadn't left her when she was carrying. Miss Della said, *Hm.* Mom said men were a dime a dozen, but those men weren't. Miss Della said, *Hm.* Because he could have, Mom said. Miss Della said, *Hm.*

Carrying what?

They both looked up. They hadn't realized I was there.

Boy, you go back into that room and watch yourself some TV. Go on, get. Don't make me get out of this chair, young man.

I held up my new cast and didn't move. They sighed and turned back to each other. Mom said "that" seemed to her to be proof enough that he was a decent man. A man not so much of distinction or refinement as of a prominent family and who had always treated her decently. She claimed that must count for something. Miss Della said, *Hm.*

Miss Della pursed her lips and let Mom talk. Mom acknowledged that it was a modest victory but merely claimed that it was a victory nonetheless and that while these weren't exactly the happiest of times, she was clutching onto it for dear life. Miss Della said, *Hm, hm.* Mom put clips in Miss Della's hair and said, *Just wait. You'll see.*

Mom reached to the counter for more clips and assured Miss Della that her man was better than most. Miss Della said, *Hm.* His brave actions at the church proved that—again and again, he'd proven it. And when would people just let up and accept that he wasn't the lecherous wretch they were making him out to be? Because it was no different than her not being the lecherous person Connie was always making her out to be. Dad had proven beyond any doubt that she could count on him in a pinch. Not to cut and run, like so many others did these days. Miss Della said, *Hm. Hm. Hm.*

Mom paused.

What is wrong with people? They've got it all backward. Him being moody doesn't mean he's in cahoots with this group or that group. He's no renegade. That's part of his charm. That his love for me is not political is a good thing. Doesn't that make his love better? More pure? Damn it, he's not political, he's pigheaded. Love isn't black or white for him. A little blinding, perhaps. But isn't that just the way it's supposed to be?

Hm. Hm. Hm. Hm. Hm. Della sat there quietly appraising Mom. Her gaze was steady, if doubtful. *Child, you light-skinned niggers are all the same. You think that just because you've weathered a few storms, you're going to be okay in a hurricane. Now, put on more of that grease and let me out of this chair. It's almost eight, and I gotta get back to the Orbachs' to wash up from their supper.*

The TV roared. I returned to the den and checked on the ball game. The last time Dad had let me stay up this late, he'd gotten me out of bed to watch Roger Maris jogging around the bases to thunderous applause. Dad had told me to pay attention. Said that I must never forget that moment, because someday I'd have kids of my own and he wanted me to be able to share with them how I was standing there beside him, my own pop, staring into the glare of the TV on the evening when baseball's longest-standing record was broken. He didn't call it baseball history—he called it human history, the history of men. He put a hand on my shoulder and said that he wanted to share it with me.

Remember Maris's home run last year?

Dad nodded. *Over the right-field wall. Three hundred and forty-eight feet. Home run number sixty-one for the year.*

Mom hollered out from the kitchen, wondering if World War III had broken out and nobody was bothering to tell her. Miss Della was gathering up her things. She joked that if Castro managed to get his hands on a missile, at least she'd go down with pretty hair. When Dad told them that Bob Burda had hit an eleventh-inning walk-off home run for the Crackers, they responded with a communal shrug.

I put my arms around Dad's waist and held him tight. The warmth between us filled me with joy. Dad shook his head and turned off the TV. Said it was time for bed—I had a big workday tomorrow. The screen went blank and Dad went into the kitchen. I stood there staring at the dark screen and thought about the time Toby and I had used a broken stack pole to tee off on the rotting peaches lying along the side of the road.

EARLY THE NEXT morning, Dad told me to sort through some stack poles. Said we were behind on a bunch of stuff and he needed me to pick out a hundred good ones by the end of the day. Once I was done, it'd be the end of sorting poles for the season. He apologized, because he knew I still wasn't one hundred percent, but asked me to just suck it up and to finish strong. Then he disappeared into the bathroom with a newspaper in hand. I didn't say anything, but I think he could tell by the look on my face that I wasn't happy about it.

The thought of picking up just one more cockamamie stack pole made me tired. A *hundred?* It would require going through a thousand to pick out that many good ones. I dragged my feet out onto the back stoop and stared out at that pile of stack poles that, no matter how many I'd sorted through and no matter how many we'd repaired, never got smaller. I resented them. They were ruining my life, and I just wanted them to go away. Why couldn't Dad just have been a stupid housekeeper or hairdresser or bookkeeper, like Mom?

Finishing strong was overrated. I'd been in the hospital, was still having medicine shoved in my face four times a day, and, frankly, was still recovering. Sure, I felt a lot better, but that was all the more reason to continue taking it easy. Apparently, it was working—I hadn't been in a hospital for three whole days just so he could dump more work on me.

I popped into the shed and riffled through the gloves and drill bits and screwdrivers covering Dad's workbench. I snatched a jar of paint thinner and a box of matches, paused in the doorway, and glanced back inside. There was a stack of boards leaning against the wall that I hadn't seen before. A big box of nails and a hammer was sitting on a chair beside it. I had no idea what he was making. All I knew was that he should have been helping me sort through stack poles instead of parking himself on the john for hours at a time while I was left to do the heavy lifting.

The pile of stack poles loomed like a mountain beside our house. It reached well above the eaves. I climbed up it with paint thinner and matches in hand, careful not to slip, all the way to the creaky top. I was momentarily distracted by the view. It was magnificent. Everything seemed familiar and new at the same time. The sun was just now emerging over the tree line. Shards of sunlight burst through the trees. The rolling hills and wide-open landscape was shrouded in an early-morning mist that had not yet burnt off. I could smell it in everything around me: the trees, the shrubs, and the dirt road, even the stack poles. I could even make out the top of a building downtown. Of all things, it was a damned church spire. It looked so small and insignificant surrounded by all this natural beauty, swaddled as it was in a sprawling countryside, connected to everything around it by threads of road.

I screwed off the top of the paint thinner and poured it out. I hadn't even wanted to look in that casket, but Mom had taken me by the hand and dragged me down the nave to the flower-draped corpse anyway. I'd never seen so many of those stupid little purple wildflowers in one place. God only knows how long it took Evan to collect them all. I spilled some paint thinner on my hands and was concerned that Mom might be able to smell it. I pulled out the matches anyway. Striking them with a broken arm was easier said than done; the whole box flew out of my hand and tumbled down the stack like it was happy to be free. I screwed the top back on the jar, and on my way back down after them, I told myself how it wasn't going to be so much a pyre as a distress call. I was sick of feeling isolated. After Derrick, Toby had practically been my best friend, but I'd gone from feeling that I'd always known him to feeling like I'd never known him at all.

I was halfway down that rat's nest of dried sweet gum when Mom hollered out for me to come in. I froze. The piled creaked. The matchbox had wedged itself among several stack poles. I stuck my arm in after it as Mom barked out again, wanting to know what I was doing. She said for me to change out of my brand-new sneakers because they weren't for wearing outside before school had started.

I looked up. *The backyard don't count! It's hardly considered outside! And if you'd get out of this stinking house more often, you'd know that!*

Mom stepped down from the stoop. She climbed atop the pile of stack poles in her house shoes and bathrobe, after me. She snatched me by the wrist and hauled me down alongside her, teetering the whole way.

What do you think you're doing, Mister? It's not enough you have a broken arm? You want to break your neck, too?

She paused. *What's that smell?*

What smell?

On your hands. Christ almighty, you been drinking moonshine again? Let me smell your breath.

I stormed off to my room and tossed myself atop my bed and curled up with my favorite comic book. When I looked up from *Sea Devils*, Snowflake was dashing around erratically in her cage. She had always been a source of comfort for me in times of family strife. Just holding her relaxed me—something about the softness of her fur, the reassurance of her heartbeat. She was anxious about something. I lifted her out and took her over to the window. I held her over the ledge and gave her a peck on the fluffy scruff of her neck and told her that I was sorry for being her oppressor. But I was a changed man now. I was finally ready to do the right thing. I leaned over the ledge and let her go. Mom's petunia bed sat beneath my window. Snowflake bounced once, but otherwise landed fine. She only took out a few flowers.

You're free! Now go!

Snowflake scampered over to the railroad tie upon which our house sat. She clawed at it.

Not up here, you idiot! That way, damn it! Go!

She looked up at me with those beady little eyes of hers and continued clawing at the railroad tie.

Goddamnit, you stupid little beanbag! Don't you get it? You're free! Now go!

A hawk carving broad circles high up in the brightly lit sky screeched. Snowflake looked confused and darted off. She had the whole open field, acres upon acres of food so good you couldn't buy it in a pet store—all the yummy dried peanuts and hay that an animal like her could possibly dream of. And where did she go? Dumb shit scurried under the house. I leaned farther out the window, the better for her to hear me.

You want me to lock you back up, is that it? Well, I'm not doing it! It ain't right!

I went into the den and sat down in front of the TV, disillusioned. All I had wanted was for her to see her newfound freedom for the peace offering that it was. Toby had always said that when something was broke, you fixed it. Here I had tried to honor his memory and done just that, and it only seemed to turn out worse.

I flipped through the channels. The only thing on was Governor Vandiver standing at a podium, saying something about having to call in the National Guard. There were lots of flashes of light bursting in his face. Cameras clicked and snapped, and flashbulbs were popping all around him. The last press conference I'd seen, General Harkins was hogging all three channels, bragging about a coming troop buildup. Dad had said for me to pay attention because the man on TV was talking about important stuff. Turner Airfield was up the road, and half of the airmen they'd need were bound to come through town on their way to training. I'd come across a few of them enjoying a little R&R at Mister Abrams's pool once or twice. Others bought half-pound bags of boiled peanuts from me on their way through town. They loved 'em. So I kind of knew them. Those were the things Dad worried about— real problems. The kind that required soldiers.

Anyway, Harkins was a real dumb shit if you ask me. Here Dad had been watching so much news yapping about the coming offensive for the last six months, I probably knew more about it than the general. The only surprise to me was that Ho Chi Minh and those damned Vietcong didn't know who the hell Walter Cronkite was.

I turned the volume down at the mention of Toby—not on TV but in the kitchen. Mom and Dad were at it again. Why did it seem that peace and harmony were only ever a highly contingent state of affairs in our house? Dad was in the kitchen rummaging through the drawers, looking for the insurance papers for the truck, all the while grilling Mom about whether she'd sent out the last payment on time.

The twenty-seventh, damn it! The premium was due on the twenty-seventh! You're supposed to know that!

Mom was holed up in the bathroom, shouting from behind the door. *Of course I know that! Keep looking. It's in there somewhere!*

I peeked in to see what she was doing and caught a glimpse of her sitting atop the toilet, secretively unclumping bills from the coffee tin. Mom slammed the door in my face and told me to mind my own business. The lock clicked. I went to the kitchen doorway. It was still hard for me to look at Dad without staring at his busted-up nose, the stitches above his eye, and the scab on his fat lower lip.

Here. Now leave her alone. She paid it, okay? It was in the bureau, mixed in with the unpaid bills.

Dad snatched it out of my hand and left for the front door. He opened it and looked around, then called me to his side. He said for me to forget about the sorting for now and told me instead to get the hammer from the shed. And nails. Said for me to bring the whole box.

I plopped myself back in front of the TV and announced that I wasn't moving a muscle—at least not until he told me what he was making. I was starting to suspect that it was a coffin, which I didn't want any part of. At least not until I knew who it was for. Besides, the governor was on the tube, saying something important—about what, I couldn't say just yet.

Dad cracked a grin and gave me an aw-shucks look. He said that he was happy to have me back to my old self.

Say, Pop, why do they have two dozen photographers there taking the exact same picture? Wouldn't it be smarter just to have one? I mean, he could share it around with the others instead of having fifty guys taking the same photo of the same man at the exact same time. Doesn't make sense to me.

Why did Pickett's Charge fail at Gettysburg? Why'd the Red Sox let Ruth go? Why is Ford holding out on fuel injection? Huey, a lot of things don't make any sense. That's just the way the world is. Might as well get used to it.

No wonder the world's going to hell in a handbasket.

Without a doubt. Huey, the world just lacks basic rudimentary skills of coordination and cooperation.

But I thought that's what kindergarten was for?

Dad nodded. He was outside, setting up the ladder beneath the front picture window. The sofa sat directly beneath it. From where I was sitting, in his easy chair, he appeared framed like in a portrait in the window. He teetered atop the ladder, fumbling around with Toby's tool belt slung over his shoulder and a board in his hands, hammering. I couldn't hear a thing Governor Vandiver was saying. Dad couldn't have picked a worse time to be putting up siding. I got up from the TV, went over to the sofa, and knocked on the window.

I can't hear the TV!

Dad had four nails poking out of his mouth. He couldn't hear me over his hammering. He wasn't interested in listening to what I had to say, and didn't seem to care about the governor's statement, either. He didn't have time for press conferences. This was a time for action. The bathroom door burst open. Mom appeared in the doorway with her coffee tin in one hand and a wad of lumpy bills in the other.

Twenty years, and this is what Toby has to show for it? That's not right, Buck—and you know it. And what the hell has all this got to do with swimming in a damned pool anyway? I really hope those swim lessons were worth it, Buck Fairchild. Because now you got people back there crying over a damned white man's swimming pool. And you know who I blame? Stanley for building that stupid damned pool and you for taking Huey to swim in it. I don't care what people say, the law's the law. And swimming in a damned pool isn't going to change a goddamned thing but where white folks go to swim!

Mom couldn't let go of that damned pool to save her life. Dad stopped hammering and pulled a nail from his mouth. He mumbled something through the glass about how first it was all about how she was going to take me there herself, and now she wouldn't let me near the place if it was the last thing she did, and to just make up her damned mind because it was confusing him. He was having a hard time keeping up with her constantly changing opinions. Said they were like clothes she was trying on to see how they fit, and when was she going to understand that they weren't going to fit her at all because they were cheap thrift-shop clothes that you buy by the pound, not the inch?

It was impossible to hear Vandiver fielding a bunch of reporter's questions. Mom began to sob. It was a strange mix of sounds: Mom crying and the TV droning and Dad mumbling with nails poking out of his mouth behind the window.

I swear on my grandmother's grave that I meant to let Toby have a go at it on his own. I just needed a little more time. A little more time, that's all! A man has got to be able to do things in his own time!

Twenty godforsaken years! And his father worked for your father for forty more—as did his father before him. And he's got absolutely nothing to show for it but this and a four-by-six plot out behind Mount Jacob! It was long overdue that you put a stop to it—and you wouldn't have ever put a stop to it. And that's on you!

I know that! You don't think I know that? I just hadn't known what I'd do without him. Okay? I don't have a problem admitting that. What's fair is fair. Of course he could have done a fine job on his own. I know that. Hell, there's no question that he knew what he was doing.

Mom sat down on the sofa and buried her face in her hands. I went over and sat beside her and stroked her back as she cried into the coffee tin. I took her hands in mine and steadied them. Dad was hammering directly behind us. It wasn't until the light started to fade in the living room that I realized what he was doing. I turned around and asked Dad if there was a hurricane coming. He said maybe, but hopefully not. Mom got up and turned on the overhead light. Dad's hammering stopped. He peeked beneath the last board yet to cover the window before his hurricane shutters cut out the last of the light coming through it.

Listen—it doesn't even matter if he did it or not. Okay? People just had it out for him. There. I said it. Happy?

XXI

MOM AND DAD'S CHECKERED PAST got dragged into everything that night. Eventually they exhausted each other's sense of outrage, the cash got put back into the coffee tin, the coffee tin got returned to the cupboard, and a tenuous quiet overtook the house. Dad was in the kitchen, sipping Mister Nelson's moonshine from a short glass. He was staring into space with a tired expression on his face. I'd come in for a glass of milk, glanced at him, then went back to my room and my *Sea Devils*. When I returned a half hour later for a refill, he was still sitting there with the same look on his face.

Dad looked down into the half-empty glass sitting in front of him, emptied it, and left the room. He mussed up my hair on his way past, reclaimed his easy chair, and flipped through the TV channels. I closed the door to the fridge and took a seat. Mom was quietly knitting at the kitchen table. She asked to see my arm. I stretched my cast out over the table and asked how she was doing. She took my fingers into hers and said that she was fine. She just wished there was more humor in our lives.

Dad was watching TV with the volume turned low and the light off in the den. The dark doorway was intermittently lit by flashes of light from the TV. Mom pressed her lips into a grin and asked if I'd read her one of my poems.

Mom always liked it when I read to her. So I dug out my notebook from my bedroom, returned to the kitchen, and leaned in the open doorway in a pair of her big Jackie Kennedy–style sunglasses. I'd gotten them from atop her bureau. Mom thought that my poems were a good way to lighten the mood. She was probably in the mood for something like Jack Benny. Unfortunately, I was intent on serving up something a little more *Prufrock*. I flipped through my notebook until I found something appropriate.

Here. We'll start with this one. It's short. You like the short ones, right? Good. It's dedicated to you, Mama. I hope you like it.

Mom sat up, pleased. I remained silent until I had her undivided attention, then began.

> *A barnacled oyster marks the spot*
> *where my dreams like carrion rot.*
> *The pearl it drifted not away*
> *like sea foam lifted from the bay*
> *but was surrendered to Old Saint Peat*
> *slain tiller at my feet*
> *where scattered pearls like dead seed lie*
> *ravenous birds try feed, then fly . . .*
> *Why saint of straw for seed did burn?*
> *In blood red battlefield upturned*
> *an empty shell marks the spot*
> *where I, his pearl, in darkness rot.*

Mom snatched my notebook out of my hand, flipped through its pages disapprovingly, then tossed it atop the table and led me into the bathroom.

You're starting to look like one of those damned renegades. Write like one, too.

Mom cut up two plastic bags and tied them around my cast without so much as looking at me.

It wasn't funny, Huey. Not one bit. Poems are supposed to be funny and light. You know? Breezy. The rhymes were okay, but everything else was terrible. Terrible.

I knew it wasn't what she'd expected, but I thought that the idea was for me to write down my feelings. I'd spent two days trying to do exactly what she'd told me. Followed her instructions to a T. Maybe a little too well. Only Mom could get that upset for something not being funny enough.

I undressed and got in the bath. Mom draped a towel over my shoulders and combed my hair back. She said that it didn't matter that Dad had Missus Mayapple when he was my age. My first day of third grade was going to be a different affair entirely. It was to be the start of a brand-new chapter.

Hot water was coming out of the cold spigot and vice versa. At least it wasn't leaking. I made the adjustment, and it felt good. I leaned back and poured some over my face. I dunked my head, careful to keep my cast out of the water, then kept still for Mom.

Why did the pastor insist that Toby was murdered when we all know he fell from Mister Buford's ladder?

You heard Pastor Meade. He said it was conjecture.

What's that?

When something sounds like it could be true but isn't. It's just like when people talk about crazy stuff like evolution, dear—we say that's conjecture. There's no accounting for what some people will believe. Mom smiled primly and kept snipping.

Well, who are we going to get to replace him?

It's still too soon to be thinking about that, dear. But I'll tell you this much—no matter who we end up with, or how hardworking and reliable and trustworthy the person, there is and will only ever be one Toby.

I splashed at the water. Part of me just wanted to shout out, *But what about me?* I knew it required a leap of faith, not to mention a great deal of imagination, but I was sure that I could be as good as Toby one day. When I asked about the people making ape noises outside the church, she went quiet. When she finally spoke, her voice was low.

Jesus only assigns each of us the burdens in life that we can bear, dear. It's important that you remember that. No matter how difficult life's challenges, you must never forget that. Besides, I'm not even sure that they were mocking apes so much as just acting like apes themselves.

Mom kept snipping.

Am I a bad person if I don't like everybody, Mama? Does that make me a bad person? I mean, I don't have to like everybody, do I?

It's not a requirement that you do. But it'd be nice if you tried.

Are you just saying that because people think you're colored?

The scissors went still. *What on earth do you mean by that?*

Because of your hair. You've got colored people's hair. I know that's why people were calling you names. Being mean to you. Saying those things to you.

Mom stood up straight. *Why, yes. Yes, I suppose some do.*

And you're sure Toby fell from a ladder?

Be still, Huey. I'd hate to snip your ear.

It must have been a really tall one. To die like that. Whammo! Smack against the ground.

A very tall one indeed. It had to be, to reach all the way up to the roof of Mister Buford's barn. He was probably just going too fast, trying to get the last of the roofing shingles up before the weather turns cold.

You said he was fixing the weather vane.

What difference does it make?

I had to think about that. Maybe she was right. I asked whether the Toby that we knew was the same Toby that all those people gathered outside the church were protesting.

I can assure you, Huey, the Toby we knew broke no law. And if by some stretch of the imagination he did, it must have been some very unjust law indeed, because I will personally vouch to you right here that he was as upstanding a citizen as any in all of Early County. And that's a fact. Lord knows he didn't have much else in life. I'll be damned if people aren't dissatisfied until they've taken his dignity away from him, too.

Mom didn't say anything else. She just kept snipping. My hair was starting to pile up in the tub, floating atop the water. Lots and lots of it just kept showering down in thin sheets. It was sticking to the back of my neck, the tops of my shoulders, and all over my arms. It even got in my ears. It was itching like crazy. I told her to stop for a second just so I could scratch. When I peeked in the mirror, I saw that my hair was so short that she may as well have been using a buzz cutter. Only I had wanted a flattop—the way Dad had it.

Hey. Watch it! You know that's not how I like it! You're taking off way way too much!

Mom's hand was suddenly stiff and her clipping accelerated. One hand held the back of my head still, and the other clipped. I felt like I'd said something wrong.

Well, don't get mad at me. I was just wondering.

The scissors went still.

No matter how different from us that Toby may have seemed to you, you must never forget that what matters most is that he was a family man whose only crime in life was that he happened to be a colored man who sought to protect and provide for the welfare of his loved ones—no different than any other man, white, black, brown, purple, or green. He was a hardworking, honest, decent family man. Just like the good pastor Meade said. No matter what others may say about him, you must never forget that. So please get it through that thick head of yours that there was only one Toby—the one we knew, loved, and trusted, and who was always better to us than he had reason to be. Why on earth is that so hard for you to believe?

I dunno.

Actually, I did. All the conflicting stories were playing tug-of-war in my head. What confused me was that I had her saying one thing, Derrick insisting on pretty much the opposite, and Dad saying something still altogether different. I was starting to wonder if maybe Toby was a mixture of all three, or none at all. What was it? Here I'd known him my whole life, and it turns out he was a stranger to me. I was starting to feel that I'd never known him at all. Love him? Hate him? Trust him? Suspect him? Did it even matter anymore? Who the hell knew which to believe? It was impossible to make heads or tails of anything anymore. The only thing I knew for sure was that he was dead—and even that I'd doubted for one panicky moment in front of S&W. And I only knew it for a fact because I had seen him lying there in that casket with my own two eyes. Truth be told, I wasn't even sure of that. He was so messed up I couldn't even recognize him. The corpse in front of me was roughly his height, so I just figured that it probably was him. Who else could it possibly have been?

Derrick had once claimed, *Once a criminal, always a criminal.* It was something about the criminal instinct—how once it got in you, there was no getting it out. There was no cure for it, no penicillin or anything you could take three times a day. You were infected for life. And like all things in life, some people were just more prone to it than others. There was nothing you could do about it, when and if you were one of the unlucky ones struck by it. Which sounded about right. Because there were diseases that I knew were just like that. Take polio, for example.

You see, petty disputes aside, what I liked most about Derrick was that he kept things simple. With him, I could always count on getting the raw, uncooked truth—not the one that had been boiled half to death and deep-fried in bacon fat to make it taste good. What I mean is, I wanted the world as it was, not as Mom desired me to see it. Her views on things required too much work for me to even begin to get my head around them. As much as I wanted to believe that Toby had done nothing wrong, the cold hard facts were starting to pile up like a bunch of thick, wavy black hair after an unwanted buzz cut. And it wasn't just Derrick. It was practically everyone. Just you tell me how so many people can be wrong.

XXII

THAT NIGHT OF THE DINNER was a turning point in our relationship and marked a coming-out period for us both. I felt good about having let Zuk get close because he knew me so much better as a result. The gamble had paid off, and not just because Mom knew how to pour on her Southern charm. Zuk just turned out to be a decent person. He'd accepted the whole gamut of things he'd been confronted with with an open mind. He understood that being light enough to frequently be mistaken for a white person was something that I was sensitive about and did not go blabbing about it to everyone at school. In fact, it never came up again. Having lain bare the skeletons in my closet, there was nothing left for me to hide, and we were closer as a result. The frank and honest recognition of our differences only made our bond stronger. The fact that Zuk was willing to look past all my dirty little secrets nearly gave me faith in the basic goodness of everyone.

The brown baby Jesus came out of hiding, as did the mousetraps and roach motels and even Mom's books—all of them except that autobiography that was so incendiary I thought the cover was made of flame retardant. The line about chickens having come home to roost was too much. The last thing someone like me needed was a race war. Otherwise, Zuk didn't care. He knew the complete me. There were no more tests or examinations or inspections to perform. He'd seen the morass of who I was and seemed to approve—the result of which was that I experienced an inner peace I'd never known. With Zuk, I could listen to Johnny Cash or Jimi Hendrix. I could eat kidney beans or black-eyed peas. I could eat roast chicken or fried chicken. I could be attracted to white girls or colored girls. I could tan or burn. Everything was fair game, and none of it mattered. He never made me feel like a walking contradiction. He never expected me to conform to some fixed idea about how a given race is supposed to be. Consequently, I was free to be myself. It didn't matter to him that I stuck out at Claremont like a cockatoo, or that there was no single box that I could easily be fit into. Zuk, as I came to call him, was a truly enlightened individual. A bona fide aesthete. A bon vivant. A free thinker, a gentleman scholar, a true philosopher in the Western liberal tradition, and as near to a free spirit as you can get in a place like Claremont. It was a breath of fresh air, like I could open my lungs and suck in all that they could hold. The stuff that I had been taught was *supposed* to happen actually happened. I suddenly understood what Mom had been saying all these years about me needing to get my head out of the sand and trust people. Looking back on it, it all seemed kind of silly. Quite frankly, I wasn't sure what I'd been afraid of. It was through the blossoming of my friendship with Zuk that I at last felt that I had a place in this world. That one flowering bond was nothing short of magical. It seemed to validate my basic human connection to everyone.

Coming home alone after school and staying locked up by myself in the apartment, alone with my books and the TV, until Mom came home was a drag. It felt like the world outside had forgotten about me. But ever since Dinner at Peola's, Zuk and I started taking the subway together after school. He'd get off at my stop because it was on his way home. We'd laugh and joke and horse around on our way past the broken-down cars parked in front of all the body shops, repair shops, and chop shops, with their iridescent pools of antifreeze shimmering over the buckled sidewalk out front, where axles to Cutlass Supremes, steering columns to Impalas, rear bumpers to Cadillacs, and tire after tire after tire lined my street and beside which some bum in an army jacket lay sprawled out cold.

We'd sidestep him on our way to the building that stood like a monolith in the foreground of the East River and Brooklyn in the distance. Jimmy would slap Zuk five and we'd talk baseball on our way up to the twenty-third floor, where we'd break out the soda we'd picked up on the way from our schoolbags. We'd sit around the kitchen table doing homework while listening to records. When we finished, we'd turn up the volume, raid the fridge, and compare fantasies of St. Michael's girls. The old lady downstairs would eventually bang on her ceiling for us to cut it out. I'd remove the record from the turntable and return it to its sleeve and we'd throw ourselves on the sofa, pooped. When all the food was gone, Zuk would pack up, and I'd walk him downstairs, out past the conga circle cluttering the courtyard, down the sidewalk past the tattered awning above which some old hag in a nightgown, with rollers in her hair, would lean out of a window with a cigarillo stub drooping from her mouth and say, *Hey Ringo. Yeah, you. The dark Beatle. I know you. Get over here. Catch. It's a quarter. Now run along and get me a cigarillo from El Paradiso's. Yeah, just one. And if Eddie's out, go across the street to Siempre Feliz. Go on. Hey! Where are you going? Not that way!*

I'd drop Zuk off at the Delancey Street subway station and watch him disappear down the stairs, then savor the walk back home. After all these years, I finally had a friend and confidant.

XXIII

I WISH I COULD SAY that on the last night of summer I was super excited about the start of the coming school year. In a way, I was. It was just that it had been so crazy that I rarely had occasion to think about anything else. So when it finally wound down and I had a quiet moment to look back and reflect on it, all I could think to myself was, *Wow*. Summer was over, and all I had to show for it was a broken arm and the three impeccably sorted piles of stack poles out back. Somehow I felt like I'd been robbed.

Sweetheart, you're probably just a little anxious because you're start-
ing the third grade. And about being cooped up in that classroom with
Miss Mayapple all day, after having been free to roam outside all sum-
mer. That's normal. All kids are a little apprehensive at first—and then
you get in there and you get in the swing of things and all the jitters just
sort of disappear and you plum forget about how nervous you were.

Mom drew the curtain, turned off the light, and told me not to worry; school was the perfect antidote for the kind of summer we'd had. I just needed to get my mind off all the crummy stuff that had been going on, was all. The classroom would be a welcome change of scenery. She sat down beside me and warned me not to listen to the things that people were likely to say about Toby. When I asked what I'd say if kids asked me how he'd gotten that way from falling off a ladder, because it seemed a little far-fetched, she fumbled for words.

Tell them the truth. Tell them he fell on the bricks Mister Buford
stacks by his barn.

His head looked like it had been cobbled together with plaster of Paris and chicken wire, Mama. Please. It sagged to one side like melted wax. I didn't recognize him. Nobody could have, except his dentist, and honestly, did he even have one?

As far as I was concerned, it could have been anyone in that coffin. No matter how much Mom had told me that I had to, I could not find it in myself to accept that the corpse I had seen was Toby. No matter how I rearranged the pieces in my head to try to fit them together, I couldn't. I knew there were going to be lots of questions at school. And I wasn't ready for any of them. So I gave her the same look that she was so fond of giving me.

There is no way on this earth for me to get from an ordinary, run-of-the-mill fall from a ladder to the corpse you made me look at. And you know it.

Mom's eyes welled. She took my hand in hers and confessed that Irma had wanted to cremate Toby but had changed her mind at the last minute. I snatched my hand away.

Oh my God.

I agree.

That's the grossest thing I've ever heard.

Sometimes the truth is gross.

Swear on the Bible?

I swear.

Put your hand on it and swear.

Mom kept a Bible on my end table. I barely ever cracked it; I had a half dozen or so comic books stacked on it. She looked up at it and hesitated, then reached over and moved the comic books aside and put her hand on it.

Cupcake, may the good Lord cast me off to eternal damnation as a blasphemer not worthy to follow in His footsteps. I swear on this holy Bible. So help me, Lord. This I do for love. This I do because deep down our world is a beautiful place and I refuse to believe otherwise. Oh Lord, please take me unto thee—unto Your bosom, body and mind, soul and spirit. And forgive me, for this I do because no matter how far we may fall, dear Father, I do require hope. And You are the great Provider of Hope. There. I said it. Satisfied?

Said what?

I wasn't sure what she'd said—seemed to me that she'd thrown in a bunch of other stuff in the bargain. Anyway, her hand didn't move. I had no choice but to take her at her word.

You mean after it had already started? Like they just had his head in the oven, then pulled it back out? Like you did with the roast the time you forgot to put cloves in it?

Yes.

Why'd she change her mind?

I don't know. Maybe because sometimes sights seen are less forgotten. She kissed me goodnight and made to leave my room.

I stopped her in the doorway. *Say, another thing I don't understand is—well—something I've been meaning to ask you for a while now, actually. How'd Toby have time for his family when he was with us all the time? And where does Evan go to school? He does go to school, doesn't he?*

I don't know.

Oh oh oh—and one more thing. That's why you never went to Mister Abrams's pool, right? Because of your hair, I mean? Just between you and me.

Mom sat back down on my bed and stroked my hair and told me how happy she was that God was looking out for me, then got up and flipped off the light. She paused in the open doorway, complimented me on the fact that the room didn't stink as much as usual. Told me to keep up the good work, and then left.

Dad came in. He confirmed Mom's story to be true when I asked. Which was a relief, because frankly I still only believed her ninety-nine point nine nine percent. Anyway, I complained to him how Mom had dragged me to the viewing and how I'd covered my eyes and looked away but she'd pulled my hands away and made me look anyway. She'd sworn up and down that I'd live to regret it if I didn't take a good hard look. I asked Dad if that were true. Because Mom had said that supposedly, someday I was gonna be glad I had. But I wasn't glad at all. It'd been almost a week, and I still couldn't get out of my head the image of that skull, the way that it had appeared to have been burnt and beaten so bad that it seemed hollow, and the scalp that had come so undone and deformed it needed to be held in place with staples and wire ties. Christ. I'd seen pictures of ten-thousand-year-old mummies that were in better shape than him.

I told Dad that I thought it unfair that I should have had to do it when he didn't have to. Then I asked him why he hadn't said a last goodbye to Toby, the way the rest of us had. He didn't say anything. When he leaned in and gave me a peck on the forehead, I grabbed him and hugged him and begged him to never leave. He pried himself from me and got up. Said I needed my ten hours and closed the door. I don't think he understood. I wasn't asking him to not leave my room. I was asking him not to leave me and Mom.

XXIV

Not only could Roy Rogers croon like a nightingale but he was a great showman—and one heck of a gunslinger. They don't make them like that anymore, Huey. Fact is, he provided a model of a sound Christian upbringing for us to emulate throughout life. Frankly, I wouldn't be the man I am today if I didn't have someone like him to look up to as a kid. Talk about the Lone Ranger all you want, but there was only one King of the Cowboys, and that was Roy Rogers.

Dad was looking over my shoulder with half a biscuit in his mouth. I glued the final puzzle piece in place, grabbed my coat, and headed for the door. Miss Della was on her way up the road. I bid her good morning. Dad strolled up beside me and raised his Thermos in her direction.

The trick in life is to always get back up, son. If there's one thing you learn from me, let that be it.

Dad headed down the steps. Mom picked up the morning paper from the stoop with a wave down the road, then climbed in the truck beside me. She had grocery shopping to do and was hitching a ride with us. It was field work for Dad and the first day of school for me. The front window was boarded up, and the house wore the hurricane shutters like a black eye. None of us said a word about the fact that we were the only ones with boarded-up windows. Dad ground the truck's gears, and we lurched forward.

Mom opened the newspaper.

Let's see. What do we have here? Oh yes. Here it is: "Social Unrest Follows 'Freedom Riders' into Akersburg; Jackson and Oxford Brace."

Mom buried her head in the newspaper. I asked if they were talking about us, but she didn't answer. The Thronateeska appeared through a stand of evergreens running alongside Cordele Road. Dad pulled into Nestor's. Mom leaned over and fussed with my sling, straightened my shirt, and wiped some crumbs from my face. She wished me luck and gave me a peck on the cheek, then reminded me that we'd survived floods, droughts, and infestations, before heading off. I shouted out, *Jesus Christ, Mama. It's only the first day of school. I'll be okay.*

Nestor was sitting on his rocker in the shade beside the latched doors of the ice cabinet. He was resting his feet on a cement parking block, sleeping. Mom headed past him, up the stoop, and disappeared inside. The door squeaked shut behind her, and its bell jingled. Nestor's eyes popped open at the sound of the bell. He ran over toward us.

We gotta talk.

Not now, Nestor.

Nestor shook the newspaper in his hand. *For crying out loud, Buck. Those kids have been staying at the Camelot.*

Dad glanced at it, then handed it back. *Stanley's got to make a living somehow, doesn't he? Just like you and me.*

Not funny, Buck. We've got a real possibility of fire here!

Gunfire?

Fire fire, *Buck. They're fixin' to burn it down.*

Nestor, the other day I had my nose broken by a mob who lumped me in with those wackos that came down on that damned bus. Before that, I had to send Huey home early from Herb's threshing. Now I have to listen to you suggesting that I might be next. Which is it, Nestor? What have I got to do to win a little respect around here?

You can't win back what you never had, Buck!

Not you, too, Nestor?

People may fight for love, Buck, but they don't do it knowing they're gonna lose.

I love her, Nestor. For me she's just Pea. Not colored. Not some "high yellow" or "mulatto." Just Pea. But everyone's always tried to make it so that I can't have one without the other. And all I got to say to that is, if anyone comes to my house tonight—so help me God—I'm ready. I'll be there waiting for them. And I'm gonna fire back.

Nestor fell back, speechless. Across the street, tiles of cardboard had been fitted over several busted-out front windows. Dad and I pretended not to see those, either. Dad pulled forward, and we continued past the sign that read MOUNT ZION TABERNACLE OF THE SECOND COMING. Main Street appeared war ravaged amid a trail of broken glass and debris. Farther down, Mister Rinkel was quietly picking up trash from around a busted-out window of a car parked in front of his shop. The shade was thick and cool. I was thankful for it. The Thronateeska appeared next to the low-rise redbrick building that was the bank, disappeared behind the hardware store, and reappeared out from behind the thin, creaking wrought-iron sign hanging over Missus Henniger's flower shop. I asked Dad to stop. He pulled over. The plate-glass door and front window were busted out, and the register was tipped over. Vases lay broken and flowers were strewn everywhere. Dad shook his head. He remarked that Missus Henniger was just a poor old spinster who had done nothing to nobody. Poor old lady. She deserved better. So what if she clutched onto archaic beliefs that were a holdover from a time that made sense to her? Wasn't her fault, was it? She just got carried off down life's fast-moving waters, only to end up in a swirling eddy that went nowhere, just like everyone else. We all can't be Plato.

Dad *tsk*ed, and we continued on. We inched our way past the sandstone brick facades and sheet-glass storefronts that I identified with. They lay in shambles. Dad stopped at the blinking yellow light at Third Street. Five colored women stood on the corner in a balding patch of grass situated between the sidewalk and curb, patting their brows as they stood in the bright sunlight, leafleting.

Dad drove slow through town. Three doors down stood a group of colored fellas. They'd all been to the service. But even if I recognized them, I didn't recognize Main Street. Dad looked over and sighed. He said that you can only go to a petting zoo so many times before you start to lose interest in the goats, llamas, and ostriches. He told me to ignore them.

Cherry to Maplewood, Maplewood to Donner, and Donner all the way up three miles to Frontage Road. Dad stayed left at the fork, and we clattered up to his turnoff.

Mind if I drop you off here?

Now that I'm eight?

Now that I'm late.

I grinned. *Fine.*

I hopped down onto dirt and gravel and looked down at Roy Rogers. He was practically waving at me.

Glue dry?

I nodded.

Be sure to mention that it has more than two hundred pieces. Edna will appreciate that. Oh, and if she asks how long it took you, don't tell her it took you all summer. She'll think you're stupid. Just say it took you the weekend.

THE CUT COTTON stalks covering the field came up to my knees, and every now and again a wispy white thread of cotton floated past. A black gambrel roof stuck out over the tree line up ahead. The almost flat slope of its top half appeared first, and then the lower, steeper slope of the bottom half. There was no sign out by the road or anything. I never did understand how people could tell what it was just by looking at it. I guess you just had to know it was there.

A hundred yards down, the cotton burrs and thin filaments scattered over asphalt gave way to a gravel lot in which stood my school. I pushed up my sleeve to make my cast stand out. It didn't hurt anymore, and I'd begun to even identify with it. As I headed around the far side of the stone foundation and clapboard siding in search of Derrick, I turned at a sound coming from somewhere up the road that was so faint I might have been imagining it. Either I was hearing voices in my head or people were singing. I cupped my hand over my eyes and strained back toward the bright sun just now blossoming over the road. A bunch of people were inching over the horizon in silhouette.

Mae and Darla Pendleton were etching boxes into the dirt with twigs we'd foraged from the adjacent wood. Little puffs of dust were billowing out around them.

Who died now, Darla?

She shrugged.

My uncle Theaster died last week. But that was in his sleep. I'd be surprised if anyone would be eulogizing him. He farted at the dinner table.

Missus Mayapple came around from the back side of the schoolhouse holding Daniel Raiford by the hand with Bobby Buford, Marcy McEllen, and Riley Daniels in tow. Marcy's face was beet red. Missus Mayapple had probably caught them being gross in the wood. School hadn't even started yet, and those hornballs were at it again.

A mailbox stood where the gravel lot, the field, and Frontage Road all met. I headed over to it and just stood there. I liked the way that wooden post felt in my armpit when I leaned on it.

Will ya look at that?

Holy moly.

Sweet Jesus.

It's got something of the Second Coming to it, wouldn't you say?

It was the most solemn spectacle I'd ever seen. I was waiting for Jesus to turn up scantily clad and dragging that wooden cross the size of a small cedar tree over his shoulder, like when he went to his crucifixion. It broke my heart to see all those grown-ups walking in procession like that—like they were following Moses to the Promised Land, except without the caravan of wagons filled with goats and chickens and sundry livestock bringing up the rear. Theo Krasinski and I exchanged a quick glance. All those colored people marching past so dignified—the intertwining chorus of their voices deep and rich, like I could reach out and touch it. Their backs were erect and heads high. Their boot heels rasped and canes knocked. Birds fluttered from a stand of nearby trees.

I checked overhead for some sort of sign like a bright shaft of light cutting through the sky, or something of the coming Revelation or Passion or some such, like a crow or something circling overhead, then rolled my eyes and laughed. Theo cracked up, too.

Missus Mayapple jerked me around and wagged her finger in my face.

But it's just a parade.

This is no parade!

She snatched at my arm like she didn't trust me to go back inside on my own, then tossed it down at the sight of boys playing stickball in the field behind me. Which was a no-no. We didn't own that field; Mister Wainwright did. And the grisliness of the scorched and half-burnt scarecrow he left sitting in the middle of it was all the proof I needed that it was best to stay out. She headed after them.

I dragged my feet on my way to the schoolhouse, kicking at the limestone, wondering what I'd done wrong.

Hugh! Burt! Over here!

I turned around. I cupped my hand over my eyes, squinting in the sun. Standing in the middle of the crowded road was a boy waving his arms. Whoever it was, I could only make him out in silhouette. He was running toward me. The road was filled with so many people they even spilled over it edges. He was zigzagging around them.

The boy emerged from the crowd marching past and just stood there looking at me, breathing hard, with that gap-toothed mouth spread wide over his face. I almost didn't recognize him without his ball cap on.

Evan?

I heard you got sick.

I couldn't tell if it was a smirk or a look of concern on his face. I wanted to be mad at him and hate him, but for some reason I just couldn't. I decided that he was concerned about me. Because he put a hand on my shoulder.

Why ain't you over there with us?

A crowd of kids flocked around. They pushed and shoved to get a good look at one of our own local colored boys, done up real fancy in a suit and tie. Someone shoved me before I had a chance to explain. I tumbled ass over end into the gully.

Go on with your nigger!

Who you calling a nigger?

Bruce Levitwerner was staring down at me with those deeply set pig eyes of his. I wanted to get right up in his face and tell him that I wasn't afraid—even if he was two grades older, he wasn't boss of me. I brushed the cockleburs from my shirt and climbed out of the gully, but before I was able to kick Bruce in the nuts, he pushed me right back down square on my ass. Which shocked the hell out of me. Once was forgivable, but twice was all out war. I turned around. Evan was running back down the road, chasing after a casket being carried away on the shoulders of eight colored men bringing up the rear.

I lay there on the ground in disbelief. There was no mistaking it. The shroud of purple flowers covering it were spilling over the sides as it hobbled off down the road atop their shoulders. I knew that casket.

Knew who was inside that casket. I hollered out for it to wait, but it was too late. It disappeared around the bend.

I scrambled to my feet and ran so goddamned fast I couldn't feel anything below my waist. I flew up the short flight of steps and into the schoolhouse. I ducked into the first door I came to. Damn it all if it wasn't the broom closet. The door was off-kilter. I slammed it several times before it finally closed. Someone was creeping around in the hallway. The door rattled. The floor moaned. I jumped out of my socks at the realization that someone was on the other side of the door, peeking beneath it.

Hubert Francis Fairchild, I know you're in there. Now get out here right this second.

Go away!

Hubert, I know that's you. Now come out.

I said, go away!

You come out of there right this instant, young man.

I'm never coming out. Now go away!

I'm standing here with a straightedge in one hand and King James in the other, young man. Do you know what that spells?

I undid the latch. Missus Mayapple was bluffing, but before I could slam the door in her face, she staggered to her feet and dragged me out the front door. We stood at the top of the steps, overlooking a loose tangle of forty-odd kids. Missus Mayapple's voice echoed out.

And on the first day of school! For shame!

A sea of white faces were all crowded together right in front of me, angled my way. Some stood with their mouths hung open, others had their lips pressed tight. My heart was knocking around in my chest like a sledgehammer. Her thick hand squeezed mine so tight her ring bit into my fingers.

Let this serve as a lesson to all of you! Never do anything that you haven't the courage to take responsibility for!

A chainsaw buzzed from deep within the adjacent wood. There echoed out the creaking sound of a limb being felled. Then all went quiet.

Now, who wants to tell me just what happened out here?

I'll tell you what happened!

Me! Pick me! I'll tell you exactly what happened!

Ooh! Ooh! Ooh! Pretty please!

We'll start with you.

Huey's a nigger!

Bruce Levitwerner!

But it's true!

Mister Levitwerner, you watch your mouth!

But I'm telling you, that nigger—!

Now you listen here, young man. I've got enough Scripture to keep you reading for a lifetime. Do you hear? I simply will not tolerate my students casting aspersions of that sort in this school. Do I make myself perfectly clear?

Yes, ma'am.

Thank you. Now, please. Anyone else?

Aw, c'mon!

    Get off it, Missus M!

        Rats!

            Bull crud!

Yeah. No fair!

    I swear on the holy Bible—it's true.

        Yeah. Another nigger practically said so himself!

      Did not!

        Did so!

            Shut up, you ninny!

Yeah.

     Am not!

       You weren't even there.

        What do you know?

        I heard it!

Me, too!

     May as well have!

      · *Was so!*

         Aw, what's the difference?

Mister Levitwerner, keep your hands to yourself! I'm warning you, I do believe I've heard just about enough out of you for one day. Good Lord, is it that difficult for you to be a gentleman six hours of the day?

No, ma'am.

Now, you may not like it, but continence is still a greater virtue than candor. Especially where slander is concerned.

Yes, ma'am.

Good. Now just who in the Lord's name is this colored boy you were talking to?

Goolsbee's boy!

Goolsbee's boy? Good Lord! And you believed him?

Who's ever heard of a nigger lying about that?

Besides, Huey ain't allowed in Mister Abrams's pool no more.

Yeah!

And my mama says that's why.

So does mine!

Mine, too!

We all know it!

Stop pretending like you don't know!

We all know!

Yeah!

Just like you're doing right now.

Yeah, Missus M.

Aw, she's just putting us on! Playing dumb like all the rest.

Stop pulling our leg, Missus M! We don't like it!

She knows!

Of course she does!

Just look at her!

Just like you're doing right now.

Even that other nigger practically said so, too!

I snatched my hand from Missus Mayapple.

I already know all that!

There was an eruption of laughter. Then everything went quiet. Derrick took off his glasses and started wiping them. Theo was wide-eyed. Everyone else seemed to be pointing at me.

It's all his fault!—Get him!!

Stop right there!

Dontcha get it?

He's why they closed Mister Abrams's pool in the first place!

No one ever broke into it!

He done it!

It was all him!

In broad daylight!

And with us all around!

While we was there!

Looking on!

He broke in!

Right under our nose!

In front of our own eyes!

My mama even said so herself!

Goddamnit if he ain't the culprit!

It was him all along!

Quiet! Mister Levitwerner, you come up front here, where I can see you.

Bruce Levitwerner begged pardon and excused himself like a gentleman on his way to the front. He stopped at the foot of the steps and stood there with his mackinaw buttoned up to his neck, in his stiff dungarees, holding a grubby red ball cap in both hands, mouth hanging open.

Much better. Now, Mister Levitwerner—is it true your mother said all that?

Bruce Levitwerner narrowed his eyes. He pressed his lips tight and scrunched his face up like an old person. That pig-faced son of a bitch. He took one look at me, then turned back to Missus Mayapple and crossed his heart and hollered out.

Yes!

My heart felt like I was squeezing it in my fist. Missus Mayapple stood in silence. We all stood in silence. She waved Bruce Levitwerner and the others inside. I looked down as Derrick brushed quietly past. Theo, too. Darla was the last to shuffle past. She had a terrible limp. She was always clunking around with that metal hardware thing attached to her shoe buckled and strapped to her ankle and halfway up her calf. You could hear her coming up the road from half a mile away, like a tank. Darla clunked past and slammed the door shut behind her. *Nigger!*

She spit the word out. I found it difficult to accept that she was talking to me. I told myself that she was talking about Evan. I remember that being very important to me as I stood there, beside Missus Mayapple.

Missus Mayapple sat down atop the stoop and gazed out over the open field, cut down and empty. It was shrouded in a gauzy haze of morning sunlight. I sat down beside her. The crud caked between the planks beneath me had little openings poked through here and there where the occasional ant maneuvered dexterously in and out. I jammed the edge of my thumbnail into one of those creases. Missus Mayapple's hair was tucked and folded atop her head, and she was fidgeting with a fingernail as she sat there in silence, listening to the gently twisting wind chime above.

For your information, ma'am, my daddy is white, so I'm white. You know that, right?

XXV

I KICKED THE WILTED BLUEBELLS scattered along Cordele Road on my way into town and wondered what it meant that all that time that I'd thought I'd known Toby, he had kept his wife and son all to himself. What kind of friend was I that I hadn't known about them?

The same five colored ladies were standing on the corner handing out leaflets in town. Why I hadn't recognized Missus Bleecker among them, I do not know. She must have had her back turned to me.

Afternoon, Missus Bleecker.

Afternoon, darling.

Missus Bleecker—today, I'm a Christian. But tomorrow, who knows?

Missus Bleecker frowned. She belonged to some fringe religion called the Apocalyptic or Apostrophic or Apologetic Overcoming Holy Church of God or something. She always left our house smelling like jasmine whenever she stopped by with a case of ointments that Mom would spend half the morning leisurely picking through. So I figured she would understand. She looked up and down the street, as if to see if anyone was looking, then held out a flier.

They teach you that at school?

I shook my head no.

Missus Bleecker fixed my hair, straightened my shirt, wiped off my cast, brushed the remaining cockleburs from my shoulder and said, *Good. You stay in school, then.* Colored ladies always seemed to like me. Colored men, not so much. Toby was the exception. I had no idea why that was. Anyway, the street was still in shambles. I folded the pamphlet and tucked it into my pocket and continued down the sidewalk.

Two blocks down, I avoided the eyes of the colored man standing in front of Ivey's, holding up a placard stenciled with the words I AM A MAN. No kidding. It's not like he had titties or anything. I took out Missus Bleecker's handbill and held it up to the side of my face and walked right past him—then did it again to the colored man walking back and forth beneath the mortar and pestle hanging from a thin, creaking sign over the front stoop of the Rexall. His placard said FREEDOM NOW. And then again to the group of people sitting on the curb in front of S&W, Indian-style, with their placards in their laps, drinking sodas and fanning themselves.

There were so many placards that it was hard for me to read them all. I weaved my way past the cramped makeshift campsite, stepped over a sleeping bag, hopped over a lantern, ducked around a teapot hanging from a campfire tripod, like I was just going about my business, whistling to myself as I made my way through them like I did this sort of thing every day of the week.

That single block of sidewalk between Ivey's and the Laundromat had practically been converted into a shanty town. I stopped right smack in the middle of it and puzzled over the sign leaning on the windowsill behind them. I'd seen it there as long as I could remember and had never really thought about what it meant. Now that I knew it was the cause of so much discord, I was trying to figure out how I felt about it.

I thought about all the people Mom was always going on about who had left town for greener pastures up north back when she was just a kid. With all her talk, I just figured that what she had said about how difficult life had been back then applied to all of us. I dunno, I guess that between the droughts, hurricanes, miserable heat, and crop infestations, I felt I could understand why most anyone would want to leave a place like Akersburg under those conditions.

My reflection was transposed over the sign: WHITES ONLY. Which made me uncomfortable. Mom's buzz cut was fine enough and my ears didn't stick out quite as much as Dad's, but otherwise I didn't like how I looked.

I pressed my face against the window. It was dark inside. Mister Schaefer was sitting all the way in the back, beside a bucket filled with cleaning supplies. Probably playing solitaire. With one dead wife and three sons in Vietnam, who could blame him? Mister Bigelow was sitting at the counter, playing cribbage with Mister Chandler. From the looks of it, Mister Chandler was ahead. I could tell by his grin. And as I stood there, mouth open, face pressed against the sheet-glass window, I noticed that Tyler wasn't there. I looked toward the back, but I couldn't see him. In his place, Mister Chambers was mopping up around the booths. He came to the door and dunked the mop in a bucket and propped the door open. He wrung it out and pointed the handle over my shoulder, as if to get my attention.

A colored fella behind me was pointing a camera at me. He was squinting into the viewfinder, squatting, moving the camera this way and that. He sure was going to a great deal of trouble to take a stupid picture. Mom and Dad usually just told me to say cheese and snapped it. *Pop*—a flash of light burst in my face. I hadn't been expecting it. I opened my eyes to a bunch of bright white dots. Mister Chambers was standing there with that mop dripping in his hands and me beside him, rubbing the afterglow out of my eyes. What kind of idiot takes a goddamned picture of a kid just standing there minding his own beeswax, contemplating some crummy damned sign in a storefront window, with an overweight Mister Chambers standing right beside him with a wet mop in hand?

Although Third Street is not the biggest street in town, it is the nicest. It's quiet and tree-lined, with a few long driveways and big houses. Some of the trees must have just been pruned, because there were mounds of clipped branches clustered along the curb. Three blocks up, I passed Missus Hildebrandt's house. A small pile of crab apples and silver maple flowers sat atop a larger one of cut grass. I kicked at the long, curvy catalpa capsules on my way past her trimmed hedges and considered that maybe I'd been a little quick to judge that fella with the camera. I mean, it wasn't every day that a perfect stranger just popped up out of nowhere and took my picture with some fancy camera like that. I just wished he'd told me to say cheese.

I cut up the street with my head in the clouds, right up there with the spires and cupolas, then came back down to earth alongside the balconies and Missus Hildebrandt, who was sitting on a wooden lawn chair wearing sunglasses and holding a sweating glass of sweet tea in front of several gentlemen from the neighborhood who were sharing a sliver of shade with her. They were patting their brows dry with bandanna kerchiefs and squinting as they chatted about those uppity niggers in town who were getting too big for their britches, fanning out like they were every day a little farther from where they started five weeks back.

Afternoon, Mister Baxter.

Afternoon, Huey.

Putnam Street is a quiet, maple-lined street with expertly paved driveways. Everyone's garbage was sitting curbside, like it did every Tuesday, mid-morning. Scotty was up the street, delivering the afternoon paper. I knew he went to a special parochial school that started a week later than the rest of us. He was slowly working his way down the street. His newspaper bag coiled around his waist every time he swung it. Two doors down, visible through a curtain billowing out of an open window, Miss Stella MacDonald was tapping out the harmony line for "Put On a Happy Face."

My mouth was parched. So I crossed over the Hofstetters' front yard and headed up the flagstone-tiled walkway and up the brick steps stained with Callery pear petals, careful not to knock over the azalea sitting there. I knocked on the door. After a minute, it opened. Missus Hofstetter peeked out. I told her that it was just me.

She begged pardon. When I just stood there looking at her, she bid me come inside before all the cool air got let out. She begged me to please not track dirt inside. So I stood just inside the now closed door and explained that I was thirsty and how I'd have used the spigot on the side of their house, but the water always comes out so hot this time of year. Of course, I could have let it run a half hour for it to cool, but by that time who knows how muddy the walkway would have gotten. Which she appreciated. Dr. Hofstetter barked out from upstairs, complaining that the afternoon paper was late.

It's not Scotty. It's Buck's boy. He's come for water.

Dr. Hofstetter appeared at the top of the stairs.

Who?

Buck's boy.

Buck's boy?

Yes.

What for?

Water.

Tell him the hose is out on the side of the house.

Oh, go back to your book.

Missus Hofstetter glanced upstairs. When her husband left the landing, she went to the kitchen and returned with a big glass of ice water. She handed it to me and asked after Mom. I stopped gulping it down just long enough to explain how Mom was getting along okay, happy to have me out of the house now that school had started up; how excited she was about me starting the third grade; and how our crop was hard going what with Toby being sorely missed and Dad being hard-pressed for a replacement because, as it turns out, good help is very, very hard to find. Missus Hofstetter seemed impatient. She shook her head and held the door open. I just stood there, looking at her.

Yes?

I also wanted to say thank you.

Missus Hofstetter pressed her lips together so hard the color left them. *Don't mention it.*

Not for the water. For helping me that day. With my arm. Remember? I wanted to show Dr. Hofstetter my cast. Thought he might wanna know that it's healing fine.

Well, he's not working today.

I headed back toward Main Street, this time on the cool side of the street, past Missus LeFranc's yapping Yorkshire terrier, all the while hopping from one band of shade to the next, trying to convince myself that maybe the summer hadn't been so terrible after all, and who knows, maybe there are worse things than a lifetime of truancy, before realizing that I was thirsty again.

Nestor had an industrial-sized fan that he kept on full blast just inside the front door. The fan stood as tall as me, and standing in front of it was like entering one of those wind tunnels NASA uses to train its astronauts. I loved it. I stood there until my ballooning shirt didn't stick to me anymore, then slid my money off the counter and went to see what was keeping him.

Nestor's boy, Ernie, was checking someone's oil. He pulled a rag from his back pocket and wiped at the windshield. The license plate was from out of town. It was just some tourist on his way to Cape Canaveral. I could spot them a mile away; the binoculars wedged on the dash were a dead giveaway. So I headed between two pick-ups, a Ford Fairlane, a Dodge Dart, a Plymouth, and a rusted-out Chevy sitting up on blocks to the adjacent service bay. He was clanging away on something in the engine compartment and called out, *Whaddya want?*

Grape cola.

Leave ten cent on the counter and help yourself.

I only got a quarter.

Nestor made change for me inside. I opened his door, felt a gush of sticky heat envelop me, took two hellacious gulps, and froze. Dad was supposed to be out in the field, trying out a man named Humphrey Moore. That much I knew. He had made arrangements with the penitentiary up the road to get a handful of inmates on loan to help with our threshing, since no one else would. Anyway, he had this pigheaded idea that he needed to see Moore work the thresher before taking him on. Mom thought that ridiculous. Who else was he gonna get? Besides, the dossier or service order or docket or whatever it was that had come in the mail said that on top of a reduced sentence for good behavior, Humphrey Moore was sixty-four years old and strong as a bull, and had been farming peanuts since before Dad could tell a peanut from a pecan. Which I suppose is why Mom had thought a trial run humiliating, even for a common criminal. Didn't bother Dad, though. Business was business. Of course, all I cared about was what he was in for—but no one would tell me that.

Anyway, Dad was headed straight for me, with some papers in his hands that he was looking over. I got the impression that he'd just come out of the bank. He hadn't seen me. I had turned on my heels, set to bolt, when he called out my name.

He looked happy to see me. He strode up alongside me, took my hand, and led me out of the sunlight and into the cool under the canopy of trees lining the sidewalk. He smiled and asked if it didn't feel better in the shade.

I snatched my hand back.

No, goddamnit, it doesn't. Okay? I like the sun! Like the way it feels on my face! So there!

Dad looked at me funny, then changed the subject. *How's Edna?*

Fine!

She sure let you out awfully early.

So?

She like your puzzle?

Loved it!

See? What'd I tell ya? Now, whatcha doing out of school this early? I hope she doesn't make a habit of it. How in the world are you ever going to learn anything if she always dismisses you this early? I swear to God, teachers hardly work anymore. Not like when I was a kid. It's the trade unions, son. They got everyone by the balls. They get days off for this, half days for that. Some teacher-development program or other excuse that they're using precious class time for. What? Is it some important person's birthday I don't know about? Or was it on account of your arm? You look a little pale. You sure you're feeling okay?

Dad took my hand. His was so big it seemed to gobble mine right up. I tugged on it and pointed at the topside of his hand.

Why am I darker than you, Pop? Answer me that. Why?

Dad begged pardon, not to me but to the colored man carrying a sandwich board. He was handing out fliers in front of the Rexall. He asked if we wanted one. Dad said, *No, thank you,* and we entered the store. The doorbell jingled, and Mister Wimple appeared from the back, wiping his hands in a white hand towel.

Whaddya got for sunstroke?

For you?

No, him.

Feeling dizzy?

I shook my head no.

Mister Wimple came around from the counter, stooped to my eye level, and tilted his head back. He was examining me from up close.

Buck, I hate to break it to you, but your boy don't have sunstroke.

Dontcha think I know sunstroke when I see it, Phil? Jesus Christ. Musta had it—what?—twenty-five times since I was his age. If there's one thing I know, it's what sunstroke looks like. The boy got real sick from that broken arm, you know. Had to go to the hospital and everything. And now he's out on a day like this, when it's so hot I didn't bother spraying acephate because the cucumber beetles aren't even troubling to come out of the dirt. And I got news for you, Phil. When it's too hot for cucumber beetles, it's too hot! The boy's got sunstroke, and that's final.

Does your face hurt when you smile?

Uh-uh.

He doesn't even look like he burns, Buck.

Heck, I dunno. Maybe his blood sugar's low. You got something sweet?

Mister Wimple handed me a gumdrop, then watched me chew on it. *Feel better?*

I shook my head. Then I nodded. I did and didn't at the same time.

If you've seen it once, you've seen it a million times, Buck. It's because school's started, ain't it? "Paw, my back hurts. Ow ow ow ow ow ow. I can hardly move." Well, son, you'll have to do better than that if you wanna outfox me. Can't say as I blame him, though. Who in Christ's name wants to sit at a desk all day in weather as beautiful as this? Besides, that Missus Mayapple hasn't changed a textbook in thirty years, Buckaroo. Can you believe it? Still using the same ones we used. Lord have mercy, she was in here Tuesday stocking up on enough Bufferin to last the entire school year, and she says to me, "How much can change in a few short years?" "A few short years?" Have you seen her lately? A few short years!

Mister Wimple slapped the countertop and ambled back around it.

I SAT DOWN beside Dad on the bench out front. The sun was a ball of fire balanced atop the Laundromat. The colored man with the fancy camera was pacing in front of S&W. He had on a sandwich board that read I AM A MAN, too. "I Am a Man"? Flashing that fancy camera around like that for all of us to see! It should have said I AM A RICH MAN. I felt like kicking him in the teeth. I just wanted my old life back.

Mister Gray emerged from the Laundromat with an armload of neatly folded clothes. He watched the man with the sandwich board pace for a minute, then continued to his car. Dad mussed up my hair.

Aw, don't listen to Phil. You just tan easily.

I looked away. *What about Mama?*

Huey, if I've told you once I've told you a thousand times—people think it's a piece of cake, but it's not, being a diamond in the rough in a small backwoods community such as ours. No, sir. Nothing worse than being a beauty in a small town. A few people love you, but most hate you. You've seen it, right? I know you have. The men want her and can't have her, and the women wanna be like her, but can't. In many respects, you're better off being born ugly, I say. The mean-spirited housewives who make it their life's work to make sure one person can never enjoy her God-given beauty—trust me, they leave the ugly women alone. And the sooner we accept it as a matter of course, the better. Okay?

Enough of that nonsense! I'm sick of it!

Dad paused. He looked startled. He recomposed himself. *Fine. What about Mama?*

Does she just tan easily?

What the hell's that supposed to mean?

You know what it means. Go on. You can tell me—I can handle it. What is she, then? I wanna know what she is.

She's your mother, for crying out loud.

So it's true?

If I've told you once, I've told you a thousand times, and I'll tell you again—no one knows. Not even her. Besides, what difference does it make?

It matters to me!

Why?

It just does!

Did someone tell you that?

They don't need to! You don't think I have eyes and ears?

Huey, listen to me. Your mother's what's known in the scientific community as a phenotypic anomaly. Okay? Someone of unknown morphology. A racial enigma—something so new they don't have a name for it yet. You watch Wild Kingdom, *right? Well, it's like a newly discovered animal that they haven't figured out where to put it in the classification system yet. Okay? So it's pointless to even bother asking. Because— well—the truth is that if people can't agree, we might never know. Now, I could make something up if that would make you happy. But I doubt it would make you happy, because you want the truth. And the truth is that no one knows. Pure and simple. So there's nothing more that I can say. At the end of the day, you're just going to have to accept that even if she is what you think she might be—which she isn't—her being one wouldn't make you one. Okay? You're just going to have to accept that you're different. That's all there is to it.*

Different, different, different! That's all you ever say. Well, I'm sick of being different!

Being different isn't a bad thing, Huey. It just means you're an exception. And the world's filled with exceptions. Now take me, for example. Heck. My skin's a little tan, too. But that don't make me colored, now does it?

I don't care if the kids at school ain't nice to me, Pop. I don't want to go to no colored school. Please, God, don't make me!

Someone said that to you?

And what about her family?

Someone said something, didn't they?

How come you never talk about them?

Because they're not around anymore.

Where'd they go?

They're dead.

Which war?

Gallstones, or something like that. None of them seemed to last very long.

How come?

They just weren't cut out for this world, I guess. Who knows?

I tried to say something, but Dad slapped the bench. *Goddamnit, son. Gallstones are things in your stomach that can kill you. And no, I don't have none. And neither does your mother.*

I closed my mouth.

Any more questions?

What about Grampa Hicks? Was he a nigger?

For God's sake, son, dontcha you see those people across the street? That's exactly the kind of talk that brought them here. Now hush with that talk.

Well?

I don't know. Maybe. I mean, God. I hope not. You'll have to ask her. But probably not.

Why?

Because it's a state of mind, that's why! Heck, I didn't make the world!

Derrick says they come in all colors. Including very light—practically white. But you say they're just stupid and lazy and you can't trust 'em any farther than you can throw 'em. And Mama says that they only come in one color—dark. So which is it?

Jesus! Just stop! Stop it already! Stop right there! You win! Okay? I give up!

Well, which is it?

For God's sake, Huey. Which is what?

Dad got up and headed off before I could answer. I ran after him.

Where you going?

I almost got hit by a car crossing Fourth Street. I chased after him past Third. He reached Nestor's. He was standing at the front door, waiting for me with the door handle in hand.

Well?

Well, I ain't gonna stand here and tell you different, if that's what you're waiting for.

So one color, then?

Christ, Huey—no! They come in all colors! Okay? Any more questions?

No.

Good. Damn it all. Thank the Lord.

Dad tugged the door open. The bell jingled. He asked Nestor if he had anything new for a penny. *For a boy in the doldrums.*

Nestor grinned out from behind the counter. *First day of school got you down?*

I squirmed out from under Dad's arm.

Someone said something awful to him today. God knows what.

Nestor handed me a peppermint. *No spoiled mood a few sweets can't cure.*

I popped it into my mouth and pulled Dad downward. I whispered in his ear from my tiptoes. He slapped a nickel on the counter and snatched up my arm and started for the door. It hiccuped shut behind us. He knelt down in front of me.

Who said that?

XXVI

HE'S NOT IN SCHOOL?

No!

Where is he, then?

He was in town with me. One second he was at my side, and the next he was gone. He just ran!

Did you run after him?

You didn't hear him come in?

I thought it was you.

Someone said something to him at school.

What?

God knows. He just started hollering at me—asking me all sorts of crazy questions.

Like what?

Then those college kids come running over, yelling, Hey, mister! Leave that boy alone! *They crowded around me. Started threatening me, said they were going to make a citizen's arrest. Next thing I know, he ran off boohooing down the street. And I'm standing there, calling out for him to wait. Yelling at them to get the hell out of my way because he's my boy. John came out of his damned store to see what was going on.*

What did you say?

Told him that he'd better go back into his fitting room and sew on another button, is what I said. I don't care if I've got to slug it out with forty acres and a damned mule, I will not tolerate being condescended to!

Not to him, to Huey!

He's not in here.

Check the back room.

He must be outside.

I heard someone come in. What's he doing out of school so early? I smell peppermint.

Follow the peppermint. Is it coming from the closet? I think he's in the closet.

Huey, is that you?

I love you, son. I love you like the earth itself. You know I'd never do anything to hurt you. Whatever I said, I'm sorry. You've got nothing to be ashamed of. You hear? That's all I meant to say. Now come out, wherever you are. I just meant you oughta watch what you wish for—if you wanna be more like me, I mean. We're not as different as all that. Look—heck, I probably got emphysema and don't even know it yet. Ain't that right, Pea?

Whose magazines are these?

Magawhat—? Oh. Toby probably left those.

What in the Lord's name are these pictures of colored girls in thigh-high lace stockings and fully exposed brassieres?

Gimme that. Huey, you in here?

Huey, sweetie, it's me. Mama. Here, look—I even made a special cake. Your favorite. That's right, cupcake. Listen to your father.

Check the bathroom. He might be in the tub. And how can you be sure it wasn't the back door you heard?

That's where I was when I heard footsteps running up the drive. The front door swung open. I thought it was you. Because I got no answer, like I get after someone's snubbed you in town.

Huey! I'm losing my patience!

You check the henhouse?

Henhouse?

What about the pump house? He could be anywhere.

Check under his bed.

His window's open, and his trunks are gone!

Snowflake's gone, too!

He ran away with Snowflake?

He's gone for a swim. Probably out by where the geese nest.

How can you be sure?

Check under his bed.

I did!

Don't shout at me!

I'm not shouting—he can't swim!

Then check for his dive mask.

Where've you been? He broke that in a million bits. And then had the nerve to give it to Irma.

Did you hear him leave?

Stop yelling at me!

I'm not yelling!

I wanna know what on earth you said to him.

He shouldn't have cried as much as he did! Okay? That's what. He was crying too damned much, and I told him so. Told him he shouldn't have hesitated to pop that Bruce kid one.

Crying?

Yes. All the way down the street. Bumping into things. And if you would have done your job, I hardly think he would have taken it so hard! Babying him all the time. He isn't made of porcelain, you know. He can take a couple of knocks. Got to. He should know by now that he doesn't have to back down from nobody.

Back down?

That boy is old enough to know what's worth crying over and what isn't. Wailing down the street like that, knocking into things. People coming out of their shops, craning their necks outta doorways to see what was going on. An embarrassment! Like we haven't had enough scenes like that around here already—and I told him so.

You said that?

Damned right I said it. Damn it all. He should have kept his chin up and taken his rightful place in line—yes, like a man!

He's eight!

Doesn't matter!

"Chin up"? What on earth happened?

The shame of having to shout out at him like that, in the middle of the street. My own flesh and blood. Saying he wished he looked more like me, saying how this life was a curse and how he wished he was dead because he didn't look more like me—Never mind fussing with your hair! Grab your coat and come on! Put a hat on it, damn it!

Stop! You hear that?
Hear what?
That.
Under the house?
There it is again.
You check under the house?

XXVII

Our house was raised off the ground by four sets of tar-treated railroad ties. Underneath was two feet of crawl space, filled with all manner of junk that had no other place to go. The most visible items poking out from under our house included four slashed tires, the remains of a busted window, a steering wheel, several oil filters, a pan seat, two mufflers, and a tractor tire draped in a tarpaulin, the creases of which held weeks-old rainwater.

I think that might have been what Mom heard. I'd bumped my head against it. As I ran home from town, I was overcome with pangs of seller's remorse. Having surrendered Snowflake to the bitter wild, I decided that I wanted her back. I knew in my heart that she wasn't ready to be set free but I'd done it anyway. I could see that she wasn't sure what to do with all that freedom, that it was too much for her little brain to comprehend. All that freedom being dumped on her all at once like that. I should probably have tested it out by giving her teaspoon-sized doses of freedom first. Perhaps let her run free in the den to start. What had I been thinking? And so strong was my desire to reclaim her that I ran into the house and grabbed a flashlight, then dove underneath that dark and moldy, godforsaken no-man's-land underneath our house in an urgent search-and-rescue mission.

Mom dug me out by my ankles. She marched me into their bedroom and told me to take a seat. I climbed atop her stiff bedcover, knowing full well I was going to get it dirty, but she told me to sit down on it anyway. Didn't seem to care. She asked what on earth I thought I was doing. I tried to explain that I was looking for Snowflake, but she didn't believe me. She kept interrupting me. Wouldn't let me get a word in edgewise. She had her mind made up that I was trying to run away and had taken Snowflake hostage, only to have lost her along the way. When I explained that I wasn't Snowflake's captor but her liberator, and that I'd freed Snowflake to roam the earth days earlier, she called me a little liar. So, yes, I guess I would consider that a turning point of sorts. Especially when she flicked that little pink slip in her hand that Missus Mayapple had given me to give to Dad—flicked it not at me, but at Dad—then cautioned him to butt out. This was for her and me to sort out. She turned to me and said, *Then what happened?*

And then she set me out. Like a dog.

You're not making sense, Huey. Your father knows Edna. She wouldn't do that.

Everyone came right out and said straight to her face why I'm not allowed in Mister Abrams's pool no more. That all that time I'd been going there, I wasn't supposed to be going there. Had no business going there. Wasn't supposed to even be in there. To be allowed in the front door—my voice cracked—*because it's against the law. That I was breaking the law. That they'd been turning a blind eye to it all this time but couldn't continue doing that anymore. And that I was nothing but a common criminal for breaking the law. And finally someone put their foot down and insisted that Mister Abrams stop letting me do it*—my voice cracked again—*and that. And that. And. Th. Th. Th. Th. That Dad stop bringing me! That. Th. Th. That he cut it out. And p. P. P. Put an end to it. So he did*—*closed it up with that st-st-st-story of someone breaking in. Just to soft—soft—soft—soften th-th-th-th-the blow! Thinking that if I couldn't swim in it, then no one could. Because that was only fair.*

I could not make the crying stop. Mom squatted down in front of me.

Did anyone lay a hand on you?

I looked down at my hands. My cast was filthy. For some reason, the sight of it made my eyes well up.

Bruce Levitwerner called me a nigger. They all did. Said none of this wouldn't ever have happened if it weren't for me. That it was all my fault.

Mom looked over her shoulder. Dad was standing in the doorway.

I've asked you not to use that word—remember?

Now, hold on—

I will not. You were very smug about it. You said not to worry because you only used it when no other word would do, and you kept insisting there's a particular type of person you have in mind when you say it and you only use it to describe that kind of person. That you don't mean to be hurtful, but that in certain cases there's no getting around the cold, hard truth of it because no other word will do, and if someone feels bad about it, then so be it. That's their problem.

Christ almighty. You asked what one was.

It wasn't honest, Buck. It was hurtful.

I told you I was sorry then, and I'll tell you again if that's what you want, because you're gonna rake me over hot coals every chance you get. A couple of stupid little slips of the tongue and all of a sudden everything's about some stupid little word. Hell, don't ask a question if you don't want the answer. You said you wanted the truth, so I told you. Lord knows if we lived anywhere else, I might understand, but—

Here?

Lord, not now.

Where I live like your hel—

Pea, please. You can't imagine the day I've had.

Does Evelyn ever so much as acknowledge me?

Pea, I'm begging you.

How about Eula? Or Mildred? Or Lenore?

Pea, it ain't exactly easy for me, either. Listen, I hate to spring it on you at a time like this, but I've got bad news. I don't think we're gonna get the loan.

I don't care about that stupid loan!

You say that now. Goddamnit! But just you wait till more coloreds start getting tools and a little credit. Where will we be then? So I went to the bank today, figuring to do something about it. Hell, two can play that game. Only it turns out some new fella Walter's brought in from one of the bigger branches in Blakely has taken over our account.

Not once in eight years, Buck. Eight years! And now you can't even say that it's all good so long as Huey goes to Good Intent.

You're not listening to what's important, Pea! This new fella's name is Frederick Hempel, right? And right off we got off on the wrong foot. He's wound tight as an acorn. When I called him "Freddy," thinking I was being friendly, he said that he preferred it if I called him Mister Hempel. So I said fine, but that that's just how we are down here, Mister Hempel. And then, as an aside, pointed out that he's not from around here, and how maybe it's different up in Blakely, but down here—well, it might be a good idea to learn how we do things down here, is all. Especially if he's gonna be our new loan officer. And all the while, he's sitting behind his desk there with his neck erect, stiff-lipped, face turning the color of an overripe mayhaw, staring at me deadpan. He told me to sit down and then, cool as a cucumber, pushes a stack of papers my way and starts asking me if I know the number for equity this and financing that and amortization of equipment as a multiple of escrow reduction times write-off value on a cost-average basis, estimates of production orders, yearly mumbo-jumbo per annum—was making my head spin, Lord knows. I told him this is a family business. I'm not some goddamned upstart like John Rinkel. Said how he better watch his mouth because I might take offense. And he better not forget it. How the hell does he think Grampa Frank got that rolling hilltop with orchards spilling out over half of Early County, anyway? Jesus Christ. Last I checked, I was still a Fairchild. I mean, I am still a Fairchild, ain't I? We been doing this for over a hundred years. I slapped his desk and told him so. Said, so what's there to know? And the way he looked at me—you should have seen the way he looked at me. I mean, the way he looked at me, well—it just—do you have any idea how that made me feel?

I bet the day your grampa died wasn't so trying.

That's right. And I'm sorry. Okay? I really am, Pea. I know that over the years, maybe some things I've said have rubbed you the wrong way. But telling things as I see them is in my blood, Pea. It's what makes me who I am.

Because there's no reason to be anything less than completely forthright in this world, because the rest is just standing on humbug pretense. And you don't believe in that.

Is that so bad?

Then how come you weren't forthright about Huey having been ousted from Stanley's pool, Buck?

What are you talking about, ousted from the pool?

Mom shook her head. My new black high-tops were choking my

feet. I'd tied them all the way up to the topmost eyelet. Boy, was that a mistake. I untied them and kicked each one off. When I looked back up, Dad was tossing his arms into the air.

Oh Jesus, Pea. That was different. We're not talking about playing around in a damned kiddie pool. We're talking about having the wrath of a community unleashed on us.

You were trying to downplay how the world's closing in on Huey here, and you know it. Which is the same reason you've been telling him all summer that he might not be able to go back there again.

Because I realize he's too young to drop off there alone.

Because you're afraid he'll get blindsided.

What are you talking about, blindsided? I want to be there with him when he learns to swim.

Which you still haven't taught him.

I've been busy!

Oh, Buck. Can't you see? It isn't like when he was a baby. People are different with him now. It's only natural that they're going to be different with him as a boy than they were with a baby. And they'll be different with a young man than they are with a little boy. Can't you see that?

Don't you think I saw it today?

And so now what?

What am I supposed to do?

March him right on down back to that school!

Dad froze. *What's that smell?*

I looked up from my bare feet. I'd taken my socks off and was massaging them, trying to get the color to come back. *Don't look at me.*

Dad sniffed. *Something's burning.*

It's the roast.

Dad went as far as the threshold. *Where's the plywood for the other windows, anyway?*

I'd fix what's already broke before I worried any about boarding up the rest of those windows.

And I thought I told you to be ready to leave.

Mom held up her finger. *Enough.*

Dad walked briskly to the bedroom window and pulled back a corner of the curtain. He peeked out.

You need to be more worried about what's going on inside than outside.

I'm not going to have this house burnt down!

Dad headed back into the kitchen and shoved his keys into his pocket, then froze in the hallway with his eyes pinned on the front door.

Did you hear that?

It's probably just a damned raccoon!

No. Someone's creeping around out there!

Dad picked up the board leaning against the wall and fell quiet. Something scuttled past the open doorway.

Snowflake!

I cornered her in the bathroom and scooped her up. She was damp, smelly, and covered in dirt, soot, and cobwebs. She'd lost a lot of weight, and her little heart was racing a mile a minute. She was looking at me bug-eyed, like she'd had a real intense adventure.

Huey! Dad was returning from the shed with more boards in hand. *What'd you do with my paint thinner?*

Paint thinner? You're worried about missing paint thinner?

What the hell's gotten into you, Pea? Huey, get out here.

Dad was at my bedroom window. He opened it and slid the ladder from beneath the window and set it upright. I returned Snowflake to her cage and filled her water and food dishes, then returned with the nails that Dad asked for. I held them up for him while he fitted a board and started hammering.

This was my granddaddy's house!

Mom was inside my bedroom, standing at the window, looking out at us.

Buck, it's what we've got between us that's going to be left in ashes if we're not careful. What little spark is left.

XXVIII

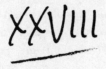

DAD WAS SITTING AT THE kitchen table, flipping through a trade journal while going on about how he was out trudging around in our fields before dawn, checking things out. After considerable back-and-forth, it was his opinion that today was the day. He glanced down at the puddle of water sitting in front of the fridge and mused that the shape of it reminded him of the reflecting pool on the National Mall. He'd had the good fortune to visit it once as a teenager. Mom was dragging a mop back and forth through it.

And Humphrey agreed?

Sure. But if I said the moon was made of Swiss cheese, he'd agree with that, too. Not like Toby. Hell, if Toby was convinced that it was too early to pull, he'd say so. He'd do the arithmetic right there in front of me, just to show me that the cost of waiting a day or two for the soil to dry out wasn't nearly as costly as the hurry I was in to get it done. You're an intelligent person. Now tell me, what the hell's the point of having someone around who can't think for himself?

Dad nudged my elbow. *Something wrong with your eggs?* He folded up his paper and pushed it aside. *You know, son, your mother and I were talking last night. Well—what I mean to say is . . . Hm. How to put this? What you've got to know—we know this is tough. Been a tough summer for us all.*

Absolutely miserable. Worst summer ever.

Yes, Pea. It has been. And we want you to know that—well. It's not easy for us, either. But what's important here, in our opinion, is that you understand that the world's not fair. That's the big lesson here.

Mom wiped her hands on her apron and pulled up a chair. *What he's trying to say, Huey, is that just because you're a little dark doesn't make you colored.*

That's right. That's what I meant to say. What I—I mean we—mean to say, Huey, is that the world's filled with exceptions. That's the main thing. And by golly, we feel okay in this day and age talking to you about it. You know what an exception is, right? No? Okay. Well, now, take your mother, for example. Her skin's a little dark, but that don't make her colored.

That's exactly right, sweetheart. Some people—like, you take that goonish Levitwerner boy, for example—don't have but two buckets to divide the world up into. It's all his little brain can handle. And then they put you into whichever bucket they see fit. And when people like you come along and don't fit in one bucket or the other, we call them exceptions.

Dad got up from the table and returned with a newspaper clipping. He spread it out in front of me. *I came across this article when I was up in Atlanta. To file the paperwork for your birth certificate, actually. Well, they got this big city newspaper up there. I forget what it's called. Does it say there? Herald or Post or Times or Tribune. Something like that. Oh, doesn't really matter, I suppose. Look along the margin there. Doesn't say? Nope? Anyway, this man appeared in it. Which, of course, didn't mean squat to me at the time. But seeing as how it was the feature story, I read it anyway. Now tell me—does he look colored to you?*

In the center of a block of text was a washed-out picture of a uniformed man squinting in the sun, carrying, of all things, a rifle. It was a Civil War–era photo, and the rifle he was holding looked like a breech-loading carbine. When Dad nudged me and reminded me what I was supposed to be looking at, I glanced up at him and said, *Nope.*

I didn't think so, either. Neither did your mother, when I brought it back home with me and showed her. Anyway, this man's name is Blind Willie McCullough. He could see just fine, by the way. So don't ask me why they called him blind. Anyhow, the thing about Blind Willie is—that you will find once you read it is—which I hope you will, because of how illuminating it is—well. Is that he traipsed around Georgia for forty years with a white woman, and no one was any the wiser. Not only that but he rose to the rank of general in the army. Can you believe it? Bless his heart, the man did every damned thing he wanted. Had a house. Four children. Shopped. Worked. Went to the ball game on Saturdays, the movie theater on Sundays. Came and went as he pleased.

So?

Which is exactly what I said. What's the big deal, right? Well here's the kicker. His mother was—you won't believe this—colored!

Sounds too good to be true, doesn't it?

Well, it should. Now do you see what I'm saying, son? When I first read this, why, I remember thinking, "Why didn't I think of that?!"

He was so bold. The way he stood up for whatever he wanted to stand up for. Just look at his eyes.

Don't even have to go that far, dear. Texture of his hair is absolutely one hundred percent normal.

Just like yours, sweetheart.

I'm sorry, but you take one look at him and all you're thinking is how normal he looks.

Mom sat down on the other side of me, the mop handle still in hand. *I understand, sweetheart. It can be a little disorienting at first. I remember how it was when I was a girl. Things were a lot different back then, of course. But I want to assure you that nowadays—well, not in all cases, of course. But in a great many, brown skin can be closer to white than it is to black. People don't talk about it much, but it's a fact. I know, I know, I know. You're thinking, "Not true." Probably because of what you hear at school. But I'll let you in on a secret—what am I saying? Don't take my word for it. Buck, do us a favor and get the Grolier's. It's in the living room.*

Dad got up and returned with the encyclopedia. He slid it across the table to me, sat down, scooted the thin metal legs of his chair up beside me, and flipped open the large book.

Let's see. What do we have here? Negotiant, negotiate, negritude—Negro. Here we go.

You don't think I know what a Negro looks like?

He thumped it. *There. See? Take a good hard look and tell me that you look like this fella.*

Dad's fingertip was covering the man's head. I pushed it out of the way. He wore a top hat and tailcoat.

Business tycoon?

No. He's tap-dancing, son.

Dad was looking down the length of his nose, examining the entry up close. Reading the small print. *Hm. "Literally meaning 'black.' A member of the black race." Interesting.*

He put both photos side by side, Blind Willie and the tap dancer. *Apples and oranges, right? Now do you see what I mean? Now, don't get me wrong, son. I wish coloreds all the best. Lord knows the world has not been kind to them. And I am speaking most solemnly on this point. I have great appreciation for the colored people, mind you. They're more reliable workers than a great many people give them credit for. And we've had a great many perfectly fine relations with a great many of our work-ers over the years. Isn't that right, dear?*

Mom nodded.

Dad snapped up the newspaper clipping.

And if I had to lump you in anywhere, I'd put you right with this one here. Not a doubt in my mind. Because he's the ticket to a better life for you. And if I have to go up to Boston or New York or Chicago or wherever old Blind Willie lives nowadays and drag him out of some nursing home myself and roll his wheelchair into that classroom with us, then I'll do that. So help me God. I'll thump this clipping down in front of Missus Mayapple with Blind Willie McCullough on one side and you on the other, because so help me God, if he gets to do it, then so do you!

Mom got up and jerked her chair in. *The law's the law, and I don't care how wrong and unfair it may be; two wrongs don't make a right. Those are the rules that we've set up to live by and respect, and just who do those people think they are, anyway, flying by the seat of their pants, practically taking over this town, making their own rules willy-nilly as they go like that? If they don't like it they should get the hell out, because we were getting along just fine before they got here. I'll be the first to admit that it isn't perfect, but I've made too many sacrifices for the little I've got, and Lord knows I wanted to go to that pool as much as anybody, but you never saw me complain about it. If I wanted to cool down, I took a cold bath, for crying out loud—was that so bad? Now they've gone ahead and planted so many ideas in people's heads they've got every colored Mammy, Tammy, and Sammy thinking they have as much right to be there as anyone. Don't get me wrong. It was madness* from the start—building an oasis like that in a backwater like this and not expecting everybody to want to come to the party. My word, this isn't Arcadia, this is Akersburg. Which is why we've got one man dead, and how many more to come? And for what? To swim in a damned pool, that's what!

Now, Huey. Your mother—what she means to say is—well, she's a different story. Okay? You know that by now, right? And that's fair enough. But God bless her tender little heart, some people actually believe she's colored. There. I said it. Whew. I know—crazy, right? But what are you going to do? Some folks are bound to think what they want to think; it don't matter if you hold a birth certificate in front of their face. They're gonna believe what they wanna believe. The question people like us have got to ask ourselves is, are we gonna let them determine how we think and ruin things for us? Now, me, I say to hell with them. Because there's no accounting for what others believe. You'll go crazy if you think there is, son. And I don't want that for you. And neither does your mother. Isn't that right, dear? What I'm trying to say is that it ain't how you look that's important, son—it's how you carry yourself. Your manner of speaking, your upbringing. That's the main thing. And to hell with what everybody else thinks. Trust me. They're gonna try and slice and dice you to kingdom come, if that's what it takes for them to be able to say what they want to say about you, as if finding one piece in a million makes them right. To hell with them. If that were true, we'd all be colored—goddamnit, we came from Africa, didn't we? Now listen here. What I'm trying to say is, Huey, people are making life a lot more complicated than it needs to be. Hell, I say if it walks like a duck and talks like a duck, then it's a duck. Right? And all I'm trying to say is, son, you're white. It's as simple as that. And anything that Edna or any of the other kids say is just dead wrong.

But—

Give your father a chance, dear. If he says he's going to fix it, then I believe him.

What you've got to understand, son, is that nothing anyone else thinks matters. Because they don't care about you like I do. And they're quick to assume the worst about anything they don't understand. Now, take me, for example. I've been down this road with Connie a million times, and there's nothing anyone can say that she hasn't already said.

254 / MALCOLM HANSEN

And she didn't decide for me then, and they don't decide for me now. I decide for myself. And my mind's made up. Had it made up before you were born. Practically had it made up the day I laid eyes on your mother. Then had it made up for sure the minute I saw this here newspaper article. And you know why? Because we're six generations of Fairchilds in this town, Huey. That rolling hilltop with orchards spilling out over half of Early County will be yours someday. And that means something in a town like this.

Seven if you count Huey, dear. Don't forget that after Trip, there was Georgette, which made four. Then there was your daddy. Then you. And Huey makes seven. Remember?

That's right, dear—almost forgot. Which is why we're gonna march you in there and set the record straight once and for all.

THE GASH OF red dirt lining Oglethorpe seemed to cut straight to the heart of the matter. Missus Mayapple and the sheriff were standing at the top of the schoolhouse steps, watching us coming down the road. We pulled up behind the patrol car. Missus Mayapple came down the steps. Dad let go of my hand and told me to wait, then got out and headed across the gravel lot, toward her.

What's this horseshit about my boy needing further evaluation for school readiness?

Buck, I don't like it any more than you do. But I've got a responsibility to everybody in this community. Not just you.

The sheriff came down the steps and joined them. Bruce, Darla, and a bunch of other kids were peering out the window behind them.

Now, just you hold your horses, Buck.

Where the hell does that leave my boy?

Well, first off, the good news is that those agitators aren't gonna be around for much longer. The bad news is that I think you're gonna have to hold out until they leave and everything settles back down. So I'm not too worried, and neither should you be. We're gonna sort this mess out.

You're doing a fine job, Ira.

Thanks, Edna. Now, Buck, let's think this through. Maybe lay low for the time being.

"The time being" being how long? A day? A month? A year?

That's a concern, Buck. And that will complicate things, no doubt. Edna?

Of course, I'm not at liberty to decide right here and now, Ira. But I'll see to it that it gets taken up with the board. I'm sure they'll want the advice of our lawyers—so as to resolve this with the least mess possible, I mean. And to everyone's satisfaction, of course.

If you ask me, Buck, why dontcha just take him on over to Eatonton and be done with it?

That's right. I don't care if you are his father; they are his people, and when that boy grows up, he'll want to be with them. Do the responsible thing and spare us all the needless spectacle.

I folded my arms atop the truck's door panel. Dad had parked so close to the mailbox that I could lean out and check the mail.

What business is it of ours if he isn't going to be much of a Negro to them? That's their business. The world is black and white, Buck. That's just how it is. I'm sure he is a fine boy, and Lord knows he probably does deserve better, but God didn't make him both so that you could pick and choose.

Lord, who made you God over that child, anyway? And where's your sense of decency, anyway? If he survives to see the day that he can think for himself, he'll think himself entitled to choose. No, you haven't thought of that, have you? Just figured he'd want whatever you want. Oh, dear. Ira, please, take this man away. It's hopeless.

Sometimes you have to be hardhearted for your own good, Buck. It's for your own good. Have the sense to see that there'll be plenty of time for a soft heart later.

Dragging us all through the mud for the sake of one boy. How selfish is that? I've been a headmistress a heck of a lot longer than you've been a father. And trust me, you don't get to be my age without learning a thing or two. It would have happened anyway, because when a boy comes into his own, he will decide for himself, and everyone knows that it's not worth taking the chance that he's going to decide against you. Now, you've gone off and knocked up a colored woman and had a child by her, and whoop-dee-do, all of a sudden, you're a loving father, so now you want everyone else to pretend that she and him are the only two niggers in town who deserve to be treated like the rest of us for no other reason than that they're yours. Well, I've got news for you, Buck—we're not the ones sleeping with her, and it isn't our boy walking around with curly hair and brown skin.

It's wavy. And he's practically white.

Who cares? Just last week, Phil joked that maybe there was something that I did to you when you two were boys. I told him that was the most preposterous thing I had ever heard. Why? No reason. He just thought that maybe I did something that turned you against us.

A hawk drifted in an updraft, high up overhead. The slow flap—slow flap—straight glide of its broad wings was hypnotizing. I glanced back down at the sound of Missus Mayapple's droning voice.

Listen, I'm going to say what I should have said a long time ago, and that is that I only ever wanted the best for you, Buck Fairchild. Told Connie myself, and no matter how hard you try, there is nothing that you can do to change that, because no matter what you think, I am not Connie. And deep down you know that, but all the same, she's right when she says that you live in the house that your grandfather built, because this is not about you and her but about him. And no matter how many times I keep telling her you're not the first man who's gone off and mucked up his life for a nigger—Lord knows it's all I can do to explain it to her, but no matter, just remember that the day after Frank deployed and she brought you to me and told me to see to it that you were raised properly, I vowed to her then and there that she could count on me, and it was with a good conscience that I swore to see after you if anything ever happened to her. And I will. And to stand by you come what may—that means through thick and thin. And I will. Which is why it tears me to pieces to have to say this. But it needs saying. Because I will—but not after your mistakes, hear? That wasn't part of the deal. So let's just hope that we can manage this. Because last week she assured me that this is not what she had in mind when she asked me to be your godmother. She said, "Edna, Lord knows I never thought that it would come to this." Which is why I'm glad you stopped by. This way I get to tell you to your face. You only have one mother, Buck Fairchild. And no matter what you may think of her, you're all that Connie and Frank have left. And like it or not, there is something that you owe them. And that is the stuff running through your veins. Someday that will mean something to you. It may not now, but someday it will. So let's hope that the day doesn't come when you have to choose between all of us and that boy. And let's leave it at that.

A cool breeze blew in through the window. I shivered. Missus May-apple started for the stairs. The sheriff slung an arm around Dad's shoulder and led him away.

She's gonna be the one dealing with all the parents, Buck. And you don't want to have your boy in a classroom with a teacher who doesn't want him there, do you?

XXIX

THE THIN RIPPLES RUNNING ALONG Cordele Road rocked me gently sideways. Half a mile up, a turnip field ended and another of the Orbachs' fields appeared. Two colored men were aerating the vast field encircling them. We followed it out for several miles, eased right at the first turnoff, and continued along another of their fields, this one covered with a smattering of hay. Dad slowed on the approach to our access road. We lumbered over its lip and continued past hundreds of haystacks arrayed in the field like headstones.

Dad pulled up beside one, hopped up and into the truck bed, and asked me for a hand. He summoned me down a rutted path and into the field. I had half a dozen pitchforks splayed in my arms, and it was all I could do to keep from tripping. I counted the tall mounds of peanut hay as I marched past row after row of haystacks. After a hundred and four of them, we entered the relative cool of our shade trees, and it was there that we arrived at a cluster of coloreds. They stared at me as I straggled up alongside Dad, cast and all, and let the pitchforks fall at my feet.

Kyle, I want you on the back lot today. Doris, you're on the front five. Art, you're on the back, too. Albert, you go with that new fella over there. Shapely, you help Doris. Maybe Kyle, I want you to be in charge today.

One by one, the men, women, and children picked up pitchforks from the pile and left, until the last one was gone. Dad picked up a shovel that lay in the dirt and headed for the thresher. I ran up ahead of him and jerked one of its knobs back and forth. Evan hopped down from atop the conveyor belt, startling me. I hadn't noticed him. He took off his cap, held out his hand, and smiled. I looked over my shoulder at Dad. I didn't know what to say.

Dad came over and asked Evan if Toby had taught him how to operate the thresher at maximum output without it overheating. Evan nodded and hopped back atop the conveyor belt and started priming it, then jumped down and began the difficult work of connecting it to the tractor.

Dad turned and left, satisfied. I reached for his hand. He signaled for me to wait. When he finished barking out orders to a straggler, he departed through a trammel of pulled peanut vines. A mess of crushed peanut pods, half-buried and withered, poked out of the dirt. The ground was covered with them. I ran up alongside Dad and took his hand.

What about Humphrey? I thought Humphrey was gonna be our new foreman.

Oh, him? It didn't work out.

Why?

A foreman's gotta do more than just follow instructions, son. He's gotta think on his feet, solve problems, manage people—all that. It's more than just coloring in the lines, you know.

I paused. *And what about me?*

What about you?

You know.

Oh. Don't worry. You two will get along just fine.

Not that.

You mean school?

Yes.

You know, I've been thinking about that, too. You know how important the next few weeks are. And how we're getting squeezed from above and below, what with every Johnny-come-lately setting up shop with forty acres and a goddamned mule, and consolidators like Herb snapping every foot of available acreage in sight. And I thought, No, sir. You're much more valuable to me here. Right here by my side is where I need you.

The thresher fired up and started spewing dust. Evan was sitting atop it. He hollered something out and gave a thumbs-up sign.

And how—what's that boy's name?

Evan?

Yeah. Evan. Well, as you can plainly see, he's still just a kid. And to be perfectly honest with you, I'm not so sure that he ever will be like his dad. I don't put it past him to cut corners, if you know what I mean. Well, if you don't, son, remember that the devil's in the details. So he's gonna need all the help he can get adjusting to how we do things over here. You know? Making sure things get done right the first time around. Why, you're an expert in that department, aren't you? And, so—well, I thought that maybe you wouldn't mind showing him the ropes. You know, as my right-hand man. You'll be sort of like a boss to him. Look at it this way—you'd be practically doing him a favor, what with his dad out of the picture and Goolsbee's place gone. Where else is he gonna go?

I'll read all my schoolbooks! I'll do all my homework! I'll never complain! I promise I will! Please! God! You gotta believe me!

I know, I know, I know. But it's not that. I swear. It's not that at all. It just works out better for all of us this way.

THE TRUCK STARTED on the first try. Dad turned on the radio, fiddled with the tuner, and started telling me about him and Connie way back in the old days of the droughts and gypsy moth infestations— how when Grampa Frank had shipped off for war, Dad was a teenager, and how for those difficult years when Grampa Frank was away, it was just him and Connie.

But you wanna know something funny, Huey? When Grampa Frank finally came back, years later, he was a changed man. But for all that war had changed your Grampa Frank's outlook on pretty much everything under the sun, it hadn't changed Connie's not one bit. She was still the same woman he'd married all those years back. No one thinks of that when they think of the cost of war. But it's true. Didn't change her one bit.

Smoke appeared over the tree line up ahead and dimmed the sky. Dad stopped talking and continued down the road at half speed. Around the bend in a clearing, off to the side of the road, sat a fire engine beside the charred remains of what had been a grain silo. A fireman was beating on it with a pickax, knocking smoking embers to the ground. There was a line of cars and trucks parked along the opposite side of the road, watching it. Dad explained that the silo had reached retirement age and that old things have to get replaced eventually. I couldn't tell if the people sitting on folding chairs eating hot dogs were happy or sad. Dad honked as we continued past. Said he recognized the fireman.

I rubbernecked as Dad sped off around the bend. I'd never seen firemen *start* a fire before. We continued on down that road with music playing quietly in the background and the tree-covered hills rolling slowly past. Several miles down, five school buses sat parked single file on the roadside. Dad pulled over at the turnoff in front of them and asked if I wanted to pick some plums before the season was over.

In the orchard, Boy Scouts were swinging from the lower branches while whistling "The Colonel Bogey March." I said no. Dad pulled back onto the road. A man was selling nuts and fruit out of the back of his truck at the next turnoff. We slowed down and pulled into Kolomoki Mounds State Park, just past him. A car with steamed-up windows was parked in the far corner of the gravel lot, and beside it a family of raccoons was taking turns raiding a trash barrel. Dad pulled in under a couple of trees. He pulled a pair of shorts from a Woolworth's bag and tossed them to me. Said it was just a little something he thought I deserved. They looked a little big, but I didn't care.

We got out, and Dad pointed at a densely vaulted wood. I followed him into the clearing leading up to it. I made my way over a damp bed of pine needles with a pair of brand-new swim trunks in hand and Dad at my side, and as we made our way through thicket and bower, Dad picked up where he'd left off about him and Connie and Grampa Frank, and how as a young man, he wanted to be an officer in the air force just like Grampa Frank, and how when he fell short, Connie wouldn't stop busting his nuts about it because it'd seemed to her that the ROTC hadn't been good for much.

Dad never talked to me about stuff like that. So I knew it was special, but even if I was sort of interested, I had no idea what any of it had to do with me. I wanted to believe what he'd said out in the field earlier that morning, but I didn't see how I could. I let myself fall behind him several paces. It was easier for me just to tell him that I was having difficulty keeping up. Dad turned around and waited patiently for me.

What's wrong now?

Why'd we bother stopping by school?

Jesus, Huey. We've already been over this a million times—to tell Edna that I needed you with me, because of how behind schedule we are. And she understood. We weren't the only ones. She just said to not be too long. And I said we wouldn't. Heck, just until we get caught up. And she said to be sure to come back for your lesson plan and books. Which I will. So don't worry.

You stood up to her, right?

Of course I did.

But I heard you!

You heard me feeling her out.

Then why didn't you say anything about it earlier?

Because it was a last-minute kind of thing.

Does Mama know?

Who do you think's going to be schooling you at home?

Wait—so I get to go back to school as soon as the harvest is over?

Yes. I said that already. This is all just until Evan gets up to speed, so don't worry.

And it'll be like nothing ever happened?

For goodness's sake, Huey. Sometimes you sure can be thickheaded when you set your mind to it. For the last time, yes, yes, and yes.

I swore to myself that I wouldn't cry. Promised myself not to let out one little tear because I was sick of him telling me that I was getting soft. But one slipped out. I couldn't help it. I tried to wipe it away, but that only made it worse.

All you had to say was that I was sick. Now everybody's gonna think it's because I'm a goddamned ni—

Dad put a finger over my lips. *Since when have I ever cared what other people think?*

He turned on his heels and continued ahead like it was all just so much water under the bridge. Like nothing had even happened.

Now, like I was saying—you know, most people, they don't believe there was much fighting down this far.

I ran up to his side, wiping the tears from my face. *During the war? Yeah.*

There was fighting down this far?

Minor skirmishes mostly. It wasn't the kind of fighting we should be proud of, so it doesn't get talked about much. But you and me, we got the story handed down to us straight from the horse's mouth. So we know better.

Don't ask me why, but I felt a little better. I think it was the mention of family.

Last year during Flag Day, Missus Mayapple said no way in heck was there any fighting down this far.

Dad swiped at the tall grass and rambled on about the time, a few years before he was born, when the Thronateeska crested during a hurricane. It continued to rise for days afterward, so high that anyone wading within a quarter mile of it quickly found himself in over his head. Akersburg was six feet underwater that summer, the worst-hit town in the area. Entire houses were inundated and swept away. Cars floated off downriver. People were left stranded on their roofs, on top of cars, and in attics. Water swirled through living rooms. Children paddled away on garage doors. Trees were uprooted and entire fields wiped clean.

Dad said that when the National Guard had been called in to help evacuate people that Grampa Frank, knowing the area as well as he did, was given charge over some volunteers. He was tasked with rescuing some cabbage farmers stuck out in hard-to-reach areas. That was what had happened to Grampa Frank when one of his underlings disappeared underwater at a blind drop-off. Sadly, there was nothing that he could do but watch as the young man slipped underwater, never to be seen or heard from again. Anyone going in after him would be doomed.

Dad's shirttail was spilling from his trousers. I grabbed at it.

Last year, on Flag Day, Missus Mayapple lined us up out front and walked us all the way down to Riverside Cemetery. You remember that, Pop?

For goodness's sake, Huey. I'm trying to explain to you how it took real courage to do what your grampa did.

We emerged out from under the dense canopy of pine trees, and Dad stopped. He gazed out at a stand of dogwoods arched over the riverbank. The sun blossomed over my face. It felt good. Dad went up to them, amazed that they were holding onto their flowers so late in the season. I stopped beside him. The swampy plain before us extended like a ledge all the way to the water's edge. I swatted at a butterfly and chased after him.

Dad knelt down to the water. *This is what I wanted to show you.*

How come?

You think a war makes heroes? Well, this is the spot where your grampa did the most difficult thing that he ever had to do in his whole life.

But what about that young man?

He drowned.

The ground was soggy and wet, and the rocks were cold and rough. Dad had brought a plastic bag and tape for me. He taped the bag over my cast, then kicked off his shoes and socks and rolled up his pants and waded in. I looked out over the murky water in awe. I was so used to my cast by that point that there was nothing that I could do with it off that I couldn't do with it on. So it had nothing to do with that. But for some reason, the charm of the water was gone. Maybe it was because it was starting to get chilly, or maybe because I just didn't trust it. I dunno. It was hard to say. All I knew for sure was that it left me feeling cold. I reached down and dipped my fingers in and ran them through the water.

If you ask me, Grampa Frank should've tried to save that young man. The Lone Ranger is always telling Tonto how it's better to die in honor than live in shame. Everyone knows that.

The water whispered past Dad's ankles. He waded up alongside me.

Whaddya say we work on that doggy paddle of yours?

Say, whatever happened to that little flag pin I got on Flag Day?

Dad tried to coax me in, but I tossed the swim trunks aside and sprinted up the shoreline, hollering out, *It's freeeeezing!* He chased after me and caught me up by the back of my trousers. I sank to the ground and sprawled out over the soft grass. He collapsed beside me.

Hear that?

What?

Listen.

I did. *I still don't hear it.*

He pointed to the murky water creeping over the shoreline.

The river is trying to tell you something. It's trying to tell you that it's not as simple as always duking it out at every turn and at any cost. Sometimes you've got to swallow your pride, just like your grampa did. He had to do it. Or else he'd have drowned, too, and no good done. And thank God that he did—because neither you nor I would be here if he hadn't. That's the wisdom of the river, Huey. It tells us to bend when there's no other way.

A FOR SALE sign was leaning in the drainage ditch in front of the Camelot. Dad pulled over beside it. A man in a checkered sport coat and hat was boarding up a window. Dad hung his arm over the door panel and asked the man if he was with the real estate agency. The man said no. He was from the bank.

We sat there, just sort of staring dumbly out from the truck as the man hammered. There was the *tap tap tap* as he started another nail, then the banging and knocking. Dad hollered out, *Mind if we have one last look?*

Go right ahead.

Dad pulled up to one of the ground-floor guest rooms and we got out. I squeezed past the stack of upside down FOR SALE signs propped up underneath the carport. The front door was open, but there was lots of junk blocking the way.

It was dark and empty inside. I crossed over to the patio door and pressed my face against the cool glass. The terrace was bathed in a golden light. The patio tables and the deck chairs were gone. The tiki bar was gone, and so was the linen cart. The pool was empty, and the patio was lifeless. I knew it was closed, but somehow I still expected to see motel guests walking around in flip-flops and bathrobes. Danny feeding the Coke machine. Missus Burns slathering on Coppertone. Aurelia knocking on a door with a short stack of towels in her arms. Mister Abrams standing under the shade of the tiki bar, showing Missus Bigelow how to make one of those fancy drinks with an umbrella in it. Dad would be standing nearby, bragging how every Fairchild had been not just a good swimmer but a great swimmer, and how that hotshot Dixon kid who had been the captain of the high school swim team was just the boy to teach me.

I slid open the glass door and stepped out. A faint whiff of chlorine hung in the air. I sucked in a mouthful of the stuff and headed for the pool. I sat down on the fat lip of the ledge and stared down at the thin puddle of gray water in the bottom, strewn with dead leaves and dimpled with indentations of water striders. I picked up a pebble and tossed it in.

Dad was out front, chatting with the man from the bank. His voice carried through the bare halls and empty rooms. He was asking after the details of the foreclosure. I remembered the time Danny Dixon had yelled out to me that the trick to treading water was to keep my arms paddling, with my head above water and "oh two" circulating through my nose. How Derrick and the Tillman kid were sitting on the ledge, splashing their feet around by the shiny chrome ladder, laughing their heads off because Danny was telling me to concentrate, and here I was flapping and flailing on my way over to him, spitting out water like a tugboat, smiling from cheek to cheek, having so much fun that I wasn't even paying attention.

Those six weeks that Danny Dixon was back from college for the summer were magical. To Mister Abrams, it was just a little something special he did for us local kids, but for us, it was like a dream come true. The ugly truth is, even if grown-ups would probably never step foot in the place again after Toby died, I would have leaped back into that water in a heartbeat.

Dad sat down beside me and asked how things were going. Sad though I was, I said, *Fine.*

He's a nice fella, that man. Said this place might go to auction.

I shrugged. *Where's Mister Abrams?*

Probably in the Ozarks for all I know.

We didn't get a goodbye card or anything?

Nope. Why?

I tossed in another pebble. *No reason.*

You're a bright boy, Huey. Tell me something. If the world went to hell in a handbasket tomorrow, does it make sense to you that it would all come down to this stupid little pool?

I reached for another pebble, but didn't answer. I knew what he meant. And he may just as well have been right, for all I cared. But as the gravel crunched under the tires and we pulled out of the parking lot, a weather vane creaked thinly in the distance. I told Dad to hold on and craned my neck to see as far into Mister Buford's peach grove as I could. But it was too late. Dad was already too far down Cordele Road for me to see anything except a perched ladder, steeply angled and disappearing, within a thick tangle of peach blossoms. Maybe Mom was right. It probably didn't even matter anymore. The lush bed of low-lying peach trees crisscrossing the neighboring foothills grew dim in the distance.

Empty buckets knocked around in the back. The inside of the truck was quiet. Dad tried to roll up his window, then remembered that he didn't have one. Field hands were back at work. A group of college kids with clipboards in hand were standing in the middle of the field, talking to them. Mister Goolsbee was hauling a stone slab and shovel up Cordele Road in his wheelbarrow. Dad tapped the horn on our way past, then slapped my thigh tenderly and told me not to worry. Mister Goolsbee would be okay. He was a survivor. Dad said that life was funny. Because as miserable as the summer had been, there was still something depressing about it coming to an end.

DAD PULLED OVER in front of the Rexall. I didn't feel like being alone, so I went in with him. Mister Wimple greeted us with a smile and warned us that he'd plum sold out of all his wide-ruled composition notebooks.

It's for his mother.

I looked up, surprised.

She lost her Bible the other day. Got away from her somehow in the scuffle. I think one of those protesters nicked it.

Mister Wimple pulled one down from atop the display case behind him, dusted it off, and handed it over. He was eager to tell us that it was annotated in red. Dad set it down beside the register and signed the receipt. Outside, the on-again, off-again weather had turned chilly. A few newly fallen leaves tumbled down the sidewalk. Dad buttoned up his coat and looked over the receipt. He seemed happy. Mom's Bible was of great importance to her, and he didn't like the idea of having to see her go without one. He held up the paper bag it was in and said that at least it was better than her old one. I had to remind him that her old one had belonged to Grampa Hicks. Dad tucked the receipt into his wallet and asked me to put on my coat. I couldn't be bothered trying to get the cast in and just hung the coat over my shoulder. Dad asked how my arm was doing. I still couldn't wiggle my pinky, but I said it was fine.

Dad said that he'd hardly recognize me once they cut the cast off.

We moseyed down the sidewalk and stopped half a block up. Mister Brines had changed the window display and we stood in front of it, admiring all the new stuff for football and basketball season he'd put in the window. Theo's dive mask was sitting off in the corner all by itself. It was marked down to half price. Dad asked if I was ready for a new one yet—said it looked like one of those fancy models, like the kind frogmen wear. He said that the split rubber strap was an awfully good feature and that it had to be good to at least five thousand feet.

I said no. I just didn't see the point. The river was already too cold to be fun, and anyone could see that the weather was going to turn soon. Besides, my old one had had a removable faceplate, too. I remembered all the times that Toby had paused from his work and strolled over to the shed, where he'd plop it down on the workbench and remove the faceplate and peel off the leaky gasket, scrape off the cracked bits of old, dried rubber, and, replacing it with anything he'd find lying around, stretch here and snip there until he was able to tuck it over the top where the metal band clamped around it, then put the faceplate back on and screw the clamp tight, then hook a finger around the strap and hold it up with a grin and say, *Good as new.*

Besides, it was going to be bad enough listening to Mom chew Dad out about the money he'd just dropped on that Bible.

Several shop windows had plywood boards nailed over them. There was not a trace of anyone up or down the street. The battered bus and the patrol car were gone. The protesters were gone from the sidewalk, and all the broken bottles and glass had been cleaned up. One of Missus Bleecker's leaflets tumbled past, got kicked up in the wind, and swirled around in the brisk air before shooting off down the street.

A cold gust of wind hit my face. Dad stooped down to help me with my coat and said the weatherman had warned of a cold front coming down from the Northeast. He'd been following it closely, said it was the sort of thing that only happens once every hundred years. Of course, we'd be okay because we'd be harvesting over the next few days, but he was concerned for Mister Harrison. He had at least three weeks till harvest, and the prospect of an early cold snap would stunt his crop so bad it wouldn't even be worth his trouble to pull it from the ground. *Son, if it's not one thing, it's another.*

The gusts of wind were cold and blustery and felt harsh on my face. I turned my back to it and flipped up my collar to keep the cold off my neck. Dad put his hand around my shoulder and said he didn't care what Missus Mayapple said.

Huey, I've said it before and I'll say it again. Your daddy being white makes you—

I stopped him midsentence. *I know, Pop.*

As long as you know that, son. I don't care what Missus Mayapple says.

I wrapped my arms around him and hugged him tight. The two of us rarely got to hang out, and doing so felt good.

Now whaddya say we get you a grape cola? Will you settle for that?

Dad led the way across the street and into S&W. I paused at the front door with the chrome door handle in hand. Down the street, three colored men and a colored woman had just emerged from the Paramount theater, laughing. I recognized them as field hands. And I found their laughter troubling because the movie wasn't a comedy. The marquee was behind them, and its big black letters were legible directly above the box-office cashier struggling to light a cigarette. It was some western where a helpless squaw gets it in the end. That's why Dad hadn't taken me to see it. He'd said that he didn't think I'd like it on account of how grown-up and serious it was. I'd had my fair share of tears, and the last thing he was going to do was pay for the privilege of seeing me sad. What I needed was a dose of hearty belly laughter. He promised to make it up to me just as soon as something funny came around.

Which is why I couldn't for the life of me understand the giddy merrymaking of those four coloreds strolling down the sidewalk arm in arm, headed straight for me, so happy-go-lucky, when they'd just seen a tragic movie like that. They were carrying on like they couldn't have cared less. No. Even worse—like it was the funniest thing they'd ever seen. I wanted to stop them in their tracks and punch them in the face. I mean, what kind of person finds it funny when a helpless squaw gets it in the end? Dad was standing inside the door. He tapped the glass and asked what I was waiting for.

WHERE WERE ALL THESE METS fans back in March, when the stands were so empty I could sit wherever I wanted? To make matters worse, three chicks in short shorts were sitting in the seats behind home plate that I'd come to think of as mine. I'm not saying that they were only there on account of our ten-game winning streak because, to be fair, they were advertising the shit out of the fact that it was the one-hundredth anniversary of big-league ball, but the two things combined sure have brought everyone out of the woodwork.

Still, the sight of those three blond chicks in face paint and tight-fitting shirts waving their blue-and-orange pom-poms made me wonder if maybe I didn't like the Mets a little more when they were losing all the time. At least then I could kid myself into believing that they belonged to me, if only because no one else wanted anything to do with them. Jimmy won't admit to it now, but at the beginning of the season he'd cast them off as a bunch of misfits. Ironic, I know. I think the fact that the Mets came to New York the same year as me is why I was a fan from day one. Not to mention the kinship I felt with a ball club mired in losses, clubhouse drama, player antics, defections, and historic misery.

It didn't matter to me that Chacón didn't know a word of English, so that Ashburn had to learn how to call for the ball in Spanish if he didn't want Chacón crashing into him out in shallow left. I was and would forever be there for the Mets and knew they would always be there for me, too. It was a tremendous feeling. There really was a ball club out there for everyone.

Shortly after the start of my fifth year at Claremont, I found a letter from Dad waiting for me on my pillow. Which, don't get me wrong, was nice. I always wrote him back immediately. I had so much to tell him about Claremont and my new best friend Zuk, because I knew that he would be proud of me. It was just that no matter how many letters I wrote or received, somehow I never gave up hope that one day he would show up on my doorstep, take me into his arms, and carry me off back home.

I kicked off my shoes, climbed atop the bedsheets, and opened it. In it, he mentioned having married a woman from Blakely. I reread that sentence three times before I moved on to the part about how Grampa Frank had broken his hip, and that as a consequence of no one being around to take care of the orchard, it was up for sale and they were all moving to Florida. I reread the whole thing a second time, just to be sure that I had it all straight. After that I just stared at it. *Married a woman from Blakely? No one left to take care of it? What the hell's going on?*

I set the letter down and decided to hell with it. It had been a year since I'd gotten a call from him, and for the last six months I had waited every single day, convinced it would be him each time the phone rang.

Mom was in the bathroom, getting ready for bed. I hid behind the doorjamb in the kitchen and crouched low to the floor so she wouldn't hear. I dialed our old number and cupped the phone. A woman whose voice I didn't recognize picked up. I froze. She said, *Hello? Who's there?* I was about to say, *Who the hell's this?* But then she said, *Is this you, Johnny? I know it's you. How'd you get this number? I told you never to call me here. I'm done with you. I'm starting a new life. Now don't ever call this number again, or I'm calling the police.*

I hung up. Mom came into the kitchen with her toothbrush in her mouth.

Who was that?

I looked up dumbly.

I've warned you about calling that Suzie girl too many times. Look at what it's doing to you. It's making you miserable.

I know that what Mister McGovern wants to hear a kid like me say is that as high as the cost of the Mets' winning streak has been to me personally, I wouldn't have it any other way because even if it's bad for me, it's good for the team and probably underachievers everywhere. But hell. Here we are in September, and the scalpers crowding around the subway entrance across from the ball park, over on Meridian Road, are asking an arm and a leg for bleacher seats. Christ. What's a kid gotta do to see his hometown team these days?

It's not pretty, and I'm not saying it's for everyone, but I snuck in amid the hustle and bustle of the beer trucks jockeying for position out by the service gates, trying to get their kegs delivered by game time. I slipped in among the trammel of heavy-lifting dollies and chain-smoking beer vendors and spent the next four hours crouched atop the john in a bathroom stall, reading the latest Steinbeck novel, waiting for the damned gates to open to the general public, all the while wondering why on earth Zuk would pass up a golden opportunity to see one of the last home games of the regular season. It just wasn't like him.

I figured what the hell and invited Mom to come. She laughed. A *three-hour ballgame? Are you serious?* She thought I was joking. Which is why it hurt a little every time I looked at the bald guy sitting beside me and wished so much that Suzie Hartwell was sitting there instead. Between innings, I'd play that awkward interaction we'd had during the game against the Phillies back in my mind, thinking about what I could have said to change the outcome. Even if I'd wanted to smack her then, I still felt that it would have been so much more fun if she were with me now. Naturally, my mind turned to how I'd dodge that bullet if I had it all to do over again, wondering if there was a way for me to keep my pride and her, too.

I'd been having this recurring dream where I was standing out at center court in our gym, during a pep rally or school assembly or something like that. You know how dreams are. You can't really tell exactly what the hell's going on or where you are exactly and have only a vague sense of place. Like it could be ten different places mixed together, quite possibly overlaid on each other, as if that sort of thing were possible. Anyway, the marching band is blaring their horns behind me, and everyone in the stands is going hog wild, having been won over by my game-winning shot at the buzzer, when none other than Suzie Hartwell swoons down from high up in the stands and lovingly tugs at my jersey as I express to all my adoring fans my heartfelt gratitude for the honor of leading us, the Claremont Lions, to yet another Division III championship.

Although there's really no telling, I figured that it probably just had to do with how much Suzie meant to me and how important it was for me to somehow measure up to her expectations. You know? For me to be good enough for her. Something like that. I dunno. Maybe I just felt a little inadequate or something. But who knows? It could just as well have meant that I had better start practicing with those kids hanging out all the time in the ball courts downstairs if I ever wanted to be anything but the team mascot.

When I told Mom, she chuckled and called it puppy love. I told her it was more than that. The thing is, there was something special about Suzie. I'd tell Mom how I'd never met anyone like her before. I explained that not even Zuk could tell you the batting averages and on-base percentages of the entire Mets starting lineup. It wasn't just that she knew that Chacón was weak going to his left side or that Bud Harrelson got a surprising amount of walks for a guy who wasn't hitting that well. Or maybe it was. I dunno. It was hard to tell. All I knew was that she was in a league of her own. Aside from a thoughtless comment here or there, she was dynamite. Besides, who's perfect? I guess maybe I'd fallen for her despite some of the things that came out of her mouth. I thought that if anyone could understand that, it'd be Mom. I guess that when all was said and done, I was just hoping that Suzie and I would get to go to another ball game together. Truth is, I was eager to give her as many chances as she'd need to show me that she wasn't really as bigoted as that day had suggested.

So yes, the Mets were very important to me. Because between Zuk going AWOL and Mom working off her newfound freedom like an indentured servant and Suzie not having called me back since that game back in May and Dad's having gotten married and moved without having the decency to introduce me to his bride, it was starting to feel like they were all I had left. Which is why I shoved the fat bitch in front of me with the big hair and shoulders like a halfback and told her to scoot the hell over. *Can I get some space over here?!*

It was bad enough that I was stuck all by myself out in the right-field bleachers, five miles from home plate, so far I needed a radio telescope to see the number on Bud Harrelson's jersey, hollering my effing brains out, knowing full well that Harrelson couldn't hear me tell him that the right fielder was playing him shallow. On one side I had the burly bald guy sloshing his beer all over my frickin' sneakers and on the other was a fuckin' Cubs fan—of all things—booing Harrelson directly into my right ear, while this fat ass in front of me had her big blue hair piled so high I couldn't see a damned thing.

XXXI

I TRIED TO ESCAPE WITH Aquaman and the Sea Devils into a cavernous underwater world for several weeks, but the loud voices from the kitchen only followed me all those thousands of leagues beneath the sea. Irma eventually got her money—Mom saw to that. The hurricane shutters came down from over the windows, gradually. First it was my room. Then, a week later, their bedroom and the front room. I was working out in our field with Evan so much I was too tired to do much of anything when I came home. I'd climb into bed with a comic book and stay there for the remainder of the night.

Over the course of those weeks, Mom brought dozens of books home from the library. There had been enough money left over after we made good on a bunch of unpaid bills for her to buy me my own dictionary. She told me I could write in it and everything. So that was nice. Mom liked to write in books. Didn't matter if it was a mystery novel or a history book; she'd write in the margins like it was her story to change willy-nilly, however she saw fit. In her version of things, it was never the butler who did it. One of the books she brought home was a slave narrative. I looked at it askance. When I asked what the heck she'd picked out that one for, she just gave me one of her looks. I wasn't sure what it had to do with me exactly. I was puzzled, but I cracked it open anyway. I flipped through it and saw that it was too difficult for me. I picked out a random word and asked, *What the hell does* ostracize *mean? Jesus Christ.* It was a grown-up book, and I didn't understand half the words. She handed me the dictionary. Turns out she actually expected me to use it. So I had no choice but to read the slave book.

In the end, I didn't write in the dictionary much at all. I preferred it clean and untarnished, the way I'd found it. But I did look up a bunch of words. When I finished the book, I just kind of sat there studying the cover. I wasn't sure if it was uplifting or depressing.

It took Mom a couple of weeks more before she came home with something on George Washington Carver. She lamented that it was even possible for me, the son of a Georgia peanut farmer, to not know who he was. She had been hinting that there was this man that she wanted me to read about. She'd been looking for something on him for weeks, trying to dig something up for me, but had difficulty finding anything about him in our local library, or even at the branch in Blakely. She finally managed to arrange it through her church to get something delivered on loan, brought down from some fancy library collection in Albany. Imagine—a book traveled all that way just to be in my hands! So of course I read that one. Anyway, I'd never heard of the man. Apparently, he was quite an accomplished scientist. Fascinating stuff, really. Curious choice for me personally, only because when she'd hinted that she was bringing home something on a scientist for me, I expected her to bring something on someone like Ben Franklin or Thomas Edison. I mean, really. Carver was interesting, but compared to those guys he was a nobody. I mean, he wasn't even the least bit famous.

There were lots of peanuts around our house during the month of August. Mom would spend nights cooking and boiling them, and Dad would station me by the side of Oglethorpe with scale, scoop, and bushel baskets of them to sell during the day. When harvest wound down, Mom and I worked together on math problems in the kitchen. She continued making regular trips back and forth to the library. I'd spend my mornings collecting seeds out back, studying the beetles and bugs around our house, and in the evenings I would rack my brain over my times tables at the kitchen table while Mom was at the sink, emptying the boiled peanuts into a colander. When the last of the water had drained, she would empty the peanuts into a grocery bag, dump in some salt, and shake the bag. We seemed to be getting into a new routine of doing things.

Then, one night, I was on the floor in my room working on a list of birds, beetles, and worms that I'd spotted on our grounds when Mom barged in and snatched the pencil out of my hand. She was bawling. I looked up and asked why. She just handed me a suitcase and told me to pack my things.

Is Dad coming?

No.

Is it something I did?

No.

Which I doubted. Whenever they argued, it always had something to do with me.

Where are we going?

On a little trip.

To Missus Muncie's?

No. Maybe a motel or something. I dunno. Ask me later.

When are we coming back?

Soon. Now hurry up.

Mom left the room. I sat there for a minute, quiet. I put my list aside and pulled open the top drawer of my dresser and shoved a handful of T-shirts, some comic books, and my home-run ball into the suitcase. I latched it shut and tried my best to hold back any tears. I was becoming quite a pro at that. I gathered up my jeans and high-tops and poked around under my bed for some socks.

I turned around at the door and, before closing it behind me, said goodnight to Snowflake. I didn't have the heart to go over to her cage and tell her what was happening. I felt it would be easier for her this way. I knew that it would be the end of her if I went over to her cage and broke the news to her face. She was much too sensitive for that. She'd be in pieces, and I wasn't sure she'd be able to put herself back together. So I just mumbled something about how important it was not to be afraid of the unknown and left. Dad had been avoiding me. When I cornered him in the bathroom, he explained how much he wished that he could come, but that someone had to take care of the farm. I told him to just stop, because I knew all that. I just wanted to be sure that he took good care of Snowflake while I was gone.

It was dark out when I stepped out of the house. I remember the sound of the crickets and the smell of boiled peanuts coming from the kitchen as I waited out on the stoop for Mom. I got into the truck with a sickly feeling in my stomach. The steel-belted radials Dad had bought made a distinct hissing sound. A blinking yellow light hung above an empty intersection in town. The eight-o'clock bus was sitting in front of the Rexall. I'd seen that bus pass through town my whole life, never dreaming that I'd one day be on it.

We weren't the only ones there. Missus Smeel was sitting on one of the shell-backed chairs, waiting for the driver to open the door. Dad stood by quietly as she told Mom about how she was off to visit a nephew a few towns over, in Rowena, who wasn't doing so well. He was sick. It wasn't clear what he had, so she wasn't sure how long she would be gone. All she knew was that she was going to stay until he got better. Mom smiled politely.

The driver opened the bus door at eight sharp. I grabbed a window seat and pressed my lips into a smile as I looked out at Dad. He was blurry. I was afraid that if I closed my eyes, the image of him standing there curbside, shouting out to me how much he loved me, would disappear forever. It was a strange feeling, him standing there looking at me like that, talking to me through the glass, telling me to be sure to brush twice a day. And to eat all my collard greens. And not to worry about Snowflake because he'd take care of her just fine—would even send me pictures. And to be sure to behave. And do as Mom instructed. And not to worry because he'd write tons and we'd talk on the phone all the time.

We pulled away. Dad grew small in the distance, then was gone. My stomach was knotted so tight it hurt. Cordele Road was unfamiliar and new in the dark. It seemed much smaller and narrower, somehow. Or maybe that was just the effect of the wall of darkness on either side of us. There was only the bright glare of the bus's headlights and the soft glow of the occasional streetlamp. Then the streetlamps tapered off and disappeared, and we were flanked by immense tracts of inky nothingness. A stretch of pines converged high above, and it felt like we had entered a tunnel. The smell of clover and milkweed seeped in amid the sound of hissing tires, and the wet asphalt reflected the soft glow of the occasional streetlamp.

Mom asked how I was doing. I smeared the tears from my face and didn't answer. She said she understood. I wasn't so sure. Up until then

I had thought that we were just going to spend the night at Miss Della's or something—that we'd be gone for a week at the most. But as the bus rolled farther and farther away from Dad, I felt as if someone were pulling my heart out of my chest. Then we turned onto a highway bathed in the glare of sodium-vapor lights. I looked up at Mom. I had no idea where we were going and was too afraid to ask.

XXXII

BIG RIGS SWOONED DOWN FROM concrete cloverleafs onto multilaned highways and filed past. Mom dozed off on my shoulder. I couldn't sleep. I cracked open *Sea Devils*, only to find myself continuously rereading page thirty-seven. It was Dad. I was unable to get out of my mind the image of him standing in front of those rusty shell-backed chairs we'd sat on together all those years. I must have eventually passed out. Next thing I knew, Mom was shoving me, whispering in my ear for me to wake up. It was time to get off.

I was squinting and my neck hurt. *Sea Devils* was crumpled up beside me, and my lap was covered in peanut shells. I flicked them off and followed clumsily after Mom with my suitcase in hand. I stepped out of the dank, airless cabin and down onto a curb that stank of piss and garbage. A black lab was dragging his butt across the sidewalk, streaking it brown. A woman dressed in two pairs of trousers and drinking from a bag walked up and asked me for spare change. Mom was standing by the shiny metal keel of the bus, putting her hair back together as she waited for the driver to open the hatch. I ran over to her. *Where are we?*

I was surprised to discover that school in New York didn't start until after Labor Day. Which I guess, in a way, was a boon. I'd just assumed that every place started when we did back home. School wasn't exactly my top priority just then, but getting a little extra summer was always a good thing. It helped knowing that I wouldn't be joining a class of complete strangers a month into the school year. I didn't want to be that oddball kid standing in the open doorway beside his teacher that everybody's staring at. I'd had that feeling once and didn't want it again.

Mom had counted on being able to get a job as a bookkeeper, but something about her not having her papers in order was holding things up. She'd found the brochure for the employment agency sitting atop the end table in our rooming house. No matter her explanations and demonstrations of all she knew about broker statements and tax returns and accounts receivable and payroll or her facility with ledgers and financial reports, everyone just shrugged and claimed that it was out of their hands without a previous employer who would vouch for her.

It's called a work history, ma'am. Certainly you must have at least one? I mean, it's obvious that you know how to use a ten-key. We just need a piece of paper corroborating the professional experience from which your skills came. It's standard procedure. It protects us in the event that you royally screw up down the road—basically saying to our clients that we weren't complete imbeciles for handing over their books to you. Surely you can understand that?

When Mom explained why she was unable to provide such a thing, the lady suggested she enroll in a class or get a certificate or some other form of accreditation. Sure, it would take her a little time, but on the other hand, she could do it with her eyes closed. When Mom explained that she didn't have money for that, her voice started to crack. She looked like she was about to start crying when the lady offered her a job cleaning office buildings instead. Her first paycheck didn't come for a whole month, at which point she discovered that the Imperial Employment Agency had deducted a quarter of her wages. Mom had never heard of such a thing. She couldn't believe that was legal. The woman from the agency said, *It's all detailed in the contract you signed, ma'am.* When Mom asked to see it, the woman got up and retrieved it from a file drawer. She smiled primly and showed Mom. Mom said yes, but it was way down toward the very bottom of a page busy with very small print. Mom had to hold the page up close to her reading glasses to be able to make out the words.

On the train ride home, Mom said that would be the last time she made that mistake. What struck me was the amount of times I heard Mom utter those very words, time and again, that first year in New

York. *Huey, it'll be the last time I make that mistake.* Come to find out, there are a lot of rookie mistakes you have to make in a town like this before you've exhausted them all.

For all the ease with which Mom had landed that cleaning job, it took another year before she finally landed at the Blumenthals'. When the lady from the agency called, she rattled on for a whole five minutes about how it was a plum assignment, and all the stuff that Mom would be expected to do, how she'd have to dress, and things to avoid saying in front of her new boss. Mom put her hand over the mouthpiece and asked if I thought she was good enough to cook for other people. I just looked at her. She took her hand from the phone and accepted the job.

For all the hoops that Mom had to jump through before the Blumenthals finally hired her, it only took a year for the Blumenthal twins to declare their undying love for her and for Mister Blumenthal to fall in love with her cooking and for Missus Blumenthal to fall in love with her cleaning and to ask what on earth she'd have to do to keep her for life. That was around the time Missus Blumenthal decided to pull some strings and get me into Claremont Prep.

Mom came home that night and poured herself a glass of *vino*—she'd started calling it that shortly after having started at the Blumenthals'— plopped herself down on the sofa, and made it sound like it'd been her plan all along. When I came to find out that Claremont was interested in me primarily because I was colored, I worried that maybe I wasn't dark enough, only to learn from Missus Blumenthal, on the taxi ride back from the guided tour, that they loved boys like me. She patted my knee and assured me that I was different, but not too different.

It didn't hurt that Mom had talked me up. She called me the next Ignatius Sancho, Satchel Paige, and Booker T. Washington all rolled up in one. If you have no idea who they are, don't feel bad; neither did I. I think they were famous accountants or bookkeepers or something. I'd never heard of any of them. I didn't realize until much later the full extent to which she'd talked me up. Which, now that I think about it, is probably why she freaked when Mister McGovern, having gotten hold of her at the Blumenthals', informed her that I'd been taken into police custody.

Mister McGovern went to great lengths to convince me that despite my standing out like a chimp in a china shop, everyone's heart was in the right place at Claremont. Which I knew in my heart to be true. Which is why I could have sworn that I was only going to get a slap on the wrist and maybe lectured about the risks of becoming just another colored boy with a criminal record.

Then an actual officer of the law arrived, with handcuffs and everything. After a couple of minutes conferring privately with Mister McGovern, the police officer escorted me downstairs. He opened the back door of his patrol car, then told me to watch my head and closed it gently behind me, kind of like Froeger's chauffeur does. So that was nice. When he got in, I told him the quickest way to my place, then explained that my mom was still at work and wouldn't be home for another three hours. He asked if I was a latchkey kid. Then he shook his head, sighed, and said he saw this sort of stuff all the time.

His name was Officer Pavlicek. I remember because I'd stared at his name tag in disbelief while he'd slapped the handcuffs over my wrists. I shouted out that I was going to sue the pants off Mister McGovern, Claremont, Officer Pavlicek, and the New York City Police Department for wrongful arrest and unlawful custody of a minor, not to mention public humiliation, slander, defamation of character, and probably fifty other things. I figured knowing the arresting officer's name would likely come in handy every bit as much as the pictures I planned on getting of my bruised and chafed wrists.

Officer Pavlicek headed north on Fifth Avenue, turned right on 125th Street, driving past all the storefront churches, juke joints, smoke shops, five and dimes, barbershops, billiard halls, and discount grocery stores they've got up there, and headed straight across the Triborough Bridge, all the while talking into his rearview mirror about how us mouthy rich kids think it's all a big joke and how we think that we have it all figured out, not realizing that the world's been handed to us on a silver platter. I couldn't help but grin. I was about to lean forward and set him straight, but then decided that I kind of liked being mistook for a Bilmore or a Hamilton. So I sat back in the thick, textured vinyl seat and kept my mouth shut and took in all the tugboats and garbage barges clogging up the East River as we blew through the tollbooth.

We pulled up to the front door of one of those special sanatoriums they have clustered together out there on Randall's Island to keep all the loonies away from the rest of us. The clean-cut colored man sitting at a desk stationed just inside the heavy front door asked if I was violent. Officer Pavlicek shook his head no and proceeded to remove my handcuffs. When he had them off, the colored man, who was dressed in all white, asked to see the underside of my forearms. He assured Officer Pavlicek that it was SOP. Officer Pavlicek obliged, then hesitated with both of my wrists in hand at the sight of my right arm. He said, *Jesus Christ, kid, your arm is bent to shit. Who do you go to for repairs, Dr. Strangelove?* He chuckled before remembering what he was looking for.

He's clean.

The colored man behind the desk nodded.

Officer Pavlicek said sayonara and left. The colored man handed me a plastic tub and instructed me to change into the clothes inside it. I looked at him, confused, and asked what I was supposed to do if they didn't fit.

I hesitate to talk about the time I spent in that facility because I'd like to someday manage to forget about it. Naturally, I was shaken. I'd just been dropped off at a fortified cement vault of a building with no way out. I wasn't entirely sure what it was exactly, although, to be sure, I was starting to have a few guesses. I was standing inside a yellow circle painted on the concrete floor. The changing area was wide open and freezing cold. Something about it made me feel like I was standing in the middle of an empty stadium. As I stood there, taking in all the steel and concrete and thick wired glass and Plexiglas and closed doors, it dawned on me what I was in store for. It was just like Mom had said: the colored man behind the desk was going to try and make me forget who I was. Which, however tenuous, was all that I had. Aside from Mom, it seemed to be the one constant in my life: I was a Claremont boy. I decided that I wasn't going to let the colored man behind the desk take that away from me. When he asked me a second time to kindly change into the clothes in the tub, I politely refused. I said that if it was all the same to him, I would prefer not to. The orderly sighed, nonchalantly picked up a black telephone, and made a very short call.

I don't think he said more than two or three words into the handset. In short order, two white men, also dressed in white, were standing on the perimeter of the yellow circle painted on the floor, looking at me. They asked the colored man at the desk where my restraints were. The orderly explained that I'd been compliant until he'd requested for me to change out of my blazer, at which point, I became belligerent. One of the men issued me a warning. He explained what would happen if he had to enter the circle. He gave me one last opportunity. I took a reflexive step back, away from him. He stepped into the circle and hurled me to the floor, pressing the side of my face against the cold cement while the other man forcibly undressed me, one clothing item at a time. When they at last had all my clothes off, including my underwear, they kicked them from the circle, wiped the sweat from their temples, and gave me the option to either go naked or put on the clothes in the plastic tub.

I changed. The two men shepherded me down a narrow hall and up several flights of stairs. They tossed me into the back of a single-file line composed of other kids my age, dressed in the same avocado color I was. The man told me to go with them. Two other men accompanied the line, one at either end of it, and they were also dressed in white. Neither took notice of me as they barked out a series of names—told this person to slow down, that person to speed up, this person to stop talking, that person to stay in line. We passed through a series of heavy steel doors and bare hallways and entered a long corridor that dead-ended at a set of double doors, where we were told to stop. I recognized the sound coming from behind the doors. It was a squeaking sound. Balls were being bounced. The guard opened one of the doors, and we plodded into a small gymnasium, single file.

THE COMMON AREA was essentially a bus terminal, repurposed. Steel-legged plastic chairs were stationed around the concrete wall on the periphery. Instead of waiting six hours for a connecting bus, I sat, alternately glancing up at the wall-mounted TV and over to the pay phone, desperate for one of the other kids to get off it. I called Mom at the first opportunity. She asked if I was okay and told me that she'd spoken with the authorities and assured me that she was doing everything she could to get me out, but that it wasn't as straightforward as one might hope, and in the meantime to be cooperative—that was the main thing.

I was in the middle of saying *Okay, okay, okay, okay* when I had to cut our conversation short. I was being summoned out into the hallway to speak with some guy dressed in slacks and a button-down who was waiting for me there. He was a small man with wispy hair and a gawky way of talking. He informed me that his name was Dr. Elias and asked me if I was aware of where I was and why I'd been taken into custody. Then he asked if I was aware of the gravity of the situation.

I nodded yes.

He asked me if now was a good time to talk.

I nodded yes.

He said, *Good.* He told the guard that I wouldn't require restraints, and the two of them escorted me through the maze of narrow concrete passageways and reinforced doors into a small, cramped office on a different floor. The guard left us alone. The doctor asked that I kindly make myself comfortable. He glanced over the contents of the manila folder in his hand and raised his eyebrows with a glance up.

Claremont Prep, eh? Not bad.

He turned back to the folder, glanced over it quickly, then put it aside. He looked at me squarely and said that on the surface, my case suggested a deep, highly suppressed underlying pathology, and that it was his job to discover the nature of those problems, which he was going to do by means of an evaluation. When I told him that I felt fine, he said that whether a single evaluation would be sufficient or more would be needed, he couldn't say as yet. In any case, I was not to worry. Although it was true that the state of New York paid his salary, he was basically working for me. He was merely to be the conduit to the state court's juvenile penal system of the important information I was to provide him and which he would evaluate so that the courts could determine the best possible course forward.

As in, what to do with me?

Correct—Hubert, is it? Yes. Correct, Hubert. An appropriate course of action, you might say. If that helps you understand it better.

Dr. Elias said that he needed specific information and insight to best serve me. He really wanted to make sure that I got it right the first time. There would be no second time. He took great pains to make that clear. He kept coming back to it—that if I wasn't careful, I would only end up hurting myself; that the only person who had anything to lose here was me. He took a tape recorder from his drawer and set it atop his desk and asked if his recording our conversation made me feel anxious. I shook my head no.

There was no need for me to worry, I was assured. He wasn't trying to make me anxious. He merely needed to record our conversation so as to accurately document my responses for the state. They would be submitted as evidence. Then he said that he wanted to talk to me a little about that, too. He would be asking me some difficult questions, but it was very important that I open up to him—that I not hold anything back. Concealing information from him would only risk hurting things for me down the road. I was to take the time that I needed with every question and answer as honestly and frankly as possible. And under no circumstances was I to fear that there might be negative repercussions to any of my answers. That was the best way that he could help me. If I didn't, well, that invited unnecessary risks.

I sat up.

Unnecessary risks? Before you go turning that thing on, mister—what's the worst that can happen? I mean, what are we talking here, exactly?

Well, Dr. Elias equivocated. *That's a tough question, honestly. And not really for me to say. But speaking to you as one human being to another, in the worst case, that could mean being taken away from your mother.*

Wha—?

Yes. Unfortunately or fortunately, whatever your opinion, the court retains the legal right to do so. If they determine that course of action appropriate, it is not only their prerogative but their obligation to do so—for example, if they thought that doing so would protect you.

When I asked Dr. Elias where they would put me, he said that he didn't know. *Could be anywhere.*

You mean, like another family?

Literally anywhere, Hubert. A family, a facility, an institution—

impossible to say. Could be anywhere. A place like this. Even jail. Impossible to say.

Dr. Elias assured me that if I were cooperative, it didn't have to be that way. But first, he needed to talk to me about a few things. He looked at his watch and said that we should get on with it because the sooner he could turn his evaluation over to the juvenile court the better. The family of the boy I'd poisoned would no doubt have the option to press charges, and stalling wouldn't help me any. The sooner we got down to brass tacks, the sooner he could provide useful information to the courts and the sooner we could be on our way to resolving this matter. Ideally, soon enough to potentially sway them from pressing charges.

Charges?

Dr. Elias nodded yes. *But this information will only help your case. Which is what I'm trying to impart to you. It's very unusual that something gets discovered in cases like this that can hurt the defendant. I simply can't imagine what that would be. That's why you need to be open with me. If nothing else, it demonstrates that you're being cooperative. And that's a good thing, right? So this is our first order of business. Are you ready?*

When I said, *Wait, wait, wait, wait, wait. Hold on with the tape recorder* and asked what the charges were, Dr. Elias hesitated. He wasn't sure.

It really hinges on whether that boy survives or not. Now, as I understand it, he's still in critical condition. But my information is several hours old already. He might be changing by the minute, for all we know. I am not receiving updates as to his condition. That is not for me to do. That is for someone else to do. Right now my job is to help you—which is why this is an extremely delicate situation. So we're going to just have to wait and see. Right now no one can really say. But if he dies, it could very well end up being aggravated manslaughter.

I was sure I hadn't heard right. *Manslaugh—?*

He nodded, gravely.

For God's sake! I was just trying to teach him a lesson!

The door opened. The doctor tried to wave the orderly off, but he remained by the door.

It's not my job to get into legal matters with you, Hubert. All I can tell you is that the prosecutor will decide what charges to seek, and a judge will decide the case, Hubert, based on evidence provided by the prosecution, the defense, and me. Now, I can tell you procedural information and am perfectly happy to do so, but none of that is going to help you right now. Right now, we have got to focus on the nuts and bolts. Our interview will be given to the prosecution at the point of arraignment to help them determine if they desire to seek charges. If they do, it will be used by the judge and jury in the prosecution of the case. That is all I can say right now.

But if he's okay—then it's all okay, right?

Possibly. But it's entirely possible, on the other hand—well, it's conceivable that they could pursue attempted manslaughter.

I wasn't trying to kill him! I just wanted him to know what it fuckin' felt like! Why can't anyone understand that?

Calm down, son. Listen, Hubert. Now we're getting way off track. I know that this is a lot to have to take in. You have no criminal record. And that's good—very good—in a case like this. I've spoken with your mother, and she sounds like a decent woman. And she's assured me that I will have your full cooperation. So I think this is going to all get straightened out. That's my honest-to-God prognosis at this point. That's what I told her. But it is in no way guaranteed. And you would be in gross misapprehension of the situation to think that it was. And I would be in gross dereliction of my professional responsibilities to lead you to believe that it was. Things can and do go wrong. The unexpected does happen. Happens all the time, in fact. Now, I think you'll agree that what you did was not normal. Can we agree that that's not who you want to be? Am I right? Because otherwise they're going to think you've gone off the deep end. And trust me, you don't want some overcaffeinated prosecutor thinking that you're in some kind of tailspin. Because he will lock you up and throw away the key because you are evidently a threat to everyone around you. Am I making myself clear? At the end of the day, if they are not confident that you are redeemable, this is where you will end up. Capisce? Okay. C'mon. You look like a good Italian boy. We'll get this all sorted out, eh? So let's get to work. I'm sure your mother's worried sick about you. And we can't have any more of that. Agreed? Good. In the meantime, let's just pray for that boy. What's his name?

Ariel J. Zukowski.

Because I understand that he is not doing so hot right now. And if he dies—and even if he lives—they may just try to take you away from your mother.

ONE DAY THE world seemed to be my oyster, and the next I was in a cold cell, listening to a man farther down the corridor shout out that it was lights out. I didn't sleep a wink that night. Yet, even if I hadn't been able to see it, there had to have been some sort of a progression. I kept telling myself that. I just had to be able to see it—but all I could make out was the dark outline of the ceiling. It was the great irony of my life that the things that I knew least of all were the things that were closest to me. After that first evaluation, Dr. Elias concluded that I would likely require others, because, as he put it, some of my problems were like a basketball that was pressed so close to my face that I couldn't even tell that it was a ball. So yes, I guess you could say that Dr. Elias helped me see that all this time, my deepest problems were akin to a basketball that was being shoved in my face.

Then one day, a pudgy administrator with a stud in his right ear came into the lounge and announced that patient number 67184-Y had been cleared for release. I looked down on my shirt. That was me. My mother had completed my discharge papers and was waiting for me downstairs. I was free to go. He said it like it was the most natural thing in the world. As if the past several days had been a cruel joke, like I could have walked out of there at any time.

Mom was waiting for me outside. I expected her to go ballistic, I really did. But she just undid her scarf and hugged me tight, like she did the day she finally got around to telling me the truth about Toby.

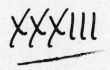

XXXIII

MOM WAS SITTING IN FRONT of Mister McGovern, boohooing about all the hours she puts in uptown at the Blumenthals' just to pay the token amount that Claremont asks of us. Mister McGovern reached across his desk and handed her a box of tissues. I slumped in the seat beside her with the dawning realization that I might not have what it takes to be a Claremont boy, after all.

Mister McGovern got up and went to the window. He gazed out at the orange, red, and yellow canopies lining the street.

We're proud of our tradition of celebrating our differences here at Claremont, Missus Fairchild. We really are.

I know that, sir.

Is there maybe something going on at home that I should know about?

No, sir.

I wished that I had some hard-knock story that would make sense to Mister McGovern—like how Mom was strung out on bennies and Dad was rotting out on Rikers. You know? Like many of the kids I'd come across out on Randall's Island. I dunno. I guess that maybe I just felt that no matter what you put in front of some people, that's all they want to see. What can I say? Maybe I have no excuse. Maybe I should have wiped my face dry and sucked in my gut and salvaged what little self-respect I had left, because maybe it's true that kids like me have all the benefits of being colored and none of the real costs. The fact is, most of my friends at Claremont assume I'm a wannabe. Not so much because I want to be something that I'm not as because the reality of what I am just doesn't make any sense to them.

Mister McGovern turned from the window.

It's a big world out there, Missus Fairchild. And believe me, your boy, Huey, here—he can practically write his own ticket. Go to any damned school he wants. Why, they're all but begging for kids like him these days. So don't get me wrong. I'm thankful to have had him.

Mister McGovern nudged his square-framed glasses up the bridge of his nose and sat atop the corner of his desk.

But Ariel didn't do anything wrong. And here he's got a collapsed lung to show for his kindness, Missus Fairchild. Because he didn't have to help Huey with his schoolwork like he did. He didn't have to do that. But he did it anyway. Did it out of the kindness of his heart. I went to visit him again last night, and the poor kid still can't even breathe on his own. He was lying there blinking like he had a fruit fly stuck in his eye. His face is swelled up so bad he looks like one of the Muppets. Broke my heart. The doctor told him not to exert himself. Then he told me one more minute and he'd have been brain-dead. Can you believe that? What Huey did to him—it's disturbing. And I had to explain to Missus Zukowski how something like that could happen at a place like this. My heart goes out to Huey, with whatever problems he has. It really does. But I cannot allow for someone to be present at this school who is a risk to other youngsters. I'm willing to go to bat for him, but only up to a point. There are limits to how far I can go, Missus Fairchild. These families pay good money for me to keep their children safe. Does that make sense to you? I hope it does.

I pitched forward in my seat. Have mercy on me, sir. I'm begging you. You gotta understand! A kid like Zuk being my knight in shining armor only made me feel worse! I won't last a day in some graffiti-covered public school filled with hooligans, where the latrines don't work because the kids shit in them. Where kids hardly ever show up, and when they do it's just to shoot spitballs at the teachers and torment people like me. They'll make mincemeat of me. I can be the Claremont boy you want me to be, sir. Just give me another chance. I'll prove it. Let me show that I will rise again, sir! Like a soaring phoenix, I will represent the triumph of the modern colored man over history. I can do it. I know I can. Just give me another chance! Please!

You're a good kid, Huey. And I like you. I really do. You're an important part of this school, son. You know that, don't you? Well, if you don't,

I'm telling you now. We're going to hate to lose you. We really are. As we say, there are no second-class citizens at Claremont. You know that.

I do, sir. I know that.

Huey, would you mind giving us a moment in private?

Mister McGovern opened the door and called in Missus Zukowski. She stopped me in the doorway and wagged her finger in my face and said that this was all my fault. There was a special place in hell reserved for people like me. Not to mention a world of other kids out there who should be so fortunate. It was only because I was colored that they let me attend Claremont with her son.

MOM LIT A cigarette, took a long, deep drag, and pulled me in close on our way down the front steps.

He's a nice man. You're lucky. He likes you and believes in you. I can tell. God knows why, because you've given him such little reason to. Lucky for you he thinks you just lack a father figure. He said he understands about your father—knows how hard that must be, to have an estranged father. But you're not the only one, Huey. He said several of the other boys here have estranged fathers, too, and struggle with the exact same issues as you.

I looked up. Dad wasn't estranged. Unreliable, maybe. Negligent, certainly. Absent, temporarily. But not estranged.

Anyway, he recommended that I contact the Big Brothers Association. Apparently they've got something set up where they provide father figures to boys like you. They come highly recommended—someone to take you out for an ice cream every now and again. You'd like that, wouldn't you? I said we're open to giving it a try. And that we're going to pay a little visit to Ariel tonight.

Tonight?

Tonight. You're going to bring him some of my chicken soup. And maybe some chocolate and flowers. And you're going to apologize. I told Missus Zukowski that I'd figure out some way for you to get over to the hospital every night to bring him a home-cooked meal until he bounces back. Told her how much the Blumenthals love my cooking. She said that wasn't necessary, but I insisted. It's the least we can do. And on top of that, you're to write down some thoughts about why you're so angry all the time. For the judge. Oh, Missus Zukowski agreed to drop the charges, all right, but I said you'd do it anyway. To show your heart's in the right place.

What about school?

Mandatory two weeks' academic probation. Regular counseling. And a fifty-page essay exploring the root causes of shame as a source of anger and a lack of personal accountability and a depleted sense of self-worth. If it goes over a little, that's okay, too.

Fifty pages? Are you crazy? That's a book!

I walked on ahead, feeling a little light-headed. I stood on the corner at Ninety-Seventh and Madison and closed my eyes. I pretended for a second that I was back home. Funny how something so far away can feel so close, and something so close can feel like a million miles away. All the honking cars zipping past in the rightmost lane, with their door handles zinging past inches away from me, put an end to that. Mom came up from behind and reminded me just how lucky I was. I shrugged. She warned me not to take the second chance I'd been given for granted.

I nodded. *I guess. But fifty pages?*

Mom's breaths were visible puffs of vapor. She clapped her hands for warmth and sighed. She knew how hard it had been leaving Dad. Said that had been the hardest thing she'd ever done.

I looked up, surprised. *Really?*

You think that was easy for me? I loved your father, Huey. I loved him very, very much. You probably don't know it, but people didn't even want us living together. We defied them and did it anyway. It wasn't easy. Our love for each other drove all of that. We'd be married now if they'd have let us. But there was not a courthouse in the state that would recognize us as husband and wife. Seems crazy now, huh? I held out hope for as long as I could, but in the end it was clear that his loyalty was to his parents. I guess I just thought that he would change. Come to find out that all that time, he'd been expecting the same thing of me. Who knows? Maybe it's good we never married.

Mom paused. She looked down at me. *You wanna go back, don't you?*

I shrugged. *I dunno. Maybe.*

If you do, I will support you in that. Lord knows things haven't been great here. But you must understand that no matter how difficult life has been for us these last seven years, this is nothing compared to what it would have been like for us had we stayed. She paused. *There comes a point in life, Huey, where the question isn't so much* What should you do? *but* What options do you have?

We crossed Fifth Avenue. It was mostly overcast, but a sliver of sun was peeking through the cloud cover, so low on the horizon it lit the bellies of a flock of pigeons gliding overhead. Mom took my hand and said that when I was a baby, she truly believed the Fairchild family orchard would one day be mine, but that the older she got, she came to realize that had never been in the cards. She shook her head at the dead leaves, stiff and curled, tumbling down the sidewalk. Mom and I entered the park at Ninety-Sixth Street and followed the first shrub-lined path we came to. We strolled through a patch of stinky ginkgos and mixed in with the ten-speeds, and the large-framed Mary Poppins bikes with their long fenders and baskets, and the tourists strolling about snapping pictures. We stopped in front of two jugglers tossing candlepins back and forth. Mom put her spare change in their cap, and we continued on past folksy guitar strummers belting out a protest song. Mom waxed philosophical about how much had changed in the last few years—how I'd gone from being a little boy to someone who would soon be a young man, and how the world around us was changing so much from one day to the next. She slung an arm over my shoulder and cursed Johnson for having lowered the draft age, but told me not to worry. Not in a million years would she let me fight that man's fight.

I stopped. *Jesus Christ. Do I look like some long-haired lotus-eating freak? I wanna go and fight!*

Over my dead body! I will not let that man get his hands on you. You hear me? If I wanted you dead I'd kill you myself. Christ, Huey. Don't be a chump! When are you going to realize that we win just by getting along? And the assholes can't even do that!

A mime was doing his routine in front of the zoo. He put his fingers to his lips and looked in our direction as we stood there bickering like an old married couple. We exited the park at Fifty-Ninth Street. I stood on the corner, staring at the perky breasts on the statue of some chick holding a fruit basket across the street. Mom tugged my arm and told me to cheer up. She said she knew just the thing to make me feel better and dragged me downstairs into the subway. We took the R train one stop and got off at Lexington Avenue. Mom took off her shawl, and we popped into Bloomingdale's. On our way up the escalator, she picked at the pilling on my blazer and fussed over a tiny hole at my left elbow and told me that I was in desperate need of a new one. I lifted my arm to demonstrate that it was only noticeable when I raised my hand with a question.

Mom didn't think that funny. Neither had she appreciated having to have it dry cleaned after I'd fished it out of the garbage can that day. Her boss at the dry cleaners, Mister Sanders, had charged her; he was still upset with her for having reduced her hours on account of Missus Blumenthal demanding more and more of her time. Mom looked down at me and said that even if it annoyed her having to shell out three bucks of her hard-earned money to pay for the dry cleaning, it was still worth it. She started in about how important it was for me to look top notch. Whether I knew it or not, people judged me by how I looked. I shrugged and told her that it wasn't like I was fooling anyone.

It didn't matter to Mom that Vernonblood, Lichenberger, and Bilmore all knew where I lived or that Zukowski was the only one who didn't seem to care. She looked at me in the prudish way she does when she's annoyed and reminded me that it was still worth spending a little extra to get the very best. What bugs me is that Mom humps away day in and day out just to buy me the stuff rich kids have, never realizing that they're dyed-in-the-wool blue-blooded boys and not just some measly peanut farmer's son, which she still manages to talk about like it's a big deal. She doesn't care if me having at least some of the stuff kids with nannies, au pairs, and chauffeurs have comes at the cost of us spending more time together, because the second I mentioned Dad and peanuts in the same breath, she started rambling on about how she had a mind to petition for back pay for all the work she'd done for him, because she should have known all along that she'd never get one red cent out of him for all her trouble keeping his books, never mind get to be a Fairchild, and when were people going to start calling her by her correct family name, anyway? She needed to start correcting people, because she was a different person than she had been back when she let it slide because it didn't seem to be worth the trouble. She was sick and tired of all the people from my school calling her Missus Fairchild all the time, when she was not a Fairchild and never would be a Fairchild because that had probably never been in the cards either. She knew that now. She only wished she'd known it then.

I snapped my fingers in her face and told her to get a grip. *What the heck are you talking about?*

You wouldn't understand if I told you.

Well, you lost me on our way past the third floor. Enough with the ranting, Mama!

Oh, hush.

There's no point arguing with her when she gets like that. Besides, it was too late. She'd already received a two-week advance from Missus Blumenthal to help with the cost of some unexpected lawyer's fees and the special psychiatric evaluations. We got off on the fourth floor and headed for the men's department. I took a seat in the wingback chair they keep in the back by the tailor's station and started to swing my feet back and forth while pretending that I was wearing a smoking jacket and puffing on a pipe like Alistair Cooke. I love that show.

Mom had been up late, taking care of the twins for half the night. She was standing in front of a three-way mirror, trying to rub out the dark circles under her eyes, going on about how the truth was that Dad always had been a hear no evil, see no evil, speak no evil kind of guy. And in a way, maybe she had been, too. But she was a much different person from who she was back then. And no, maybe New York hadn't turned out like all the fancy stories she'd been told, but we'd make something of it still. We just needed to give it more time. Where there were second chances, there was hope. And New York seemed to be giving us a second chance. Mom flashed me a smile— the kind that can light up a ballroom, which to my mind, was just another New York City abstraction that I had never been to. Right up there with Carnegie Hall, Lincoln Center, the Statue of Liberty, the Empire State Building, and the Apollo Theater. Anyway, even if you can kind of tell that life has been a little rough on her, she's still the most beautiful woman in the world. Honestly, I don't know how she does it.

An older gentleman in a double-breasted suit and comb-over strolled over and asked if he could be of service. Mom asked after a Mister Castiglioni. The man raised an eyebrow, nodded his head slightly, and said, *Speaking, madam.*

Mom informed Mister Castiglioni that he came highly recommended from Carol Blumenthal. Which seemed to make an impression. Mister Castiglioni checked his watch and then escorted us into a fitting room. Mom handed him the blazer she'd pulled from a rack. Mister Castiglioni recognized the crest on my lapel, complimented me on my academic accomplishment, and instructed me to kindly change into the one he was presently holding open for me.

I slipped my right arm in quickly. The infection where the bone had poked through the skin had left an ugly scar, but the worst part was how crooked it had healed. I'll never forget the look on Mom's face when the doctor at the New York Hospital cut off the cast and saw my bow-shaped forearm. She was as shocked as he was. There she was, planning to celebrate the occasion with Chinese takeout, and she turned irate with those two big bags of food in her hands. I could tell that she wanted to throw them, but of course she couldn't waste food. She'd joked on our way up the elevator to the pediatric orthopedics floor, telling me how it'd be a quick in and out and that of course the Chinese food would still be hot by the time we got home. She had no idea that my arm was going to end up looking like a corkscrew— that's what she'd called it. Dad had never told her that he'd foregone the procedure that would have corrected that issue without having consulted her.

Dr. Cohen, who had no idea about any of that, asked if it had happened while we were on vacation in Mexico; he'd attended a conference in the Yucatán once and could sympathize. The Mayan ruins in Chichén Itzá were amazing, but you didn't want to end up in a hospital there. When Mom grunted and said, *No, no, no, no, no, no, no. It happened right here. In the United States,* Dr. Cohen looked both ways and said under his breath that he didn't necessarily advise it, but judging by what he saw, she could probably sue for malpractice. *This is egregious, ma'am. There isn't a judge out there who wouldn't be sympathetic to this.*

Mom didn't care about the money. She wanted my arm to be straight—which Dr. Cohen explained was resolutely impossible. Took Mom three weeks before she was able to climb down from the angry tree. I learned that term from my court-appointed social worker, Tabetha, who urged me to visualize myself climbing out of a tree next time I got irate. Said it helped to trigger something calming in the brain. I asked if it could be any kind of tree I wanted, and she said sure, why not? I settled on a palm tree. They seemed pretty damn near impossible to get out of. Long story short, Dr. Cohen said there was a fifty-fifty chance that I would regain sensation in my pinky. It's been seven years now, and it still just kind of hangs there, useless.

All this is to say that my bent-to-shit forearm got a raised eyebrow from Mister Castiglioni. Thankfully, he didn't feel the need to comment. Instead, he blithely snapped at the blazer's hem with his fingers and, with pins in his mouth, said,

Whose kid?

My eyes fell to the floor.

The Fairchilds'.

I don't know that family. What business are they in?

Peanuts.

Mister Castiglioni raised an eyebrow, impressed. *Peanuts? I once had a customer who was in peanuts. Now, this was a great many years ago, of course. I think his son went into politics. Or maybe it was his nephew. Anyway, he used to come in all the time, trying on some double-breasted number, and would always talk about his boy. I think he was doing some type of missionary work for the UN, if I'm not mistaken. Who knows? Might be a congressman now, for all I know. Any relation?*

I waited for Mom to correct him, but she just said that she wouldn't know and otherwise let him believe whatever he wanted. After all her talk. I was starting to sense that maybe everything had changed and nothing had changed. Mister Castiglioni finished with the chalk marks and poking me with pins and informed Mom that it would be ready at four thirty, then bid us to kindly give his regards to the dear Missus Blumenthal.

Mom pulled me in close, and on our way out of the heavy glass doors, I closed my eyes and wished the day to last forever. With all the time we had together when we lived back in Akersburg, I'd never once gone for a stroll with her down Main Street. What made strolling down Lexington arm in arm with Mom magical for me was that no one bumping into us knew or cared whether or not my folks were married, or why they'd split, or what color they were or how much money they made. We strolled down Lexington like two kindred spirits and would have done it together every day if it wasn't for the fact that she practically lived at the Blumenthals'.

I didn't care if all the men in business suits shoving their elbows and knocking their briefcases into me as they passed assumed she was my nanny. And honestly, I don't think Mom did, either. It was still nice. As we walked down the busy street, weaving through the hustle and bustle of midtown pedestrian traffic on a drab weekday afternoon, I thought that maybe the pickle I'd gotten myself into had something to do with the realization I'd had that it was better to be some run-of-the-mill, just-off-the-boat foreigner from Krakow, or wherever the hell Zukowski's folks were from. They actually thought they were better than me. It didn't matter to them that they hadn't been off the boat fifteen years and were from some godforsaken far-flung place that I couldn't even pronounce, or that they still spoke Polish around a dinner table packed with aunts and uncles and cousins while Missus Zukowski peeled potatoes barefoot in the kitchen of their split-level, stand-alone duplex out in Canarsie. None of that mattered. I mean, really? Does that kind of bullshit happen in other countries? Even the one they left?

Even if it were true that I'd only gotten to go to Claremont because I was colored, I didn't exactly appreciate having my face rubbed in it. The worst part for me was that even if Zukowski knew better, the rest of his family hadn't been here long enough to and didn't understand about our delicate history of human bondage, and frankly, they could not have cared less. Missus Zukowski was too busy celebrating her son's recent accomplishments in the land of opportunity to be bothered to give a shit about that. As far as her merry band of scorekeepers were concerned, the point totals spoke for themselves.

Zukowski's family hadn't been here for much longer than I'd been alive and had already achieved what had taken Mom ten generations. Trust me, none of that was lost on me. And none of that would have mattered, not one lousy bit, except for the fact that Zukowski's enlightened worldview wasn't enough to keep him from cashing in on the advantage unfairly conferred unto him when it mattered most. He had no problem using the color of his skin to curry favor with Suzie Hartwell when she came to both realize and resent that I'd misled her about mine. And yes, that pissed me off. I knew that what I'd done was wrong, but so was he. I was being mocked and maligned on a daily basis for having the gall to use the color of my skin to gain advantage where it concerned getting into Claremont, and here people like Zuk pulled shit like that all the time and weren't even aware of it, much less feeling pangs of guilt about it.

Listen, I'm not going to sugarcoat it. I was having a hard time, socially, those first few years at Claremont. I know that what grown-ups want to hear me say is that it's a great time in our country's history to have brown skin, what with a kid like me in school here and the nation on the mend now that we've got all that happened back in Akersburg behind us. But I was pissed. Tabetha has assured me that it's okay if I come clean about the racism I've experienced at Claremont, that I can only bottle things up for so long before they just explode. Even if I'd gotten pretty good at ignoring it, when *nigger* was murmured anonymously under someone's breath, it still hurt. I dunno. Maybe it was just that I no longer had an Evan around to absorb that particular shock.

Which is why I had no choice but to explain myself to Mom. I told her how devastating it felt when I saw Suzie Hartwell and Zukowski walk up the stands in the gymnasium and then sit together, arm in arm, at a pep rally. How I calmly made my way through the crowd and walked over to him and tapped him politely on the shoulder, and when he turned, I socked him one. Right in the teeth. I don't know. Seeing the two of them together like that—it just triggered something ugly in me. I just sort of blew my top. I guess I just realized that having nothing in common but a lack of belonging is not enough to base a friendship on. I deserved better. My only regret was that I'd let Hamilton and Bilmore egg me on, which had me feeling like I was their chump. Of course I knew that guys like them just want to see a fight. I dunno. I guess I'd just finally reached a point where I didn't care anymore. Didn't matter that it took five years—they'd finally succeeded in getting me to behave the way they'd predicted I would all along. As they said, *That's just what niggers do.* I looked up at Hamilton and Bilmore and said, *Happy?* and walked off with blood on my hands.

Mom stopped me in my tracks.

Oh my Lord. You didn't. Please tell me you didn't. Oh, no. You did? You did that? How did I not find out about that? Mister McGovern was wrong. It's not a father figure you lack. It's the father figure. You lack Jesus Christ in your life, son. I'm sorry, but it's true. You do. I sense a black hole somewhere deep inside you—a very, very dark place. Absolutely, positively Godless, I'm afraid. Starting tomorrow, you're going to start reading the Bible again. We're going to start with Leviticus. I think that'll be good for you. Every day. And cartoons be damned—you're going to make time for church on Sundays. And not just on Christmas and Easter, either. Every week. You hear me? For crying out loud! Does his mother know about that?

The only answer that I could offer was a shrug. The truth was, I didn't know. On our way across the street, the late-afternoon sun was shining a lustrous amber light between the tall buildings. Mom rubbed her hands together for warmth and cursed the cold and said how eight years sure was a long time to have cloudy judgment, and how Dad hadn't given her one red cent for child support all these years, and how she was sick and tired of being nickel-and-dimed to death, and how people down there probably still don't want people like them living together and now she hadn't got a legal claim to any of it. *Nothing. Imagine! Rights, my A-S-S.* She wasn't allowed to protect herself financially and here she was taking care of me all on her own and Dad never sent one red cent in any of those letters, and now he probably had some other woman doing his books for him. Mom gave a manic laugh, then stopped and snapped me around in the crosswalk right in the middle of Lexington Avenue.

You don't think I heard her? What she said to you in the doorway of Mister McGovern's office? I've been working around people like that for seven years, mister. And you don't think I've heard that talk before? Don't you believe it. Or seen the look of judgment on her face when she said it? Listen here. You have every bit as much right to be at Claremont as Ariel. Every single bit and then some. It's like one man steals a house from another man, and we say, fine. The authorities find the man guilty and send him to jail, and we say justice is served. But his son gets to keep the house. Okay? In short order, the son has a child and decides that he wants a second house. Except now, the man who's had his house stolen finds himself competing for a home loan with guess who—the thief's son. Only the thief's son has a house to offer up as collateral against a second mortgage, and the man with whom he's competing for the loan does not. Now, the banker doesn't care one way or the other about that first home. He only cares about getting his money back. And after all, the son didn't steal the house that he lives in. His father did. So why should he be penalized unfairly? We all know that you can't punish the son for the sins of the father. Which is why he gets to live in that first house. But I'll be damned if he gets to use it to bootstrap his second home when there is still a man out there who has been robbed of his fair chance at his first! And I don't care if Zukowski has nothing to do with the provenance of that first home, either. Because it was stolen, and they strolled into it like they've got the Midas touch, when all they've done is stumble upon a damned fire sale. Nothing more!

An emotional bottle, having inadvertently come uncorked, was spilling over, and Mom was desperate to catch every drop. I wasn't following half of what she said, but it didn't seem to matter. Lexington Avenue may as well have belonged to her.

I'm going to tell you this once, sweetheart, and then I'm never going to tell it to you again. So listen well. Any person you know who has not had a family member enslaved is at a two-hundred-fifty-year advantage over you. Okay? Not the other way around. You must understand that one simple fact. You have ancestors—blood relatives, real people, connected to you by blood and history—who were enslaved, who had their families, language, labor, freedom, possessions, and identity taken from them by force and used to the advantage of everyone you see around you right here, right now. That is, everyone but us. So do not ever let anyone talk to you like you're some goddamned drain on society. Ever! That would be like scorning the man who has built your house for not owning one himself. That's just wrong. The only thing you oughta be worried about asking any of them is what the hell they have to show for the last two hundred fifty years of their advantage. And I don't care if for those two hundred fifty years their ancestors were in Europe or Asia or Russia or on Mars or wherever, because I can guarantee you that they were not in chains. Your Grampa Hicks once reminded me of that fact. And now I'm reminding you. I probably should have reminded you a long time ago, but I was too busy trying to be someone I'm not.

The honking grew loud enough to break through Mom's ranting. She pulled me out of the way of traffic, onto the sidewalk.

You want fair? I'll give you fair. If I were to go down to Akersburg now and demand my fair share of all the work I put in for your father, some magistrate would laugh in my face, and they'd look at me like some two-bit hustler trying to game them. I'm nothing but a hussy to any of them. No different than someone who was his one-night stand. You hear me? A fly-by-night. An easy come, easy go. Me? Oh, what am I saying. You probably don't even know what that is.

Yes, I do.

I was too proud to ask for help early on, but let me tell you, I'm not too proud to ask for it now. Only now it's too late. If I were to do that now, people would talk like it never even happened. They'd probably have something cute to say like, "Oh no. You must be mistaken, Miss. We never let any of our coloreds cohabitate with Caucasians in Akersburg back then. That sort of thing simply didn't happen." Or like, "Well, why didn't you get yourself a marriage license, darling, if you loved him so much?" As if people like us never lived together. As if it never happened. Please! Because if there is one thing I've learned, it's that life in this country is like living on a dollar-store inflatable you're constantly having to blow up unless you want to sink. There's not a day of rest. It's a perpetual assault on my basic humanity. And it's exhausting. All just to keep this damn floaty above water, when it seems like other people are hell-bent on tearing into it with a knife only because if they can't have it all to themselves, then they don't want anyone to have it.

Listen. You never got to know your Grampa Hicks. But you know me. And I'm telling you, you get to be whatever the hell you want. You've earned that much. It's not for me or anyone else to say. All I want to see you do is take back what's rightfully yours. That's all. Lay claim to *it like others before you have not been able to do. And if anyone tries to stop you, make them get out of your way. You owe that much to your Grampa Hicks. They've rearranged the world to put themselves in front of you. They never asked for your permission. Don't ask for theirs. You don't owe them anything. And it's high time some of that comes back around for us.*

Mom snapped me back around and dragged me down the sidewalk and reeled off a list of stuff she wanted to pick up while we were out. She should have written it down, if you ask me, what with the box of tampons, eyeliner pencils, two wide-ruled notebooks—make that two dozen flowers for Zuk—special hairspray, two blush markers, and an eraser for me. Which she said we should get two of, since I was bound to make a lot of mistakes when I got around to writing my essay. I told her that maybe I should type it. She said to get them anyway. Called them the bare essentials. I could tell that she was more desperate for my eventual return to Claremont than I was.

Which is only a half truth. Listen, even if I feel resentful and a little conflicted about Claremont it's just because I'd had somebody whisper *nigger* to me under their breath in a crowded room one too many times. Even though its painstakingly cultivated sense of exclusivity exacts a toll on people like me because we know we will never share in its aristocratic heritage, I'm still thankful that I have the experience of going there. I guess that maybe at the end of the day, I love Claremont much in the same way that I loved Mister Abrams's pool. I see it as a keyhole through which I get to peek into a life bursting with possibilities that would otherwise never be known to a kid like me. I'm thankful for it because even though it was never truly mine, it has, in a perverse way, become a sort of home away from home.

Even if I know that elitism is wrong, the floor-to-ceiling burnished wood paneling, ivy-covered wrought iron and redbrick out front, and portraits of stately men wearing powdered wigs and dinner coats puffing on meerschaum pipes are still kind of cool. I guess I've come to dig them. Stalwart slave-owning criminals and crooks though Mom claims many of them to be, they've all become a part of who I am, and they have as much a claim on me as anything else. Which is why they mean every bit as much to me as they do to Vernonblood and

Lichenberger, and have, with time, become every bit as much a part of me as them.

We stopped at the corner of East Fifty-Seventh Street and waited for the signal. Across the street a marquee was lit up like a blast furnace, so bright Buzz Aldrin could probably see it from outer space. *The Wild Bunch* was showing. Mom reached into her coat pocket and pulled out her coin pouch. She unrolled each of the five curled-up singles stuffed inside, all the while telling me how she'd once found herself at the Blumenthals' building uptown without subway fare home and swore she'd never make that mistake again. I remember how exhausted she was by the time she got home. I had to fend for myself that night. She was out like a light on the sofa, with her overcoat still on and spit-up baby food staining her dress and her pumps brushing up against the box of cereal I'd balanced on the sofa arm amid the soft flicker and glow of Dick Cavett announcing his first guest of the evening.

Mom tucked her coin purse away and proclaimed how sad it was that all the western stars she'd grown up with were over the hill. With John Wayne contemplating retirement and Jimmy Stewart right there behind him and Gene Autry out of the picture, who would save the day? *They don't make them like they used to, Huey.*

You can say that again.

The light turned, and we crossed with the herd. Mom said it wasn't every day that you got to see the end of an era. She linked her arm with mine, and we headed for the theater.

I pulled at her coat. *Can't people like me be a new generation of cowboys?*

Mom laughed. That was a good one. All the same, she agreed that I could be her cowboy any day. Which, frankly, offended me. It was something in the way she said it—like it required too much imagination. Then what the hell was she sending me to Claremont for?

You've got it all wrong. Cowboys are only as good as the challenges they face and swear to overcome, come hell or high water. It's the big heart and unyielding courage in the face of insurmountable odds that matter. That's what's made this country great. Don't you know anything? I can be a cowboy. Anybody can be a cowboy. That's the point.

Mom was still chuckling. A little too long, if you ask me. She thought

I was being cute. She said she just wanted me to be more realistic, was all. Said I had my head in the clouds too much. If there had been a can there, I would have kicked it. Mom led me across the street, and we popped into Woolworth's. She grabbed some flowers for Zuk and a protractor and erasers for me and some tampons for herself.

Mom was tapping her feet to the music emanating from overhead while we were waiting in line. She said she'd like to try her hand at something different—maybe go back to school and study to become a certified public accountant. She could work on contract for small businesses. Handle all their back office needs—kind of like she did for Dad, only now she'd get paid good money for it.

That'd be nice, wouldn't it?

I opened a bag of chips and stuffed some in my mouth. *Great.*

I just love sitting down in front of a clutter of receipts, invoices, bank statements, and payroll reports—tapping away on an adding machine—figuring out where all the money is going.

I unwrapped a stick of gum and shoved it into my mouth. *If you say so.*

What—you don't think I can do it? Or you think I can but that it's beneath me? I can't tell which.

It's not that. You're a modern woman, I see that. Anyone can see that. You can do anything that you set your sights on. And have the right to. So it's not that. It's just that—well. I paused. *It's not that I think you should be home, cooking and cleaning, or anything like that. It's just that I wonder—well . . . I mean . . . what about me?*

What about you?

How can we both be in school at the same time? Where's the money going to come from? And when are we going to have time to hang out? Besides, whatever happened to doing people's hair? Didn't you like that? Don't get me wrong; I'm all for you leaving the Blumenthals. But. Well. I just thought that, if you do leave the Blumenthals, well—I dunno. I guess I just thought that somehow you'd find your way back to doing people's hair. Why would you just give something like that up, when it used to be such a big part of your life?

Mom sighed.

First of all, I hated the work. Second of all, I checked into it, and I'd have to rent out a chair somewhere and I'm not doing that. Third of all,

I need a change. And I'd like to try something that I actually enjoy for once. Of course I'll need to ease into it, silly. I was just thinking long term. This kind of a move would take a while to materialize. It wouldn't happen overnight.

I shrugged. It was as much of a blessing as she was going to get from me. We stepped to the check-out counter. Mom unloaded our stuff from the basket and asked if I'd mind waiting for her outside. She was going to ask to speak with the manager about the HELP WANTED sign leaning in the window. It said to "See Cashier." The matinee didn't start for another half hour, and she'd been talking about changing jobs for the last year. Who knew? Maybe they had some sort of training program that would jump-start her new career.

The woman behind the counter was ringing up our items. I looked up at her as I stuffed my pockets with the gum, chips, Milk Duds, and Mike and Ikes I'd gotten for the movie.

Are you sure this is right? You're able-bodied and capable and you want equal pay for equal work. Trust me, I get it. What's there not to get? You want a job where you get the respect you deserve. I guess I just thought that—well. I mean, I just think of you as being more of a people person. And besides, how can you be sure that you're not doing it for the fancy business cards? Or the novelty of having "CPA" tacked on at the end of your name? Or the allure of maybe even having your own LLC one day? Or for the promise of maybe flying high with the corporate jet set one day? That's where it all leads, right? All just so that you have a fancy story of your own to tell someday? I mean, if you're doing it for me—you don't have to. Please. God, don't do it for me. I just thought you liked doing people's hair, is all. Because there's absolutely nothing wrong with doing people's hair. And it just seems so much more manageable. Because you can do it from home. I could even help find you customers. And that way—well—we could have a lot more time together. I dunno. I guess I was just hoping to eventually get my mom back someday. You know? Have more time together. To talk and stuff. Kinda like we're doing right now. Jesus. You're all I've got.

The cashier was taking her time, doing a price check on the flow-ers. Mom was digging money out of her purse. She looked up and sighed.

You wanna know something, Huey? Math was my favorite subject in school. I liked reading. But I loved math. Did you know that? You wanna know what I loved about it? I loved how everything starts out messy but ends up nice and neat. Other kids would make fun of me. Especially the boys. I don't know why. I think it was because I was so much better at it than any of them. I didn't mean to be, but I guess it just made them feel insecure. So I wasn't too popular with many of them. So I backed off that stuff, because I didn't like being made fun of any more than anyone else, and the unfortunate result was that I never did much with it in school. I just sort of played it down and let it fall by the wayside. The only time I used it since was to help your father. And every time I'd sit down at the kitchen table with the ledger, I got a rush of excitement. Because I knew it was important, and because I just loved how I could see the story that all those numbers were telling me. It was never difficult for me. Because none of them ever lied. And ever since we've been up here, I've felt this longing. I used to think that it was for your father. But now I realize it's not—it's for that darn ledger. Can you believe it? Does that sound strange to you? Well, it's true. When we first arrived here, we simply couldn't afford to go without a paycheck. We had no place to live yet, no food, nothing. But now it's different. It's taken me a long time, but I finally know what I want in life. That's what I want, Huey—I want my life to be like a math problem that starts out messy but ends up nice and neat. At some point in this lifetime of mine, I'm going to have to do something for me. Nothing splashy. Nothing fancy. Not some get-rich-quick scheme, not some pill that you take that solves all your problems. Just a small step in the right direction. You asked how I know it's the right decision for me. Well, that's how I know.

I turned for the door. Mom waved me back and handed me her umbrella and told me to take it, in case.

She blew me a kiss at the door and told me to wish her luck. I leaned into the spatula-style door handle and looked up at the sky—gray as it was, at least it wasn't raining. It was something that Mom would say. I wasn't even sure how I felt about her eternal and unbending optimism, but it seemed to be rubbing off on me. So there I was, on the corner of Fifty-Seventh Street and Lexington, standing on the sidewalk outside Woolworth's in the bitter cold, holding a white paper bag with one hand and a bouquet of lilies, carnations, and buttercups up to my nose with the other. I buttoned up amid the honking cabbies jamming the three-laned avenue in front of me, and the hectic flow of pedestrian foot traffic and grumpy sidewalk vendors wobbling past with their steaming hot dog carts. The clipped strides of women in heels hauling large shopping bags. I'd just about gotten the last of the potato chips out from between my teeth and was feeling pretty good about that, and sort of got to thinking about what I'd write in this essay of mine, which was already starting to weigh on me a little and, as you now know, turned out a little longer than it was supposed to. You see, I knew more or less that I wanted to say something about the summer seven years back, but I wasn't sure what exactly to say or how to say it. I just knew that it was still weighing heavily on me. I guess that in a way, you could say that writing this damned thing has helped me figure out that what was so humiliating about that whole summer wasn't the bone-aching inevitability of it all, or the fact that school was segregated, or even having been the last person in town to discover the truth about who I am. It was the way I'd been forced onto a bus and shipped willy-nilly out of town on the overnight express, under the cover of the darkness—jettisoned without a say like a dead leaf kicked up in the autumn wind. I hated the fact that it denied me the wiggle room I'd need to make up an excuse to save face. You know, like, a dear old relative of Mom's had fallen ill in a neighboring town and so I had to go assist in her convalescence and liked it so much I decided to stay. Better yet, Dad could have said that it might be a long while before I returned. Even if Theo and Darla and Derrick would hardly have cared, that didn't matter. What mattered was that it look like the actual leaving had been my choice. I figured I was owed that much. Of all the lies I've ever told myself over the years, that was the most important—the one I carried with me from day to day. You know, the only one that ever really hurt to give up. I may live on the twenty-third floor of a housing project in the East Village, but Akersburg is still my home, and deep down I know that's where I belong.

I could have just kicked myself when it started to drizzle. Damn it all. I knew I should have brought my galoshes. I fumbled with Mom's umbrella, all the while asking myself why oh why I had believed in that asshole right up until the bitter end, and now no letter had come since the one I'd sent him back in April. I was getting a little worried because it was starting to seem like maybe life had moved on for him, and here I was spinning my wheels, getting in all sorts of trouble. When I asked Mom if four unanswered letters was a lot, she said not for him. I was starting to think that maybe I should just suck it up and write Dad a fifth letter, just to be on the safe side. Because it's entirely possible that he just figured that I was doing fine without him. Except that it's been over a year since he's so much as called, and like a complete douchebag I'm still waiting, as if that's ever going to happen. Which is why I think I've got no choice but to bury the hatchet, let bygones be bygones, and start accepting that I'm never going back.

What a flimsy fucking umbrella. It took me five minutes to get the goddamned latch free, and then it just sort of reluctantly flopped open. A man carrying a cardboard box filled with all sorts of useful things for people walking around Midtown in the rain popped up in front of me and held out a new umbrella. He offered to sell it to me. I told him that I had too many cheap umbrellas. Sure, I was irritable. Just look at my thirty-dollar shoes.

Acknowledgments

IT'S BEEN A LONG ROAD to this book, and I am forever grateful to those who have traveled down it with me. I am immensely indebted to Mildred Zambrano, for suffering through the many frustrations of the early days. To Amy and Jim Houran, for always keeping their door and hearts open to me. To Nancy Heiser, for giving me a sense of direction when I needed it most. To Jess Chen, for being an amazing godfather to my sons and a load-bearing beam for my family. To Paul Beatty, for teaching me how to be a completionist. To Victor LaValle, for his generosity in giving me a year of his time. To Jaida Temperly, for understanding where I was trying to go, and for her commitment in helping me get there. To Joanna Volpe, for taking over the reins with a steady hand. To Todd Hunter, for taking a leap of faith with me, and under whose stewardship—with special thanks to Molly Lindley Pisani—this book came into full bloom. To Ramsey and Wren, who never had a say in what they sacrificed for this to happen, and for loving me in spite of it. Most of all, I want to thank my wife, Maja, for sharing her sharp mind and extraordinary heart. She showed me what love, compassion, and forgiveness mean. That this book exists at all is testimony to her generosity as a wife, mother, friend, reader, editor, and muse.

And to Faustino, who lay at my feet as I sat in a bungalow in the Argentine Pampas working on an early draft. I wish he was still here.

ABOUT THE AUTHOR

MALCOLM HANSEN was born at the Florence Crittenton Home for Unwed Mothers in Chattanooga, Tennessee. He was adopted by two Civil Rights activists, and his family lived in Morocco, Spain, Germany, and various parts of the United States. Malcolm left home as a teenager and, after two years of high school education, went to Stanford, earning a BA in philosophy. He worked for a few years in the software industry in California before setting off for what turned out to be a decade of living, working, and traveling throughout Central America, South America, and Europe. Malcolm returned to the US to complete an MFA in fiction at Columbia. He currently lives in New York City with his wife and two sons.

THEY COME IN ALL COLORS

MALCOLM HANSEN

This reading group guide for *They Come in All Colors* includes an introduction, discussion questions, and ideas for enhancing your book club. The suggested questions are intended to help your reading group find new and interesting angles and topics for your discussion. We hope that these ideas will enrich your conversation and increase your enjoyment of the book.

INTRODUCTION

The year was 1962. As Freedom Riders brought protests to the quiet farming town of Akersburg, Georgia, eight-year-old Huey Fairchild's parents assured him of his identity. He was no different from his friends, who were white. Years later, as a student at New York City's ritzy Claremont Prep, Huey finds that he can no longer deny the truth: he's part black. As reality for Huey becomes inescapable, so does his anger. But can he heed his estranged father's advice—*That's the wisdom of the river, Huey. It tells us to bend when there's no other way*—or will he allow his pride to get the better of him?

TOPICS AND QUESTIONS
FOR DISCUSSION

1. Discuss the structure of the book. What's the effect of alternating between fifteen-year-old Huey's current life and that of his eight-year-old self? Did learning about Huey's past help you better understand his current actions? Did your feelings change about Huey's attack on Zukowski upon learning why he did it?

2. Did you find the plot of *They Come in All Colors* relevant to today's headlines? If so, how?

3. How does the incident that transpires between the Freedom Riders and the white townsfolk in front of the S&W reflect the sociopolitical environment of the time period? Consider its impression on young Huey, as well as on the white and black residents of Akersburg.

4. There are several moments in the story that hint at Huey's feelings toward his mom. When he was young, he proclaimed: "Mama's the dark one in this family. Not me. I'm normal, okay?" (p. 69) When he's a teenager, he forbids his mom from coming within ten blocks of his school. Why is it so important for Huey that his mom blend in? How do you think this affects Mrs. Fairchild?

5. What does Toby represent for the Fairchild family? What does Toby represent for the black and white residents of Akersburg?

Why do you think it was important for him that Huey be more self-aware about his race?

6. Despite their physical differences, Huey and Zukowski share a lot in common. In fact, it was their similarities that brought them together in the first place. Compare and contrast Huey and Zukowski. How did the incident at the baseball game affect their relationship?

7. At the core of *They Come in All Colors* are themes of identity and family. How do the events that transpire in Akersburg affect the Fairchild family—more specifically, the relationship between Huey and his father? Do you think Huey's anger as a teenager stems from his lack of a father figure?

8. At Claremont Prep, there are people, such as Mister McGovern and Clyde (the school's colored janitor), who remind Huey that his presence at the school is unique. Do you think these interactions affect the ways in which Huey measures success?

9. In what ways does Pea's character evolve over the course of the book? Consider the way her role as a parent changed from Akersburg to New York City.

10. Huey's encounters with Evan—Toby's son—are often violent. What do you think fuels Evan's anger toward Huey? Are there any parallels between Evan's actions toward Huey and Huey's actions toward Zukowski?

11. Do you think Huey's parents did the right thing by keeping him in the dark about his biracial identity? Why or why not? How did his parents' decision shape his transition into adulthood?

12. On page 244, Huey recounts to his parents what happened at school: he was outed by his classmates for being black. He also reveals the accusations against his father—that he was the one who circulated the story of a break-in at Mr. Abrams's pool. Describe the significance of this scene and its effect on everything thereafter. How do the revelations impact the family's ability to move on?

ENHANCE YOUR BOOK CLUB

1. *They Come in All Colors* has been compared to *The Secret Life of Bees* and *The White Boy Shuffle*. Read these titles with your book club and compare them to *They Come in All Colors*. Are there any similar themes? In what ways do you think these books are alike?

2. Have an open and honest conversation about race and identity with members of your book club and/or at home with your family and friends.

3. To learn more about Malcolm Hansen and read reviews of *They Come in All Colors*, visit his website at malcolmhansen.com.